THE THIRD SIN

Pleasure is the highest good: the group who called themselves the Cyrenaics embrace the hedonistic principle until the death of one of their members from an overdose. Sobered, the group went their separate ways. One headed for Canada, another disappeared and a third was believed to have committed suicide – at least until his body turns up in the wreck of a car swept up on the Solway mud flats. The murky relationships among the Cyrenaics, revived when they start returning from a party, bring more suffering and death. DI Marjory Fleming faces obstruction and hostility. Can she piece together the puzzle before someone else dies?

THE THIRD SIN

THE THIRD SIN

by

Aline Templeton

Magna Large Print Books
Long Preston, North Yorkshire,
BD23 4ND, England.

British Library Cataloguing in Publication Data.

Templeton, Aline
    The third sin.

    A catalogue record of this book is
    available from the British Library

    ISBN   978-0-7505-4115-2

First published in Great Britain by Allison & Busby in 2015

Copyright © 2015 by Aline Templeton

Cover illustration by arrangement with Arcangel Images

The moral right of the author is hereby asserted in accordance with
the Copyright, Designs and Patents Act, 1988

Published in Large Print 2015 by arrangement with
Allison & Busby Ltd.

Magna Large Print is an imprint of Library Magna Books Ltd.

Printed and bound in Great Britain by
T.J. (International) Ltd., Cornwall, PL28 8RW

For Jennie and Hugh, and Matti and Bill, with much love

'I have done that,' says my memory. 'I cannot have done that,' says my pride, and remains adamant. At last – memory gives way.

Nietzsche

CHAPTER ONE

October 2012

Julia was wild that night, her long blonde hair streaming as she danced like a maenad among the trees.

Jen watched her warily. She was high. Well, they all were, all the Cyrenaics, of course, but Julia – oh yes, Julia was beyond that – way beyond. She had thrown off her coat despite the cold and she'd just tripped on a tree root, gnarled as an old man's foot.

'You'll break your ankle, J,' Jen shouted. 'Chill, for God's sake!'

Julia turned. Under the bleached moon her face was all white planes and black shadows, her eyes pits of darkness. She laughed a great, joyous, uninhibited laugh.

'Chill? How can anyone chill on a night like this?' She flung her arms wide, embracing the universe, the whirling galaxies overhead. There was an edge of frost tonight and above the angled branches of the trees the black bowl of the night sky was studded with diamonds.

Tonight you could almost hear the music of the spheres, Jen thought, interwoven with the restless muttering of the trees. The rest of the Cyrenaics drifted around her: Connell, Will, Skye, Randall, Kendra. Only Kendra's husband Logie was

13

missing, running the pub.

Skye was laughing and dancing too, a sprite alive with energy. 'I'm floating,' she called. 'I don't need to touch the ground!' Then she stopped, staring up at the sky, a mood swing making her suddenly serious. 'We're so small. We're so – so *nothing*. We're ants – ants to be stepped on.' She ground her own small foot into the leaf mould.

Was that what started the first wave of unease among them? Afterwards, Jen couldn't remember, but her sensory exhilaration began to fade, along with the effects of the last spliff.

'How come we don't see this every night?' Skye tilted her face up to Will who was standing nearby.

'Light pollution,' Will said. 'Too many lights, everywhere.'

'Oh, for God's sake, spare us another eco-rant!' Randall wasn't high; the cigarette he was smoking was the kind you could buy across the counter but he'd got drunk tonight instead, drunk and belligerent. He was younger than the rest of them and something had definitely put him on edge; perhaps it was Skye, spirits restored, twirling herself into Will's arms to be gathered into an embrace. 'What are we going to do now? Just stand around in a wood all night? OK, we've seen the Dark Skies effect – who's coming back to the pub?'

'Slow down! Just feel the night.' Connell's voice came from deep shadow, under a towering Scots pine, on the edge of the group. As usual.

All Jen could make out was the bulk of his darker shadow and the paler smudge of his face: bad, beautiful Connell who didn't play their little games with anyone except Julia. She felt a stab of

14

pain at the thought. And she could, indeed, feel the night, like invisible fingers creeping about her, chilly, sinister. She gave an involuntary shudder.

Kendra moved across to Will, her brother-in-law, and Skye. 'Will, you were going to point out the planets,' she said. 'I can do Orion, up there – see?'

Will turned away from Skye, his attention caught. 'The Plough next, then.' He put his arm round Kendra's shoulder, directing her gaze. 'Look, high up – higher. Got it?'

Randall gave a disgusted snort, throwing down his cigarette and stamping it out. 'That's enough communing with nature for me. I'm cold. Anyone coming back to the cars? Skye?' But Skye twirled away again, throwing him an impish glance over her shoulder.

Jen was cold too, and there was too much going on tonight. She felt the tensions in the group tingling like nettle stings on her skin. If she and Randall left, it might break up the party. *Before something happened.*

Why was she thinking that? It was foolish, of course, just the effect of the dramatic surroundings of ancient trees, moonlight and darkness. Even so, she'd be a lot happier once they were back in Logie Stewart's smartly decadent gastro-pub.

'I'll come,' she said, then looking round, 'Where's Julia?' It was ten minutes since she'd seen her disappear among the trees.

'Off to worship the gods of the grove, no doubt,' Connell said in that dry, sarcastic way he had.

Jen's eyes went back to him. She didn't really

15

like him – not *like*, no – and she wasn't sure that any of the others did either, apart from Julia, but he got the stuff for them. And did Julia like him – or was the relationship built on need not inclination? Julia was getting in deep these days.

'Come on then, Jen.' Randall put his arm round her shoulders. 'Let's leave these morons to gape. I left a bottle in the car.'

She could smell the drink raw on his breath; you always could if you'd been inhaling rather than drinking yourself, and she wasn't sure how much she wanted to find herself alone with a Randall who had something to prove to Skye and had declared his intention of getting drunker still. She was beginning to feel spooked, though, and she allowed him to sweep her along.

They went in single file along the narrow track they had followed to the clearing until the broader forestry track that cut a swathe through the trees opened up ahead of them.

An owl hooted, another owl answered and twigs crackled in the depths of the forest as if people were walking beside them unseen. Jen drew a little closer to Randall's tall, broad-shouldered silhouette, glad now that she wasn't alone. It was a relief when they turned downhill and she could see Will's 4x4 parked lower down the slope.

The sound that reached them, a horrible sound, a sort of choking, gurgling cry, froze her to the spot.

'Dear God, what was that?' Jen could feel blood draining from her face.

Randall looked pale too in the moonlight, but he said only, 'A rabbit, probably. They scream, you know, when the stoat gets them.'

'Yeah, I guess,' she said, but when she turned back he followed her. She didn't break into a run, not until she heard the voices calling, 'Julia! Julia!'

They reached the clearing again. The others were all there together, Connell in the middle shouting, 'Julia! Where are you, you silly bitch!'

'Have you seen any sign of her?' Kendra demanded.

Randall shook his head. 'What was that noise?'

It was Connell who said, 'Some animal, I guess.' But he went on, 'I think we'd better just check on Julia, though, in case she's got lost. The way she was going on, she could have tripped and knocked herself out somewhere.'

He was sweating, Jen noticed with an almost clinical detachment. What had he given Julia tonight? And, more importantly, where was she?

'Fan out.' Will took control, directing them out on different angles. 'Don't go too far and get lost yourselves.'

The cries began echoing all through the forest: 'Julia! Julia!' Jen found herself shivering convulsively, with cold and with nerves. She had to force herself to move on through the multiple paths ahead, avenues of trees that beckoned then withdrew the invitation in a snarl of brambles and nettles, straining her ears for a cry of, 'I've found her!' that didn't come.

Slower, slower. She was putting her feet down very deliberately now but even so she almost trod on her.

Julia was lying across a path, little more than a track, splayed out on her back, her top pulled off one shoulder as if she had been too hot. Her teeth were bared in a grimace and her face was suffused and sweaty. In the relentless moonlight her eyes gleamed, wide and glassy.

Jen didn't have to touch her to know she was dead. But with a shudder of revulsion she bent to pick up the limp arm. It was hot – scarily hot – but there was no pulse and she dropped it again as if it had burnt her fingers. Then she screamed.

Later, it all came back to her in flash frames. Connell, grim-faced, being comforted by Skye. Will, a policeman himself, unable to look his colleagues in the eye. Kendra, who had summoned her husband, clinging to him in tears. Randall, looking like a scared teenager, explaining to his mother on the phone. Then later, Julia's mother, small but dignified, holding herself upright despite her stick, her sternly handsome face rigid with the determination not to break down here.

Jen had been the last to give her statement; the others had gone, and when Mrs Margrave's eyes swept over her it felt like a scorching flame. Until then, Jen had felt detached and emotionless, as if she were viewing the dramatic events from behind a pane of glass; now she burnt with shame.

In her heart of hearts, Jen had somehow always known that their relentless pursuit of pleasure would end badly. Baudelaire's *Les Fleurs du Mal* had been their literary bible and now they were seeing the flowers of evil indeed. And from somewhere a voice from that older bible came murmuring, 'The wages of sin is death.'

And not Julia's alone. Connell was charged

with drug dealing and culpable homicide and two days later his car was found in the car park by the lighthouse at the Mull of Galloway, a letter to Julia's mother taped to the steering wheel. Will, sacked from the police force, went off to Canada and Skye, without a word to her parents, left home and vanished.

Randall, the baby of the group, prospered in his job with an Edinburgh merchant bank and Jen, still teaching in the little school at Ballinbreck, nursed her grief and pain and anger and learnt to live with the ghosts.

It was only in 2014, the Year of Homecoming, that the shadows began to stir.

On television it seemed such a cheerful, harmless invitation: the pictured Scots, either bonny or famous and sometimes both, calling the exiles home for a party, for a love fest of mountains and lochs and ceilidhs and pipe bands and whisky – so warm, so welcoming, beaming into homes worldwide in thousands of advertisement breaks.

The Year of Homecoming! Visit Scotland!

'Where's the remote?'

At the snarled question Heather Denholm, already stiff with apprehension, began a futile patting around the sofa she was sitting on.

'I-I don't know, Donald. You had it last–'

'Oh, for God's sake!' Her partner flung himself out of his chair to turn off the set then stormed out, his face contorted with what you might assume to be anger but she thought could be pain. With this VisitScotland commercial constantly appearing it was going to be a difficult year.

If it had been her daughter who had disappeared and for two long years she'd had no idea if she was alive or dead, she'd certainly have found the thought of happy reunions with returning loved ones hard to take.

So it was natural enough that he couldn't bear it – even if it sometimes sounded as if he hadn't … well, actually *liked* her very much.

The flyer delivered to the doorstep along with a couple of catalogues was on its way to the recycling pile when the headline caught Jen Wilson's eye.

'The Year of Homecoming in Ballinbreck,' it said and she read it with mounting unease: a village party inviting the diaspora to return, held at Ballinbreck House.

A shiver ran down her back. Why, for God's sake, would you want to do that? Why try to bring back the people who had left, rake up a past that was better forgotten – much better?

She looked at the signature – Philippa Lindsay. Philippa, who liked to refer to herself as the 'Lady of the Manor', though with a light laugh to show she was using the term ironically, whose Lady Bountiful moments had been few, far between and carefully calculated.

So what was in it for her? Why would Philippa want to provoke a reunion that would risk opening up old wounds?

Then suddenly, she knew – knew as if she had read the mind behind the message. A fit of rage shook her; she crumpled up the flyer and threw it in the bin, as if destroying it could somehow destroy the thought behind it.

It wouldn't, though. There would be people in the village with family overseas or in London or even closer at hand, in Glasgow or Edinburgh, who would welcome the idea of a grand reunion. The Lindsays, for once, would be popular.

If it happened, the seething emotions that had settled to an uneasy calm would break out all over again. She had to try and stop it.

Jen went to her laptop, clicked Create Mail, then hesitated. Could it do any harm? Probably not, though it might not do any good. She tapped out her message, took a deep breath and despatched it.

The speed of the reply surprised her. What it said left her shocked, bewildered and very, very angry.

Logie Stewart looked up from his laptop. 'That's Will saying that with all this Year of Homecoming stuff he might pay a visit back.'

'Oh, really?' Kendra said. Her voice sounded perfectly calm, her face was tranquil, as if the thought of her husband's brother coming home was a matter of no more than mild interest.

'Amazing that he feels able,' her husband went on, a slight chill in his voice. 'After all that happened.'

'After all that happened,' she echoed. 'Yes, amazing. Do you want a cup of tea?'

She didn't wait for his answer before going to make it. As she filled the kettle she found her lips shaping the words that Will had quoted to her all

21

those years ago: *he that would keep a secret, must keep it secret that he has a secret to keep.*

It was only words written on a piece of paper, but it had been folded up, put in an envelope, addressed and sent on its way and its seismic effect was starting.

So be it: *Fiat justitia, ruat caelum* – Let justice be done, though the heavens fall...

CHAPTER TWO

March 2014

Philippa Lindsay was taking trouble over her appearance today. She took her Max Mara silk-cashmere sweater, a delicious warm red, out of its protective bag and paired it with designer jeans and a smart little DKNY jacket; her audience would be impressed that she'd taken so much trouble – or they should be, anyway. Poised, as-sured: that was the effect she was channelling, and if she established her authority right from the start it would be less likely that anyone would argue over the arrangements she had decided on already.

She was pleased, too, with her hair: the new shade of ashy blonde was what her hairdresser had vulgarly called 'classy, not brassy' and though Philippa wouldn't quite have put it that way her-self, it worked. She touched a little concealer under her eyes and then completed her make-up with a soft-red lipstick to match her sweater, enhancing her rather thin lips just a fraction over the edge.

She'd been scrupulous about working out too – not a trace of flab – and she was still looking good; fully ten years younger than the date on the birth certificate she didn't care to look at, she told herself. She didn't register the grooves of disappointment that soured her mouth or the little temper lines that had hardened between her well-tailored eyebrows.

Brimming with confidence, she went downstairs to breakfast.

Her husband, sitting at the table with a bowl of cereal, looked surprised. 'I didn't know you were off somewhere today.'

She turned from spooning coffee into a cafetière to look at him with a frown. 'I'm not, Charles. I don't know what you mean.'

'You don't usually treat the locals to designer stuff. The only time I ever see you wearing it is when you want to impress your friends in Glasgow.'

Philippa had naturally high colour and her cheeks flared in rivalry with her sweater. 'That's a silly and spiteful remark. I have to look after my clothes because as you don't hesitate to tell me, we're not made of money.' She left the words, 'And whose fault is that?' hanging in the air.

It was a pity if Charles was in one of his spiky, sarcastic moods. Since he never listened to local gossip she'd managed to put off telling him what was happening, but soon he was bound to find out and she'd decided it would be wise to break it to him before he found out.

'Actually, today I'm making an effort because we're planning the Year of Homecoming party.' She said it casually, apparently concentrating on pouring the water over the coffee grounds.

It was Charles Lindsay's habit to ignore his wife's activities as far as possible, more or less in self-defence, but this was going too far. 'I told you before, Philippa – no! I thought you'd dropped it.'

She threw him a glance over her shoulder as she pressed down the plunger of the cafetière. 'There's no point in saying no. It's too late. I sent the flyer round ages ago, and there's been a good response. I've invited everyone to hold it here.'

Charles choked on his cereal. 'You've ... what?' he spluttered.

Philippa gave him a small, triumphant smile. 'I told you that was what I was going to do.'

'And I told you not to! For God's sake, Philippa, what are you trying to do? Wasn't there enough trouble before?'

He pushed back his chair and jumped up to confront her. His pose might have been intimidating if she hadn't been taller than he was, and she took advantage of that to look down on him pityingly.

'I should have thought you'd have realised by now that there was no point in bullying me, Charles.'

He struggled for words. 'Bullying – me bullying you! That's a sick joke, do you know that? You bully everyone. It comes as naturally to you as breathing. Do you know what they think of you in the village – how often they dive down a side street if they see you coming?'

The tide of colour rose in her cheeks again. 'That's a lie. They're happy enough to come to the things I arrange. And I can tell you people are really enthusiastic about this.'

'That's because you've offered to host it here. And apart from anything else, that's a bad idea. One way or another it's going to run us into expense and with the economy the way it is we don't have the money for lavish, manipulative gestures.

'I'm not sure why you're set on this, but any reason I can think of is frightening – playing games with people's lives. Sometimes I think you're crazy – power crazy.'

Philippa gave a silly titter. 'Power crazy – that sounds very grand! You flatter me.'

'Not really,' Charles said tiredly. 'When we were in the nursery we just used to call it wanting your own way, and you've never grown past the infantile stage. You want your own way all the time.'

'Why don't you leave, then?' she said shrilly.

He had turned to walk out; he swung back. 'Because you own half the business and you'd collapse it for sheer vindictiveness. That's the only reason, believe me.'

Philippa was left staring at the door he had slammed, feeling for once a little shaken. She was no stranger to marital rows, but she'd never known Charles be – well, vicious.

She still wasn't going to pay any attention. He'd get over it. Her hand was shaking, though, as she poured out her coffee.

Ballinbreck, on the shores of the Solway Firth between Balcary Bay and Abbey Head, was a picturesque fishing village, the haunt of smugglers in days gone by and now generally prosperous enough. The pretty harbour, home mainly to leisure craft, was a draw for tourists to support the small hotel and self-catering cottages as well as a couple of artists' studios, craft shops and galleries.

The seventeenth-century houses, harled and whitewashed or colour-washed in a spectrum running from pale cream to deepest blue – with one unfortunate shade of purple – were looking particularly charming in the watery spring sunshine, Jen Wilson thought as she walked along the main street.

There was a 'Chocolate and Cupcakes' fund-raiser at the little local school where she taught and her Primary 4 pupils had been high as kites about it for days. Cupcakes were definitely beyond her but she'd made enough chocolate crispies to ensure obesity and dental decay for fully half the school.

She loved occasions like these. The mums would be out in force today, and the grannies, as well as a number of other people who realised that the home baking on offer would be seriously underpriced, but whatever the motive it brought people together. The village was growing, with a good number of new houses spreading round the back, and charity events were a bridge for the 'incomers' to get into the local community.

The woman who ran the general store and post office had promised an iced and decorated cake to raffle, so Jen went in to collect it, admired it effusively, and was just on her way out carrying it carefully when she all but bumped into Philippa

Lindsay, hurrying in.

'Oh – sorry, Jen,' Philippa said. She didn't look directly at the other woman, moving round her to pass.

Jen put a hand on her arm. 'I hear it's going ahead – the party.' Her voice was cold.

'Oh, yes, the party.' Philippa gave a false, social laugh. 'It's proving very popular, giving the village a sort of focus for this year, you know? A lot of people are arranging family visits round about it. Well, you know how it is with the young – it's more tempting to come and see the wrinklies if you know your friends are going to be there too. And it's a community thing – you know how sentimental expats are. It's going to be a shot in the arm for the local economy.'

'Very public-spirited,' Jen said. 'What I want to know is, did the fish take the bait?'

Philippa's thin lips tightened. 'I don't know what you mean. If that's your attitude, you don't have to come.'

Jen held her gaze steadily until Philippa's eyes dropped. 'Oh no,' she said. 'You invited me. I'll be there.'

She walked away.

April 2014

Eleanor Margrave had smelt bad weather all day. After a bitter March of relentless frost and snow it had turned sultry and today the air felt thick, oppressive. A headache was gripping her skull like a vice.

It was late afternoon when she heard the first dull moaning of the gathering storm, a complaining wind from the south-west, muttering and grumbling. Looking out from the sitting-room window of Sea House across her strip of garden to the Solway Firth, narrow at ebb tide and muddy-brown under low, sullen clouds, she could see the scrubby trees above the shoreline starting to sway as the wind rose, then to bend and twist.

The spring tide would be turning now down the estuary, racing over the sand flats with the driving wind, faster than a horse could gallop, according to local legend. She wanted to listen for the roar of its arrival but when she tugged at the handles to raise the sash window with her rheumaticky hands it had no effect.

Even with the window shut, though, she could hear the rushing waters now and when she craned her painful neck to look west, there was the line of surf with its cloud of spray encroaching on the sand flats with menacing speed. She sat down to watch; it thrilled her, just as it had thrilled her when she'd been taken down to see it as a child, being given dire warnings about its dangers.

The first fat spots of rain slammed on the windowpanes and even as the low breakers started to cover the shore the wind noise rose with the storm screaming in from the Irish Sea. Though it was only six o'clock the light went rapidly and she found herself sitting in darkness. It had turned cold again and the bleakness outside made her melancholy.

Eleanor got to her feet and limped slowly into the hall that ran from the front to the back of the house. With a door at each end, the draughts were fierce on a night like this and she shivered as she crossed it. The Aga kept the kitchen cosy, though; ever practical, she had pretty much lived here during the cold spell but she'd been pining for the long light evenings in the sitting room watching daylight fade to a glimmering gold on the sea outside, trying once more to capture even a hint of its glory on her sketch pad.

Sighing, she made her supper and ate it in the chair by the stove off a folding table, watching the small TV set up in one corner. They were advertising the Year of Homecoming extensively now and she watched with a small, cynical smile. In the run-up to the vote on independence for Scotland, no heartstring was to be left untugged.

At least the headache had cleared and the warmth eased her painful joints. She found herself nodding over the killer Sudoku she tried to do every night, to prove to herself that her brain was still working, jerking awake with a 'Tchah!' of annoyance each time.

She was dozing when the peal of thunder broke directly overhead and she woke in a panic, convinced the ceiling was falling down – something to do with her dream. She sank back in her chair with a gasp as the room lit up with a lurid flash of lightning and seconds later heard another, just as loud.

The old house had withstood storms for two hundred years and Eleanor loved them. She always watched the moods of the sea from her window as if they were dramas with a celestial cast played out for her especial benefit and it looked as

29

if tonight they were lining up for a spectacular. She went back to the chair in the window of the sitting room, picking up a throw from the back of the sofa and wrapping it round herself.

The *son et lumière* was, she judged, more or less at its height with forked lightning flickering every few moments and the crashing rumble of one thunderclap barely fading before the next took its place. The sea below her was tossing, white-capped, under hissing sheets of rain, but the tide had turned again and the shallow waters were making their slow retreat.

Gradually, the intervals between strikes grew longer, the rumbling fainter as the electric storm moved on. Show over. She yawned, ready for bed now; satisfied, replete almost. Storms were always cathartic, as if wildness outside somehow purged the emotional storm that had raged within her ever since Julia's terrible decline into drugs and death.

As she got up she caught a movement out of the corner of her eye, just to the left of the house. She turned her head, peering into the darkness, but could see nothing. A trick of the light, perhaps, a shadow thrown by distant lightning flickering behind a waving tree. She folded up the throw and put it back neatly over the arm of the sofa, but she felt a little unsettled. It was almost midnight; she had no near neighbours and with the nearest house quarter of a mile away, no one could have a reason to be about in weather like this. No good reason, anyway.

She was not by nature nervous, and anyway, you couldn't afford to indulge your imagination when you lived in this sort of isolation. She'd just go and check that the doors were locked then make herself a cup of tea and take it up to bed with her–

The knocking on the front door was alarmingly loud in the silent house. She stood in the hall staring at its unrevealing back in fright.

After a moment, it came again, louder, more imperative.

She would be crazy to open it without knowing who was there, she thought, suddenly conscious of her frail body, her brittle bones. Even if she went to an upstairs window and looked down she wouldn't be able to see because there was a porch over the doorstep. She could pretend she wasn't here or hadn't heard – but then would they just break in?

There were keys in all the doors leading on to the hall. She could lock these, retreat upstairs, call the police on the phone at her bedside, but it could take half an hour or more for anyone to reach her. And what if they cut the phone line? There was no signal for her mobile here.

Her heart was fluttering. When she went to lock the nearest door, her hands were shaking so that it was a struggle to turn the key and when the beating on the door began again she jumped so that she knocked it on to the floor. This time, though, she heard the sound of a woman, a child, even, wailing desperately.

Eleanor was no fool. There were criminals who wouldn't hesitate to use a decoy to gain entrance, and even women who were evil themselves. But you could die of exposure on a night like this and

31

there was no other shelter. She switched on the outside light, fixed the chain across the door then very cautiously opened it.

The figure on the doorstep was small and slight – and alone. A woman – a child? It was hard to tell. Not threatening, anyway, and clearly distressed, with a livid bruise on the left cheekbone. She was wearing a thin jacket and jeans and she was shockingly wet, dripping as if she had come straight out of the water. Her hair, plastered to her head, was long and curling; as Eleanor released the chain to admit her she saw that her eyes, wide with distress, were as grey-green as the sea itself.

A mermaid, she thought, like the little figurine that had sat on her mantelpiece since a visit to Copenhagen twenty years before. She waved her inside.

'What on earth's happened to you? You'd better come through to the kitchen, where it's warm.'

The girl glanced up at her blindly; she was shivering so much that her teeth were chattering loudly enough to be heard. There was no colour in her face and for a moment Eleanor thought she might even collapse, but she made for the Aga as if with an instinctive response to its heat, huddling against it like an animal.

'I'll get a towel,' Eleanor said, retreating. She was glad to have a moment to collect herself.

Had the girl really come up out of the sea, after a shipwreck, perhaps? Boats came to grief sometimes in these tricky waters – but no, if she'd waded out just now she would have been filthy with sandy mud, and she was only wet. Been walking for a long time, then, while the storm was on?

Under the kitchen light it had been clear that she was older than she'd looked at first – late twenties, early thirties, even. It was also clear that she was in shock and at risk of hypothermia. She'd have to stay the night, until she was fit to contact her family or friends.

Yes, Eleanor knew her duty but it was with a certain reluctance that she set about fetching towels and bedlinen from the airing cupboard and turning on a radiator in one of the spare bed-rooms. The girl would need to get out of those wet clothes too, so she took a thick pair of pyjamas out of her chest of drawers, gave a long-ing glance at her own cosy bed, and switched on the immersion heater for a bath.

When she got back to the kitchen, the girl was standing as she had left her. She didn't seem to notice that her clothes were steaming; she was still shivering and still looking blank.

'What you need is a brandy,' Eleanor said, handing her a towel and going to the larder. There should still be brandy left from mince pies at Christmas and though it was a year or two old it shouldn't actually have gone off. 'I think you should get into a bath as soon as possible too but the water won't be hot enough just yet. Sit down and drink this and I'll make a cup of tea. I know I could be doing with one.'

The girl was dabbing at her hair with the towel but she looked at the glass as if she had never seen one before and took a moment to grasp it. Eleanor took her by the arm to urge her into the chair beside the Aga. Her passivity was quite alarming.

'Now tell me what's happened,' she said gently.

'Did you have an accident?'

She got no answer. The girl was still staring at the brandy; it was a moment or two before she put it to her lips, swallowed and shuddered, then took another sip.

At least the convulsive shivering was subsiding. Suddenly it occurred to Eleanor that she could be foreign, failing to understand what she had been asked. There were a lot of middle Europeans in the area now; she tried German, without result, then French, then miming.

'Eleanor,' she said, patting her chest, then 'Your name?' pointing. When there was no response, she pointed to the bruise, now spreading in vivid glory. 'Accident?'

It seemed more as if the girl was disconnected than as if she didn't understand. As Eleanor made tea, she kept up her attempts to communicate, but without success. The most she got was a shake of the head at a plate of biscuits, but the girl drank the brandy and the mug of tea. It was only when Eleanor turned back from making a hot-water bottle that she realised she had begun to cry silently.

There was no point in asking her questions. 'It's time you were in bed,' she said briskly. 'Come on.'

The girl got up and followed her. She had a canvas rucksack that had been set down at her feet; it was still soaking wet but when Eleanor suggested she left it by the range to dry she shook her head violently, clutching it to her and holding on grimly.

'Fine, if you want to keep it with you. But you'd better empty it and spread out your things to dry – it's soaked through.' Feeling ruffled – did the girl think she was going to steal something? – Eleanor took her upstairs, pointed out the bathroom, the pyjamas, the bedroom, put the hottie in the bed then left her and went back downstairs.

She'd have to try again in the morning to find out what this was all about, once the girl's shock had worn off a bit and she wasn't so tired herself. There really was something very strange about her and she remembered her own fanciful reaction: that here was a mermaid come ashore.

It was only as Eleanor was dropping at last into an exhausted sleep that she remembered the fairy tale: the mermaid was dumb. In exchange for her human legs, she had given her voice.

It was a beautiful morning after the storm, though wrack thrown up into the narrow garden below Sea House bore witness to its power. Eleanor got up with the burden of her unwanted guest hanging over her: she really must find out where the girl had come from – and where she would be going to, as well. She'd done her duty in succouring the distressed but she certainly wasn't issuing an open-ended invitation to stay. It was still early, though, so she got dressed as quietly as she could. After what had clearly been an ordeal last night the girl needed all the rest she could get.

But when she came out of her bedroom the door to the spare room was standing ajar. The curtains were open, the room was empty and the bed was tidy, with the flannelette pyjamas neatly folded on top. There was no sign of her visitor.

Eleanor sat down heavily on the bed, her knees suddenly weak. Would she go downstairs to find her credit cards and her car gone and the house ransacked? The saying 'Sooner or later, one must pay for every good deed' was ringing in her ears as she hurried downstairs as quickly as her creaking joints would let her.

But downstairs everything was in its usual place. It was as if her unexpected guest had been a figment of her imagination – or perhaps, she thought with a nod to fantasy, had merely vanished into sea foam. That a mermaid in legend was famously an ill omen she put firmly out of her mind.

The onrushing tide that had played with the car as if it were a dinky toy, tumbling it over and over as it swept it far up the Firth, retreated slowly. The car settled on its side, then with the next tide, less violent, rolled on to its roof. At last, abandoned on the sandy flats, it settled into the soft silt.

Inside it the man's battered body, unrestrained within the car, settled too, settled and stiffened.

CHAPTER THREE

May 2014

Was there anything, anything at all, more enjoyable than sitting in a pavement cafe on the Rive Gauche on a sunny Saturday morning in spring, people-watching through the thin blue haze of smoke from a Gitane with a knock-your-socks-off espresso on the little zinc table in front of you? If there was, Louise Hepburn couldn't think what it would be.

She came to Paris as often as her work as a detective sergeant in the Galloway Division of Police Scotland allowed to see her mother, though Fleur didn't reliably recognise her any more, slipping into a cruelly early twilight in the care of the *religieuses* at a convent nursing home near her sister Coralie. She seemed content enough there and calm, her moments of unhappy confusion mercifully brief.

Louise had found it very hard to let her mother return to her homeland from Scotland; theirs had been a close and loving relationship and her sense of loss was acute. Her visits to Paris had been clouded by dread of what further deterioration she might find but over time she had learnt a sort of acceptance that allowed her to take pleasure again in the city she had always loved since childhood holidays with her mother's family.

Now she stretched luxuriously like a cat in the warmth of the sunshine, her eyes half-closed, then hearing her name spoken looked up to see a tall young man coming along the pavement towards her, raising his hand in greeting.

Embarrassed, she sat up. 'Just caught me basking,' she said awkwardly. 'Great to see you, Randall.' Then, before she could help herself she blurted out, 'Goodness, you've changed!'

He laughed easily. 'The beardy student look doesn't go down very well in business circles.'

Louise had seen his photo on Friends Reunited, then Facebook, but she hadn't seen the *tout ensemble*. Randall Lindsay was pinkly clean-shaven

37

now and wearing a pale-blue shirt in thick, expensive looking cotton with a coral-pink cashmere sweater knotted loosely round his shoulders.

Oh, very BCBG, Louise thought dryly. *Bon chic bon genre* – good style, good class; the very uniform of the French upper-middle. Even his scruffy student look at Glasgow University, she now remembered, had been very carefully on trend, and as Randall gestured to a waiter she began to regret her impulse to contact him.

They had known each other a little at uni having discovered they both hailed from Galloway, though he came from the smart sailing territory in the south while she came from Stranraer where the sailing was mostly done in ferry boats to Ireland. When she discovered he was working in Paris, Louise had thought meeting up sometimes might be fun; her aunt had a busy social life and her cousins had left home so she was often at a loose end on her visits.

Having ordered his coffee, Randall was studying her. 'Now, you haven't changed a bit. Still the same crazy girl, I bet!'

He said it in an admiring way, but she almost had to sit on her hand to stop it going up to smooth her dark curly hair, which had a will of its own. She knew her own student look had been casual to the point of indifference, owing a lot to Oxfam, but she would have hoped that her Diesel jeans and Karen Millen top might at least have spelt out a change of style.

'So,' he was going on, 'what are you up to these days? You didn't say on your page.'

'No,' she admitted. 'I'm a bit careful. Trolls get

in everywhere–'

'Tell me about it!' Randall leant forward eagerly. 'I didn't put the merchant banking bit on mine. You in the same business?'

Now she really was regretting her sociable impulse. 'Not exactly. I'm in the police. Detective constable.'

He gave a low whistle. 'Wow – a copper eh? What the hell took you in that direction? Not much money in it – with your degree you could have been a lawyer.'

'I could, yes.' She knew she sounded frosty. 'But when I looked into it, I realised that this seemed much more interesting and challenging. And it is – I wouldn't give it up for anything.' She couldn't resist adding, 'And I like the fact that it's public service.'

'Very laudable.' Randall's lips twitched in a little, patronising smile. 'And I'm sure you've had a lot of fascinating cases.'

'Yes,' she said flatly. 'And you – what bank is it you work for?'

He told her. He had been based in the Paris branch of a British bank for the past year, a chance to use his degree in French.

'And what brings you to Paris? Are you sleuthing? "On a case"?' He indicated quotation marks, looking elaborately round the cafe and indicating a blameless French pensioner. 'Now that old guy there – in your professional opinion, doesn't he look distinctly suspicious?'

'Not really,' she said coolly. God, what a prat! If she got up and walked out it would be rude to the point of downright aggression, but she was

39

tempted. Fighting the impulse she explained about her mother. 'I come over to see her occasionally,' she said, playing it down in case he suggested a regular meeting.

'Shame I didn't know sooner. I could have whisked you round a bit. But in fact, I'm more likely to see you back home.'

Louise was surprised. 'In Galloway? Didn't think that would have been your scene any more.'

'Oh, I pop back from time to time, you know.'

She thought he looked oddly shifty as he said that – perhaps ashamed of admitting to going anywhere so uncool. But he was going on, 'And my mother is taking this Year of Homecoming stuff terribly seriously – there's a three-line whip out for some grand event she has in mind, so that was it, of course. Did you ever meet my ma?'

'I don't think so.'

'You didn't, then. Once seen, never forgotten. Most people bear the scars for years afterwards.' He laughed. '"She Who Must Be Obeyed", you know? People in the village run when they see her coming.'

Looking at her son, Louise could well believe it. His air of confident authority probably went down well in banking circles but it was getting right up her nose. She shifted the conversation to mutual acquaintances until she felt able to look at her watch and claim another engagement.

Randall looked disappointed. 'I thought we could run this into lunch. Come on, chuck your date! I go to this great little place near the Bourse – the patron gets the foie gras straight from his brother's farm. Oh – my treat, of course.'

As if it was charity to a humble copper who couldn't possibly afford the local he usually popped round to from work, Louise thought, and if that was meant to impress her he'd really blown it. 'I'm afraid I don't eat foie gras,' she said coldly. 'I'm lunching with my aunt and I couldn't possibly let her down – she's getting on a bit and I couldn't disappoint her.'

Louise crossed her fingers surreptitiously as she spoke. Her *Tante* Coralie would have had reason to be surprised to hear that, not to say annoyed, since she was currently lunching with two equally youthful looking and elegant Parisiennes in their own very chic local bistro. However, Louise felt sure she would forgive the slur if it allowed her niece to escape this objectionable young man.

Randall got to his feet reluctantly. 'Too bad. Well – see you at the other end, then?'

'Absolutely. Great to see you,' Louise said with what enthusiasm she could muster and left, giving an airy wave before he could complete the move he was making to kiss her.

He probably won't bother, Louise told herself as she headed back across the river and bought a baguette from a stall near Notre Dame to eat in the Square du Vert-Galant and contemplate the bustle of the Seine.

The tourist season was just starting to get under way and the *bateaux-mouches* were plying their trade up and down, though there were still more tourists in the glass-roofed cabins than hardier souls braving the river breeze on the open decks.

She lit up once she'd finished eating. How strange it felt, sitting here and knowing that the

41

day after tomorrow she'd be back at police headquarters in Kirkluce, Galloway, having to huddle
round the back by the dustbins to smoke her
Gitane, probably in pouring rain. It really was
high time she gave up. She might even do it.

'What I don't understand is why they requested
you,' Detective Superintendent Christine Rowley
said petulantly. 'I told Tom Taylor I'd be happy to
review their processes in the case and you would
have thought he'd have jumped at the offer of an
experienced senior officer.'

It was a wet Monday morning, but DI Fleming's gloom had been lifted by the invitation to
take a look at a murder case in Dumfriesshire
that had been going on for some time without
apparent progress.

She was trying to conceal her pleasure, though,
saying, 'Mmm,' as non-committally as possible,
though she could have explained that the superintendent – known to her officers as Hyacinth
after the redoubtable Mrs Bucket – had gained a
reputation for being toxic that went well beyond
the bounds of Galloway. Rowley had come from
Edinburgh and was unwise enough to make it
clear that in her eyes the job out here in the sticks
was only a stepping stone to promotion back in
civilisation.

Instead, Fleming said with careful tact, 'He
probably felt that doing it at superintendent level
would be overkill. It's an informal request and
with all the constabularies being technically
merged into one force now this is more like asking
a colleague to brainstorm than calling in a formal

case review.'

Rowley pouted. 'The merger wouldn't have happened at all, if I'd had any say. Now we're just a division instead of a force – indeed, a sub-division of that division – our successes are going to get blurred.'

'Our failures, too,' Fleming put in, with malice aforethought.

Rowley's sallow skin took on an unattractive flush; she had gone blonde recently which somehow made her skin tone muddier than ever. 'Compared to other forces – when there still were other forces – it's a shining example of my good practice, but who will notice that now?'

Here we go again! Once Rowley began on a lament for the diminution of her prospects of becoming a chief constable since there was only one now for the whole of Scotland, it could take quarter of an hour out of the working morning.

Fleming seized on a pause for breath. 'Anyway, I'm to get in touch with Detective Super-intendent Taylor, is that right? I'd better do that now before I get caught up in sorting through the weekend reports.'

Escaping, she headed for her office on the fourth floor of police headquarters in Kirkluce, a market town on the main road between Newton Stewart and Stranraer. She took the steps two at a time; she'd become more conscious of the need for fitness since her husband Bill's heart attack last year. She was tall – five-foot ten in her socks – and she'd carried the weight that had crept on more or less unnoticeably. She was getting her athletic figure back now, though, and with the intrusive grey hairs in her chestnut crop judiciously camouflaged, she felt she was limiting at least some of the damaging effects of middle age.

And the new task was good news. There had been something of a lull recently and she'd had to take on her share of the chores that were the tedious side of modern police work. Skilfully managed, this assignment could even provide her with an excuse to palm off the statistical return that was currently lying reproachfully on her desk to someone else. With hope in her heart Fleming shifted it to one side as she sat down.

She knew why Tom Taylor had asked for her. He was in his late thirties, young to have made super – another reason for Hyacinth to be snarky about him – and he was new to the job. They had met at a course geared towards bringing together several neighbouring forces before the Police Scotland reforms came into operation. He had sought her out to ask about her most recent murder case and they had been deep in discussion when his senior DI Len Harris appeared, a sharp-featured man with a neat pencil moustache, every hair of it bristling.

He clearly saw this cross-border détente as fraternising with the enemy and was embarrassingly chippy with his senior officer; though Taylor was wise enough not to rise to provocation the atmosphere became uncomfortable and Fleming made a tactical withdrawal. Since then Taylor had come to her with a couple of queries, which by tacit agreement she had not mentioned to Rowley; she would be very surprised if he'd mentioned them to Harris either.

However, she knew no more about the case in

question than she'd read in the press releases: a man's body had been found in a battered car stranded on mudflats off the Dumfriesshire Solway coast last month, just after a storm and a particularly strong spring tide. Given the conditions, the presumption of accident had been the obvious one: the car, perhaps on one of the low roads running right beside the Firth, had either misjudged a corner or been swept away by a tidal surge and the notoriously treacherous Solway had claimed another victim.

A later release had announced that the police were treating the death as suspicious, but with nothing about it to attract press attention, it had merited only a small paragraph in the Scottish papers. Since then Fleming had heard nothing more and it was with considerable interest that she dialled the number she had been given.

Detective Superintendent Taylor answered the phone himself, his voice brightening when he heard her voice.

'Marjory! Thanks for getting back to me. I take it Christine told you what this is all about?'

'Not really, no, except it's to do with this body that was discovered in a stranded car.'

'That's right. Oh, I can send you over the reports if you agree to get involved, but if I brief you on the situation over the phone now I can speak in confidence, I hope.'

'Of course.'

'The car was reported stuck on the mudflats near Newbie – treacherous stuff, we nearly lost a tractor trying to get it off. The boffins tell me that from its condition it had been thrown about in

45

the water but as usual they're reluctant to commit themselves to anything more specific than that, given the weather conditions at the time.

'Anyway, it finished upside down with the corpse in a corner of the roof.'

'No seat belt?'

'Presumably not. None of them was broken. Of course, that's not of itself significant. As you and I both know there's all these morons with a death wish out on the roads who don't use them – the body was a vivid example of what happens if you're unrestrained when a car goes out of control.' He paused.

'I sense a "but",' Fleming prompted.

'Yes, a but... He didn't die in the accident. The pathologist is prepared to be specific, for once – he was killed with a single blow to the back of the head. The weapon was round and very solid. Could even have been a cosh but there's no sign of it – either removed or washed away after the car entered the water.'

'A cosh – could be a professional? Right,' Fleming said slowly. 'Do we know if he was driving?'

'Inconclusive. Lots of smudges on the steering wheel but no clear prints. His prints were clear elsewhere, though, so it was presumably his car. Anyway, that's the story, basically. But we have a problem, Marjory. We're embedded in the mudflats, you could say.

'The car's number plate was false – it's all too easy to get them on the Internet, so that was a dead end. The engine number wasn't any use either; the original owner sold it in a private arrangement five years ago. Now nothing's happening. It's like Einstein's definition of insanity around here – repeating the same action and expecting different results. I've got dozens of lads out there duplicating investigations they've done already. And this is the bit I will deny flatly if challenged – I have absolutely no confidence in Len. He's sloppy, he hasn't an idea to take forward, he's going round and round in ever-decreasing circles and acting like a Rottweiler guarding a bone and he won't let anyone else take over. He's been so offensive to his DCI that she's off with stress.

'I need your help.'

Suddenly it didn't seem quite such an attractive proposition. 'And what makes you think he'll let me take it away without taking my hand off first?' Fleming asked.

'I'm going to have a very straight talk with him. If we haven't some progress to show for the time and the money in the next couple of weeks there'll be an official case review, with his methods scrutinised. I think he's scared himself – he's actually a very insecure individual.

'You've got a good record. Now we're all meant to be working together, I want to tap into that. Please, Marjory – as a favour to me.'

'Let me recap,' Fleming said dryly. 'You don't know where the car came from, you don't know when it happened, you don't know who the body is–'

'Oh, we know that,' Taylor said.

'Do you?' Fleming was surprised. 'I haven't seen anything about that.'

'No,' he said, a little awkwardly. 'We haven't

announced it yet. Dragging our feet a bit, I admit. The thing is, going by the DNA records we have he's been dead for two years.'

When the doorbell rang, Heather Denholm was peeling potatoes. 'Can you get that?' she called through the open door to the sitting room. 'My hands are wet.'

Her partner Donald Falconer, who was watching the six o'clock news, grunted and got up. She heard him cross the hall to open the door, wondering who their visitor was, ready to abandon the potatoes and be hospitable if necessary.

Someone on TV was reporting on a new protest about fracking somewhere but she could hear none of the normal sounds of greeting from the hall. Curious, she put down the potato peeler and came out of the kitchen, wiping her hands on a towel.

Donald was standing very still by the open door, staring at the girl on the doorstep. At first glance she looked to be no more than a teenager, dressed in skinny jeans with a black-and-white striped T-shirt and a grey waistcoat, worn open. Her dark hair was piled loosely on top of her head and she was very pretty, with striking blue-green eyes and delicate features. Looking more closely, Heather realised she was older than she had seemed and the thought suddenly struck her. Could it be...?

'Well, well, well,' Donald said heavily. 'Fancy that.'

The woman's smile didn't reach her eyes. 'Hello, Dad.'

Heather came forward. 'Are you Skye? Oh, I'm

so pleased to see you! Your father has been so worried about you, all this time.'

Donald shot her a cold look. 'Have I?' he said ominously. 'Oh yes, perhaps I have. It had just slipped my mind – the searches in case you'd had an accident and come to grief somewhere, the phone calls to the hospital and to everyone I had ever heard you mention, the police enquiries that had them questioning me as if I'd done away with you myself. You didn't think of maybe just phoning or sending me a text to say you weren't at the bottom of the Solway Firth with your pal Connell?'

Skye bit her lip. 'It was ... difficult,' she said.

Donald drew in his breath but before he could say anything Heather cut in. 'There's no need to stay standing on the doorstep. Come in, dear. I'm Heather.'

With an uncertain smile Skye shook the hand held out to her but her eyes went back to her father's face and she only stepped over the threshold once he had stepped aside.

On the news, they were talking about a royal visit now. Donald killed the programme and sat down in his usual chair while Heather fluttered about, ushering Skye to a seat on the sofa.

'Would you like a drink or something, dear?' she offered.

Skye shook her head.

'Whisky,' Donald said.

As Heather scurried to the kitchen to get it she heard Donald say, 'And are you going to tell me where you've been?'

'No.' Skye's voice was flat.

49

'You don't think you owe it to me?' Donald's voice had risen. 'It killed your mother, you know. Proud of that?'

Heather felt tears come to her eyes. That was cruel – and not true, either. How would the poor girl feel after an accusation like that?

Hostile, apparently was the answer. 'I heard it was cancer, actually. And you'd both made it very clear to me that I wasn't welcome at home any more after what happened.'

'You're surprised? The reports after the inquest – disgusting! And if you think you can just swan back here, come home as if nothing had happened–'

'I don't. A lot happened and everything changed. I only came to tell you I was back in the neighbourhood before one of the neighbours did.'

'Why did you come back at all, then?'

Donald sounded rough, angry, but Heather could hear the hurt in his voice. He was still hopeful, wasn't he, even now – hoping that, after the blazing row he needed to have with the daughter who had turned her back on him in this ruthless way, the air could be cleared and some sort of healing could begin.

'I wanted to.'

Through the open door Heather could see that Skye had stood up.

'Oh yes!' Donald gave a bitter laugh. 'That was always your only thought – what you wanted. Never mind anyone else. It didn't occur to you that after the shame you brought on this family I might appreciate it if you just stayed away?'

'Leaving you to relish the thought that I was

probably dead? I didn't think of that, no, though I probably should have.'

Heather heard the hurt in her voice, too, and almost groaned aloud. Why did people do this sort of thing to each other? Pride, probably. She'd never been much tempted to pride, herself. It only seemed to cause pain and misery, as far as she could see.

She'd poured out Donald's whisky already but as she heard the front door slam she unscrewed the cap of the bottle and added another measure.

'What did he say?' Jen Wilson asked, though her friend's drooping shoulders and the look on her face gave her the answer already.

Skye Falconer shrugged. 'Same old, same old. I'm rubbish, and basically he'd rather I was dead.'

'I'm sure–' Jen was about to go on, 'he wouldn't,' but on reflection thought that he very likely would. She'd felt bad about keeping Skye's secret after all the fuss about her disappearance but when a guilty conscience prompted her to go round to see the Falconers, their reaction – a tirade of abuse from Donald, tight-lipped anger from his wife – convinced her that they were more enraged than heartbroken. She left feeling justified in keeping her promise of silence

'Come and have a drink,' she said instead.

Skye nodded listlessly and followed her through to the kitchen. As Jen fetched a bottle of Sauvignon out of the fridge she said, 'She seems nice, his partner. Can't imagine why she took up with him, to be honest. She seemed quite keen to welcome the black sheep but he just wanted to know why I'd come back at all.'

It was the question Jen had been longing to ask too but it had seemed inhospitable when Skye, badly bruised, thin and strained, had turned up on her doorstep one morning.

'I'm looking for sanctuary. Promise you won't tell anyone I'm here – now or ever?' she'd said, but she'd only shaken her head and begun to cry silently when Jen tried gently to find out why. It had seemed pointless, even cruel to persist and Jen couldn't but sympathise with this poor little shadow of Skye's former self. An imp, a sprite: those were the sort of words people had used to describe her, drawn to the sparkling personality and charm. They wouldn't say that now.

She was having bad dreams, too, but the first time Jen woke to muffled groans and a startled waking cry and went through, Skye hadn't welcomed her. 'Sorry – did I wake you? Just a dream,' was all she would say and there was nothing Jen could do but wonder.

She'd always felt that Skye's love of pleasure, which had drawn her to the Cyrenaics, had had a sort of innocence about it, unlike Jen's own attraction to the darker glamour of decadence. What had happened to Skye had been like breaking a butterfly upon a wheel.

Today had been the first time Skye had left the house since she came. 'Pretend I've only just arrived – promise, on your honour? Promise? I want him to think I dashed round whenever I got here. I just had to let my face heal first.'

Jen suspected that she had needed time to recover from whatever had caused the injury as well, and soothed her with a solemn promise.

Skye had been an ideal guest, appointing herself housekeeper so that Jen had the luxury of coming home from a tiring day to a clean house and a meal, but she had said nothing about moving on. Now, as they sat at the table with their wine, Jen said, 'So what next?'

Skye looked down at her glass, turning it in her hands. 'Would it be awful to stay a bit longer? I just need some time to think – get my head straight. I'd help with expenses, of course – I've got money...'

Jen was far from sure that she did. 'Of course you can,' she said. 'And you more than earn your keep. It's been total bliss being spoilt.'

The relief on Skye's face was obvious. 'Thanks, Jen. Don't know what I'd have done without you.' Then she smiled and she suddenly looked younger, her face impish once more.

'Let's celebrate! As far as my father's concerned, I'm dead. We have to hold a wake.'

They both laughed but Jen gave a sudden shudder as she went to fetch the bottle from the fridge to top them up. 'Oooh – goose walked over my grave.'

'*My* grave, you mean,' Skye corrected her and they both laughed again.

CHAPTER FOUR

DS Tam MacNee parked his car and walked across to the police headquarters, Galloway. He was, as always, wearing a white T-shirt, jeans and trainers with a black leather jacket and recently he'd been asked by a cheeky DC if it wasn't time he gave up trying to be James Dean – a man of his age?

He'd got a dusty answer. MacNee had been much the same age as the ill-fated star when he left the uniform branch and adopted it as a uniform of his own. He intended to go on wearing it until they did the whip-round for his retirement party. Possibly even after that; it was a few years yet before he'd need to decide.

Today he was in a sullen mood. His wife Bunty's Aunt Jessie was coming to stay to give her put-upon daughter some much-needed respite and as well as having to watch Bunty working herself into a frazzle – the old besom didn't seem to know slavery had been abolished – he'd have to bite his tongue for two whole weeks if he wasn't going to make the situation even worse for his warm-hearted, long-suffering wife. And to protect Bunty, he'd chew his tongue off at the roots, if that was what it would take.

Added to that, the latest Scottish independence referendum poll had been alarming and he couldn't even have a good moan about that, since

Fleming had banned discussion of it in the team. 'Too many people feel too deeply about this one,' she'd said. 'Feelings are running high and taking sides would affect operational efficiency.'

She was certainly right there. Conflicts within her team of four detectives caused problems – you only needed to look at all the tiptoeing round they had to do because DS Andy Macdonald and DC Louise Hepburn seemed to be permanently at each other's throats, and it was just a mercy that DC Ewan Campbell was normally so silent it would have been hard to work out if he had a problem with one of the others. But it was frustrating when you wanted to let off steam about the stupidity of the folks who couldn't see things your way.

He wasn't looking forward to his shift, either. He'd to be in the district court this morning which meant sitting around wasting his time until the case, a minor charge of theft, was called or more likely went off because the accused hadn't got out of bed to come to court. It wasn't as if he didn't have plenty other stuff to get on with – not that he wanted to do that either, since most of it would involve writing up a report on a credit-card fraud.

His day, however, improved almost immediately when he arrived in the CID room to find a message that a plea of guilty had been entered in the theft case, and improved even more when DI Fleming came looking for him a little later.

'How are you placed this morning, Tam?'

MacNee brightened. 'Me? Oh, I'm fine. Nothing that wouldn't wait.'

'Come with me, then – five minutes? Something's come up. I'll explain in the car.'

As she left, DC Hepburn who was working at a computer nearby, looked up enviously. 'Some people have all the luck. I spent all yesterday catching up with stuff that came in over the weekend and I'm not finished yet.'

'Och well, you'll be used to it so you'll not mind doing a wee bit of tidying up on the credit-card case, will you?' As Hepburn drew breath to protest, he went on, 'Thought not. That's my lass – you're a wee stotter, so you are. I'm just forwarding it to you now.'

He logged out, picked up the black leather jacket he had slung on the back of his chair and strutted out, giving her a wink over his shoulder and whistling through the gap in his front teeth.

Hepburn groaned. 'Why me?' she demanded of the room in general, running her hands through her hair so that it looked even wilder than usual. 'Why is it always me?'

DS Andy Macdonald, dark and unsmiling, paused on his way out to a house-breaking to say, 'Punishment for past sins,' as if it was a joke. It just didn't sound like one to Hepburn, the way he said it.

'It's a bit delicate, this one,' Fleming said as she drove out of the car park, heading for Dumfries. 'Hurt feelings on every side. The super thinks Tom Taylor should have asked her to do this, not me, and his inspector is very aggressive and is probably even now working on the hissy fit he's going to throw the minute I appear.

'Taylor's idea was that I should do it on my own

but I insisted on bringing backup – I'm taking you along to ride shotgun, basically.'

'Should've brought my *sgian dubh*,' MacNee said happily.

'Just as well you didn't. Since it's only licensed for carrying in the top of your sock when you're in full Highland dress, I'd be forced to charge you with possession of a knife and you know you get the jail for that.'

MacNee laughed. 'Here! You're in a good mood.'

'So would you be. I've got John Purves conned into taking over the statistical report that's been haunting me for weeks.'

'Funny you should say that. Same here – Louise. Anyway, fill me in on this lad that's going to set about you.'

'Len Harris – do you know him? Dapper, thin moustache–'

'Not Lucky Lennie Harris, who used to be in Glasgow? He was a PC when I moved to Galloway, famed for never actually being on the spot when it got down and dirty. I heard he'd left – in fact, I think I might even have seen the fireworks from the farewell party from down here.'

'Oh no!' Fleming was dismayed. 'It never occurred to me you might have previous where he was concerned. Maybe I should have brought Andy Mac – or Ewan, better still.' Given his pathological addiction to silence it was hard to quarrel with DC Ewan Campbell.

'Och, it was just one or two wee minor disagreements,' MacNee said cheerfully. 'It was years ago – he'll likely have forgotten all about them by now.'

Fleming gave him a doubtful look. 'I hope

you're right. He didn't strike me as the forgiving and forgetting type.

'Anyway, this is the situation.' She explained about the car being found in the Solway Firth on the mudflats near Newbie three weeks before and the forensic evidence of murder, and then the identification of the body as Connell Kane who had staged his own suicide after he was charged with drugs offences, with a charge of culpable homicide pending as well.

'Oh aye?' MacNee raised his eyebrows.

'Supplying drugs to a girl who OD'd two years ago. From what I've seen of the investigation, Harris is majoring on just two angles: trying to find out where Connell appeared from after two years presumed dead, and investigating the area near where the car went into the water. Nothing's come of either approach but he won't accept it – keeps saying that's all they need to know and it's just that they haven't interviewed enough people yet. It's become a matter of pride and he's blowing the budget to prove himself right.

'He's intimidated his DCI to the point where she's on sick leave, and though Tom Taylor is a nice guy I don't think he's got a grip on Harris. When I met them together the man was impertinent and got away with it. Even as a mere inspector, I wouldn't have taken it from someone junior.'

'Don't think I ever heard anyone describe you as a "mere" anything,' MacNee said dryly. 'You're maybe a farmer's wife but you're the kind that would cut off tails with a carving knife and not bat an eyelid.'

'I just believe in the broken windows' theory,'

58

Fleming said in her own defence. 'Ignoring the trivial leads on to big problems later. Taylor is desperate now because if there isn't major progress in the next couple of weeks it'll mean an official review and from what I've seen they'd shred him. So that's where we come in.'

'So where do we start?'

'We're meeting Harris at the police garage where they took the car after they pulled it out, so we can take a look at it. The forensic report on it is exhaustive but there's nothing dramatic and apart from Kane's own, no fingerprints that check out on the database.

'There were two or three things I picked up on. Harris seems to have put far too much weight on a sighting of a grey car being driven through Annan with a driver and passenger, both male, who seemed to be having a row – shouting, the witness claimed, though she couldn't hear what it was about. She didn't notice the number plate or even the make of car, but on the basis that Annan isn't far from Newbie, there have been days and days of house-to-house in and around the area and from there down to the Solway coast where the car was found. The car was grey right enough and I don't doubt the witness, but it still seems a flimsy foundation for such a full investigation.

'There's no fingerprint evidence to suggest who was driving, but since he was hit from behind – quite likely coshed – he was probably in the front, unless he was out of the car when it happened. And interestingly, though there are unidentified fingerprints on the other safety-belt releases, on the steering wheel there are only smudges.'

'Someone wiped it? So someone we know already, maybe?'

'Might just be someone ultra-cautious. Anyway, Harris's theory is that this all happened after they were seen quarrelling in Annan, and the men were both in the front. It's only four or five miles to the coast. In that space of time the murderer would have needed to get behind his victim somehow – get himself into the back seat, or get the other man to step out of the car and turn his back.'

MacNee snorted. 'When they were having a collieshangie – yelling at each other? Aye, right. He'd have to be daft.'

'They'd be travelling on minor roads, some of them so small you'd practically be driving through a farmyard, but no one saw or heard anything – they seemed to have checked every house on the route. Some twice. I'll give Harris that, at least – he's thorough.'

'Hmm.' MacNee considered that. 'OK, let's just assume chummie's got himself there and no one's noticed. He's put his car with the body into the river and now he's miles from anywhere. What happens then?'

Fleming nodded. 'Exactly. Was there another car travelling with him, maybe? You're very obvious walking on country roads; any passing car would notice you, unless you dived into the hedgerow – I suppose you could do that, and just keep walking. And then there's the killer question – the car was badly damaged after being rolled around in the water, but how the hell would you manage to drive on to mudflats without getting solidly bogged down immediately you left the shore?

'When I got the report yesterday I took a look at the Solway tides and current charts. They found the car the day after a spring tide and when I checked the weather records there was a strong wind blowing right up the Firth the night before. With the head of water that would produce it could have gone in anywhere, Tam – carried on to the flats at Newbie by the strength of the tide.'

'So you're saying he's blown the budget on a wild goose chase?'

'Apart from what he's spent trying to establish where Connell Kane had been since the last time he died, yes. And that hasn't delivered any results either.'

MacNee whistled through his teeth. 'Here – you know you said you were worried I might get up his nose? Once he's heard what you're going to say, I'll be his new best friend by comparison.'

DI Len Harris didn't seem to feel anyone was his friend. He greeted Fleming with barely concealed hostility and MacNee with open aggression.

'Can't think what they imagine I'm going to learn from you, MacNee. You weren't even CID in Glasgow.'

There was nothing MacNee enjoyed more than a bit of aggro. 'Och well, Lennie, I've maybe been learning all the time you've been wondering why you should,' he said cheerfully.

Fleming shot him a warning look that he took care not to see as, with Harris walking stiff-backed before them, they went into the garage workshop where the car was being kept securely as a crown production.

It was certainly in a battered state, the paint abraded and the windscreen as well as two of the side windows stoved in. The tyres were ripped and twisted and the doors, buckled by impacts, had obviously been forced open to allow the SOCOs a full examination.

'Not much to learn from that, as you see,' Harris said.

Fleming walked round it, studying it carefully. 'And in your view, the car – what, was deliberately driven on to the flats with the corpse inside it, somewhere around here?'

He began to explain about the eyewitness, but she cut in. 'Yes, I've read all the background. But it did occur to me – could it have been just a passing grey car, nothing to do with this at all?'

A flush of colour came to Harris's face. 'Yes, of course. But you have to say it was suggestive – two men quarrelling, the right area–'

'Of course, absolutely,' Fleming said soothingly. 'If the car was driven into the water at Newbie–'

'If? How else would it get there?'

'Well, it was just the timing – the weather, you know.'

'Oh yes, the weather.' It was plain that he hadn't thought about the effect of the spring tide; he coughed, then went on, 'You've formed some theory, have you, because of the weather?'

'Not exactly a theory, just a thought about keeping the options open. With the spring tide and the wind direction, it's conceivable that the car could have gone in further down the estuary and been swept up here.'

Harris had a very prominent Adam's apple and it bobbed up and down as he swallowed. 'Er, well, of course I did consider it. Naturally. But that would make the search almost impossible – we can only work on information received.'

Fleming sensed MacNee moving restlessly, heard him draw in his breath to speak and interposed, as she thought tactfully, 'It's always the problem, isn't it? Look, is there somewhere we could go for a cup of coffee and talk this through?'

'Oh, I suppose so. The station's just round the corner.'

'There'll be a space in the car park there? Fine, we'll drive round and see you inside,' Fleming said.

As she drove off MacNee gave a low whistle. 'Man's a liability. Seems to think a detective's job is to sit and wait till someone comes and tells him what happened. Starting from scratch, then, are we?'

'With the trail cold and the budget blown already,' Fleming agreed grimly. 'Fun, fun, fun.'

In the gleaming, stainless-steel kitchen at the back of The Albatross pub, Logie Stewart was preparing for the lunchtime service. He was in a bad mood; he always was when it came to wasting his considerable talents on the day-to-day, boring stuff, the food that would appeal to the passing trade or the less discriminating local clientele. The Albatross might be a destination restaurant as a result of his culinary skill but a tasting menu event once a month, parties in the chic private

63

dining room upstairs and fine dining à la carte wouldn't keep your head above water, particularly before the tourist season got going.

With a bad grace he topped steak and ale pies with puff pastry, put them into the oven, set the timer, then turned to the small, frazzled looking woman who was chopping vegetables.

'The onions for the lasagne, Maggie – where are they, then?'

She put up a hand to wipe her streaming eyes. 'Sorry, sorry, not quite finished yet, Logie. Won't be a minute.'

He glared at her. 'No, you won't be, will you? Nearer ten, judging by the pile that's waiting. Heaven send me patience!'

With an exaggerated gesture of despair he swung round to fetch the mince from the huge industrial refrigerator and he was leaning into it when his wife Kendra came into the kitchen and greeted him. He didn't turn round.

'Kendra – good. Grab a chopping knife, will you? Maggie's on a go-slow, apparently.'

Maggie made an incoherent protest as Kendra said, 'Oh darling, I would, of course, but I'm just on my way to a hair appointment in Castle Douglas. Sorry face, look!' She made a little moue and pointed to it.

He surveyed his wife as he brought the meat back to the working surface. She wasn't classically pretty but her vivacity was very attractive. Her hair, slicked back into a neat brown bob, looked as it always did.

'Doesn't look as if it needs it to me,' he muttered.

'Darling, if I waited until you noticed that it needed it, I'd be having people pointing at me in the street,' she said, laughing. 'See you in the afternoon sometime.'

'Oh, fine.' His tone was grudging. 'Is that brother of mine lounging about next door, then? Tell him he can come and give me a hand to earn his keep.'

Kendra turned in the doorway. 'Oh, sorry again, love. Will's cadged a lift with me. He's got an appointment with the bank – something about transferring money from Canada. Bye!'

Logie grunted, then turned his attention to the unfortunate Maggie. 'For God's sake, are you not finished yet? Give me what you've done so I can get started with this.' He grabbed a handful of onions and tipped them into the oil in the frying pan.

His mind, though, was on other things. He hadn't exactly shed tears when Will had announced he was emigrating. As a founder member of the Cyrenaics Logie had, of course, endorsed the pleasure principle, had been as ready as anyone to take advantage of the joys of sexual freedom – but he had drawn the line when it came to his wife and his own brother.

They had assured him, laughing, that they – well, couldn't. 'He's my *brother* – well, all but,' Kendra had giggled. 'Ugh!'

It was what Logie wanted to believe so he'd accepted it at the time, fighting down the inclination to start watching them, counting the 'brotherly' hugs and affectionate exchanges. Affection worried him; that was very different from the

65

casual pleasure that was the Cyrenaics' creed.

The scandal that had followed Julia's death changed everything. They'd all grown up suddenly, avoiding each other, living it down as best they could. And if they felt that life now was dreary and flat, after the rich excitement of those heady days, they didn't talk about it.

Bizarrely, it had done wonders for the business; the ghouls had come to gawp and then gone away spreading the word about his cuisine. He'd planned to redecorate the private dining room upstairs with its sombre walls and silver-framed mirrors but it had proved so popular he couldn't afford to, even though marketing decadence seemed sordid now. The other benefit was that Will had gone to Canada and he could relax.

Now Will was back. He hadn't changed in those two years, years in which Logie had grown stouter and balder and wearier with the punishing hours a chef has to keep.

He tossed the onions in the pan and glanced irritably at his helper. 'Finished the onions? Hallelujah! Bring the rest over and then get the cheese out of the fridge and start grating.'

The tantalising aroma followed Kendra as she tripped out to the car. Will, taller and considerably leaner than his brother with a clever, humorous face, was leaning against the car. He straightened up as she reached him.

'All right?'

Kendra smiled up at him, her brown eyes sparkling. 'Fine. I'm all yours.'

Detective Superintendent Taylor had obviously

asked to be alerted when they arrived, appearing just as they sat down in Harris's office in the smart, modern Dumfries Division headquarters.

From the look on his inspector's face he was about as welcome as sleet at a barbecue but he ignored that, greeting Fleming and MacNee warmly and asking if Harris had ordered coffee for their guests. 'Just about to,' he said stonily.

'Tell them an extra cup, will you? I'd like to sit in on this.' He pulled across a seat from the farther end of the room. 'Marjory, any thoughts?'

It wasn't the way Fleming would have chosen to handle it but perhaps this was all to the good. However tactful she was, Harris was going to be resentful; spending time on smoothing ruffled feathers was a luxury they couldn't afford and he might be more inclined to cooperate in the presence of his senior officer. Might be.

'It seems to me we need to widen the scope of the enquiry. The investigations round Newbie have been carried out very thoroughly, of course,' she attempted a half-smile at Harris but got only a cold stare, 'but since that hasn't yielded anything useful and since we can't be sure that this was where the car went into the water, I suggest that we consider playing the man instead of the ball. We could—'

'We've tried that,' Harris interrupted rudely. 'There's no trace of Kane that we can find, since the suicide note.'

'I thought perhaps we could take it back to the time before he disappeared – who were his contacts and so on. There are quite a number we can readily follow up because of the investigation

67

following Julia Margrave's death.'

'Have you done that?' Taylor asked Harris.

It was clear that he hadn't, hadn't even remembered the woman's name. 'Not in that sense,' he said.

As MacNee opened his mouth, clearly to ask him in what sense he had, exactly, Fleming shot him a quelling glance and he subsided.

'We'll have all the reports on file,' she said. 'I can send them over to you, of course.'

'Excellent!' Taylor was beaming.

'Can't see the point,' Harris said stubbornly. 'As far as everyone's concerned, he was dead, wasn't he? They won't be able to tell us anything useful.'

The man was impossible. Taylor was shifting in his seat and Fleming was biting her tongue when the Force civilian assistant came in with coffee, giving her a chance to consider how she was going to take this forward. By the time the business with milk, sugar and biscuits was over she had made up her mind.

'I'm sorry, Len, that's not a helpful attitude. Your approach has resulted in the investigation running into the sand and I can't help if you are simply planning to be obstructionist. And I'm going to have to ask you, Tom, to decide who is in charge. I have to have the authority to direct operations.'

Harris's face reddened. 'That's an outrageous suggestion! I'm the senior inspector here and while obviously I have to consider ideas you put forward, you have to convince me that they have merit.'

'No,' Fleming said flatly. 'I take charge, or I

withdraw. Tom?'

Taylor looked from one to the other, his discomfort evident. 'Len, Marjory's a very successful and experienced senior investigating officer. We're extremely grateful to her and to DS MacNee for coming in and I'm sure you'll cooperate.' He directed an anxious smile at Harris, but getting no response he went on, 'You see, since our own SIO – that's DCI Brotherton, Marjory – is signed off sick for a spell, technically we need one to run this, at least until she returns.'

It was less than the ringing endorsement Fleming had been hoping for and she wondered what would happen the next time Harris got Taylor round the back of the bike sheds.

His face rigid with anger, Harris said, 'Until she returns.'

'Good,' Fleming said. 'With DSI Rowley's permission I can get my team on to interviews that fall within the Galloway division, though I think you might have to have a conversation with her about budgets, Tom.'

Taylor smiled ruefully. 'No doubt. Still, cooperation's much simpler now than it used to be when we had our own little fiefdoms.'

MacNee, who had been held uncharacteristically silent by the power of his superior's eye, snorted. 'Not quite sure our super sees it that way, sir.'

Harris had been simmering behind his desk. 'And what am I supposed to do meantime?' he burst out. 'Sit twiddling my thumbs, until you graciously solve the whole thing on the basis of feminine intuition?'

There was a silence, as Fleming waited for Taylor to intervene. He didn't, only looking from one to the other with a sort of nervous despair.

Before Fleming could stop him MacNee said, 'Why not? Getting out a crystal ball wouldn't be a lot more useless than what you've done already.'

Fleming could only hope that Harris had taken his blood-pressure pills that morning since from the colour of his face it looked as if apoplexy might be imminent. She said coldly, 'I don't think this sort of exchange can help the progress of the investigation. Could I suggest that as well as the further plans you have no doubt formulated, you could get teams to check the low roads round the Solway coast, to see if there's any indication of damage where a car might have gone in. If we could establish that it would give us a better focus for enquiries.'

'An excellent idea,' Taylor said heartily. 'I'm sure you can get that moving, Len.'

'It's your call, if you think it's a good idea wasting time on that nearly three weeks after it happened.'

The words 'And whose fault is that?' hung in the air but Fleming and MacNee resisted the temptation to utter them.

She got up. 'I'll get on with this, Tom. I'll let you know what progress we make.' She nodded coldly to Harris and they left.

As they walked back to the car, Fleming said ruefully, 'Well, that was a train crash, wasn't it? I didn't do very well, getting drawn into dramatic confrontation.'

'Och, rubbish! You gave him his head in his lap

and his lugs to play with, as the saying goes, and he was needing it. A fine performance. *From scenes like these, old Scotia's grandeur springs,* eh?' MacNee was grinning as he quoted his beloved Burns.

CHAPTER FIVE

'No,' Detective Superintendent Rowley said. 'Oh no. If Tom Taylor thinks he can just breeze in and appropriate my officers to boost his clear-up rate – which, I may say, is very far from impressive – he has another think coming. I'll take it up with the Chief Constable, if necessary.'

Afraid this would happen, Fleming had rehearsed her argument carefully before she took it to her superintendent on Wednesday morning. In Christine Rowley's head there was a sort of mental score sheet: will this boost my chances of professional promotion, or not? If the verdict was negative, she'd block this at every turn.

Admittedly the case didn't fall within the old constabulary boundaries but those weren't supposed to exist any more, and if Harris was left in charge it was likely to remain unsolved unless the perpetrator turned up holding his hands out for the cuffs. Now Fleming had got her teeth into it, seen a way forward and made plans for the next steps, she was very reluctant to give it up.

'I think,' she said delicately, 'that perhaps this is just the sort of cooperation the CC is keen to encourage. He's been very insistent about it and I'm sure he'd be impressed that the Galloway Division was so ready to support his ideas.'

Rowley hesitated, still unconvinced. 'And suppose you can't get a result any more than they can? It's an unnecessary risk to my excellent record, Marjory. I admit you've done quite well in the past–'

'Thank you,' Fleming murmured, quite overcome by this encomium.

'But that doesn't mean you couldn't come unstuck on this one. No, I shall phone the CC and explain the situation.' She paused, struck by a sudden thought. 'I suppose I could point out that you're coming to it after they have failed and very likely made a successful outcome impossible. That way he could see I was keen to implement his policy but any failure would be Taylor's fault. Yes, that would do.'

Amazed yet again at the unselfconscious transparency of Rowley's ambition, Fleming found it hard to know what to say but Rowley, having established a strategy, was going on. 'So, what steps will you be taking?'

On the principle that the less she knew, the less able she was to interfere, Fleming said, 'Now you've given it the nod I'll go and sort out the details. I'll be wanting my own team on this – Macdonald, Campbell, Hepburn and MacNee, of course – and I'll brief them later. Fortunately we're not at full stretch for once, and the Dumfries team will be doing a lot of the legwork for us.'

'So I should hope. And we'll be billing them for our time as well. I'll get on to the CC just now and as long as his reaction's favourable I don't see why you shouldn't go ahead. But remember, Marjory, this is very important. I need to be able to show continued successful outcomes, so don't let me down.'

On the way back to her office, Fleming gave herself a stern talking-to. It was immature even to entertain the thought of making blunder after deliberate blunder, just to wreck Hyacinth's career.

Randall Lindsay walked into the hall of Ballinbreck House and called, 'Hello! Anybody in?'

There was no answer. They were probably at the warehouse at the other end of the village where there was storage and office space for their online home decor business, along with a shop.

It had been set up with the last of his father's family money and it was Philippa's eye for stylish and unusual home accessories that had made it a thriving business, though since the downturn things hadn't been going well. That gave him a sick feeling in the pit of his stomach.

Randall went up the stairs two at a time to his bedroom. It was still a shock when he went in, even though he knew his mother had expunged all trace of his childhood when he left home. The room was now an elegant guest room with French-Grey walls and white bedlinen, piled with vintage lace-trimmed cushions instead of the bunk beds and bookshelves and pin boards he still saw in his mind's eye.

With a petulant movement he threw the cushions on the floor and lay down at full length on the bed, not taking his shoes off. They were probably muddy – it was pouring today – but he didn't care. God, he hated this place!

He glanced at his watch. Half past four. It would be half past five in Paris and he'd be making an assessment of how much more he needed to clear from his desk before he could pop round to the cafe that was their local for a pastis before they decided where to eat. His gut twisted at the thought.

He heard the front door opening and then his mother's commanding tones. 'Randall – you're home? Where are you?'

He heaved himself off the bed. 'Yes, Mother. I'm upstairs.'

'Come down, then. I've got a list of things I'll need you to do. I'll put the kettle on.'

What about, 'Welcome home, lovely to see you?' He swore, then glanced at the smears of mud on the pristine white cover. He seized the corner and used it to wipe the rest of the mud off his shoes.

Why was it that at the sound of his mother's voice he became a sulky schoolboy again? He was an adult, he didn't have to take her pushing him around any more. He could just walk out of the door and go—

Go *where?* a nasty little voice inside his head murmured. Trying to ignore it, he thrust his hands into his pockets in an attitude of nonchalance and went into the kitchen.

The kettle was singing and Philippa was standing at the island unit in the Smallbone kitchen that wasn't quite so designer smart after fifteen years: he could still see the scar on one of the cupboards he had secretly kicked in a fit of impotent rage on his last visit home and there were chips on one or two of the drawers as well. It wasn't like Philippa to tolerate imperfection and he felt another qualm.

When he came in she was frowning over a clipboard and looked up, smartly blonde, carefully groomed and with that familiar cold blue gaze. It was presumably his imagination that the temperature in the house had suddenly dropped.

'Get some mugs, will you? I want to go over the list with you.' She took it over to the table and sat down as, seething, he made tea and brought it to her.

He looked round. 'Where would I find biscuits?'

'Biscuits? Oh, there aren't any. Your father and I don't eat them.'

And of course, it never crossed your mind to make any provision for me? he thought but he wasn't looking for aggro just at the moment.

'Right,' Philippa said. 'The first thing is the flower beds round the lawn. They're a bit out of hand and though we can't assume it'll be a good day we'll want to shove people out into the garden if it's possible.'

'Why can't the gardener do it?'

'Gardener – what gardener?' Philippa gave a mirthless laugh. 'Laid off last year. You'll just have to get your hands dirty – unless you'd care to spend some of your lavish salary on getting him back?'

It had all gone, along with what they'd paid him to go. Gritting his teeth, Randall said, 'Ha, ha. Funny. I suppose I'd better give it a shot.'

'Oh yes, you'd better. And then I want you to

clear the hall and the drawing room – get all the good furniture out to the barn before the peasants get drunk and start falling on it. Get your father to help with the bigger stuff. And clear the shelves too – I don't want any of my bibelots falling prey to sticky fingers.'

'What's all this about, anyway – what's in it for you, going to all this trouble?' he said sulkily but she ignored his question, only flushing slightly and making an impatient noise. 'All right, then. Clear the garden, clear the house – anything else?'

She gave him a tight-lipped smile. 'Oh, very likely. How long are you staying, anyway?'

He felt himself tense up. 'Not sure. I've got a bit of leave piling up so I'll probably hang around for a bit.' *It's my home, it's where I grew up...*

'Oh.' Philippa's voice went flat. 'Well, I suppose we can find something for you to do for your bed and board after Saturday's over.' She had been studying her list; now she looked up sharply. 'Everything's all right, isn't it?'

'Yes, of course.'

'That's good. Hurry up with your tea and I'll take you out and show you what needs doing.' She got up and looked at him impatiently. 'Come on, then.'

Randall drained his mug then followed her, feeling drained himself, empty, a hollow shell of misery.

With all their different assignments, it was mid afternoon by the time Fleming was able to assemble her team in her fourth-floor office in the police headquarters in Kirkluce.

She always kept three chairs in front of her desk, with another two set beside the table in the farther corner. There were usually four officers in the team she liked to work with but the arrangement gave her officers a choice of where to sit – something she found instructive. Perching on the table was sometimes evidence of a desire, probably subconscious, to use its height to dominate the meeting; taking one of the other chairs when there was one by the desk available was usually a sign of disengagement.

She studied them as they came in: Louise Hepburn, bright, vivacious and untidy as always, came in chattering to Tam MacNee. They sat down in front of her just as Andy Macdonald arrived. He was a sound man, Andy, if a bit unimaginative. He must be hitting forty now, though with his dark buzz cut he still looked a lot younger than that. Fleming stifled a sigh as he ignored the vacant chair next to Hepburn in favour of one nearer the table, it was an indication of the friction within the group.

She had tried banging their heads together, but the best she had achieved was only a sort of armed neutrality. She was very reluctant to split up the team; they were both valuable to operations and their abilities were complementary, so however irritating their infantile spats might be she just had to accept it, ignore it and keep them out of each other's hair as far as possible.

DC Ewan Campbell, slight, red-haired and freckled, was last and with a sideways glance at Macdonald, took the seat next to Hepburn.

Fleming explained the background to their latest

assignment. 'Our immediate priority is to trace the people here who were involved in Julia Margrave's death. I'll circulate a copy of the inquest proceedings.

'Briefly, the situation was that she worked for a merchant bank in Edinburgh but came down to Galloway most weekends to stay with her mother who has a house on Balcary Bay. She was into drugs and her death was ascribed to a combination of cocaine and Ecstasy.'

Hepburn pursed her lips in a silent whistle. 'Not smart.'

'No,' Fleming agreed. 'Drug-taking seems to have been standard in this group that called themselves the "Cyrenaics" – does that mean anything to anyone?'

'Louise is the long-dead tongues expert,' Macdonald said. 'She'll know.'

It was the sort of joking remark anyone might have made – Hepburn's degree had included law – but she coloured at the sneer in his voice.

'I do, as it happens,' she said coldly. 'They believed that physical pleasure was the only good and maximising it was the only rational purpose of life. Drugs nowadays, I suppose, but then sex, good food, good wine–'

'See their point,' Campbell made one of his rare interjections.

MacNee grinned. 'Not just sure they were thinking of a Scotch pie and a wee half at the time, Ewan. Sounds to me like a recipe for disaster.'

'It's pretty much a list of the Seven Deadly Sins, isn't it,' Macdonald said.

'Certainly the third one,' Fleming said thoughtfully. 'Greed, that's what this is, really – greed of every kind and in this case the consequences certainly were deadly. But we need to ask ourselves what relevance all that had to the reappearance of Connell Kane – if any. There may well be none, but what we are trying to establish is whether anyone knew where Kane was over the past two years.'

'If he was a dealer he'd have contacts,' Macdonald said. 'Easy enough for him to disappear.'

Hepburn picked up on that. 'With friends like that, they could be behind his death as well, if he put a foot wrong. If a cosh was used it's a pointer in that direction – not the sort of thing you get on the shelves at Homebase, is it?'

'Good point,' Fleming agreed. 'DI Harris has run checks but only locally. It would be instructive to find out if any of the Cyrenaics knew where he got supplies from – it could be Glasgow, say–'

'Or Edinburgh.' MacNee bristled, as usual, at any slight on his native city. 'Plenty of big boys in Edinburgh too.'

Fleming stifled a smile. 'Of course. So that'll be our first line of attack – though they may not know–'

'Or won't tell.' Campbell's remark was, as usual, to the point.

'Could be afraid to incriminate themselves,' Macdonald said. 'When it comes to drugs, what most people do is distance themselves as far as possible. "I didn't know anything about it, just took a puff occasionally on someone else's joint." You can write the script.'

Hepburn looked sceptical. 'One of their mates

died from drugs – you could probably find one or two people who held that against Kane. Might be happy enough to give us chapter and verse.'

'Didn't do it at the time, did they?' Macdonald pointed out, but Hepburn was ready to argue.

'Too dangerous then. You said it yourself – they'd try to show they'd nothing to do with it. Now they'll know we won't try to prosecute for possession for private use and might be more ready to talk.'

'If you say so.' Macdonald crossed his arms, a shut look on his face. Fleming sensed MacNee moving impatiently in his seat and said hastily, 'Either of those may be true. It's also possible that some of them won't be happy that he's been killed. To us he was a drug dealer, scum, but they could have seen him as a friend.'

'Or it could have been one of them killed him,' Campbell said.

'A friend of Julia's, say.' Hepburn picked up on the idea. 'But how did they get to him? And what brought him back to the area?'

'Business?' Macdonald joined in. 'For all we know, he may have still been operating in the drugs trade quite close by–'

'And if someone who wanted revenge for Julia discovered that, they could have seized their opportunity, arranged a meeting–'

'They were friends, after all, he wouldn't necessarily suspect anything. You could get him in a car, say you were taking him to the pub or something–'

'Right! That would work.'

Fleming exchanged a sidelong glance with

MacNee as Macdonald and Hepburn went on tossing the idea around. She didn't think it would prove to be as simple as that but it was the first amicable exchange they'd had in a long time and she was happy to let it run.

At last, the speculation petered out as they came up against the practical problem of taking it forward and Fleming took over.

'We've got several theories running now – good. Anyway, this is the current position. Jen Wilson and Logie and Kendra Stewart are still living locally. Logie wasn't there that night but he ran the pub where the Cyrenaics met. Skye Falconer disappeared immediately after Connell Kane staged his suicide–'

'Is there a connection?' Hepburn asked.

'Could be. She's still on the record as missing but as she was an adult and there were no suspicious circumstances it wasn't followed up. Her father Donald lives in Ballinbreck and by now she may have turned up without him bothering to tell us.

'Will Stewart was a police sergeant and of course was kicked out. No record of him after that. The last of the group, the youngest, works for a merchant bank so we can trace him through them – Randall Lindsay–'

Hepburn sat bolt upright in her chair. 'Randall Lindsay?'

They all stared at her. 'Know him?' Fleming asked.

'I'm afraid so. He's in Paris – I made the mistake of contacting him on Facebook because I'm over there quite a bit, seeing my mother, and I knew

81

him slightly at uni. Tosser!' She spat the word.

Macdonald looked amused. 'What did the poor guy do? Stand you up for a date?'

Fleming had to repress an impulse to kick his shins – and hers, as Hepburn replied, *'Au contraire,'* choosing a French phrase to irritate him. 'I walked out on the date he was offering. He's a smug, patronising toff with a superiority complex and he brought me out in a rash after five minutes.'

MacNee patted her arm. 'Don't hold back, hen. Why not tell us what you really think?'

'Sorry. But honestly, he is a slimeball. Someone else can interview him – I don't want him crawling all over me again.'

Amused, Fleming said, 'I'll see what I can do. We're not shelling out for a trip to Paris just yet anyway.

'I've got a meeting tomorrow that I really can't get out of and I'm going to go back to Dumfries today to have a no-holds-barred conversation with DSI Taylor now we've got the go-ahead.

'Andy and Ewan – I want you to talk to Jen Wilson and Donald Falconer, Skye's father. Tam, you and Louise can take Logie and Kendra Stewart as a priority. Anything else may have to wait – there's no overtime on this one as yet. Tomorrow you'll have time for any follow-ups that are needed. Let's hope we get a lead from at least one of them. Any questions? No? Right. Report back to me – I should be out of the meeting by then.'

As the others filed out, MacNee hung back. 'Thought we'd a breakthrough in the kindergarten for a wee moment there.'

Fleming sighed. 'Andy can't resist needling and Louise's back goes up like a cat's and she starts spitting. But they're both useful, Tam.'

'Oh, aye. If you ask me, they're enjoying it.'

'I'm not,' Fleming said bitterly. 'And it's all right tossing ideas around but I don't think we're even beginning to skim the surface with this one.'

DI Len Harris came out of DSI Taylor's office in the Dumfries Headquarters with a thunderous look on his face. He hadn't expected to have a problem with him once he got that bitch out of the way, but Taylor had shown the stubbornness of the weak man, insisting that Fleming took control.

'The thing is, Tom, the lads won't wear it,' he had said confidently right at the start. 'She's coming in on to our patch–'

'We're not supposed to have patches any more,' Taylor pointed out.

Harris's jaw tensed. 'Yes, of course. No one's readier to cooperate than I am. But it's a question of man management. She needs to be tactful, tread carefully, not come in throwing her weight around.'

Taylor shifted in his seat. 'Well, I'm sorry. I suppose she can be – well, a bit abrasive, if you like. But we've no alternative, Len. What have we got to show for what we've spent already?'

'For God's sake, this is a complex case! We're not going to come up with the answers right away. This comes across to me as you having no confidence in your own people. No wonder that morale is at a low ebb.'

'Is it?' Taylor winced. 'Well, I'm sorry about that. But I can't do anything about it, Len–'

'Not can't, won't,' Harris had retorted. Leaving his superior officer chewing his lip, he walked out.

He'd called a meeting earlier before going, as he thought, to get the lines of authority sorted out. The Dumfries Division detectives would be there waiting for him now that he had failed and the prospect of humiliation left him seething with impotent rage.

He couldn't take Fleming on openly without Taylor's support and truth to tell he was almost at a standstill on the investigation, unable to think where to go next, if the grey car really did prove to be the distraction Fleming obviously thought it was. He had almost reached the CID room when desperation produced the inspiration he needed.

If she wasn't able to crack it either, they would blame her not him, and it was still in his power to spike her guns at the operational level. It would be pure joy to watch her fail.

An expectant silence fell as he came into the room. He knew there were mutterings within the CID already about the way things were going and while he had his own men, the men he could count on to back him, there were others – the two female detectives, for instance – who would go over to the enemy given half a chance. He even saw one roll her eyes to the other as he came in; he'd make them pay for that later.

'Right, lads,' he said. 'We've been shafted. Apparently we're not good enough to investigate our own cases without Galloway coming in to tell

84

us what to do. Of course we're humbly grateful. Forelocks will be tugged whenever she appears.'

One of the female detectives sat up sharply. 'She? Is it DI Fleming?'

Harris glared at her. 'Yes, it is, as it happens, Weston. Friend of yours?'

DC Lizzie Weston met his gaze without flinching. 'No, but she's got a pretty good reputation.'

'Then of course we must be very grateful to her for condescending to come, mustn't we, lads? Grateful and very, very humble.'

That got a sycophantic titter and Harris went on. 'Our first instruction is that we're to comb the banks of the Solway. Sounded to me like work for the uniforms but she's decided we're to do that while she applies her elevated mind to doing the thinking for us.' He was pleased to hear a little murmur of resentment.

'She's got a theory the car went into the water somewhere else, miles away and travelled on the tide like a surfer. As if, but she's the big boss now.

'So I'm detailing you, Weston, and your little friend Jamieson to work your way down the banks of the Solway, checking it out. She'd probably like you to make it a fingertip search, to make sure you don't miss anything.'

He waited for a laugh that didn't come then went on, a little tetchily, 'Well, apart from that we'll carry on with enquiries as we've planned. We haven't traced the grey car yet and we need to pull out all the stops to find where the man came from. I'll be circulating his mugshot and you'll be briefed tomorrow on your allocations. Any questions?'

DC Weston put up a hand. 'The banks of the Solway – does she want us to go on down into Galloway?'

Harris knew the answer to that one – yes. 'No,' he said. 'There's plenty of detectives in Galloway suited to doing the brain-dead stuff. Lucky we've got a couple here too, eh lads?'

As he walked out smirking, DC Weston said crisply, 'Prat!' Harris heard her but chose to ignore it, filing it under 'Insults to be avenged'.

There was a warm fragrance coming from the kitchen as Jen Wilson came home late after a parents' meeting – definitely onions, possibly tomatoes too, she thought happily.

'Something smells wonderful,' she called as she dumped her bags in the hall.

Skye Falconer appeared from the kitchen. 'Tuna casserole,' she said. 'It's just from tins. If you've had time to shop today I'll do something a bit more substantial for you tomorrow.'

Jen stifled a sigh, then turned back to the bags she had put down. 'I did a trolley dash round Spar in my lunch hour. We'd better get the milk into the fridge but then I could murder a glass of wine. I'm shattered. You wouldn't believe the illusions some people have about their little darlings and my brain hurts from trying to find a tactful way to tell them that wee Damien isn't dyslexic, just thick, which is hardly surprising given his genetic inheritance.'

Skye took the bag from her. 'Looks like putting a glass in your hand would be an act of mercy. You go and put your feet up.'

'You're a star.'

Jen went through to the little sitting room, where there was a fire burning in the old-fashioned grate. It wasn't a cold day but it was drizzling and grey outside and with its small cottage windows the room was dark. Before, when she had come back to an empty house and a grate full of dead ashes it had often seemed so unwelcoming that Jen would settle in the kitchen, which was in a bright modern extension at the back. Now she settled cosily by the fire in her favourite armchair – second- if not third-hand but plumply cushioned – with a pleasurable groan.

Skye was working hard at anticipating her every want. It was like having a very superior housekeeper, but Jen was troubled. She'd thought once the bruising had gone and she'd seen her father, Skye would stop hiding. But this morning, when Jen suggested she should go to the shop, Skye had shrunk back.

'No, no, I can't! No one must know I'm here! You haven't told anyone, have you?'

Jen hadn't, in fact. It had been a busy time at school; no one there knew Skye and in any case she made a point of never talking about anything related to the tragedy.

'No,' she assured her. 'But Skye, you can't live indoors for the rest of your life. Have you some sort of plan?'

Skye ignored the question. 'Promise you won't tell anyone I'm here! Just till I decide what I'm going to do. Promise!'

'Well, of course, if you insist–'

'Thanks, Jen. I don't know what I would have

done without you. Do you want an egg – scrambled?'

'Scrambled would be lovely,' she had said. It wasn't the time to tackle Skye, when she was so fragile.

The trouble was, Jen couldn't see that she was getting any less fragile – she'd heard her sobbing in her room again last night. Skye tried to cover it up but she was showing all the signs of depression; her hair was stringy and though Jen had offered to lend her clothes since she had only brought a small rucksack with her, she'd refused, alternating two sweaters and jeans. As a loyal friend, all Jen could do was to wait in patience until Skye felt better or was ready to explain.

And now there was something she had to mention to her – something that had niggled at her all day. She didn't know how Skye would take it – or even whether it would come as news to her or not.

When Skye came in, she brought a plate as well as the wine and the glasses and offered it to Jen, looking at the little pies on it slightly dubiously. 'I hope these are all right. I'm getting quite into cooking now and I just wanted to try making them.'

Jen bit into one and pronounced it delicious. There were definite compensations for being patient.

Skye took her glass and sat down. 'Tell me about your bad day,' she said, just as if she'd found a handbook on how to be the perfect wife.

Jen seized the moment. 'Oh, too boring to talk about,' she said. 'But I'll tell you who I bumped into in the shop – Will! I didn't realise he was back from Canada.'

The colour drained from Skye's face. 'W-Will?' she said, and her glass dropped through her fingers and spilt on the rug.

'Oh – oh, sorry, h-how clumsy!' she stammered, jumping to her feet. 'I'll get a cloth.'

Jen stared after her blankly. When Skye returned with the cloth, she had regained control of herself. 'Here we are,' she said, dabbing at the rug. 'Glass must have been slippery with condensation.

'I didn't realise Will was here – he must have decided to come back for the Homecoming party. That's good.' She straightened up. 'The casserole's ready, so we'd better eat before it spoils.'

Picking up her glass and the rest of the nibbles Jen followed her friend through to the kitchen, feeling a bit dazed. It didn't look as if Skye was going to be any more forthcoming about this than she had been about anything else.

CHAPTER SIX

DI Fleming drove back frowning after her meeting with DSI Taylor in Dumfries. It had been very unsatisfactory – in fact, when she thought about it, the man himself was pretty unsatisfactory, clearly desperate for her to rescue an investigation from disaster but too feeble to stand up to the pressure from Len Harris.

He'd shown the whites of his eyes when she'd

suggested that she should have a briefing session with his detectives.

'Oh no, Marjory, that wouldn't be wise. The lads just wouldn't wear it.'

'Wouldn't wear it?' She raised her eyebrows. 'Do they have a choice?'

'Well, of course not, not exactly, but you have to understand the problem. Morale is very low just at the moment and I can't risk undermining it any further.'

Suppressing her impatience, Fleming said, 'Don't you think their morale would improve once they felt the investigation was getting somewhere?'

He seized on that. 'Absolutely. I couldn't agree with you more. So if you can show them some progress first, they'll feel quite different and then, of course, you'll have them in the palm of your hand. Right?'

Kicking herself for not seeing that one coming, she had to acquiesce, though she couldn't bring herself to say 'yes'. 'Mmm. As long as DI Harris understands the position. I'm hoping he will be starting on the Solway search tomorrow. The more manpower we can assign to that the better – perhaps uniforms could be drafted in as well?'

Taylor was on more comfortable ground. 'I've emphasised that is priority, I assure you. And I'm sure Len has it well in hand – he's very efficient, you know.'

Efficient and obstructive – not a reassuring combination. Still, once she got her own team reporting they might come up with something that would give her ammunition against him – she was starting to see this investigation as a war zone –

since at the moment it was plain there was little point in arguing.

Fleming moved onto the next item on her list. 'I was just wondering, Tom, when you were giving your next press conference. Once we get Kane's name out there, along with a mugshot, we can enlist the public as our eyes and ears.'

It was such an obvious step to take that she couldn't think why he hadn't done it before, but he took on the look of a hunted rabbit.

'Oh dear, yes. I suppose I have to. But it'll bring the press down on us like an avalanche. I can hardly bear the thought.'

She remembered suddenly that he'd been given a rough time over a badly managed operation that had led to a bank robbery case collapsing. Well, they'd all had their moment in the *Sun*, as the saying went. She said briskly, 'Better give it to them before they come and get it. First rule is to control the information out there.'

He was huddling miserably in his chair. 'Oh, I know I'll have to—'

'When? Tomorrow?'

'Oh – oh yes, I suppose putting it off won't make things any better. Unless,' he sat up, 'we wait until you come up with something to offer them, Marjory—'

'Won't do. I have people going out tomorrow asking questions about Connell Kane and the press could be round baying for blood by tomorrow afternoon.'

Taylor sank back down in his seat. 'I take your point,' he said wearily. 'All right, tomorrow morning.'

She had left him plunged in gloom and no doubt wishing he'd never thought of drawing her in and taking on Len Harris – whose voice Fleming had recognised in Taylor's replies – or even, probably, of applying to be a detective superintendent in the first place.

She didn't stop in at the station in Kirkluce and after five miles had reached the turn off for Mains of Craigie, the hill farm that her husband Bill, following his father and grandfather, had farmed all their married life. It was sheep mainly, with young beef cattle bought in for fattening and a couple of the lower fields laid down to winter feedstuff.

Their son Cameron was all set to continue the line into the next generation, though at the moment his career as a Scottish international rugby player and a professional with the Glasgow Warriors took precedence.

After Bill's heart attack last year they had all walked around on eggshells, though the doctors had assured him he'd made an excellent recovery. Cammie had talked about giving up rugby to take on his share of the farm work but Bill had threatened to have another heart attack if he did any such thing. Cammie would be near enough to give a hand at the busiest times and Bill had Rafael Cisek, his right-hand man, the rest of the time.

Marjory blessed the day Rafael had come, especially since he had brought his wife Karolina with him from Poland. She kept the farmhouse in perfect order and provided delicious meals that made up for Marjory's notorious skills' deficiency in the kitchen. The meals were low-fat now and aggressively healthy; she gave a small, wistful sigh as she remembered Karolina's belly of pork and the dumplings whose light-as-a-feather innocence belied the wickedness of their ingredients.

Still, keeping Bill fit was considerably more important than her own decadent tastes. After the shock of his illness he had become less confident, more inclined to fuss about minor problems; he never said anything but she knew he hated it when she came home late and tired. He did seem to be improving, though, and with Cammie at home so much there was lots of light-hearted banter at the supper table.

Their daughter Catriona had said she would be home from Glasgow University this weekend too – that was good. She had also said she was bringing a friend, a young man who was studying social sciences with her. That was...

Perhaps 'interesting' was the best word. Something about the way Cat had mentioned it had made Marjory suspect this wasn't just a random friend, and she thought she had sensed a faintly defensive note in her daughter's voice.

Their relationship had been uneasy for a long time. Bill's illness had brought them closer together but Cat's placements alongside social workers dealing with 'problem families' had fostered her distrust of the police force, which put a number of topics off limits if they weren't going to descend into the sort of arguments that upset Bill. Marjory had a sinking feeling that the weekend guest wouldn't be sympathetic to her views on dealing with crime either.

Bill, though, would be looking forward to seeing

his daughter so he'd be in a cheerful mood to-night. Summer was on its way too, and it was the off season for Cammie so he came home from his Glasgow flat quite regularly. She wouldn't spoil things just yet by telling Bill that she was taking on another investigation which would, no doubt, result in her coming home late and tired even more often.

As Marjory turned off up to the farm she suddenly realised she was very hungry – it had been a long time since lunch. It had been dreary all day, with grey light under an overcast sky, and now a drizzling rain was falling, so she did hope it wouldn't be salad tonight. Karolina's salads were a long way from the limp lettuce, sliced cucumber and hard-boiled egg of the station canteen but however imaginative and interesting they might be, when it came right down to it they were still, well, just salad.

'Louise!'

Louise Hepburn turned from the bar where she was waiting to get in the next round of drinks. The girl whose birthday they were celebrating was holding up the mobile Louise had left on the table and now she could hear the police siren ringtone she'd thought was funny when she installed it, though she was beginning to get tired of people turning round and staring.

'Thanks, Chrissie.' She came back to the table to take it, glanced at the unfamiliar number then answered, walking with her finger in her other ear as she went to a quieter part of the bar.

'Sorry, who did you say?'

94

'Randall. You know – Randall Lindsay.' He sounded impatient.

Groaning inwardly, Louise said coolly, 'Good gracious, Randall! Are you phoning from France?'

'No, of course not. I told you I'd be coming home – remember?'

'Vaguely.'

'Well, I'm home now, in Ballinbreck. God, what a dump this place is! I can't imagine why anyone lives here.'

Louise could feel her hackles rising. 'Quite a nice little place, as far as I remember. Look, Randall, I can't chat just now. I'm out with friends. What did you want?'

'Oh, all right then,' he said petulantly. 'I told you my ma was organising this Homecoming party. It's on Saturday and I wondered if you would like to come? Give me a bit of moral support and someone to talk to apart from the peasants.'

It would be childish to say that she'd rather have her fingernails pulled out one by one. 'Sorry, Randall,' Louise said. 'I'm afraid I'm busy. Got to go – bye!'

She changed her mind about the glass of white wine she'd been going to order and made it a vodka shot instead. She needed something with a kick to stop her shuddering and get the taste of the conversation out of her mouth.

The pub restaurant at The Albatross was busy tonight. Kendra Stewart, managing front of house, was doing what she did best – chatting up the punters.

Her brother-in-law watched her from across the

95

room where he was grudgingly acting as waiter. Logie had made it clear that while he was staying with them it would be a working holiday but Will resented the overtones of servitude that went with the job – and it showed. He wouldn't have minded so much if the clientele hadn't been, almost without exception, middle-aged, overweight and dowdy.

You'd never think to look at Kendra now, making great play with her velvet-brown eyes and fluttering her eyelashes at a well-upholstered gentleman, that she had a tongue like a whiplash when she chose to use it and that the staff were terrified of her.

She was clever, too: now she was drawing the man's wife into a female conspiracy of amusement at his susceptibility. She left them laughing and moved to another table, casting a practised eye round the restaurant as she did so and nodding a waitress towards a table where a guest was looking round for attention. The waitress jumped and hurried to respond. Oh, Kendra was quite something.

Will was a little afraid of her. It had been different before, when sleeping together had just been part of the free-love philosophy, and ignoring Logie's bourgeois objection to it was a private joke. He'd never thought of it as an affair; now he was realising that she had.

Perhaps she'd been possessive about him even then but with so many other distractions he hadn't noticed. Now he was feeling stifled.

There was a table waiting to be cleared and he moved to do it before he too earned a dagger-look for inattention. The woman at the table was, for once, pretty and he favoured her with a charming smile when she complimented him on his efficiency and made a joking response.

Suddenly Kendra was at his elbow, hissing in his ear, 'Can you get that cleared as quickly as possible, Will? The table over there hasn't had their order taken.'

Surely she hadn't taken exception to him laughing and joking with an attractive woman? Oh yes she had. She was still watching him covertly as she chatted to the guests at another table. He felt a surge of alarm.

God knew, he hadn't wanted to come back. When he left he'd vowed never to set foot in Scotland again, let alone Ballinbreck. He'd never thought he'd have to. But with the long shadow of the past threatening to engulf him, what else could he do?

As he took the plates through to the kitchen Logie, sweating at the range, snarled, 'For God's sake, pull your finger out, Will! There's plates waiting at the pass.'

A feeling of claustrophobic panic threatened to choke him. 'Need a breath of air,' he muttered, blundering out of the back door.

He had an open ticket to Canada in his wallet. He could walk out right now – but he couldn't. Not yet.

It was quite a way down to Ballinbreck on the Solway coast so MacNee had suggested an early start, keen to get out the house before Bunty's auntie came down to breakfast. Her habit of issuing too much information about the workings of her interior during the night was enough to put a man off his porridge.

Hepburn had been happy to agree. She was living now in a pleasant rented flat in the centre of Kirkluce, which meant that MacNee's 'early start' was about half an hour later than her usual when she lived with her mother in Stranraer and had to commute.

She was looking a bit pale this morning, though, and she polished off a bottle of water in the first five minutes in the car.

'Heavy night?' MacNee said without sympathy.

She pulled a face at him. 'Nothing I can't handle. I'm young, you see, and we can take it. You probably could – once upon a time.'

And fair enough, she might be hung-over but she was still fizzing with fresh thoughts on the theory she and Macdonald had discussed at the briefing.

He listened indulgently. Even if long experience had taught him that there was no point in developing theories before you had some evidence to base them on, throwing ideas around was Hepburn's role and he was happy to listen.

'Do you think you could really have a situation like that, where everyone was casually sleeping with everyone else, without some people seething with jealousy?'

'No,' MacNee said flatly. 'It's human nature.' If anyone had ever so much as made a move on Bunty he'd have had him by the throat.

Hepburn nodded. 'Right. I've been thinking about the Happy Valley set in Kenya in the 1940s, you see. Did you ever see that old film, *White Mischief?*'

'Not that I remember,' MacNee said dryly. He'd never been one for the cinema and after Bunty insisted he take her to *Gone with the Wind*, he'd never been back.

'They were hedonists like that, with all the drug culture and wife-swapping and stuff, and that ended in murder. The jealous husband was charged but he was acquitted, though everyone knew he'd done it. It's officially unsolved – let's hope that doesn't happen with this one.'

'This isn't the films, though. The guy was a dealer. It's a lot more likely just to be a dirty row over drug money.'

'Well, I know that, of course. But you have to admit the background really suggests there could be any number of motives...'

It was amazing how long a woman could go on talking if you made the right noises, MacNee reflected. They were getting close to Ballinbreck by the time Hepburn ran out of speculation.

'Where is it exactly that we're going?' Hepburn asked.

'The pub's just on the outskirts of the village. The Albatross. Funny name for a pub – not many albatrosses around here. I suppose calling it The Seagull would be a bit downmarket for a posh place.'

'The Albatross!' Hepburn exclaimed. 'That'll be Baudelaire, of course.'

MacNee looked at her uncertainly. The young kept coming up with these new words you'd never heard of. Usually they meant either wonderful or awful.

'French poet,' Hepburn explained kindly. 'Sort of a high priest of decadence with poems called *Les Fleurs du Mal* – the flowers of evil. All dark and angst-ridden – I loved them as a teenager. "The Albatross" was one of the most famous – about how the poet is scorned in ordinary life.'

MacNee nodded. 'Right enough – happened to Rabbie Burns too.'

Hepburn laughed. 'From the little I know of his activities, he and Baudelaire would have got on just fine. Oh look, there it is! And look at the sign!'

The sign didn't show, as MacNee had expected, the magnificent bird soaring in flight, but clumsy-looking on the ground instead, head lowered and great wings dragging on either side.

'That's the poet when forced to walk not fly,' Hepburn said happily. 'You know, Tam, this could be a really interesting case.'

Far from sharing in her enthusiasm, MacNee's heart sank. Burns's poetry was one thing, arty-farty intellectuals, red-hot about their human rights and entitlement to deference, were quite another. The alternative theory, favouring the dark and dirty underworld of drugs, was looking positively enticing by comparison as he drove into the car park.

'Going to be a right doss, this, going off for a jaunt to the seaside,' DC Debbie Jamieson said gleefully as she was driven out of the Dumfries police HQ car park by DC Lizzie Weston. 'First time they've let us off together without a sergeant – no one to check on what we've done and we can take all day – probably tomorrow as well if we play smart. Where do you fancy for coffee? There's a caff in New Abbey that does cupcakes.'

Weston shook her head. 'No way. We're going to be the ones who find out where the car really went in the water. OK, it might take a couple of days but we're going to check every single bit of the shore that we can reach, even if it means going down miles of dead-end one-track road and then coming back again.'

Jamieson stared at her. 'But Harris'll never know if we did it or not. It'll be like a revenge on him for all the stuff he's put us through.'

'Sometimes you're dead naïve, Debbie. Don't you get it? That's what he wants – us not to find a place where the car could have gone in. If we do, it means DI Fleming was right, when the whole point of this where he's concerned is to prove she's just as useless as he is. He's probably reckoning on us going off to muck about.'

Jamieson was mutinous. 'We will if I've got anything to do with it.'

'Since I'm driving, you don't. Look, I've heard about Big Marge Fleming and she's a class act. If we get this one right I could maybe ask her if I could transfer to the Galloway division. I don't want my career ruined because Harris treats me as if I'm just a totty.'

'I don't want a career. A job does me fine – and frankly I'm thinking about looking for something else anyway.'

Weston looked at her in astonishment. 'You're not! What could you find that's better than this? Look, here we are – this road goes down to the

Solway.' She turned down a narrow side road as she spoke.

'What about my coffee?' Jamieson complained. 'Oh well, if you insist. But if we find it early, we're not going back till the end of the shift.'

'With you there.'

When they came near the Solway shore, the road ended in a farmyard. 'Back we go,' Weston said cheerfully. Jamieson only groaned.

It was a very attractive-looking pub. The original charming Victorian cottage had been enlarged with a two-storey extension at the back but it was in keeping with the style, the harling finish a pristine white, and the window boxes and tubs all round, bright with flowers.

There was, however, no sign of life; the front door was uncompromisingly shut and there was no doorbell and knocking produced no response.

MacNee looked at his watch. 'Nine o'clock, and nobody up,' he said. 'What's that about?'

'Probably about not finishing work till after midnight.' Hepburn wandered off round the back as MacNee peered in through the windows of the bar but came back to report that the kitchen, too, was deserted and it hadn't been any good knocking there either. 'Do they even live here?' she asked.

'That's the address they gave the court. And those windows right above the bar – those look like they could be bedroom curtains.'

'We could throw a stone at them,' Hepburn suggested.

'Oh aye, and put it through the pane instead? I've a better idea.'

MacNee went back to the car and started leaning on the horn. Seconds later, the curtains rattled back and a furious face appeared at the window, tugging at the catch until it yielded and he could fling it open.

A plump, bald-headed man, red with fury, leant out. 'What the hell do you think you're doing?'

MacNee stepped out of the car. 'Mr Stewart? Sorry to disturb you, sir. Police.' He held up his warrant card. 'You weren't answering the door.'

'Of course we bloody weren't! We were asleep. What time is it, anyway?'

'Four minutes past nine, sir.'

'Oh.' He turned to say something over his shoulder to someone in the room, then called down, 'Perhaps you could come back in half an hour – give us time to wake up and get dressed.'

'Afraid not, sir. We don't mind you in your dressing gowns.'

'You may not, but I do. Are you refusing to come back later?'

'Not exactly refusing, sir, but we have many calls on our time and it's important that we talk to you as soon as possible.'

MacNee saw uncertainty on the man's face. 'What's it about, anyway? If it's about some licensing infringement–'

'No, sir.'

'What, then?'

'We'd rather talk to you directly. It's a serious matter.'

Logie Stewart stiffened visibly. Then he said, 'Oh, all right, then. I'll come down, though I can't imagine what it's about.' He shut the window.

MacNee grinned at Hepburn. 'There, you see? Smart thinking, not brute force. That's what gets results.'

The man who opened the door looked only half-awake, his eyes puffy with sleep and a growth of stubble on his chin, but his dressing gown was a resplendent red with a gold-tasselled tie-belt, with slippers to match. MacNee introduced himself and Hepburn and walked in.

'This had better be important,' Logie Stewart said tartly. 'This way.'

The pub was very smartly furnished with highly polished wooden tables and shining brass around the bar and dark-blue upholstery on the banquettes and chairs. Sailing prints on the cream walls suggested a nautical theme, presumably in tribute to the seabird outside, but there weren't any of the usual ropes and anchors, or even imitation portholes. Tasteful, MacNee supposed they would describe it, though he'd have called it dull. He preferred his pubs to have a bit more life about them.

It still had the slightly fetid smell of yesterday's alcohol and sweaty bodies. As Logie waved them to seats at a table near the door, he went round opening the windows wide. He had his back turned to them as he said, 'What's all this about, then?'

'Connell Kane.'

It was deliberately brutal; MacNee had expected the man to spin round, but he didn't. His back went rigid, but he went on to open another window and his voice sounded casual.

'What about him?'

104

'We just wondered if you had seen him recently?'

He turned at that. His expression was guarded, but he said with some force, '*Seen him?* Since he's been dead for a couple of years it would be a bit tricky, wouldn't it?' He sounded sarcastic but he was definitely uneasy as he came to sit down at the table.

'So when was the last time you saw him, then?'

Logie shrugged. 'Not sure I can remember. Somewhere around the time poor Julia Margrave died, I suppose.'

'You weren't at the hearing in court?'

'No. Look, I really had very little to do with him – he was just another customer.'

'And a member of the Cyrenaics, like you,' Hepburn said.

Logie's face coloured. 'That didn't mean anything. It was just a sort of joke, a passing idea.'

'For a passing idea, it seemed to have quite a history, according to the report on the inquest.'

He looked at Hepburn with dislike. 'I wasn't at it. And I was here, in the bar, the night Julia died. That was just the tragic consequence of her drug problem – I don't see what it's got to do with me. And anyway, what's this nonsense about Connell? Are you telling me he's still alive?'

MacNee ignored the question. 'What were you doing on April 14th?'

Logie froze, but MacNee didn't read too much into that. Being asked by the police to account for your movements made even the purest soul tense up. He filed it away, though.

'How on earth would I know? In the restaurant, probably. What day was it?'

105

'Monday.'

'Ah, then I wouldn't have been – we're closed on Mondays. So...' He shrugged. 'Could have been anywhere.'

'Need to push you to think, sir.'

'Perhaps my wife might be able to help.' He jumped up; there was no mistaking his eagerness to get away. 'She must be dressed by now – I'll go and fetch her.'

MacNee didn't see any need to stop him, but as he went towards the back of the room the front door opened and a woman in a pink overall appeared. She hesitated, peering curiously at the officers.

'Oh – Sandra!' Logie said. 'You'll be wanting to get on with the cleaning.' He turned to the officers. 'Do you mind going upstairs to the restaurant? You won't be disturbed there. Light switch on the left.'

MacNee and Hepburn climbed the stairs he indicated.

'Did he know or didn't he?' Hepburn murmured. 'Couldn't make up my mind.'

'Some gut reactions, but I couldn't be sure what they meant. Cool customer, that one.'

The restaurant on the next floor was a cavern of darkness. MacNee fumbled for a second then found the switch. They both gasped.

The long room was all purple and silver, the walls so dark they were almost black and the velvet drapes covering the windows and the upholstery of the chairs true imperial colour. There were silver-framed mirrors on every wall, causing glittering reflections that went deeper and deeper towards infinity. And then there were the botanical prints.

MacNee stopped in front of one. It showed the cross section of a mottled pink, fleshy plant, formed like a cup with a pool of liquid in the bottom, a trap where the helpless bodies of flies floated, slowly dissolving.

He read the inscription. 'Pitcher plant. Yeuch!'

'This one says it's a sundew. There's a wasp or something entangled with it.' Hepburn walked along, studying them. 'This is a Venus flytrap–' She stopped. 'Of course! These are symbols of the Flowers of Evil that I was talking about. This room's practically the definition of decadent. You can see why it's a destination pub – people love that sort of thing.'

'I don't. Put me right off my mince.' MacNee spoke lightly but it was making his flesh crawl. He went across to the window and pulled back one of the drapes. 'That's better. Let's get some daylight in here.'

But he was beginning to have a worrying feeling about the likely effect of daylight on the situation they were starting to explore.

CHAPTER SEVEN

'We'll do Falconer first,' DS Andy Macdonald said to DC Ewan Campbell as he drove into Ballinbreck. 'He's retired so he should be at home, and being a teacher Jen Wilson'll be busy first thing – taking the register and stuff.' He paused. 'That's if they take the register now. They always did when I was at a school.'

Campbell snorted.

'Oh, I know, doesn't prove anything. When I was in primary you could still get the strap across the back of your legs – you'd get locked up for that now.'

'First left, then,' Campbell said, pointing to the street name.

Donald Falconer's house was in a smart new development at the back of the village. They could hear the sound of a vacuum cleaner as they rang the bell and the door was opened by a sweet-faced woman with very bright blue eyes and a fluff of grey curls who greeted them with a friendly smile when they showed their warrant cards.

'Oh, police,' she said with the happy confidence of the blameless. 'What can I do for you? Donald? Oh, the neighbourhood watch, is it?'

Not waiting for an answer, she led them towards the back of the house. 'He's in his study. Keeps him out from under my feet while I get on,' she confided, then opened the door.

'Police to see you, dear. They've discovered your guilty secret!' She ushered them in, then went back to her hoovering.

Donald Falconer put down the newspaper he was reading and stood up. 'Don't recognise you,' he said brusquely. 'Not from the local station, are you?'

Macdonald explained. 'Wondered if we could have a word with you, sir.'

A look of caution came over Falconer's face.

'Ah. Is this about my daughter? I suppose I should have reported it to you immediately. She's turned up, like a bad penny. I'm sorry you've had to come all this way for nothing but I'm impressed that you're still working on it.'

Awkwardly, Macdonald said, 'I'm glad to hear it, sir, but it's not about that.'

Falconer looked alarmed. 'Dear God, she's not in trouble again, is she?'

'Again?'

'The dreadful business over that girl's death – Julia Margrave. It was bad enough then. Is she going to bring more shame on us?'

'She's in no trouble at the moment, as far as we know. We weren't aware she was back in the neighbourhood.'

'I didn't know myself until she dropped in, calm as you please, on Monday. Not a word of apology for what she'd done to me and to her poor mother.'

'I see. Do you know where she's staying, then?'

'She didn't tell me and I didn't ask. I didn't want to know.' The man was almost visibly bristling. No fatted calf for Skye, it seemed.

'Is there anyone you can think of who might know?'

Falconer sniffed. 'She was always thick as thieves with Jen Wilson. She was another of them – and still teaching children. Should have been sacked when it all came out.'

'We'll follow that up.' With a glance at Campbell Macdonald got up. 'Thank you for your cooperation. Just one last question – when was the last time you saw Connell Kane?'

'The drug dealer? I'm happy to say there wasn't a last time, since there wasn't a first time either. I'm not ashamed to say I was delighted when I heard he'd done the decent thing and killed himself.'

'Not very effectively,' Campbell said as they went out, leaving him staring after them.

Primary 4 was proving challenging this morning. Someone was having a birthday and since the mother had been thoughtless enough to hand out invitations to the party to some children and not to others, there were first hurt feelings to be soothed, then tears from the birthday girl when one of those not included was nasty to her.

Jen Wilson grimaced at the teaching assistant. 'Roll on break,' she muttered, just as the door opened and Mrs Pearson the head teacher appeared.

'Miss Wilson, could I have a moment?'

'Yes, of course.' With a murmured, 'Sorry!' to the assistant she went to the head's study, wondering what was so urgent that it couldn't wait for break.

There were two young men there and Mrs Pearson gave Jen an acid look as she came in.

'These gentlemen are from the police. They want a word with you.'

Jen's heart sank. She wasn't the head's favourite person; she'd almost lost her job two years ago and she still hadn't managed to live it down.

'I'll leave you with them,' Mrs Pearson said frostily and withdrew.

Swallowing nervously, Jen sat down, nodding as the taller officer introduced them and the red-haired one took down her details.

'Just a few routine questions,' he said reassuringly. 'I know you've got a class you're keen to get back to.'

'Not necessarily,' Jen said wryly and he gave an easy laugh.

'I can understand that. Don't know how you do it. Now, you knew Connell Kane – is that right? When was the last time you saw him?'

She didn't need this. 'It was a long time ago – definitely after the inquest; I know, because he was very distraught. I think it was probably a week before he committed suicide.'

'I see,' Macdonald said. 'And you haven't seen him since?'

She met his gaze squarely. 'No. I was very upset because he must have felt abandoned by us all, to do that–'

'I was meaning more recently.'

She frowned. 'How could I have? What do you mean?'

'It seems that Mr Kane staged his suicide.'

'Staged it? Do you mean – he's still alive?'

'No, I'm afraid not. He was found dead in a car that was washed up on the sands near Newbie a short time ago.'

Jen felt suddenly dizzy. Her head was light, light, as if it might float away. 'Dead?' she managed to say. 'An accident?'

'No. This is a murder enquiry.'

The room was spinning now. She pitched forward out of her chair in a dead faint.

DC Hepburn took an instant dislike to Kendra

Stewart. As she crossed the threshold in a way that demanded the adverb 'trippingly', she began the sort of 'little me' act that would set any right-thinking woman's teeth on edge. Her admittedly enviable eyelashes were being batted at MacNee, of course, in the mistaken belief that this would soften him up.

'My husband says you're asking about poor Connell,' she said. 'I don't understand – he died two years ago.'

'So you haven't seen him since, then?'

'Well, of course not,' she cooed.

From her tone, she'd only just stopped herself adding the word, 'Silly!' Hepburn said coldly, 'Obviously we wouldn't be asking you if that was the case. It seems that his suicide was faked.'

'No! I'm astonished.'

She produced the sort of astonished expression that made Hepburn wonder if she was big in the local amateur dramatic society. She must know already; there was no way Logie wouldn't have realised and told her.

'Where were you on Monday April 14th?' Mac-Nee asked.

The eyelashes came into play. 'Goodness, Sergeant, I've no idea! I haven't consulted my diary but I don't remember that I was doing anything special. I was probably here with Logie. That's our day off – the pub's open but the restaurant's shut – and we usually just have a quiet supper at home, with a box set, maybe.'

'Anyone vouch for that?' MacNee's tone was sharp and she looked hurt.

'I shouldn't think so – unless the sous chef had

to consult Logie about something.'

'We can check. So – are you saying that you were both here on that night?'

'No, I am not! Don't try to put words into my mouth, Sergeant.' The simpering facade vanished, her mouth tightened and her voice suddenly became hard and businesslike. 'I am saying that I don't know. I am certainly stating categorically that I haven't seen Connell Kane for two years and that I had no idea that he wasn't dead. Is that clear?'

'Perfectly, madam. This is a murder investigation so it's important that there should be no misunderstandings.'

Hepburn eyed Kendra closely as MacNee said that, but it didn't tell her anything. She sounded shocked as she said, 'Murder!' but the big brown eyes were cold and watchful.

'Are you aware of other contacts he might have had?' Hepburn asked.

'Not recently, no. Obviously.'

'Before that?'

In the moment of hesitation, Hepburn could almost read the words, 'How much do you know?' passing through Kendra's mind before she said, 'I'm sure you have the names of his contacts here.'

'Suppose you tell us anyway.' From the edge in MacNee's voice he didn't like her any more than Hepburn did.

'Oh – poor Julia, of course. She knew him much better than the rest of us did. Connell rather kept himself to himself, you know? And Randall – Randall Lindsay. He and Julia knew him in Edinburgh when they were both working at one of the merchant banks – I forget which.'

MacNee shot a glance at Hepburn but she had her notebook out already. 'They introduced him down here?' he said.

'Yes, that's right. He stayed with Randall sometimes, I think. Julia stayed with her mother who wouldn't have approved.'

'Why was that?' Hepburn asked, faux-innocent.

'The drugs, of course. We were all really worried about Julia, you know. It was all Connell's fault.'

She stopped. Pause for calculation, Hepburn thought cynically, as Kendra's voice went girly again. She really wasn't sensitive to atmosphere.

'Perhaps it's naughty of me to say this, Sergeant, but I wasn't a bit sorry when I thought he'd killed himself and I'm not sorry now he's dead. There!'

MacNee benefited from another sidelong look. He didn't take it well.

'You knew he was dealing drugs, then. Where was he getting them from?'

She recoiled as if he had struck her. '*I* don't know! How would I know? I had nothing to do with it, nothing.'

MacNee drew breath to speak. Going for the throat on Kendra's own drug use wouldn't be productive and Hepburn stepped in. 'Who else was involved at the time, Mrs Stewart?'

Kendra was pouting now. 'Well, there was Jen Wilson – she teaches at the school here so you could always ask her. She and Skye Falconer who disappeared just around that time were always very thick. That was about it.'

'Apart from you and your husband, of course,'

114

Hepburn said.

'Well – we were rather semi-detached members, you know. It was good business for us, having them all meeting here. And we were married, so a lot of the ... well, social side passed us by, really.'

If she does the eyelash thing on MacNee just once more, Hepburn thought, he'll deck her. His voice was positively savage as he said, 'By "social side", do you mean sex, Mrs Stewart?'

'If you want to call a spade a bloody shovel,' she said with distaste, 'then yes, I suppose so.'

'And I've noticed there's one person you haven't mentioned so far,' MacNee went on. 'Your brother-in-law.'

'Oh, Will?' She trilled a casual laugh. 'I'd sort of been discounting Will because he's working in Canada. And of course he was in the police force before that so I'm sure he wouldn't have had anything to do with Connell's – activities.'

Yeah, sure, Hepburn thought. If he hadn't booked Kane when the first spliff appeared, it probably meant he was more in the know about where it came from than anyone else. Pity he was in Canada.

'Can you give us an address for him?' she asked, her pen poised over her notebook.

For the first time, Kendra showed real uncertainty. 'Yes, I could, but actually – well, he's over visiting.'

'Really!' Hepburn and MacNee spoke together.

'Where is he, then?' MacNee went on.

'Staying with us. Philippa Lindsay's organised this Homecoming party and last week he just decided to pop over for it.'

'I see. Thank you, Mrs Stewart, that's all for the time being. Could you send him up to speak to us now, please?'

'Oh, I think he's gone out. He was putting on his coat when I came upstairs. We didn't know you'd be wanting to see him,' she said with a little, satisfied smile.

Tight-lipped, MacNee said, 'And when do you expect him back?'

'Expect? Oh, I never presume to expect Will – he's a free spirit. If there's nothing else I can help you with, I'll see you out.'

As Hepburn and MacNee walked back to the car he said, 'See her? If it was her had been murdered, I'd not be surprised. Another ten minutes and I'd have done it myself.'

'This is the border with Galloway,' DC Jamieson pointed out as DC Weston, apparently oblivious to where the limit of their Dumfries Division territory was, drove on. 'Harris told us we didn't need to go further than this, Lizzie. We can turn back now – if we don't we'll be late off our shift.'

She was feeling mutinous. The cup of coffee hadn't materialised and she was beginning to feel sick, going down these endless twisting little roads.

DC Weston paid no attention. 'I don't care what he said, Debbie. I need him to be wrong about where the car left the road. Then he'll have to get us to show DI Fleming where it was.'

'Maybe it was where Harris thinks it was.'

Weston gave her a scornful look. 'Course it wasn't. If a car drove on to the sands there it'd have got bogged down in the mud long before it got to where they found it. Everyone knows that – it's just he won't accept it because he can't think what to do next.

'I tell you what – there's a cafe at Rockcliffe and if we haven't found it by then we'll turn back. And we'll say we haven't managed to finish checking and ask to be detailed on this tomorrow – no, listen,' as her companion protested, 'I promise tomorrow we'll start with a bacon butty.'

Jamieson looked at her pityingly. 'You're mental! Going all the way round the Solway coast will take a week – two weeks. You'd never get away with that.'

'I know. But it's likely it wouldn't be as far as all that, to end up at Newbie. I want to give it a go, anyway. I tell you what – if I haven't found anything by the time we reach Kirkcudbright tomorrow, I'll stop. Here's another little road. This one looks promising.'

'No, it doesn't,' Jamieson said bleakly. 'Like I said, you're mental.'

Macdonald was still sweating slightly as he drove off from Ballinbreck Primary. 'Never had a witness faint on me before. Doesn't look good – next thing she'll be complaining about police brutality.'

'Didn't look the sort,' Campbell said.

'We can always hope.'

He was probably right about Jen Wilson. At least he'd managed to catch her before she actually fell and had laid her out on the floor while Campbell went to fetch the head teacher back, and when Jen came round she was apologetic rather than hostile and insisted on going on with the interview once

117

she'd had time to recover.

'It was just the shock,' she'd explained. 'First you saying that he wasn't dead, then that he was now – stupid, I'm sorry.'

'I should have broken it more gently but I didn't realise you'd be so upset,' Macdonald said.

'No, no. It was probably low blood sugar as well – I was needing my chocolate biscuit at break. There's no reason at all for me to be overcome – we were never that close.'

'So can I take it you haven't seen him since he faked his suicide?'

'No, I haven't.'

'Going back to that time, do you know where he was getting the drugs he supplied – any contact he might have had in the past?'

She shook her head. 'Sorry. It's – it's not a past that I'm proud of. I find it hard now to believe we were as foolish as we were and if I knew anything that would help, I'd tell you.'

'Which of you might want him dead?' Campbell said.

The question took her aback. 'Julia's mother, I suppose. But she's an old lady – walked with a stick, I remember. Apart from that, no. But he was into drugs – if he went on supplying, this could be a deal that went wrong, couldn't it?'

She wasn't a stupid woman and she seemed truthful. 'We're keeping that line of enquiry open,' Macdonald assured her. 'Now, we just need to know where you were on Monday April 14th this year.'

Jen frowned. 'April 14th – the date rings a bell. Oh yes – that was just before the Easter break,

118

wasn't it? I was in school all day, of course, and then a few of us on the staff went out for an end of term meal.

'Is there anything else? I'd really better be getting back to my class,' Jen said, getting up.

'Just one more thing. We spoke to Skye Falconer's father this morning and he said she was back in the neighbourhood. Do you know where she's staying?'

'Oh. Well, I'm sworn to secrecy but I suppose I have to tell you she's been staying with me. She doesn't want people knowing she's here, not until she makes up her mind what she's going to do.'

'So we would find her at your address?'

'Yes.' Then she added hastily, 'though of course she might be out.'

She definitely looked shifty as she said that. He'd said only, 'Thanks very much, Miss Wilson. I hope you'll be all right, after this.' But as they had walked out to the car he'd said to Campbell, 'What would you bet she's on the phone to her pal now?'

'Dead cert. Bet she won't be there, though.'

And when they reached Jen Wilson's house and rang the bell, sure enough there was no answer.

'Told you,' Campbell said smugly.

'Maybe she's just gone out, anyway,' Macdonald said. 'Why did you think she would try to avoid us? Do you think there's something going on there? I thought Wilson was truthful enough.'

'Probably was. Said she hadn't seen him. Didn't say she didn't know he was alive. Only passed out when you said he was dead now.'

It was a long speech for Campbell, but when

Macdonald thought about it, he was perfectly right. Campbell usually was.

'That didn't take long,' MacNee said cheerfully as they drove out of the car park by the restaurant. 'Next stop Randall Lindsay's parents. They'll have his Paris address – have you got theirs in the notes?'

'Yes, I suppose so.'

Hepburn sounded reluctant and MacNee shot her an enquiring look. 'Problem?'

'Actually, he's back at home on leave. He phoned me last night to ask me to this stupid Homecoming party his mother's organising.'

'Couldn't have mentioned this before, I suppose?'

'I was hoping someone else would be detailed to interview him. He's loathsome, Tam, and I think he sort of fancies me, which is really creepy.'

'Grilling him's not exactly encouragement, is it? If you were in uniform, now – that might be a "phwoar!" factor. But hang on – I suppose he might be into this dominatrix stuff–'

'Tam! You're not taking this seriously.'

'No,' he grinned. 'Where's the house?'

'Oh, all right then,' she said sulkily. 'Back into the village, right along the high street, just past the speed limit sign, turn right, first left.'

She had intended to punish him with silence but it didn't seem to be having any effect and after a minute she gave up.

'Why do you think Will Stewart did a runner when he heard we were asking questions? Did you know him before?'

'Didn't, no. Never came across him until there was all the stuff in the papers about him being involved in that group. The red tops loved it but it didn't do the Force's reputation any good.

'My guess would be he wants to flush us out, find out what this is all about before he talks to us. He's been a cop – he'll be pretty savvy. Doesn't necessarily mean he's got anything to hide. Maybe he's got the sort of job in Canada that could be affected by another scandal here – security, or something.'

Hepburn looked disappointed. 'Still seems pretty suspicious to me – him coming back just at the time when Kane was killed.'

'We don't know that,' MacNee pointed out. 'That was weeks ago. She said he'd only arrived last week.'

'Maybe,' she said darkly.

'Easy enough to check. Is this it here? Nice, eh?'

It stood on its own beyond the other houses in the lane, backing on to fields, a large, sprawling Victorian house with a conservatory-style kitchen extension at the back. He drove up the short drive and parked on the sweep of gravel at the front.

The garden was extensive but poorly kept, the gravel weedy, the shrubbery beside it overgrown and what had once been a herbaceous border choked with weeds, though a wheelbarrow and a spade suggested that someone was tackling the problem.

'You could do worse,' MacNee said naughtily. 'Play your cards right and you could–'

'Oh, shut up, Tam!' Hepburn slammed the car

door and went to ring the doorbell.

There was no response. 'They're out!' she said triumphantly, heading back to the car.

MacNee ignored her. 'Maybe round the back, working in the garden,' he said.

But there was no one there either. Hepburn, sitting smugly in the car, called, 'Have to leave it for today. Someone else's turn tomorrow.'

Lurking in a little alleyway a hundred yards from Jen Wilson's cottage, Skye Falconer peeped out to watch the police drive away.

They wouldn't give up; not seeing them today only meant that she'd have to wait for their next visit, dreading the knock on the door. But she couldn't think straight, not yet, so she'd done what she always did when trouble came – bolted, as instinctively as a frightened animal.

They had gone now. Skye walked slowly back to the cottage and let herself in. She had to sort herself out, calm her nerves. Right now. They could be back at any moment.

It was a lovely morning and the sun was warm in the tiny garden at the back. She made herself a cup of coffee then carried it outside and sat watching the tits squabbling over position as they pecked at a fat ball hanging on one of the shrubs. She forced herself to relax, shutting her eyes and turning her face up to the sun, listening to the chirpings and tweetings.

She couldn't afford to be paralysed by shock; she'd allowed herself too much of that already. Staying with Jen for the rest of her life wasn't an option. She had to get herself back into the real world somehow, not wait till she was dragged out of her fugue of denial, kicking and screaming. This was the wake-up call.

Skye sat up straight in the hard little garden chair and took a sip of the coffee she'd made so strong that she gave a little shudder as she tasted it. Strong – she had to learn to be strong too.

Rejoining the world. There was the Homecoming party Jen had talked about: everyone would be there, all together, and the gossips could have their field day all at once. She didn't trust Philippa Lindsay – you'd be a fool if you did – but whatever her motives might be that could be the answer to Skye's problem. She couldn't control the outcome but it would force her out of deadly inaction.

When Jen had phoned, like the loyal friend she was, to tell her that the police were coming to talk to her, she'd obviously been worried that Skye would do exactly what she had done and tried to reassure her. Once Jen got back from school she'd ask her exactly what the police needed to know, prepare just what she was going to say then maybe even take the initiative by phoning them, apologising for being out. Then she'd sign on and start looking for a job. Whatever you had been through, life went on.

And she'd go to the Homecoming party. It wouldn't be easy; she gave a little shiver at the thought, but she wasn't going to waver. That was a firm decision.

She finished her coffee and took it back into the house. She'd have to plan what to wear, then. Jen, bless her, would no doubt offer to lend her something but anything that fitted Jen's much taller, sturdier frame would swamp her; she wanted to look confident, not pathetic.

A scruffy sweater would not really do. There was a smart top somewhere at the bottom of her bag; she tried to block out her memories of wearing it in happier times. It would need laundering.

Skye went upstairs to dig it out. She had never got round to unpacking the rucksack; putting things in drawers had seemed like settling in and she wasn't doing that. Now she tipped it on to the bed and pulled out a crumpled silky T-shirt in a greeny-blue colour that matched her eyes. There was a chunky glass necklace that she'd worn with it as well and she laid them out together. Yes, that with jeans would do.

Skye started stuffing things back into the bag, then suddenly stopped, a thrill of fear going through her. She hadn't seen it – where was it? It should have been there. Perhaps it was in a pocket somewhere – but she knew it wasn't, really.

Even so, she checked, shook everything out, poked into her make-up bag. Where could it be, where could it possibly be?

Then she realised and she went cold all over.

CHAPTER EIGHT

'Will Stewart, Randall Lindsay, Skye Falconer – coincidence that none of them were available for questioning?' DI Fleming said.

Her meeting, for once, had ended early and she

124

had called in her team for a debrief before the end of their shift.

'Don't believe in coincidence,' MacNee said.

Macdonald nodded. 'Certainly wasn't any doubt in my mind that Jen Wilson was planning to warn Skye that we were on our way. Wonder why she needed to?'

'Will Stewart definitely knew we were there and asking questions. Whether he tipped off Randall–' Hepburn pulled a face. 'Little though I like to give that creep the benefit of the doubt, it's possible he'd genuinely stepped out.'

'It'd be useful to know,' Fleming said. 'They were close-knit in the past; they may have kept up the connections – or maybe this has prompted them into contact again. And if so, is that significant?

'We won't have the advantage of surprise tomorrow but at least you shouldn't have anyone passing out on you, Andy. It'll hit the media tomorrow – DSI Taylor has given a press conference and there was a lot of interest. He's desperate for some sort of progress now, but on the face of it we haven't come up with anything much to offer him, just people who professed to be shocked, whether genuinely or otherwise.

'I've had the drug squads in Glasgow and – yes, Tam – Edinburgh alerted to see if his fingerprints and mugshot make any connection there, and I've got DSI Taylor to circulate those to all the stations in the whole Dumfries and Galloway areas to see if there's any chance he's known to them under a different name.'

'Huh! You'd think they'd have done that already,'

Macdonald said and MacNee rolled his eyes.

'Well – we won't go into that,' Fleming said diplomatically. 'Now, tomorrow we need to get the interviews we didn't manage today sewn up. I'll take that on with you, Tam – I want to get a feel for the place. Louise, chase up phone numbers and arrange the appointments first thing. Then you can be on sifting duty – I'm expecting calls tomorrow once this goes out on the media and the switchboard can't be expected to sort out the nuggets from the dross.'

She smiled at the disgruntled face of her young officer.

'How many tons of pitchblende was it that Marie Curie had to shovel to get a smidgen of uranium?' Hepburn said. 'Bet I'll manage to beat that.'

'Just as long as you come up with the goods,' Fleming said. 'Andy and Ewan, I want you on background. Check everything you can about the Cyrenaics – jobs, family, record of course, if any. The inquest report will give you a starting point – and check out the address Kane gave when he was charged. I'd like to find out where he stayed when he was down here too–'

'The Lindsays, sometimes, according to Kendra Stewart,' MacNee said. 'So maybe we're needing a wee word with Randall's mum as well.'

Fleming nodded. 'Right. Fix that too, Louise.'

Hepburn nodded glumly and MacNee said, 'Cheer up, hen. You weren't wanting to interview him anyway.'

She brightened slightly. 'If I never see him again it'll be too soon. At least that means I won't have to.'

It was only afterwards that she remembered George Eliot's dictum that among all forms of mistake, prophecy is the most gratuitous.

Fleming had ordered the newspapers to be sent to her desk first thing on Friday morning and she was poring over them now. They made grim reading.

DSI Taylor and Dumfries Division had been savaged, as she had guessed they would be, for sitting on the information about Connell Kane for such a long time. She'd seen him looking frankly terrified on the TV news last night and now phrases like 'bungled operation' and 'rabbit in the headlights' were being thrown about. They had loved rehashing the original scandal – with pretty girls, sex, drugs and tragedy, and now a brief resurrection before a murder, it was all their Christmases come at once.

She sighed. As she drove in this morning, there had been a couple of the local stringers lurking hopefully at the front entrance but it didn't look as if the big boys had picked up on Taylor's mentioning that she was now involved with the operation.

They might well be down at Ballinbreck, though, trampling all over the patch she was planning to investigate herself this morning, and she sighed again. Transparency was one thing; having someone constantly breathing down your neck and making the job they were blaming you for not doing all but impossible, was quite another.

The phone rang. Finding that DSI Taylor wanted to speak to her was hardly a surprise but it certainly wasn't going to improve her morning.

'Yes, Tom?' she said wearily.

'Have you seen the papers?'

'Yes, Tom.'

'It's simply outrageous, that they can print stuff like this. I should sue...'

Fleming let him bluster on, making soothing noises. At last she said, 'I'm afraid we simply have to accept that's what they're like and until we can show some progress we just have to take it.'

He pounced on that. 'Have you come up with anything, Marjory? They'll want at least a statement today and I need to have something to give them.'

'It's the preliminary stages here,' Fleming reminded him. 'We're still lining up interviews with Kane's contacts that we couldn't see yesterday. We have lines of enquiry, but– No, Tom,' as he interrupted with an eager question, 'absolutely nothing I could share with the press.'

Before he could argue, she went on, 'What about your end? Have the uniforms made any progress with finding where the car went in?'

'No. Harris said he had people out yesterday but found nothing. He's still convinced you're barking up the wrong tree there.'

Yes, he would be. 'That's disappointing. How far have they got?'

'I can't tell you that. Harris is in charge; I'm sure he'll see it's all done properly. He's very efficient, you know.'

'Yes, you said. And he hasn't made any more progress on the lines he's following either?'

'I don't think so. I'm sure he'd have told me if

he had. And if there's anything you come up with, you'll get in touch at once Marjory, won't you?'

'Of course.'

Fleming put down the phone and sat back in her chair, frowning. Perhaps she'd been too wedded to the idea that the car could have entered the river lower down, just the way Harris had been wedded to his theory. She still didn't believe his worked, but she had to admit that a car might have left the road somewhere, or been pushed in, without leaving significant traces for the searchers to find. And she wasn't absolutely sure that Harris would tell her if they did.

For once it looked as if DSI Rowley's fears were justified. She could see this one going very wrong for her. From the sound of it, Harris wasn't changing his position and when – if – she had information that had to be shared with the media, the attention and the responsibility for the case would switch to her – and he'd do his best to make sure it did.

Unless today's interviews turned up something more useful than yesterday's, it was going to be her head on the block.

Kendra Stewart tiptoed into Will's bedroom, pausing to push the silky floral kimono she was wearing over a low-cut nightie a little wider open to give a better view of her impressive cleavage.

Will was on his back, sprawled almost diagonally across the double bed, his mouth half-open. He was giving small, puffing snores and she giggled as she went across and kissed his stubbly cheek.

He woke and shot bolt upright so suddenly that

she had to duck to avoid his head making contact with her nose. He didn't seem impressed by this romantic way of being returned to consciousness.

'For God's sake, Kendra, what do you think you're doing? Logie–'

'It's all right, sweetheart, he's downstairs.' She sat down on the bed. 'Give me a kiss.'

Will pulled the bedclothes up round his bare torso in an almost maidenly gesture of self-defence. 'He could come up at any time. Anyway, I need a shower.'

He got out on the other side of the bed and pulled on a towelling robe over his pyjama bottoms.

'Not necessary, darling. It just adds to your animal magnetism. You'll wash away all those wonderful pheromones.' Kendra followed him across the room.

God, she really couldn't take a hint, could she? He'd thought he was safe enough in his own bedroom – at least first thing in the morning when her husband was within earshot.

'No, Kendra,' he said irritably. 'I'm really not in the mood. Was there something you wanted?'

She gave him a suggestive look. 'Apart from you? Well, actually I came up to tell you that the police phoned to say they want to see you at eleven. And from the sound of it, you'd better be here.'

'Fine.' He headed for the bathroom, leaving Kendra sitting on the bed pouting.

It was a good, powerful shower. Will stood under it, letting it beat on his head as if that might wash away the tormented thoughts.

Kendra was going around like a cat on heat; it

was getting so obvious that Logie was set to explode any day now and a simple statement of Will's own indifference to her wasn't going to fix it – indeed, Logie was quite capable of taking that as an insult. He'd seen marrying Kendra as a triumph over the younger brother who'd always been famous for his ability to pull, without asking himself why she'd agreed.

Thinking back, Will suspected that once she realised that commitment wasn't in his vocabulary, she'd seen the marriage as a way of stalking him. And from the way she was going on, it looked as if she reckoned she had Will where she'd always wanted him now and he was very much afraid that when the accusation came she would own up to it gladly, say it was true love and expect him to express delight and whisk her back with him to Canada. Her self-confidence, and her insensitivity, were boundless. And she wasn't his only worry.

But once he'd shaved and dressed he felt better. He could handle Kendra, surely, and he couldn't see any problem with the police. He'd been smart enough to avoid his former colleagues yesterday and he'd pumped Logie and Kendra so that he knew what they were going to ask and it seemed straightforward enough.

All he had to do was play it cool and in a week's time he'd be back in Canada. And Kendra, with any luck, would be five thousand miles away.

'Kirkcudbright we stop – you promised, right?' DC Jamieson said as she got into the car with DC Weston outside the Dumfries Police HQ. 'And you owe me for this one – I didn't shop you

131

when we swore blind to Harris that we hadn't gone on into Galloway.'

'OK, promise,' DC Weston said blithely. 'It's a nice day for a run in the country anyway. Would you rather be spending today going round Annan for the fourteenth time trying to find someone who hasn't already been questioned about seeing men quarrelling in a grey car? The lads are fed up to the back teeth with it. We'll get bacon butties in Dalbeattie. That'll cheer you up.'

Philippa Lindsay put down the phone and turned to her son, who was sitting at the kitchen table wearing an out-at-elbow sweater and jeans that were baggy with wear, looking gloomily at a plate of muesli as he contemplated the day ahead.

'That was the police,' she said slowly. 'They want to speak to us both. What's that about?'

'The police? How – how would I know?'

But his face registered alarm, dismay, even, and his mother homed in on that immediately, the tension in her face relaxing.

'What have you done, for God's sake?'

He pushed back his chair and jumped up. 'Nothing! Absolutely nothing!' He licked his lips that had suddenly gone dry. 'What have you done, for that matter?'

Philippa ignored that. 'You always were a rotten liar! You might as well tell me. I'd been wondering why you were planning to spend all this leave that you talked about at home – you never have before.'

Randall's face flushed with colour. 'I haven't

132

done anything, I told you. It was just a bit of a misunderstanding—'

'Oh yes, and you've lost your job? I thought you had. God, that's all we need! Do you know how strapped for cash we are now in the business? It's your future too, sunshine, and it's on the brink of going under. Unless people start spending we're all finished. I'd been counting on you for another injection of capital.'

'You wouldn't have got it,' her son said unpleasantly. 'What have you ever done for me?'

Philippa glared. 'Done for you? Where do I start—'

'You sent me to the local bog-standard, when you could well have afforded to send me to a decent school. I got where I did through my own sheer hard graft—'

'And blew it all on your own too, it seems.' Philippa gave him a nasty smile. 'So – give me a clue. Just what sort of "misunderstanding" was it that has brought the police down on us?'

'They said they weren't going to do anything!' Randall cried. 'Like I said, it was a misunderstanding. I filled in a form wrong, that was the thing – just sent some money to the wrong place—'

'The wrong place? Dare I guess – your bank account? Dear God, Randall! You always were a fool.' She shrugged. 'Oh well, have to take your punishment like a man. If we're going to go bottom-up I don't suppose having a son with a criminal record will really matter.' She turned away to pour herself a cup of coffee.

The callousness stung him. 'Anyway,' he said

133

savagely, 'if it's about my problems with the bank, I don't know why they'd be wanting to interview you. Maybe it's nothing to do with that at all.'

'Don't be stupid! What else would it be?' she said.

Leaning heavily on the banisters, Eleanor Margrave lugged the Hoover up the stairs, paused to get her breath back then went to fetch sheets out of the linen cupboard to make up the bed in the spare room. She was looking forward to the weekend; as she counted out pillowcases and towels she thought happily about Biddy's arrival this afternoon.

They'd been at school together, their friendship forged in the art room, and one of their particular delights was the sketching holidays they'd shared over the years. They were both reaching the stage of decrepitude where holidays in Greece or Italy caused them more anxiety than pleasure, but as Biddy's Lake District and Eleanor's Galloway were both artists' paradises their weekends continued.

Where to go tomorrow, though – back to one of their favourite spots or find new ground? There was a lovely view she'd discovered on a hill looking right out over the Solway... She was humming happily as she went back to the spare room.

It was a very good thing to have visitors, she reflected: it made you do the housework you tended to neglect when it came to the rooms not in regular use. The sun shining in highlighted the neglected state of the polished surfaces and she was ashamed to see that there were dust bunnies under the bed. It would never do for Biddy to find those.

She hadn't actually been into the room since the night of the storm, except to strip the bed the day after, and she'd almost forgotten about her little mermaid – the woman who had disappeared as suddenly as she had appeared in the first place. She'd hoped at the time that she might come back to explain – the mystery had intrigued Eleanor for days – but she never had.

With the bed made up, she switched on the vacuum cleaner, going meticulously into the corners of the rooms and pushing it under the bed. As she did so, the machine's tone changed. When she pulled it back out she saw that a folded sheet of paper had stuck to the nozzle.

Something the mermaid had dropped, perhaps? Something, even, that might give a clue to her identity? Her curiosity freshly aroused, Eleanor unfolded it then realised that she would need her glasses to read what it said. She tucked it in the pocket of her skirt, gave a final flourish with the Hoover and took it back downstairs.

The paper seemed to be a letter. It was heavily creased, as if it had been folded and refolded several times. Reaching for the glasses she kept beside the Aga, she put them on and read what was written on it.

It was lucky she was near her chair. Her legs went as if she had been poleaxed and she dropped into it struggling for breath, with her heart racing. Fighting for calm, she closed her eyes but she could still see the words she had read, as if they had been written on the back of her eyelids in letters of flame.

What was she to do? The police – but did she really want to start that up all over again? What difference would it make? She hadn't even attended the inquest. Julia would still be dead and she had been so much the author of her own destruction that any desire for what was now fashionably called 'closure', but used to be known as revenge, had left Eleanor long ago.

She'd talk it over with Biddy when she arrived. Biddy's advice was always very sensible. She must just put it to the back of her mind.

But somehow she couldn't. There was a question that niggled and niggled at her. She made scones for Biddy's tea, but she forgot to put in the baking powder and they came out of the oven looking more like pancakes than scones.

She looked at them despairingly. She needed an answer and until she did she was going to think of nothing else. There was no point in going on until she'd ruined the Victoria sponge as well.

She went to the phone and dialled Biddy's number. There was no answer and she didn't leave a message; Biddy would be on the first leg of her journey now. She'd see her soon enough.

But oh, she did quite desperately want to know whether that was what had really happened to Julia, even if she never did anything about it. She wasn't sure she could bear to wait.

'Breakthrough, sir!' DS Duncan was smirking as he came into DI Len Harris's office in the Dumfries headquarters.

Harris eyed him warily. Duncan, in his experience, was a smartass whom Harris suspected of being behind the muttering campaign about lack of progress and there was something about that smirk that suggested to him the breakthrough in question might not be altogether good news, for him at least.

'Spit it out, Duncan,' he said.

'There's two men come forward after the newspaper appeal, sir. They didn't come sooner because they were embarrassed–'

Harris wanted to put his hands over his ears, scream, 'La-la-la-la-la, I can't hear you!' He felt sick as Duncan went on with his report.

Yes, the men had been driving a silvery-grey car through Annan at the time in question. Yes, they had been having a screaming row. One had accused the other of pocketing his winnings from the betting shop and the other had denied it, but in the end it had all been sorted out.

'What do you want me to do?' Duncan finished.

'Book them, for a start,' Harris snarled. 'Wasting police time.'

'Right,' he said, turning to go.

His alacrity rang alarm bells. If the details of the amount of police time they had wasted came to the attention of the media, Harris would be hung out to dry.

'Wait,' he said. 'Just give them a bollocking and leave it. Don't want to discourage citizens who come forward with information, however long it takes them to get round to it.'

'So what's the focus of our enquiry now, sir?' The sergeant was all innocence.

'You'll hear at the appropriate time. I want

those statements on file before the afternoon meeting.'

When Duncan had gone, Harris put his head in his hands. He'd known he was getting nowhere, had realised that days ago, but he hadn't been able to see what else to do. It had actually been a bit of a relief when Fleming was called in; he'd hoped he might find some way of picking her brains that meant he could still present new lines of enquiry as his own initiative. Until she came up with something fresh he'd just had his officers relentlessly marking time – and they were getting restive.

He'd accepted, with some bitterness, that the time and money spent had been wasted but in the general confusion of a difficult case it could be airbrushed out. Even in his worst moments he hadn't thought that he would be proved so definitively wrong.

That didn't mean *she* was right about the car, though. As long as there wasn't evidence to prove her theory, he could muddle through – and having allocated two little airheads to the search and ordered that the search stopped at the border with Galloway it would be cruelly unlucky if anything turned up.

But now he'd have to go and tell Taylor. He was feeling sick again: humiliation always affected him that way.

'Isn't that beautiful?' DC Weston said as they turned on to the road that looped down to Balcary Point, along the bay and then on through Ballinbreck.

No one could argue with that. The tide was ebbing so that the sand flats showed through, golden against the blue of the Firth under a wide, wide sky with only a few fluffy clouds. On the shore there were drifts of orange-brown wrack among grey rocky outcrops and as they watched a heron took off, flapping low up the estuary on its majestic way.

'Yeah, great,' Jamieson agreed, then looked at her watch. 'How far to Kirkcudbright now? I'm needing my coffee.'

'Not far,' Weston said with a sigh. 'Then I suppose we'll have to give up.'

'Too right we do. You promised. Aah! Lizzie! What the hell are you doing?'

Weston had slammed on the brakes. 'Look at that!'

The side of the road sloped down gently towards the shore. There was scrubby growth all along the verge, bushes and alders wind-shaped and stunted by the salt air. Where Weston had stopped there were broken branches, a hawthorn uprooted and beside it two deep tracks heading down on to the sandy foreshore.

'That's it,' Weston said. 'We've found it. I can't believe it!'

Jamieson was impressed. 'You could even be right. What do we do now?'

'Go back and tell Harris. Forget your coffee.'

'You think he's going to be pleased?' Jamieson was doubtful. 'He told us to stop at the boundary.'

Weston was driving on, looking for a place to turn. 'I don't care whether he's pleased or not. This is evidence.'

Weston and Jamieson were actually excited, the stupid little cows, bouncing into his office looking for a pat on the back.

'Tell me where it was you found it,' DC Len Harris said.

'About four miles short of Ballinbreck, two miles off the main road.' Weston frowned. She'd told him that already.

'And where is Ballinbreck? Remind me.'

Jamieson gave Weston a warning look but Weston didn't notice. 'On the Solway, sir. You turn off at Auchencairn.'

'And where is Auchencairn?'

She was with it now. She dropped her eyes. 'In – in Galloway, sir.'

'And what were your orders, Weston?' His voice had risen.

'To stop at the boundary.'

'And did you?'

'No, sir.'

'So what have you done?' He was yelling at her now.

'Disobeyed orders, sir.'

'And what's the penalty for disobeying orders?'

'Being – being charged, sir.'

'Yes, being charged.' His eyes were bulging and his face was bright red as if he might have a stroke at any moment. He jumped up from his chair, unable to sit still.

Weston cringed, as if she were afraid he would strike her, but however much he might like to, he wasn't crazy. He went past her, stamping across to the window and staring out blindly, his back

140

turned as he took deep, calming breaths, trying to control himself. He couldn't afford to lose it completely.

When he turned back, he was trembling with the effort to sound reasonable. 'I'm prepared to overlook it, this once. I daresay you thought you were using your initiative, but there's a time and a place for that. I'll go down and evaluate this myself. That's all. You can go.'

He could hear the relieved exhalation from them both.

Jamieson said, 'I'll get the report to you immediately, sir.'

'No need for a report. I'll report on it myself.'

As they went out he wiped the sweat from his brow. This was a disaster and he wasn't entirely sure he'd managed to contain it. They'd looked at each other as they went out.

'I really thought he was going to hit me there. Pity he didn't. I'd have had him.' Weston's voice might be shaky, but she was still defiant.

'Mmm,' Jamieson said.

'He's not going to pass it on, is he?'

'Probably not. Look, Lizzie, it's above your pay grade. It's his decision. This has got us into big trouble and that's it, as far as I'm concerned. Just leave it, OK?'

'It's important evidence! How can we just ignore it?' Weston's face was mutinous.

Jamieson stopped. 'Do anything else and you're on your own,' she said and walked away down the corridor.

CHAPTER NINE

DI Fleming glanced at her watch as she drove into Ballinbreck. 'Just over an hour – not bad,' she observed with satisfaction. 'Who's first on the list?'

MacNee consulted the notes. 'Skye Falconer. Staying at Jen Wilson's house.' He gave her directions.

'Nice wee place,' Fleming said, looking up and down the High Street. 'Haven't been here for years. Hard to imagine it having been a hotbed of drugs and decadence.'

'Probably still is,' MacNee said darkly. 'It's the same with folk – the quiet ones are the worst.'

Fleming laughed, pulling up outside the cottage. 'Now, let's hope she's in this time.'

She was. The woman who admitted them greeted them with a nervous smile. She was small and slight, her hair piled up into an untidy knot on the top of her head. Her eyes were striking, blue-green, rimmed with dark lashes, and she had neat, pretty features, though Fleming noticed with interest that her face seemed pinched and drawn, as if she was under some sort of strain.

Fleming made the introductions and Skye led them through to the kitchen at the back of the house and they sat down at the kitchen table.

'I'm sorry I was out when you came yesterday, but I didn't know to be in.' She spoke airily, but her hands were gripping each other tightly.

She'd been looking straight at them. As she finished the sentence, she looked down and off to the left; if she was right-handed, that was a classic psychological indicator of lying. At the same time, her right thumb stroked her left several times.

Fleming didn't believe her. And it was useful to learn a witness's 'tells' early on: it told you what to look out for.

She began, 'I expect you've heard what has happened to Connell Kane? Right. Did it come as a shock?'

'We'd all thought he was dead. Anyone would be shocked by what's happened.'

A very careful reply. 'Were you close to him at the time of Julia Margrave's death?'

'Not really. Julia was the only one he was close to. Randall knew him quite well too. He was around, of course, but...' She shrugged.

'Know where he got the drugs from?' MacNee asked and Skye bit her lip.

'Look, I'm ashamed of what happened but I wasn't in deep, like Julia. I'll admit to the odd spliff but that was the extent of it. I'd no idea about suppliers or anything.' Her hands fluttered innocence.

Fleming wasn't ready yet to put the boot in with 'That's what they all say'. Instead, she asked, 'Did you have any contact with him, either immediately after his pretended suicide or more recently?'

She wasn't halfway through the question when Skye suddenly looked round as if she'd remembered something and got up. 'No, I didn't,' she said over her shoulder, then, 'I'm sorry – I should

143

have offered you coffee before. Would you like some? I made a fruit loaf yesterday.' She switched on the kettle – using her right hand, Fleming noticed with interest.

MacNee, always a sucker for home baking, brightened but before he could speak Fleming said, 'Thanks but no thanks. We've several interviews to do this morning. Do you know where he was, what he was doing? Why he came back?'

Skye's eyes went down and left again. 'No idea,' she said.

She wasn't at all a good liar. 'I think you do,' Fleming's voice was gentle.

Skye's eyes went wide in panic. 'Why should you think that? I told you, I didn't know he was alive, so how could I know where he was?'

'Know any of his contacts?' MacNee put in.

'No! No! I told you I didn't.'

'I'm not sure I believe you,' Fleming said, then softened her voice, leaning forward encouragingly. 'Look, we're not accusing you of anything. It's just that someone you knew has been murdered, and I think you may be able to help our investigation. You probably know that withholding information is an offence.

'I'm going to ask you again: did you know anything about Connell Kane, his whereabouts or his contacts over the last two years?'

It didn't work. Skye said flatly, 'I told you I didn't. You can ask me as many times as you like but that'll still be the reply.'

She was steelier than Fleming had thought. 'If that is your considered response I will have to accept it. For the moment. You disappeared yourself for a long period of time, leaving your parents to instigate a police enquiry. Where were you?'

Skye hesitated. 'Is this relevant?' The hands were gripping each other tighter than ever and the thumb was twitching again.

Playing for time, Fleming thought. Skye hadn't expected that question. 'Yes.'

'It's – well, it's complicated. I was all over the place – France, Spain – I was in Spain for quite a long time. Italy too. I just had a sort of double gap year, picking up casual jobs and getting away from it all.'

'And why have you come back to it all now?'

'Oh – tired of living out of a rucksack, I suppose. You can't go on being a bum forever. And I was starting to think about that when I picked up an email from Jen telling me about the Homecoming party and I thought it would be a good way to get back in touch.'

Skye had spoken fluently, her eyes wide and fixed on her questioner. Liars often believed that a straight gaze was convincing. Fleming wasn't convinced.

'I see,' she said. 'Then we have to ask you where you were on April 14th?'

'Sorry – dates don't mean anything when you're constantly on the move. Still in Spain, I think, or maybe France.'

'When did you get back here?'

'Last week. I just descended on poor Jen out of the blue to scrounge a bed.'

'I see.' Fleming got up. 'We'll leave it there.' The third degree could come later. 'Thank you, Miss Falconer.'

145

As they got back into the car, MacNee gave a low whistle. 'How much of that did you believe, then?'

'Not a lot. Easy enough to check up on her if we need to – not smart to say you were out of the country if you want to cover your tracks. But people have different reasons for lying, Tam, not necessarily linked to murder.'

MacNee sniffed. 'Maybe. But as Rabbie said, *"There's nane ever feared/ That the truth would be heard/ But they whom the truth would indict."*'

Philippa Lindsay had a cup of coffee waiting for them in her very posh kitchen. No home bakes here, MacNee thought sadly as he accepted a cup of the kind of posh coffee that made your mouth pucker.

Her son, slouched at the table looking sulky, was wearing the sort of clothes that posh people wore that in a better-ordered world would have folk pointing at you in the street and laughing – red cord trousers and a pink shirt. Comfortable with his own sartorial choices of jeans, white T-shirt and a black leather jacket, MacNee was finding it hard to stop his lip from curling visibly.

Philippa was being very gracious. 'What's this about, Inspector? If you want to interview my son first, I'll make myself scarce.'

Randall, MacNee was interested to see, gave her a look of loathing as Fleming said, 'No, there's no need for that. A lot of the ground we want to cover concerns you as well, Mrs Lindsay.'

They both went very still. Then Philippa said smoothly, 'Of course. I'm delighted to help you

146

in any way.'

'You knew Connell Kane, I understand.'

'Yes.' Philippa's response was guarded; Randall looked definitely taken aback.

'Have either of you seen him recently?'

'How could we? He's dead.'

'He is now,' MacNee said. 'Seen the news to-day?'

'My dear man,' Philippa said lightly, 'I haven't had time to think about anything other than this Homecoming party for a week. Perhaps you could explain.'

MacNee's hackles were rising and on the whole he was grateful for Fleming's hasty intervention to explain. It didn't do to go into attack-dog mode too soon.

'Good gracious, how absolutely extraordinary! Didn't the police suspect he might have faked his death to escape justice at the time?' Philippa raised her carefully groomed eyebrows.

'I can't comment on that,' Fleming said. Her hackles seemed to be rising too. 'Can I take it that you are saying you knew nothing about this?'

'Well, of course I didn't.'

MacNee looked at Randall. 'What about you – laddie?' he said, as revenge for 'my dear man'.

He didn't rise to the provocation. He sat up, saying with heavy irony, 'Oh, am I allowed to say something too? I thought Mummy was going to do all the talking for me. No, as far as I was con-cerned he was dead. I saw him at the inquest but that was the last time.'

'That's right, the inquest,' MacNee said. 'Was he staying with you then?'

'Staying here? That man? Of course not!' Philippa's voice was shrill. 'I wouldn't give him house room after what happened to Julia. Her poor mother – and it was all his fault.'

'But I understand he stayed here on previous occasions,' Fleming said.

'Who told you that?' Randall demanded.

'Don't be silly, Randall, they won't tell you,' Philippa said. 'He only stayed here once or twice, Inspector, as a friend of my son's. I had no idea what he was doing.'

'Oh yes you bloody did! You were always hanging round the Cyrenaics, trying to be included, puffing on joints with the best of them. It was embarrassing!'

Philippa's colour rose. 'That's not true! You always were one to say things for effect.'

There was, MacNee decided, nothing he liked more than a floor show, when the witnesses did the job for them. He said provocatively, 'Can we get this straight? You're saying your son's a liar, he's saying you are. Are we meant to assume no one's telling the truth about Mr Kane?'

It was a Laurel and Hardy moment: the way they were glaring at each other, you could almost read the 'Here's another fine mess you've got me into' thought bubble above their heads.

Then Philippa said, 'I'm sorry, that was a misunderstanding. When I said I didn't know what he was doing, I mean that I didn't realise the strength of the stuff he was supplying to poor Julia.'

'Well, neither did I,' Randall said unconvincingly.

Fleming, clearly deciding that the fun had gone on long enough, stepped in. 'We're not really concerned with Mr Kane's operations at that time. What we are anxious to find out is where the drugs he was supplying came from. I understand you and Julia Margrave knew him in Edinburgh, Mr Lindsay?'

Randall shifted uncomfortably in his chair. 'Just Julia, really. I wasn't much into drugs – a bottle of bubbly has more of a kick, as far as I'm concerned. And if you think a dealer is going to give you any clue to his sources, you're quite remarkably naïve.'

'You and Miss Margrave worked together at a bank in Edinburgh, is that right?'

'Yes, Rutherford's.'

Why, MacNee wondered, had that particular question made the man uneasy? 'That's the bank you're still with?' he prodded.

There was no mistaking the unease now. 'Yes, that's right.'

'So you're just having a wee break?'

'That's right. The party, you know – couldn't miss that.'

Philippa Lindsay was studying her fingernails.

'So when did you come back here, Mr Randall?' Fleming asked.

'On Wednesday.'

'You weren't here on Monday April 14th?'

'Why on earth would I be? I work in Paris.'

'Thank you. And you, Mrs Lindsay? Where were you on that date?'

Philippa shrugged. 'At work, certainly. We have an interior design business and I would be there

149

most of the day and early part of the evening. Then home, grab something to eat, fall into bed, I suppose. That's the usual pattern. I don't think I had any sort of social engagement.'

'And someone can vouch for this?'

'My husband, Charles. And there are a couple of women who work for us – they do shifts.'

MacNee and Fleming exchanged glances. It was the first time they'd heard about a husband; only Philippa had been mentioned before.

'Perhaps we could speak to him now?' Fleming suggested.

'I'm afraid he's away on a buying trip.'

'But he'll be at this party, I take it?'

Randall laughed. 'You think? She's having it over my father's dead body – oh, not literally. At least,' with a malicious glance at his mother, 'I hope not. He says he doesn't know why she wants to have it and to be honest neither do I.'

Philippa compressed her thin lips. 'I'm doing it because I have a duty to the community that comes with the property. And there is still a huge amount of work to be done for it, particularly in the garden, Randall. Unless there's anything more you need from us, I'd be very grateful if you allowed us to get on with it. I've got a dozen people to see this morning.'

DSI Taylor, masochistically reading newspapers in his Dumfries HQ office, looked up eagerly as DI Harris came in. 'Something to report?' Then, as he saw the look on Harris's face, 'Oh.'

'You could call it progress of a sort.' Harris was on the defensive. 'We've eliminated one line of enquiry. The two men who were quarrelling in the car – they've come forward.'

Dismay made Taylor bold. 'But for God's sake, man, that wasn't just "one line of enquiry" – it was pretty much your only line of enquiry! What the hell am I supposed to say in the next press release?'

Harris's jaw tightened. 'I thought bringing in DI Fleming was going to transform the whole investigation, but what has she come up with – nothing!'

'Well, nothing so far,' Taylor was forced to admit. 'What about the searches on down the coast? Have they reported yet?'

'Wild goose chase, like I said it would be.'

'Nothing at all?'

'Nothing.'

Taylor ran his hand through his hair despairingly. 'So where do we go from here, then?'

'Better ask her, Tom. She's in charge of the operation – you said it yourself.'

'I have asked her. But of course she's only had a couple of days–'

'Three, counting today.'

Stung by his relentless negativity, Taylor said, 'The day's not over yet. Let's look on the bright side – Marjory's doing a series of interviews today and there's still time for something to come up that may change the whole thrust of the investigation.'

'This one should be good,' Fleming said as they drove through Ballinbreck to the Stewarts' restaurant at the other end of the village. 'I'll be interested to see the place, for a start, after the way you and Louise described it. And coppers who go over to the dark side are always interesting too.'

MacNee snorted. 'You think? Money, usually – that's all.'

'OK, but that's often just part of it. The job's hierarchical and breaking the rules is a way of putting up two fingers, and if it makes you a profit on the side too, well and good. And it could be just that Stewart wanted to be in on this Cyrenaic group and had to go along with it. It hinges on how much he knew about Kane's suppliers.'

'They'll have toasted his toes about that during the internal enquiry,' MacNee said. 'Can we get access to it?'

'Not sure,' Fleming said. 'Legal problems with that, I suspect. We'll just have to grill him ourselves – though he's certainly given himself enough time to have his story absolutely straight.

'Oh, there it is.' She drove into The Albatross car park.

To Fleming's disappointment they were taken not upstairs to the restaurant with its velvet drapes and nasty prints, but through to the private quarters at the back by a cleaner in a pink overall who was obviously bursting with curiosity.

Will Stewart was waiting for them in a pleasant sitting room with a view on to a small private courtyard, bright with pots of geraniums. He got up to shake hands, smiling affably, and said to the cleaner who was lingering in the doorway, 'Thanks, Sandra – that's OK.' Reluctantly, Sandra withdrew.

'Bit embarrassing, this,' Stewart said, getting in

152

first. 'The classic bad apple, me, I'm afraid.'

'Were you, Mr Stewart?' Fleming said with some interest. 'How bad?'

Stewart laughed easily. 'Make it Will. Mr Stewart's my brother. Oh, not rotten to the core. Just a few little bruises round the edges.'

'How would you define "bruises"?'

'Turning a blind eye, I suppose. Of course I knew about the drugs and you wouldn't believe me if I said I didn't indulge. Weed certainly, the odd line of coke, but the equivalent of social drinking if the laws in this country were halfway realistic.'

His manner was relaxed, almost chummy. 'I'm not here to debate the law,' Fleming said coldly. 'Where did it come from?'

He gave her a sideways look. 'Well now, do you think I wouldn't have taken great care not to know? That kind of knowledge doesn't do you any good, if you're a cop. They start expecting awkward favours.'

That, Fleming thought, had the ring of truth, but MacNee said, 'Worth it when it's good money, though?'

'You didn't know Connell Kane, obviously. He wasn't about to cut anyone in on his deals. All I can tell you is that he was Edinburgh based, so I assume that's where it came from.'

Fleming felt, rather than saw, MacNee's triumphant glance at this exoneration of his native city. That line of questioning wasn't getting them anywhere and she changed tack.

'Did you see Mr Kane at any time after his staged suicide?'

Stewart shook his head. 'No. I was as aston-ished as anyone else when I heard about it.'

'Did he tell you what he was planning to do?'

Again, he shook his head. 'Kept his cards very close to his chest. None of us knew him, really, Inspector, except Julia – well, Randall too, I suppose. But it didn't seem odd at the time that he should kill himself knowing he was respon-sible for the tragedy – he never had eyes for anyone except Julia.'

'And the rest of you, Mr Stewart?'

'Well – we were young and foolish, as the saying goes.'

'Forty-three, you were,' MacNee said flatly. 'It's on record.'

For the first time, Stewart seemed put out. Then he gave what was, Fleming had to admit, a very charming smile. 'They say forty is the new thirty, though, don't they? But I suppose I was just immature.'

Long experience had made her impervious. 'However immature you might be, you must have realised that for a police officer to become in-volved in a group like the Cyrenaics was courting trouble?'

'Mmm. But look at it this way. I was single, I had a job that kept me in a place that isn't what you could call exciting. There was this group of fun people gathering in my brother's pub – you expect me just to go to bed early every night saying, "No, no, I can't have a social life, I'm a police officer"?'

Fleming was quicker to recognise the red her-ring than MacNee, who had started to argue

154

about what constituted a social life. She cut in before Stewart could respond. 'You have a job in Canada now, I understand?'

'That's right.'

It was the shortest answer he'd given so far. 'What do you do?'

He paused. 'I don't want my present employer being told that the police are asking questions so I'm afraid that without compulsion I won't tell you.'

He was well within his rights and it wasn't that important. 'So when did you return?'

'I arrived here last week. Friday. You can check it, if you like.'

They were getting nowhere, and MacNee was definitely becoming restive. 'What on earth would you want to come back for? You'd been drummed out of the place, more or less.'

'Not quite, Sergeant.' Stewart sounded annoyed. 'The police drummed me out, granted, but this was my home for forty-three years, my brother lives here and I have a lot of friends, some of whom will be here for this Homecoming party. Since I didn't want to be exiled from Ballinbreck for the rest of my life, I thought it would be a good opportunity. All right?'

He'd answered what they asked him, apparently readily. Either he was truthful or he was a very good liar. Or – Fleming considered the possibility – they hadn't been asking the right questions. After checking whether he had tipped off Randall Lindsay about their visit, and getting a look so blank that she had to believe it was genuine, she thanked him formally and then they left.

'What did you make of him?' she asked Mac-Nee as she drove off.

'Sleekit,' MacNee said, using that useful Scottish word that means both smooth and sly.

'Not just well prepared?' Fleming said. 'I think he's clever, certainly. But I wouldn't be sure it's more than that.'

'Sleekit,' MacNee repeated firmly.

Biddy James glanced at her watch as she slowed down to turn into Eleanor Margrave's gateway. Ten past four; she'd made very good time – she'd always driven rather too fast – and it had been a golden afternoon for the drive, the Solway scenery at its sparkling best. Perfect sketching weather.

She was looking forward to the weekend. Her circle of old friends was sadly diminished now and it was only really with Eleanor that she could go back to being young and silly again. Under the depressing weight of general expectation you found yourself compelled to be boringly sensible but she and Eleanor could still reduce each other to helpless fits of the giggles.

Young she might be at heart but the feeling didn't extend to her rheumaticky legs. She unfolded herself painfully out of the car, holding on to it until she could reach her stick.

Eleanor's front garden, shielded by a thick hedge, was impressive as usual, given the salt spray and the winds. Pale late narcissi and tulips, primulas and bluebells were all making a show under pink and red rhododendrons and on the wall of the old house a clematis was ready to burst into flower. Biddy paused to admire it, then rang the doorbell.

There was no answer. Eleanor usually had the door open by the time Biddy got out of the car but she was a little earlier than she'd said. She waited knowing that, like her own, Eleanor's mobility wasn't good, but after a moment or two she rang the bell again, for rather longer; maybe her hearing was becoming a problem too.

Still no reply. Eleanor's car was there, so she couldn't have dashed out for something she'd forgotten, say. She must be round the back, though Biddy was puzzled. There wasn't really a garden there, just a stretch of the riverbank where she sometimes hung out washing but Eleanor would hardly be doing that when she was expecting a guest. Leaning heavily on her stick she went round the corner of the house, negotiating the rougher terrain with some difficulty.

The tide was on the turn, with only a narrow strip of shore below the drying green. Eleanor wasn't there either. Biddy's heart skipped a beat. At their advanced age, it was bad news when a friend who was expecting your visit didn't answer the door. Perhaps Eleanor had fallen, or ... or worse.

She turned to go back to the house, intending to peer through the windows. Then a movement in the water caught her eye, a flutter of rags undulating moved on the waves. Rags, and a huddled – something.

Shaking and feeling sick, she hobbled over to the edge of the grass. 'Eleanor!' she cried, though she knew there would be no answer. Her friend's face looked back at her from a tangle of seaweed, suffused and swollen, with bulging eyes that were glassy and staring. On the pull of the tide, the body drifted a little further out, then further still on the next retreating wave.

CHAPTER TEN

The word had spread rapidly round Dumfries CID that the lead they had been following had petered out. As DI Len Harris came in to take the afternoon briefing he could sense the discontented, almost rebellious mood, with even his most loyal supporters looking away as he came in.

He had spent years keeping them in check with bullying and threats; he reckoned they would still find it hard to take him on unless he gave them the opportunity by seeming weak.

Act it, become it. Harris swept confidently through them to stand before the whiteboard, beside the pictures of the car and the corpse, the blue fibre-pen notes and the arrows for action that now meant nothing. He seized a rag and wiped them all off.

'We've achieved the first stage of the investigation,' he said. 'For those who don't know, we've managed to eliminate the car seen in Annan from our enquiry. You did a good, thorough job around the area, lads – well done.

'That frees us to go on to the next stage. Known previous associates – that's the name of the game. I've instigated enquiries already so the

Galloway force have begun carrying them out on their patch.

'As you know, the super in his wisdom has decreed that DI Fleming takes charge of this one, so we're more or less hamstrung until she gets round to making decisions instead of mouthing off.'

They had been very silent. When Harris said that, he could feel a ripple of discontent. He went on hastily, 'Of course, I have my own ideas. Hotels, B&Bs; I want them all checked. Show them the mugshot, get them in conversation. Remember Kane would be using a false name, remember there may be staff who are off duty. Don't rush it this time – get them chatting. Questions?'

There were a couple, easily dealt with. Weston's hand, waving at the back, he pretended not to see and swept out again. There was sweat on his forehead but he couldn't risk getting out a handkerchief to wipe it until he was back in his office.

He hadn't got far down the corridor when she came up behind him. 'Sir...'

He didn't stop. 'Yes, Weston?'

'The tracks, sir – the place the car went into the sea...'

Harris turned round. 'I didn't mention it, Weston, because it was utterly pointless. I checked it out, as I said I was going to, and they couldn't have been made by a car. Did you study the tracks on the shore?'

'I didn't think there were any.'

'You see, that's the problem. The reason I can't rely on you, Weston, is that you're sloppy. When

159

you looked at them properly it was clear it had been something like a quad bike with a trailer, going down on to the shore – to get seaweed for fertiliser, more than likely. The farmers do that all the time.

'I've overlooked the insubordination but I'm seriously concerned about the lack of attention to detail. You'd better shape up or we'll have to consider whether you have a future in the Force.'

He swept on, leaving Weston gaping.

At the Kirkluce afternoon briefing the mood was more upbeat generally, though Hepburn was having a moan about her assignment.

'Of all the wastes of a day! I'd no idea we had so many nutters around. There was actually a psychic offering her help; she'd had a vision of a man wringing his hands and wailing and he was telling her that his murderer's name began with B. And there was another one from a B&B down near Manchester who claimed he'd been staying there last week. Tricky. And those were pretty much the best of them.'

'Indeed. So – no uranium?' Fleming asked.

'Not a trace.'

She looked at Macdonald and Campbell. 'You two? How did you get on with the background checks?'

'They seem to have led a disappointingly blameless life,' Macdonald said. 'We trawled the records but no joy, apart from a speeding conviction for Randall Lindsay. Logie and Kendra Stewart, Jen Wilson – all here, doing the jobs we know about since Julia Margrave's death, but we've no handle as yet on where Skye Falconer or Will Stewart might have been. We did turn up one interesting little piece of news, about Lindsay, though – I spoke to his boss in Paris and he's left the bank. Wouldn't say why – just said that the decision had been mutual. Sounded pretty tight-lipped about it, though.'

'Ah!' MacNee said with some satisfaction. 'That's not what he told us. I jaloused there was something there from the way he was twitching when it came up. Seemed surprised when he realised that it was Kane we were asking about, too.'

'Fingers in the till, from the sound of it,' Fleming said.

Hepburn was grinning. 'Couldn't happen to a nicer guy. He'll have to learn how the other half lives now.'

'I've got an appointment with one of the senior executives at the headquarters in Edinburgh on Monday,' Macdonald said. 'I'll check out Julia Margrave's professional background as well.'

'Excellent.' Fleming said. 'So you and Ewan–'

Campbell cleared his throat. 'Er ... not me.'

'It's your day off, isn't it. But I think we could swing some overtime–'

'It's not that. I've an appointment. Medical.'

They all looked at him with concern. 'I hope it's nothing serious,' Fleming said.

'No. Back Tuesday, probably.'

MacNee, uninhibited by social convention, said, 'What's wrong, lad? Spit it out.'

Campbell went pink. 'Just piles. OK, laugh.'

No one did. 'Bad luck,' Fleming said and passed on quickly. 'Right, that will be you going with

Andy on Monday, Louise. All right?' They both looked at their feet, saying nothing.

'There are one or two areas to follow up after our interviews this morning.' She gave them the general details and went on, 'We were both convinced that Skye Falconer was lying. I don't know exactly what she's lying about, or why, but we need to lean on her and find out.

'We haven't had any result from the searches along the shoreline. It was a long shot, but I had been hoping we might be lucky. DSI Taylor said he'd be putting a full team on it so they should have covered the ground – we certainly haven't the manpower to check ourselves.

'I'd have liked to go on with this over the weekend – ask a few questions round the village, try to tap into any gossip – but the super's put her foot down about overtime. If the media focus shifts to us here she'll have to, but for the moment she's quite relaxed about leaving Dumfries to take the flak for lack of progress. That's all I have for the moment. Questions?'

'Why now?' Campbell said.

'What brought him back, you mean?' Fleming said. It was, as usual, a good question. It had come up before but in organising the routines of investigation they hadn't taken time to consider it.

'Risky thing to do,' Hepburn said. 'He was known in the area and his photo had been in all the papers. He could have been spotted just going into a shop.'

'So what was it that made him take that risk? Was he meeting someone?' Macdonald said.

Hepburn picked up on that. 'There was this

Homecoming party. Maybe it was the focus –
they'd all have gathered then. Does it mean we're
looking just at the people who came back for it –
Randall Lindsay, Will Stewart, Skye Falconer?'

'I don't think so. It's this weekend, isn't it? He
was actually killed well before. Could be that it
was to prevent him meeting someone who was
coming back.'

Hepburn was impressed. 'That's a fair point,
Andy,' she said.

Fleming watched with a quiet smile as they did
the job she had picked them for – generating ideas.
If they would just cut out the constant needling –
and, of course, being cooped up in a car all day on
Monday would probably bring out the worst in
them both, but she wasn't going to pander to their
prejudices by sending Tam instead of Andy.

'That's food for thought,' she said, when they
had talked it out. 'I'll let you go. There won't be a
briefing on Monday morning. I'm going to have
to go and talk to the Dumfries CID – get them a
bit more directly involved doing interviews in the
village since we can't do that ourselves. Tam, I'll
want you to come with me.'

MacNee grinned. 'Feart you'll get a dagger in
your back?'

'You think you're joking,' Fleming said. 'Anyway, have a good weekend, all of you. And good
luck on Monday, Ewan.'

Campbell nodded glumly as they filed out.

Biddy James thought she was going to faint. Her
head was spinning and her legs were trembling so
that she thought they might collapse under her.

163

But if she went down on uneven ground, how would she ever get up again? She mustn't give way, she mustn't, she mustn't, for Eleanor's sake as well as her own. Grasping her stick with both hands for support, she forced herself to take deep, calming breaths. 'There's nothing wrong with you except nerves,' she told herself sternly, being of the generation that despised mental weakness.

The dizziness passed off and Biddy stumbled back to the car. Phone. She must phone the police. She had an awkward stretch into her car to reach her handbag, clutching at the roof for balance, then lowering herself to sit sideways on the driver's seat while she scrabbled through it.

She persisted in having a smartphone, though her family kept telling her she should have one that had bigger numbers, more suited to clumsy old hands. She regretted scorning the advice now, when her hands were shaking so much, but she succeeded at last. But when she switched it on, there was no signal and now she remembered Eleanor had told her that.

What was she to do now? And every moment that was wasted, the dreadful, implacable waves were pulling Eleanor further and further out. Not that she would care, anyway, not now. Tears came to her eyes.

She banished them, blew her nose, wiped her eyes and considered the possibilities. There was a phone in the house and perhaps the door was unlocked. Awkwardly, she levered herself to her feet again and walked shakily over to the front door.

The handle didn't yield. The back door, perhaps? But she quailed at the thought of negotiating the rough ground again, and then the steps that led up to it. At that moment a car passed along the road.

I'll hail a car, Biddy thought, her heart lifting a little at the thought of being able to pass the responsibility to someone else. She'd never played the age card before, had found herself bristling sometimes when well-meaning help was offered. She'd be glad enough to be considered old and frail now.

She walked to the gate. Another car passed just as she reached it but she didn't have time to flag it down. Then the road was empty.

The minutes ticked by with agonising slowness. It seemed a long time before a car came along and the woman driver, seeing her wave, stopped and lowered the passenger window, smiling.

'Want a lift, dear?'

Biddy was humiliated to find the tears starting again. 'It's my friend,' she said. 'I think she must have fallen in the river. She's drowned. Oh please, please could you go round and see if you can stop her being swept away?'

'Oh my goodness!' She jumped out. 'That's awful! And you're shaking – you need to sit down.'

Biddy indicated her own car and allowed herself to be helped back onto the driver's seat. As the woman headed off towards the river, she leant her head sideways against the seat back and shut her eyes, thankful that at last there was someone to take charge. Bizarrely, she found herself drifting into sleep and woke with a start to find that the woman had returned and was wearing a puzzled expression.

'Round the back, on the shore, did you say, dear? I can't see anything there at all. Are you sure?' She looked at Biddy doubtfully. 'You didn't just dream it, did you? Sometimes it's so difficult to tell when you just wake up. Maybe your friend has just gone out...'

She had the sort of kindly, indulgent tone that people so often adopt as if being elderly were the same as being feeble-minded. Irritation stiffened Biddy's resolve as nothing else could have.

'Oh no, my dear,' she said with a certain hauteur, pushing herself upright. 'I do assure you she was there. The waves were already dragging her away. We need to contact the police so they can get the coastguard out, but there's no signal here.'

The woman still looked doubtful, but she said, 'My house isn't far away. I'll take you there and call them. Now, if I took your arm do you think you could get up, dearie?'

Pride, and her hatred of being thought old and feeble, got Biddy out of her car and onto her feet before her rescuer had finished her sentence.

Will, with a bad grace, was setting up tables in the pub for the evening meal. There had been a bit of a row with Logie when he'd tried to get out of it; his brother was on edge – well, frankly, they all were – and their relationship hadn't been that close to start with. Now, with Kendra all over Will like a rash, Logie was ready to pick a fight about anything except his wife's relationship with his brother, being too afraid of what the outcome might be to open the subject.

Will was entirely with him on that, even if it did mean giving up his evenings to save his brother a waitress's wages. It wouldn't be for long, anyway. He hoped.

When his mobile rang he glanced at the number, not recognising it. 'Hello?'

'Will.'

A throaty voice, loaded with some sort of meaning, one he didn't recognise. 'Yes, speaking.'

'It's Philippa, Will.' The voice held a hint of reproach.

His heart sank. 'Philippa, goodness! Great to hear from you. How are things?'

'Oh, all the better for your being around. The grapevine, you know? But why didn't you let me know you were back for the party?'

'It's been a bit frantic since I arrived. The pub is busy – you should see me at the moment, setting up the tables. Never saw myself as a waiter, really. In fact, I should really be–'

She didn't wait to let him make the excuse. 'Oh, I know things must be tricky at that end. Kendra always talks as if you're her personal property. But what about sneaking out later, just for a drink? Renew our ... acquaintance?' She gave a little laugh.

Oh God, what had he got himself into? 'Philippa, nothing I'd like more but I couldn't let Logie down.'

'Tomorrow lunchtime, then?' she persisted. 'Remember that little place up near Gelston?'

Yes, he remembered it. All too clearly. It was part of that terrible madness that had somehow taken possession of them all two years ago, and he was paying for it now.

'Tomorrow's no good, either,' he lied. 'I'm meeting up with an old chum – we'll probably make a day of it.'

'Oh.' Philippa sounded put out. 'That's a shame. But you'll be at the party, at night, won't you?'

'Of course.'

'I'll see you there, then. Oh Will, it's just so good to hear your voice. I couldn't believe it when you just disappeared like that, without a word. Naughty man! I shan't let you get away with that again.'

Philippa was too old to be kittenish. Much, much too old. She'd had a certain mature charm back then, but now she must be – what, fifty, fifty-five? He said hastily, 'Looking forward to it. Sorry, have to go.'

He was feeling slightly sick as he picked up another napkin to fold over a knife and fork.

He wasn't what she'd expected. Marjory Fleming had been sent on training courses that would, if they were any good, have eliminated any inclination towards stereotyping, yet when she was considering the 'friend' who was studying social sciences along with Cat she had been guilty of thinking in terms of long hair, a duffel coat and earnestness.

Nick Canton's dark curly hair was short and neat; his clothes were the sort of smart casual a girl's parents might approve of, without looking old-fashioned to someone his own age. He was nice-looking, tall – always seen as an asset in the Fleming family – and he had a pleasant speaking voice. What wasn't to like, for even the fondest mother?

Bill, having shared Marjory's own reprehensible expectations, was both surprised and delighted. Nick listened politely, laughed in the right places, and said nothing to disagree with his host.

So why didn't Marjory take to him? She didn't like it that Cat, too, was letting Bill make comments that would normally have had her jumping down his throat. She didn't like it that Cat was on edge, shifting uncomfortably in her seat.

She couldn't put her finger on it until Bill began enlarging on his view that if people would just get married and stay married, half the social problems would disappear. It was hardly a new topic of discussion around this dinner table; Cat's opposing views had always been volubly presented.

She said nothing; Nick agreed, and suddenly Marjory understood.

He was laughing at Bill. He knew Cat's opinions; he was now trying to lead Bill on to the point where he would look foolish in his daughter's eyes. Marjory saw Cammie suddenly shoot a sharp look at Nick and then at her, his eyebrows slightly raised.

The young men had been getting on all right before they sat down. Nick was a rugby fan but, he admitted in self-deprecation, no use as a player. 'I tended to stay out on the wing where I wouldn't get my shirt so dirty,' he had said and Cammie, from his position of natural superiority as a number eight, had remarked that wingers were all like that.

It was, Marjory thought, as if Nick was analys-

169

ing them, working out just how to play it – definitely manipulative. He'd made no attempt at engagement with her as yet beyond common politeness and Marjory had taken very little part in the conversation. It might be interesting to see what his tactics towards her would be.

It was. When he turned to her, it was with a question of such naked hostility that she almost gasped.

'What about you, Marjory – what do you think about traditional marriage? With a job like yours, family would always have to take second place.'

So she wasn't to get the charm treatment. What hurt was the realisation that while Bill and Cammie must be either undermined or brought on side to make him surer of Cat, her mother's opinion didn't matter. She glanced at Cat and saw her eyes fall.

She was used to hostility, though – thrived on it, professionally. 'Depends what you mean by second place, Nick. Do you mean you don't approve of women working, that you think a father can't provide supportive care? That's a very old-fashioned attitude, I would have thought?'

Nick coloured, and she saw his eyes narrow. 'No, not at all. Of course women have the same rights to work as men.'

Marjory laughed. Time to take the gloves off. 'Ah,' she said. 'You've been talking to my daughter, obviously. The children were both at nursery when I started work again after Bill positively begged me to get a job instead of directing all my energies into organising him. I do admit I can never guarantee that an emergency won't arise.

170

But look at this pair' – she gestured at Cammie and Cat – 'fine, upstanding young people, I'm sure you'd agree, Nick, so I can't have done everything wrong.

'Now, anyone ready for pudding? It's Karolina's *szarlotka*, Nick. That's her wonderful apple pie, specially in honour of our guest.'

Marjory went to fetch it. Perhaps she'd gone too far, but the sort of conversation where words and intentions were at odds left her feeling deeply uncomfortable. Queasy, almost. And no one, but no one, was going to be allowed to patronise Bill.

Cammie got up to help her pass round. Under cover of the conversation that had started up again round the table, he muttered in her ear, 'Go, Ma!'

As usual, given Bill's early start, it wasn't much after half past nine when they went up to bed, leaving the clearing up to the young. As they climbed the stairs, Bill said happily, 'Nice young fellow, that! Seemed to have his values straight. Maybe he'll knock some sense into Cat.'

'Mmm,' Marjory said. How do you tell your husband that someone is making a fool of him and he hasn't noticed?

The Portling coastguard rescue boat from Colveig had been called out, though as they went upriver the chief rescue officer was sceptical. Even as he dutifully scanned the shores where the mudflats were gradually being exposed, he said, 'This may be a wild goose chase. Apparently the woman who phoned in said the wifie who reported it was elderly and might be confused. She didn't see anything to confirm it and apparently there wasn't a bank or anything someone could have stumbled down. We'll probably find the old girl's pal is just out shopping or something.'

He glanced at the chart in front of him. 'We should be coming up almost level now.' He put the binoculars to his eyes again, then said sharply, 'Hang on, what's that?' He pointed. 'Over there, Sandy. Take her in closer.'

It was only a few hundred yards downstream from the reported site, stranded on a mudbank – a dark pile of sodden material, a mud-streaked, water-bloated face. With the tide still relatively high it was one of their easier retrievals.

'Poor old dear,' the chief said. 'Just tripped, probably, and got swept away on the tide.'

Today, though, the waves were lapping the shore as gently and rhythmically as a mother rocking her baby to sleep and as the body was dragged on board one of the men said, 'Not unless she'd tied something round her neck and tightened it first. Take a look at this, Chief.'

The blackened, indented line in the corpse's swollen neck was eloquent evidence of a violent death.

'Oh,' the chief said uncomfortably. 'See what you mean. Looks a nasty business. I'll radio ahead – get them on to it right away.'

Skye had made a chicken pie for supper that night and she was making a lot of fuss about it – her first attempt at pastry, she said. She went on about whether it was crisp enough, and crumbly enough, until Jen, who had needed to find four different ways of saying it was delicious, realised this wasn't really about the pie at all. There was something she was trying hard not to talk about and she could make a good guess at what that was.

Skye was in a funny mood, nervy and artificially bright. There was no mention of the police until Jen said, 'How did the interview go this morning?'

'Oh, the interview?' Skye gave a little laugh. 'I'd forgotten all about it. They were fine, just like you said. No problem.'

'That's good. Did they ask you why Connell had come back?' she said. She kept her voice light, casual.

Skye got up to clear the plates. 'Yes, but of course I said I didn't know, that you could never tell why Connell did anything.'

'That's certainly true,' Jen said, with a pang of pain. 'Are they coming back to see you again?'

'Don't think so,' Skye said, dumping the plates in the sink and running water over them. 'Oh, by the way, I've decided to come to the Homecoming party after all.'

'Really? Oh, that's such a good idea, Skye! I've been worried about you, you know, shutting yourself away here.' She paused. 'Does ... does Will know?'

'I decided to give him a surprise. And after that I'm going to get myself sorted out – look for a job and get out of your hair.'

'Don't be silly,' Jen said. 'You're welcome to stay as long as you like. It will be a sore blow to have to go back to living with my own inadequacies, I tell you.'

But she was under strain herself, longing for peace just to sort herself out, not to have to keep up a constant front of calm and cheerfulness. She would be glad when Skye left. She couldn't help but see her as the stormy petrel who had presaged the storm.

Bill had, as usual, fallen asleep whenever his head hit the pillow. Marjory, her mind active not only with her family concerns but with the case which seemed to be nothing but loose ends at the moment, was still awake when her phone rang at quarter past ten. She jumped out of bed and carried it on to the landing to answer it, though she thought it probable that nothing short of a bomb exploding directly overhead would wake Bill out of his first sleep.

It was Inspector Mike Wallace, from the Kirk-cudbright police station. She listened intently as he explained the situation.

The police surgeon had pronounced a woman pulled from the Solway officially dead, and the pathologist had unhesitatingly assessed the cause of death as strangulation. She had been unofficially identified as Eleanor Margrave.

Marjory reacted with shock. *'Margrave?'* Her mind started racing. Margrave – Julia – Connell Kane. Connections, connections.

'DSI Rowley has agreed that you should be SIO,' Wallace was saying. 'Can you get down tonight, Marjory?'

'Yes, of course,' she said mechanically. 'With you shortly.'

She went back into her bedroom to collect her

174

clothes, dressed speedily and went downstairs.

Cat, Cammie and Nick were still up, chatting in the sitting room. When she opened the door Meg, who had been sleeping in front of the fire, jumped up and came over to greet her.

'Don't tell me,' Cat said with the edge in her voice that always made Marjory wince, 'it's going to screw up the whole weekend. As always.'

Nick looked up with a sardonic smile. 'Are you going to say, "There's been a *murder?*".' He rolled his r's in imitation of Taggart.

'An elderly woman has been strangled, if you think that's funny,' Marjory said. She didn't care that her response had produced an awkward silence, or that she heard Nick say, after she'd shut the door, 'That was a joke, for God's sake. Needs to lighten up a bit, your mum.'

She lingered long enough to hear Cammie's response. 'Ever seen someone who's been strangled? I haven't either, but I know I wouldn't like to. That's what Mum's just gone to deal with and I don't think I'd be giggling about it either.'

She only just managed to whisk into the kitchen out of sight before Cammie opened the door on his way upstairs.

CHAPTER ELEVEN

Laid out under the harsh lighting of the morgue Eleanor Margrave's face was almost navy blue, the whites of her eyes suffused with leaked blood. Her small, elderly body was frail, thin and bony as a bird's, the limbs looking fragile enough to snap.

She had probably once been a handsome woman, DI Fleming thought, looking at the high cheekbones and the straight, elegant nose. Her reddened eyes would once have been a bright blue, though they were hooded and faded now.

According to the pathologist, there were no signs that she had fought back, taken by surprise presumably by a much stronger assailant.

The helplessness of the old, their vulnerability – she thought of her own mother Janet, in her eighties now, and felt the same kind of protective anger that always seized her when there were injuries to children. Eleanor Margrave deserved justice and Fleming felt an odd little surge of pride that the job she did meant that the duty to deliver it was hers. She made a silent vow to Eleanor that if she failed it wouldn't be for lack of trying.

'Thanks,' she said, gesturing to the mortuary assistant to cover the body again. 'They've done the photographs?'

The woman assured her they had and Fleming left to drive back to the police station at Kirkcudbright. Inspector Mike Wallace was waiting for her with the photographs spread out on his desk.

Fleming winced as she looked at them. 'It was brutal, Mike. She was a frail old lady – couldn't even resist.'

'Wouldn't have left a mark on her assailant, the pathologist thinks. Surprised when she was standing with her back turned.'

'Then dragged out to the river for disposal?'

'Even carried, possibly – she didn't weigh much. The light was failing so we couldn't search for tracks – fingertip stuff tomorrow, I suppose?'

Fleming nodded. 'So we've got at least a pointer to time, wouldn't you say? The body must have been meant to be swept away downriver, maybe even out to sea, so we could very nearly assume that it would be at high tide – there wouldn't be much point in laying a body out in full view on the shore below the house.'

'I'll get someone on to checking tide tables. And first thing tomorrow – local interviews, I suppose – see if anyone saw anything useful?'

'Right. And I'll get my team going back over the connections with her daughter's death – you remember Julia Margrave?'

'Oh, of course! I knew the name was familiar. Poor lady – it can't have been easy if the girl was a druggie even before she OD'd. So – that body in the car at Newbie, the drug dealer – do you think there's a connection with that?'

'We've got nothing on him, as yet. I've been helping Tom Taylor in Dumfries. But let me say this – all the main characters in the drama of Julia Margrave's death have recently come back

177

to the neighbourhood. And I have a nasty, distrustful mind when it comes to coincidences. The woman who found her – is she still around?'

'We took her to a hotel for the night. Quite old and very shaken but she was determined to give her statement. Perfectly clear and coherent – she's a feisty old bird.'

'We can talk to her tomorrow. Anything else tonight?'

Wallace shook his head. 'We've got security in place down there and a duty car on site. They've been round the neighbouring properties, and Mrs Margrave was seen in her garden around twelve-thirty. I'll get some rotas worked out now and have teams in place at first light.'

Fleming got up. 'I'll do the same. I'll be calling staff in and I'll get down to the site whenever I've had the morning briefing.'

As she headed back to her office in Kirkluce, she tried to control the random ideas that kept sparking in her mind and focus on the central point. Julia Margrave's death was the direct link between Connell Kane and Eleanor Margrave. Surely it must all stem from that?

She had been puzzling away at the question Campbell had raised again at the meeting – why would Kane have come back to the area? He might not have realised that there was a threat to his life but he would certainly have known that he was in danger of being recognised and arrested. Macdonald and Hepburn had talked about the Homecoming party, which might draw the Cyrenaics together again, but it was hard to believe that Kane would take the risk for the sake of a get-together fondly recalling old times.

Unfinished business. The words sprang to mind. Yes, it just could be that, and perhaps the Homecoming party might be key – and, now she thought of it, there was an inside track she might be able to persuade Hepburn to use.

But it was hard to understand why a blameless elderly widow should now be lying shrouded in a chilled steel box in a mortuary.

The evening, Louise Hepburn thought, had gone rather well. Her date was both attractive and amusing – there weren't a lot of those around in Kirkluce – and they'd had dinner in a new little Italian restaurant, lingering so long over their meal that they had to be thrown out when it closed.

The pub they'd adjourned to had a late licence and they'd carried on the conversation, going on to their taste in films. There was one they both fancied showing in the Newton Stewart cinema that week and they'd just agreed to go together the next night when a ping from her phone signalled a text message.

It could be an emergency summons. With a sinking heart she said, 'Sorry,' and glanced at it. 'Sorry,' she said again, pulling a face. 'I'll have to make a call. My boss.'

She carried the phone through to the back. Murder was a priority, date or no date.

Fleming was surprised to get her response. 'I thought you'd get this in the morning – we're not doing anything more tonight. But since you're there, Louise...'

Fleming gave her the background, then went

on to outline her idea.

Hepburn listened in horror. 'It's awful about Mrs Margrave, of course. But I really can't stand Randall – it would be absolute purgatory,' she said, though she recognised that this was a feeble excuse. She listened as Fleming explained that of course this wasn't an order and that she must make up her own mind, but...

She said glumly, 'Yes, boss,' and put the phone down.

She glanced at her watch – half past twelve. Too late to take up an invitation you had so rudely spurned the day before yesterday – and she wouldn't have been so rude if she'd known she'd have to change her mind.

It was humiliating – but on the other hand, it would give her the chance to be right at the heart of the investigation, with an 'in' that no one else would have, a temptation she couldn't resist. She'd phone Randall in the morning.

Then she went back, with dragging feet, to explain to her date that the cinema tomorrow was definitely off.

DSI Taylor was whistling as he pressed the lift button to take him to his office in the Dumfries HQ first thing on Saturday morning. He was still looking uncharacteristically happy when DI Harris presented himself in response to an urgent summons.

Harris wasn't happy. He was feeling deeply conflicted: on the one hand, it was a considerable relief to know that media attention would this morning be switched to the Kirkluce headquarters and not directed at the lack of progress at Dumfries; on the other hand, he'd definitely have to let Fleming take full charge now and go swanning around being the great detective.

'Heard the news?' Taylor was infuriatingly chirpy.

'Yes.'

'That's good, don't you think? Takes the heat off us, anyway.'

'I suppose so.'

Taylor looked suddenly more uncertain. 'But Len, it seems as if the investigation coming our way was accidental – it obviously stems from this place in Galloway. Fleming will be dealing with it and we can shut down the operation at this end, rescue the budget – maybe even bill Galloway division for some of the work we've carried out. Don't you think?'

Harris shrugged. 'I'd have liked to show her up. She was riding for a fall with her attitude here – I was looking forward to a good laugh at her briefing on Monday, watching her trying to get my lads on side. It's about time she was taken down a peg or two. But still, if it means we're off the hook–'

'All but, I should say. At least no one's going to be interested in us for the next bit, anyway. Shame we can't prove the car went into the Solway there as well – if someone had managed to place it on their patch we could wash our hands of the whole thing.'

It hit Harris like a punch to the jaw. 'Surely – surely they'll move on from us anyway,' he managed.

'We-ell, maybe. The danger is that they start digging back and suggesting that if we'd got Kane's murder wrapped up all this wouldn't have happened. But let's look on the bright side and assume they won't – I'm not going to let it depress me, anyway.'

Suppressing a terse rejoinder to little Pollyanna, beaming across the desk, Harris went back to his office brooding. He was seldom entirely honest with himself; a deep-seated sense of inferiority made him respond to any criticism with raw aggression and he flatly refused ever to admit to failure. In this case, though, he could see how vulnerable he was.

It was greatly in his own interests that the whole operation at this end should be forgotten. On the other hand, how could he go back to Weston and tell her that he had lied to her, and that her evidence had been not just relevant but very possibly crucial? The site she had named was, he now realised with a further sinking of his spirits, just two or three miles from Eleanor Margrave's house.

The short answer was that he couldn't. Not only would it be a totally unacceptable loss of face, it would leave him wide open to a charge of misconduct and Weston – nasty, weaselling little creature that she was – would be just the person to do it.

No, he would have to pretend it hadn't happened and look on the bright side as sodding Pollyanna had suggested. It didn't make him feel like beaming, though.

DI Fleming's team had assembled in her Kirkluce office by eight o'clock. There was to be a general briefing at nine o' clock, but after an update from Inspector Wallace she had decided to get them out on interviews immediately.

'The first line of enquiry is obvious. We need to know exactly where all three Stewarts, both Lindsays, Jen Wilson and Skye Falconer were yesterday afternoon. Of course, we have to keep an open mind; there may be others involved that we don't know about as yet or this could just have been the result of a break-in or a random attack. But taking Connell Kane's murder into account, it's a good working hypothesis that this is related until proved otherwise.

'Now, timing. A neighbour reported seeing her in the garden as she drove past around twelve-thirty and Bridget James, who was coming to stay for the weekend, arrived just after four o' clock. The pathologist can't narrow it down much – assessing a body that's been immersed is tricky – but the tide was at the full at about three-thirty. For the moment at least, I think we go with the theory that the body wouldn't have been laid out on an open shore, so mid afternoon – say three to three forty-five looks like the crucial time.

'I'll take the briefing and then I'm going to Eleanor Margrave's house. Tam, I want you and Louise to talk to Bridget James then join me there. Andy and Ewan – take the Lindsays and Skye Falconer and Jen Wilson. Wilson was probably at school though, of course, we need to check that she wasn't off sick or something. Then report to me at the house and we'll take it from

183

there with the Stewarts. All right?'

'Maybe they'll feel they have to cancel the party,' Hepburn said hopefully, and Fleming grinned.

'Oh, I think we need to assure them that there's no need. I think it could be extremely instructive. We'll have our own spy in the camp,' she explained to the others, indicating a grimacing Hepburn. 'Louise has nobly agreed to go to it as Randall Lindsay's guest.'

Macdonald and MacNee burst out laughing, earning themselves a death stare. 'Was he pleased?' Macdonald said provocatively.

'Confused, mostly,' Hepburn said. 'I got him out of bed to tell him. And once he hears what's happened and puts two and two together about why I wanted to come, it could get very sticky. I don't suppose any of them will be very pleased.'

Fleming said sharply, 'If you're at all worried, forget it. I don't want to put you in an awkward situation.'

'I'm quite looking forward to it now, actually,' Hepburn admitted. 'There'll be plenty of other people there and I can look after myself.'

'If you're comfortable with it, fine. But if you sense trouble, get out. And that's an order. Right. Questions?'

'I didn't hear the early bulletin on the news,' Macdonald said. 'What did it say?'

'No more than that the body of an elderly woman had been recovered from the Solway yesterday evening. No name or definite area, so the media interest will be low at first, but once the stringers get hold of it and the connection with Kane's murder comes out, attention will

184

certainly build.'

'But it's possible that it's not general know-ledge?'

'Certainly possible. But of course the grapevine will be working overtime. I should think if any-one went into the local store in Ballinbreck this morning they'll have heard all about it. Anything else? OK – good luck.'

After they had left Fleming turned to drafting instructions for the briefing. With the apparent link between the two murders, this was going to be a major investigation right from the start. For extra manpower they might have to use Dumfries but at the moment she hoped to run it using only the Galloway force. She didn't trust Harris and it was entirely possible that he would be deliberately obstructive. But even as she ran through the de-tails of deployment, Hepburn's comment niggled at her. She'd suggested her going to the party without giving it enough thought; it had merely seemed a good inside track, a way of observing the interactions of their suspects. But if her theory that both murders had somehow sprung from poor, sad Julia Margrave's death was right, the killer was likely to be present and unlikely to appreciate an 'off-duty' police officer among them.

It wasn't likely she'd actually be threatened in the middle of a party. If there was some un-pleasantness Hepburn was an experienced officer now, well able to look after herself. Even so...

She didn't have time to sit here agonising. Not with the briefing in half an hour and only the barest of details sketched out.

In the Dumfries briefing room DC Weston listened with blank disbelief as DI Harris told them that the investigation was being stood down.

'Our connection with Connell Kane's murder seems to have been tangential at best. DSI Taylor and I have agreed that we will stand ready to offer any support that Galloway needs in their operation – though I expect DI Fleming's feminine intuition will solve it all in the next couple of days.'

There was a sycophantic titter from a couple of Harris's toadies but the general mood was sullen. They all knew that their time had been wasted and they all knew whose fault it was; that was unmistakable and Harris was uneasy, hurrying on to talk about a warehouse break-in that had happened the night before.

Weston put up her hand. He showed no sign of planning to call on her so she said loudly, 'Can you tell us where this woman's body was found, sir?'

He looked at her with a sarcastic sneer. 'Speaking too quickly for you to follow, Weston? In – the – river. All – wet. Are you with us now? That's everything.' He named a couple of officers he wanted to see and left.

Weston looked for DC Jamieson. Since their foray into Galloway, Jamieson had taken to avoiding her – not deliberately cutting her or anything, just not coming to sit beside her in meetings or seeking her out at breaks. It hurt; they'd always formed a protective alliance against the automatic chauvinism of many of their colleagues and Weston had noticed she was sitting with the group that had obligingly sniggered at Harris's gibe about DI Fleming.

Now as Weston came towards her Jamieson hung back, turning to make a remark to one of them, pretending not to have seen her one-time friend.

Weston was not to be discouraged. 'Debbie!' she called. 'Have you got a minute?'

Jamieson said, 'Sure,' and came over to her, though from the laughter she left behind her Weston suspected she had rolled her eyes before she did.

'It's this thing about the car–' Weston began.

'I thought it might be. Lizzie, you're obsessive about it. You heard what Harris said – it was a quad bike, going down to get seaweed. Now drop it, will you?'

'He said there were tracks on the sand. There couldn't have been – the tide comes right in there twice a day.'

'Well, maybe someone had only just been down that morning.'

Weston shook her head stubbornly. 'The broken branches were withered. It had happened long before that.'

Jamieson scowled at her. 'You think what you like. I'm not having anything more to do with it, because I'm not stupid. If you try to take on Harris I won't back you up.' She walked off.

Weston opened her mouth to pursue the argument, then shut it again. She wasn't going to take on Harris – she didn't have a death wish. There was no point in going to the super; he had about as much backbone as your average jellyfish.

She was going to take it direct to DI Fleming. And given half a chance, she'd ask her if she'd back a transfer into her division.

She checked the number, then slipped outside to make the call. 'I'd like to speak to DI Fleming, please,' she said. 'This is DC Weston.' The operator brushed her off with professional ease. 'I'm afraid she's not available. I'll put you through to the duty sergeant.'

'No, I'm afraid it has to be DI Fleming. It's personal.'

'Sorry. She doesn't take personal calls on this line. If it's "personal" no doubt you have her private number.' There was no mistaking the cynicism in the woman's tone.

It wasn't going to work this way. Weston thanked her politely – she might find herself working alongside the woman, after all. She'd just have to think of some other way to get this through.

Having prepared himself to be gentle and sympathetic to a poor, traumatised old dear who would need a lot of reassurance, MacNee was taken aback to find a tall, formidable woman instead. There was a stick by her chair, admittedly, but her back was ramrod straight and she had eyes so piercing that he almost winced as she turned them on him.

Bridget James – Biddy to her friends – had been, apparently, a senior civil servant in the Ministry of Justice and MacNee, who had automatically straightened his own back when she declared a particular interest in how things were done under the different judicial system in Scotland, realised he had called her 'madam' five times in four sentences. Hepburn had settled quietly into the background, hoping to avoid notice, but Mrs James's laser gaze swept over her too.

'You've made your official statement already, madam, so this is informal,' MacNee explained. 'This morning we'd just like you to talk us through what happened, if you would.'

'Of course. I'll explain the background first, as succinctly as I can.'

Unlike most elderly ladies, she understood the meaning of the word and delivered a clear and concise account of her friendship with Eleanor Margrave and their sketching parties. When she had finished, she waited for questions.

MacNee's mind went blank. The woman was mesmerising him; it felt as if he was being interviewed and failing to come up to scratch.

Hepburn came to the rescue. 'Was there any reason why Mrs Margrave might have been in the back garden?'

Mrs James nodded approvingly. 'Sound question. No. It wasn't really a garden, just a strip of rough ground between the house and the river. There was a drying green, but I don't think she used it at all now. The ground is very uneven and like me poor Eleanor wasn't very steady on her feet. She told me years ago that she'd bought a tumble drier. Now, I'll tell you exactly what happened, shall I?'

'Thank you, madam,' MacNee said humbly as another well-structured report was presented to them.

When she finished, she looked at them expectantly. 'I'm sure you will have a lot of questions. Fire away.'

This time, both MacNee and Hepburn began to speak at once, then both stopped. Mrs James looked amused; the steely eyes, MacNee realised, had quite a twinkle once you got used to her.

'I'm old-fashioned,' she said. 'Ladies first.'

Hepburn hesitated, glancing towards him; that wasn't quite how it worked in the police force but MacNee gave her an encouraging nod.

'Did you and Mrs Margrave keep in touch?'

'Oh yes, every couple of weeks or so – mostly, these days, to compare our aches and pains, I'm sorry to say. That, and discuss the latest batch of old friends who have popped off.'

She seemed quite calm about this but Hepburn, a little thrown, murmured, 'Oh dear, I am sorry. Er, well ... did she mention any problems she had had, any disagreements with neighbours, say, over the past few weeks?'

'She didn't really have what you'd call neighbours. The nearest house was quite a distance away and Eleanor didn't go about much; her mobility was even worse than mine is. She certainly didn't mention any problems and that would be unlikely anyway. I doubt if she saw any of them, except in passing. To be honest, I don't think she had friends at all locally. She led a very quiet life.'

'Was that since her daughter's death?' MacNee asked.

Biddy's face softened. 'Oh dear, Julia! She was the loveliest little girl, you know – the dream daughter, pretty, clever, charming. Spoilt, of course; Eleanor married late and she had never expected to have a child at all, then her husband died when Julia was six.

'What happened to her was such a tragedy, and even before that her poor mother had had to watch her destroying herself in slow motion, totally helpless. We talked about it a lot and I got her the best advice I could find, but it was no use. The girl would deny it flatly and Eleanor was afraid of losing her completely. Somehow she was still holding down her job and I always hoped that age would bring her to her senses, but she never got the chance.

'Eleanor withdrew at that time – ashamed, I think, and feeling responsible, though I always told her that nowadays there's nothing you can do at that stage. It's a very wicked world.'

'So there wasn't anything she told you that might suggest a reason for what happened?' MacNee said.

'I wish there were. I haven't been very helpful, I'm afraid.'

It looked as if there was nothing more to learn. MacNee reassured her and got up. 'Thanks very much. And if there's anything you remember, anything unusual, say, no matter how small, you'll contact us?'

'Of course. I–' Biddy stopped suddenly. 'Wait a moment...'

'You've thought of something.' MacNee sat down again.

'Eleanor's mermaid.'

'Mermaid?'

'Oh, it was just a curiosity, really, but it was certainly unusual. She was quite intrigued – phoned to tell me all about it. There was a big storm one night, a few weeks ago–'

MacNee stiffened. 'Not on the 14th of April, was it?'

'Could have been, I suppose. In fact, that would be right! I was talking about the opera I'd been to the night before and I'm pretty sure that was the 14th. I can check my diary, of course, but I clearly remember telling Eleanor the tenor should be taken out and painlessly terminated.'

MacNee and Hepburn were both on the edge of their seats. Don't go off about the opera, keep to the subject, MacNee begged silently, but he needn't have worried.

'There was a knock on the door late that evening – almost midnight, I think she said. Eleanor hadn't gone to bed – she's always been a night owl. There was this girl on the doorstep, soaked to the skin, with a very bad bruise on the side of her face. She took her in, tried to find out what had happened, but she wouldn't speak, not a word, just cried. She was in shock, Eleanor reckoned, and she popped her up to bed with a hottie, meaning to quiz her in the morning once she'd recovered a bit. But when she got up the girl had vanished. She was a bit worried, she said, that some of her household goods might have vanished with her, but no – she'd just gone. Eleanor never found out who she was or what had happened.'

It was a fascinating story. 'Why the mermaid bit?' MacNee asked.

'Oh, that was just Eleanor's fancy. She was pretty, with long hair and sea-green eyes, she told me, and she was wet as if she'd come out of the sea, though she wasn't muddy, apparently, so it could only have been the rain. She reminded Eleanor of the Little Mermaid statue she bought in Copenhagen once.'

'We'll certainly keep that in mind,' MacNee said. He asked a few more questions but nothing further emerged. He noticed that Biddy's shoulders were starting to stoop and the strong old face was showing signs of fatigue. Time they left her.

As they went back to the car, Hepburn said, 'Wow! Quite a lady!'

'Scary, frankly. Wouldn't like to get it wrong if she was in charge. But what's this Little Mermaid thing anyway?'

'It's a statue on the seafront in Copenhagen. Hans Christian Andersen, you know? He wrote a story about a mermaid that fell in love with a prince and went to a witch to get legs but she'd to give up her voice in exchange and then pain like knives stabbed through her with every step she took.'

'Doesn't sound like a bargain to me.'

'Especially since he then went off and married a suitable princess instead of the mermaid and something horrible happened to her – I can't exactly remember what. It was all rather sick, really. It was in a Ladybird book I had and I hid it at the back of the bookcase because it made me so sad.'

'Everybody – aww! Poor wee soul! All right, all right – you were only little. But now we have to work out what this particular mermaid could have been up to, late on the night of the storm, with a bruise on her face.'

CHAPTER TWELVE

The scene of crime officers were working in Eleanor Margrave's house and a line of uniforms was doing a fingertip search on the back garden and the foreshore when DI Fleming arrived.

Inspector Wallace was there already directing operations and he briefed her as she struggled into paper coveralls. 'There's expensive stuff in the house but nothing appears to have been taken, or even touched. There's absolutely no indication of forced entry. We found both doors were locked, but the front door locks when you shut it anyway. No sign of a weapon as yet and there certainly wasn't a violent struggle of any kind. She was probably half-dragged, half-carried across to the shore; there are a couple of short parallel grooves that could have been made by her heels but no footprints as yet and they're doubtful if they'll find any. The ground wasn't wet enough to hold an impression and of course the tide's come in to wash away any marks on the sand.'

'If the tide was full, as I've been guessing it was, she might have just been dropped in from the bank,' Fleming said. 'And I've seen the pathology report. The ligature was gone, and he doesn't think from an initial inspection that they'll find fibres. There was nothing at all to suggest she had resisted, nothing under the fingernails, so we're not likely to get help from DNA.'

Wallace raised his eyebrows. 'Someone she knew, then?'

'Certainly someone she knew well enough to open the front door to and then turn her back on, unless she wasn't in the habit of locking her back door. Perhaps your lads could check on that to see if anyone knew that she was in the habit of being casual about security – though I think most old ladies these days are so scared by *Crimewatch* that they lock everything and go back twice to see that they've done it.'

'Of course.'

Fleming went on past him, giving her name to the officer with a clipboard beside the front door as she went in.

Sea House was like Eleanor Margrave herself, she thought. A handsome house, with good bone structure: high-ceilinged rooms with the period features that made house hunters drool, and it had been treated with respect. The walls were all washed with classic Georgian colours – pearly grey in the stone-flagged hall, dark red in the small dining room and pale celadon green in the drawing room, which was hung with what looked like rather good watercolours in gold frames as well as a couple of family portraits. The antique furniture was elegant rather than comfortable and there was a collection of china in a Georgian corner cupboard; though Fleming wasn't expert enough to know what it was she was sure it was precious.

There were more modern pieces, too, on shelves and occasional tables that Fleming guessed were things Eleanor had chosen herself, rather than inherited. She had a good eye; there was some lovely chunky glass and a charming sculpture of a seal in polished granite, sleek and sinuous.

Heart-rendingly, there was also a small table covered with photographs, all of the same person – a pretty blonde girl who featured as a mop-headed toddler and a small child grinning to show the gap where her baby teeth had been, right through the teen years to a studio portrait of a beautiful young woman in an academic gown. A shrine to her dead daughter, Fleming thought with a pang.

But it was the wide bay window that drew you whenever you entered the room. Avoiding the SOCOs dusting for prints, Fleming went to look out.

It was a truly stunning view, all blue and gold on this bright spring day with the sun glinting on the Solway and the banks of whin across on the other side.

And Eleanor Margrave had liked it too. Beside the chair in the window there was a small stand with a sketch pad displaying an unfinished watercolour, not as expert as the framed ones on the walls but pleasing enough. There was a tray of paints and a brush beside it; she had been planning to come back and complete it.

Fleming felt the catch in the throat that she often felt when there was evidence like this of a life suddenly cut short. Eleanor might have been an old lady but there were still things she wanted to do. No doubt she'd been looking forward to her friend's visit as well.

She went through to the kitchen. Here there was more evidence of Eleanor's age than in the other rooms: she had probably retreated in here during the winter. There was a powerful reading lamp behind the chair drawn up close to the Aga, a magnifying glass beside it with a pile of books on the sort of table you could pull across your knees, a small TV just opposite.

And here, just beside the sink, a SOCO was kneeling on the floor taking samples. He looked up, offering to move aside but Fleming shook her head. 'I can see enough from here, thanks.'

Indeed she could. It was eloquent; the large Aga kettle was sitting in the sink, half-full, with its lid on the draining board. Eleanor had been making a drink for her visitor when she had been attacked. An unexpected visitor, then; having an Aga herself, Fleming knew that if someone was coming you had the kettle hot, sitting on the range to be brought forward to boil. But it had been someone she knew, or someone she felt must be given hospitality, at the very least.

'Was the water running when you all came in?' she asked the SOCO. He said it wasn't.

'It may have been the killer who turned it off,' she said. 'Can you see that the area is meticulously fingerprinted, please.'

Fleming went back out into the hall that ran down the centre of the house. There was another small room on the ground floor that seemed to be a sort of study and the SOCO there was sitting at a neat roll-top desk going through papers. On the other side of the room there was a long cupboard; above it were several framed sketches, signed neatly with 'EM' in the right-hand corner – the ones Eleanor had been pleased with, presumably. When Fleming opened the cupboard with her gloved hands she saw that this was where Eleanor had kept her artist's equipment, the brushes, the paints, the sketch pads, beside a wire tray holding other, presumably less-favoured paintings. She closed the door again.

Upstairs there was nothing to detain her. Eleanor's bedroom was immaculately tidy, almost impersonal; one of the spare rooms, presumably intended for her friend, had fresh towels laid out on a chair and a bunch of spring flowers in a bowl on the dressing table.

It looked as if what evidence there might be here would have to come from the forensic investigations in the kitchen and she could only hope that something useful would emerge.

There was nowhere to park when DS Macdonald and DC Campbell arrived at Ballinbreck House. A dozen cars were parked outside, half-on, half-off the verges so that the road was obstructed and the entrance to the drive was blocked by a delivery van from an off-licence.

'We should get Traffic to come along and sort this lot out,' Macdonald muttered, driving past to find a more appropriate stopping place. 'We'll be halfway to Balcary before we can stop at this rate.'

'Walk'll do us good,' Campbell said and earned himself an exasperated glance.

'Some of us get our exercise running,' Macdonald said pointedly, 'and it shows.' Campbell's love affair with Scotch pies was starting to take its toll. 'Oh, here we are. This'll do.'

When they reached the house, it was heaving like

an anthill. The weather, clearly, wasn't reliable enough at this time of year to have tables laid outside but there were people erecting a motley selection of small garden tents and gazebos on the lawn in front of the house and a couple of half-oil-drum barbecues were standing ready on the gravel.

Weaving their way through the helpers coming and going, Macdonald and Campbell went up to the front door. It was open and since there seemed little point in ringing the bell they went straight in. One of the helpers stopped and looked at them enquiringly.

'We're looking for Mrs Lindsay or her son,' Macdonald said.

'Kitchen – Philippa's there. No idea about Randall.' The helper bustled on.

They could hear a clear, commanding voice as they reached the passage that led to the kitchen. 'I'm afraid you can't have the fridge for white wine, Peter. We'll need it for the sausages and burgers. You'll have to get ice from somewhere and find a tin bath...'

Macdonald and Campbell had no hesitation in identifying the woman they were looking for. She was tall, as assured looking as her voice had sounded, and when they came into the busy kitchen she was facing in their direction. 'Yes?' she said sharply. 'What do you want?'

They produced warrant cards. 'Mrs Lindsay? DS Macdonald and DC Campbell,' Macdonald said. 'Just wanting a word, if you don't mind.'

Philippa's carefully shaped eyebrows shot up. 'A word? Just now? Oh, I don't believe it! This is absolutely surreal. I spoke to someone yesterday and I've nothing to add to what I told them then. My good man, we have more than a hundred people coming here tonight. I'm afraid I don't have the time to spare.'

It was a positive pleasure to say, 'Sorry, Mrs Stewart. I must insist.'

Her eyes narrowed. 'When did this become a police state? Am I to expect that if I refuse, you will arrest me on some trumped-up charge?'

'Obstruction, you mean?' Macdonald said, unmoved. 'Well, we could, madam, but I'm hoping we won't have to. Is there somewhere quieter?'

Philippa gasped, as if she were at a loss for words. Activity had stopped round about as the helpers exchanged glances and after a moment she collected herself. Ignoring them, she turned to one of the women.

'Fiona, I'm going to have to sort out whatever ridiculous thing it is that these men want – probably something to do with health and safety. Can you be an angel and take over here? I'll get rid of them as quickly as I can.'

She said, 'Come this way,' with a look that was, Macdonald thought, the kind you would direct at something brought in on the sole of your shoe. He grinned inwardly. Getting someone thoroughly irritated was an excellent way of putting them off balance.

Philippa led them upstairs to what seemed to be some sort of snug, a small room with not much in it beyond a couple of sofas, a coffee table and a large flat-screen TV. From the glimpses Macdonald had seen of the rather grand rooms on the ground floor, you'd need somewhere like this if you ever wanted to loosen your tie.

She waved them to one of the sofas and sat down herself on the other one. 'Now,' she said icily, 'perhaps you'll be kind enough to tell me what all this is about. I have to say I have found your attitude very surprising.'

'I do apologise, madam. I hope this won't take up too much of your time. Can you tell us where you were between the hours of twelve noon and four p.m. yesterday?'

'Yesterday? I doubt if I can, really. As you can imagine, I was dashing about. There has been a great deal to organise, a good number of people to see. I'm not sure that I could give you chapter and verse.'

'I'd be obliged if you could try.'

'Oh, really! Very well then. I spent some time here with two of my helpers, then I went into the village to pick up a couple of things in the shop. I couldn't tell you the exact time but perhaps the shopkeeper will remember. Then I spoke to one or two people in the street – I'm not sure how long that took. After that I know I came back to the house–'

'This would be at what time?'

'Good gracious, *I* don't know. I don't go about with a stopwatch. After that I drove to Kirkcudbright – I had to check on delivery times for the wine and glasses.'

'Didn't just phone them?' Campbell said. 'You being so busy.'

She looked at him as if surprised he could speak. 'No. I had one or two other things I wanted to do there as well.'

'Such as?'

'Oh – personal shopping, if it's any of your business. Look, what is all this about?'

'Let's work this out,' Macdonald said. 'You don't know when you left for Kirkcudbright. When did you get back?'

'Around four o'clock, I think. Shortly after that, perhaps.'

'Can anyone vouch for that?'

Philippa shrugged. 'Most people had gone home but I think Fiona McCarthy was still around. She might recall the time.'

'Thank you. That gives us a useful starting point. A uniformed officer will come round to take a formal statement and at that time you will be asked for names and contact details of the people who can confirm your account.'

She gave him a level look. 'You're treating me as if I were guilty of something. I demand to know what it is.'

'Do you know Mrs Eleanor Margrave?'

'Yes, of course. She comes into our warehouse shop sometimes – she has very good taste.'

'You're friends?'

'Not friends, no – just acquaintances, really. Has – has something happened to her?'

Macdonald couldn't make up his mind if that was an innocent question; she had asked it with just the degree of anxiety you might expect when someone had started putting two and two together, but it wouldn't be hard to fake that.

'I'm afraid her body was recovered from the Solway yesterday and we are treating her death as suspicious.'

Philippa's hand went to her mouth. 'Oh no! How dreadful! You mean – not an accident or suicide?'

Macdonald repeated that they were treating the death as suspicious. 'Is there anyone you can think of who might have had reason to want to harm Mrs Margrave?'

He was expecting the answer he got, that it was unimaginable that anyone would. He nodded. 'Thank you. We won't take up any more of your time, Mrs Lindsay. We also want to speak to your son.'

She was on her feet before he had finished the second sentence and when he did, she gave a short laugh. 'Good luck, that's all I can say! I've been looking for him all morning – had a dozen things I wanted him to do, but he's made himself scarce. When next I see him I'll tell him you're looking for him. And now if you'll excuse me...'

As they walked back to the car, Macdonald said, 'What did you make of that? Cool as an iceberg. I've no idea whether she was lying or not, but from her account of her movements she could have had the time, if she had a motive. Anyway, we'd better report back to Big Marge and see what she wants us to do about Randall.'

DS MacNee and DC Hepburn had just arrived at Sea House when DI Fleming finished her inspection and was struggling out of the overalls and stripping off her plastic gloves to drop in a bin by the side of the path. She walked down to the gate to meet them.

'How did you get on with Mrs James? Was she

able to give you a coherent account?'

For some reason that was funny. 'You could say,' MacNee said dryly. Hepburn nodded. 'She's what you'd call formidable. Ran some government department.'

Fleming was interested. 'A battleaxe?'

They looked at each other. 'Not quite – firm but fair, probably. In a scary sort of way,' Hepburn said. 'She'll make a great witness.'

'So – anything useful?'

'Not directly,' MacNee said. 'She arrived, she saw the body in the water, she hailed a passing car and the driver called in to us. There was a wee bit of background – Julia was a spoilt child, Eleanor felt ashamed of what happened. But Mrs James came up with something that could be of interest.' He relayed what she had said about Eleanor's mermaid.

Fleming too was intrigued. 'That's fascinating. Raises all sorts of interesting questions. I wonder if she made any record of it? There was a SOCO going through her papers so we should get those before too long.

'Now, did you see Macdonald and Campbell? No? They may be a while, with both the Lindsays to interview. Tam, I want to have another go at Skye Falconer so you can come with me. Louise, I'd like you to go back to Kirkluce. Inspector Wallace has sent through some interviews with neighbours and I'd like you to check those out, and anything else that comes in. But go off at the end of your shift. You'll be working tonight at the party and you ought to have a break.'

'Wish me luck!' Hepburn rolled her eyes, but

took the car keys from MacNee.

'I do wonder about the mermaid,' Fleming said as she and MacNee set off along the road to Ballinbreck. 'This could be highly significant.'

'Aye – the night of the storm, and the shock and bruising. The sort of thing you might expect if she'd been in some sort of accident, maybe – like a car going off the road with a murdered man inside it.'

'It's just a pity the Dumfries lads didn't manage to pinpoint where the car went in the river. It was a long shot, of course, all that time afterwards. That's the house there, isn't it?' She drew in to park.

It wasn't Skye Falconer who opened the door. 'Jen Wilson?' Fleming asked.

The woman's face was sombre and she waved them in at once. 'I thought probably someone would be round because of the Julia connection. What a terrible thing – poor Mrs Margrave.'

'You've heard, then?'

'I went to get some rolls for breakfast and it's all over the town. Is it true?'

Fleming repeated the usual mantra and Jen called through to the back of the house, 'Skye, it's the police,' as she showed them into the sitting room at the front.

'Perhaps we could talk to you first.' When Skye appeared in the doorway, Fleming said firmly, 'We'll speak to you later on your own, Miss Falconer.'

Skye was looking tired, with dark shadows under her eyes and she directed a look at her friend – helpless, appealing? – as if she hoped Jen would argue, but then withdrew.

'I think this is probably quite straightforward,' Fleming said as they sat down. 'Can you tell us where you were yesterday between noon and four pm?'

'At school, of course. It was probably after four when I left, so I suppose it was around quarter past, twenty past maybe, by the time I got home.'

'I see. Do you have a car, Miss Wilson?'

'Yes, but I always walk to school.'

'The keys are kept – where?'

'On a hook in the hall, by the door. Wait a minute – you don't think Skye had anything to do with this? She wouldn't–'

'We don't think anything at this stage, madam. We just ask questions. Was Miss Falconer here when you got back?'

'Yes, she was. And she'd just made scones too,' Jen said. 'So I should think she'd have to have been here for some time, wouldn't you?'

Fleming made a non-committal noise. 'Can you think of any reason why anyone would wish to harm Mrs Margrave?'

'Of course not! I'm sure she never did anything to hurt anyone. And it was so sad for her, with Julia too. You just can't believe that something like this could happen.'

Jen Wilson's eyes filled with tears. Now Fleming looked at her closely, she looked pale, as if she too had not slept well.

'I think that's all. Thank you for your cooperation. Could you please tell Miss Falconer we'd like to see her now?'

Skye's elfin face was set in mulish lines when

she came in. She sat down opposite the officers and folded her arms in a classic defensive gesture.

'I didn't borrow Jen's car yesterday afternoon, if that's what you're saying. I was here all day.'

Fleming felt faintly annoyed that Jen had warned her of the question. 'Can anyone vouch for that?'

'No. There's no one else here, when Jen's at school.'

'So you didn't leave the house at all, or have any visitors?'

'No.'

'Did you know Mrs Margrave?'

'Not really. I don't think any of us did. I've never spoken to her. I only saw her the night it happened – I don't think she came to the inquest.' She was studying her fingernails.

'Sure about that?' MacNee said sharply.

She glared at him. 'Quite sure.'

'I just want to go back over what you said the last time we spoke,' Fleming said. 'You said you had been abroad. When did you come back to this country?'

Skye was obviously flustered. 'I – I don't know what I said. I told you it was very vague – I was just drifting about. I didn't come up to Scotland until ten days ago. Jen can tell you.'

'Miss Wilson can confirm when you arrived here. I'm asking where you were before that?'

'Like I said, I don't know exactly. I spent a few days in England after I got back, just coming north.'

'Anyone who can say where you were?'

'No they can't!' she said wildly. 'I was just picking up a lift or two, coming up here – all right? Slept rough a couple of times. I was a bit broke.'

'So when do you estimate you crossed the Channel?'

Skye pursed her lips. 'I told you, dates don't mean much when you're travelling.' Then she said, with an air of triumph, 'I can tell you I was still in France on my birthday – April 22nd. A nice guy bought some cheap fizz.'

'Don't remember his name, I suppose?' Mac-Nee's cynicism was obvious.

'Dave,' she said coldly.

Fleming had no doubt at all that she was lying now – and Skye was getting better at it, too, with fewer of the body language giveaways. Practice makes perfect.

She said, 'I'm going to repeat two questions, Miss Falconer, and I cannot stress too much how important it is that your answers to them are accurate and truthful. I'm going to ask DS Mac-Nee to make a note of them. Do you understand?'

There was no flicker of response.

Fleming waited for a second then went on, 'Where were you yesterday afternoon?'

'Here. All day.'

'When did you arrive here in Ballinbreck?'

'About ten days ago. You can ask me as many times as you like. The answer will still be the same.'

'Thank you.' Fleming got up. 'For the moment, that's all.'

Skye walked to the door and called through the hall. 'Jen! Could you come for a minute?' then when the kitchen door opened said, 'Can you just confirm to them that I arrived here ten days ago?'

She'd outwitted them. Her back was turned; they couldn't see Jen's face, couldn't judge the look that passed between them and they couldn't stop her asking the leading question.

There was a tiny pause, but only a tiny one. 'Yes, of course,' Jen said.

When Skye turned back to face them, the sea-green eyes were wide and limpid. 'All right?'

Back in the car, MacNee said, 'She's a piece of work, isn't she?'

'Certainly is,' Fleming said grimly. 'She's getting better, too. I don't believe a word she says and we have to ask why the lies are necessary. We'd better check everything that's checkable: ferry passenger lists, passport control – though given how porous our borders seem to be, not finding her name wouldn't prove much.'

'And the only wee vague kind of alibi she has is that she'd just made scones, says Wilson. How long does it take to make a scone?'

'You're asking *me?*'

'Sorry, daft question. The Stewarts now?'

'Yes. And let's hope if they're in the mood to tell lies that they're not as good at it as she is.'

Skye went through to the kitchen and switched on the kettle. 'I need coffee after being given the third degree like that. Make one for you?'

Jen followed her slowly. 'Skye, why did you ask me to say you just came back here ten days ago?'

'Because they came on like the Gestapo and as an innocent person, I don't have to account for my every movement to the police. All right?' She sounded very fierce.

'All right,' Jen said. But as she fetched the coffee mugs dark and ugly thoughts were beginning to stir.

CHAPTER THIRTEEN

Fleming and MacNee had gone by the time Macdonald and Campbell arrived at Sea House. They hadn't told the duty constable where they were going and Macdonald was frowning as they went back to the car.

'I guess I'd better phone the boss and see what we've to do next. If she's doing the other interviews herself she'll maybe send us back to the station. There'll be stuff coming in by now.'

Campbell grunted. 'Haven't finished here.'

'Look, I don't like paperwork any more than you do but if Randall Lindsay's bunked off we can't interview him, can we?'

'Find him.'

'Yeah, find him – how?'

'Where would you go?'

'To get out the house when my mum was expecting visitors? Find a cafe that sold bacon butties if the pubs weren't open, I suppose. Well, maybe it's worth a try.'

He drove back to park in the village. They drew a blank at the first coffee shop where the clientele consisted of a retired couple and a table with pushchairs forming a sort of palisade for a posse of young mums. The only other one, rather scruffier, had the smell of frying that had Campbell's nostrils flaring like a hound scenting truffles and as well as a group of elderly men with red tops folded to the racing page there was a tall young man wearing red cords and looking distinctly out of place.

He looked up warily as they came in then, as they approached his table, sat back in his chair, pulling a face. 'Oh, not again!'

Macdonald could never quite work out why it was that people he had never seen before so often seemed to recognise him as police even before he spoke. He was wearing a perfectly ordinary shirt with a zip-up jacket and jeans; perhaps it was going round in a pair that gave it away, like the Mormons.

'Mr Lindsay?' he said. 'Could we have a word?'

Conversation at the other table had stopped. The two old men with their back to the room swivelled round, ready to enjoy the sideshow.

'Outside, I think?' Macdonald suggested. Lindsay nodded curtly, put down some money on the table with a gesture to the waitress and followed them out.

Macdonald introduced himself and Campbell and showed his warrant card. 'Perhaps we could talk in the car? It might be more private.'

Lindsay sneered. 'Oh, great idea! And have it all round the place that I've been arrested for whatever crime it is you have in mind to fit me up for?'

The rash that Hepburn had said Lindsay brought her out in must be contagious; it was afflicting Macdonald as well. 'Where do you

211

suggest, sir?'

'Oh, for God's sake! *I* don't know. If we go back to the house we'll be trampled underfoot by the old She-Elephant and her host of minions. You want to talk to me – you find somewhere.'

It was hard not to crack a smile at his spot-on description of his mother, but keeping a straight face was a professional skill. 'Could I suggest we use the car, but drive to some quieter spot outside the village? It's unmarked; there's no reason why it should attract attention.'

'Oh – if you insist. I'll walk until I'm leaving the village and you can pick me up.'

He set off as Macdonald walked back to fetch the car with Campbell. 'Poor Louise!' he said. 'I thought she was exaggerating, but if anything she was playing it down.'

It only took a few minutes after they had picked up Lindsay before they found a field gate where they could draw in and park.

'Get on with it, then,' Lindsay said. 'Spending time with police officers isn't one of my favourite pastimes.'

'And why is that?' Macdonald, turning round in his seat, asked blandly.

'Can't think. Oh, yes I can. I got a particular distaste for it when I realised I was being used as a stooge by one of your little friends.'

'Don't know what you mean, sir.'

'Oh, yes you do. She's blocking my calls so if you see Louise you can tell her not to bother coming to the party tonight. I don't know what she thinks she's going to spy on but she won't get a very cordial reception. Distinctly *un*cordial, in fact.'

The raw hostility in his voice was alarming. Even as Macdonald ignored this and went on to his first question, he decided to phone Louise himself and tell her to forget it.

'Where were you between the hours of noon and four p.m. yesterday?'

Lindsay bristled visibly. 'And why should I have anything to do with that?'

'"That"?' Macdonald raised his eyebrows. 'You know about Mrs Margrave's death, do you?'

'Well, duh! It's all over the town, but I don't see why you should pick on me. I hardly know the old bat – haven't set eyes on her for years. Anyway, I've been in Paris most of the time. Why should I have come back in a homicidal frenzy and killed first Connell Kane and then Julia's mother?'

'I don't know, sir,' Macdonald said. 'Perhaps you could tell us.'

Lindsay groaned and struck his forehead theatrically. 'Never joke with the plods. That wasn't a confession, Sergeant. That was me being funny.'

'I hadn't realised.' Macdonald earned himself a suspicious glance. 'So – your movements?'

Lindsay groaned again. 'I was just – around. After lunch I went to do an errand for my mother in Castle Douglas – there's a butcher there who was giving her a good deal on sausages for the barbecue. Then I just – didn't go back. Not until about five when I reckoned the worst would be over.'

'And where did you go when you "weren't going back"?'

'Drove around. Went along to Kippford, had a

213

walk along the shore, that sort of thing.'

'I have to press you for details of times, and anyone who might be able to vouch for your whereabouts.'

'*Whereabouts?* God, who says "whereabouts" nowadays?' Macdonald could see a flush of annoyance appearing. 'I told you – it's vague. That's because I haven't done anything. If I had, I'm sure I'd be able to give you a minute-by-minute alibi vouched for by witnesses.'

'Not as easy as you make it sound, I'm afraid. So there's no one at all who can back up your account of where you were after you collected the supplies from the butcher?'

'No, there isn't. So?'

'But you estimate that you came back shortly before five o'clock. Did you notice anything as you passed Sea House?'

Lindsay stared at him. His face was getting redder, his blue eyes starting to bulge a little; he clearly had quite a temper. 'Trick question, is it? I should have seen a police car or tapes or something, should I? Well, tough. I didn't come back that way. I came back through Kirkcudbright. All right?'

'Adding a good ten, twelve miles to your journey? Rather an odd way round to go, wouldn't you agree?'

'I was wasting time, for God's sake! Oh, go on, arrest me, why don't you?'

'We're not in the habit of arresting people unless we have some reason for it,' Macdonald said, adding provocatively, 'I'm not sure why you should be so upset about such a simple, routine request.'

He thought for a moment that Lindsay might lose it and land a punch – taking him in would be a real pleasure – but with an obvious effort of will Lindsay controlled himself.

'Don't you?' he said unpleasantly. 'I should have thought, with all the training courses funded by the long-suffering taxpayer these days to keep you from actually doing any police work, you'd have had one on empathy by now.'

'Not so far, sir. Now, we'll be sending someone round to take a formal statement from you. I take it you won't be going anywhere for the next few days?'

'No. Is that all? Can I go now?'

Macdonald was just about to agree when Campbell said, 'Julia Margrave – good pals, were you?'

Lindsay, who had been leaning forward in his seat ready to get out, slumped back. 'What on earth has that got to do with this?'

'We're not saying it has,' Macdonald said. 'It's just a question.'

'Oh, just a question. Well, this is just an answer. We knew each other slightly when we were young and then we worked together – she was my boss. She helped me get the job, in fact, and I was very grateful to her. Yes, we were friends and yes, I was very upset when she died.'

'Going back to Paris soon, then?' That was Campbell again.

Randall's face turned a dark, mottled red. He said, with reluctance, 'No, actually, since you ask. I've decided it doesn't suit me – I'm looking for a new job.'

'Turf you out, did they?'

'No, they didn't. I resigned.' He opened the door of the car. 'That's it. I haven't anything more to say to you, except' – he leant forward to push his face closer to Macdonald's – 'you can tell that little bitch to stay at home. We won't be welcoming gatecrashers and she'll regret it if she tries.' He got out and slammed the door.

Macdonald whistled softly. 'Seriously nasty. I'm going to tell Louise she can't go.'

Campbell gave him an ironic glance. 'Good luck with that,' he said.

The Stewarts were all so elaborately cooperative, so willing to help in any way they could, that both Fleming and MacNee came away from the interview deeply suspicious.

They had interviewed them together; when they suggested seeing them individually, Kendra had said earnestly, 'Well, of course, Inspector, if that's what you want, but you know it's all really just a sort of jigsaw. We were to and fro during the afternoon and it will be easier to sort out the time frame if we're together. I'm sure you'd find it helpful.' She had directed a winsome look at Fleming that left her feeling faintly queasy.

It was true, though, that the pattern that emerged was one of a group getting ready for a busy weekend, in the kitchen, in the pub and in the restaurant upstairs, which was being prepared for the next evening's fine dining.

Logie was in the kitchen all afternoon, along with an assistant. Kendra and Will were working separately but were never, they claimed, out of sight of each other for more than about quarter of an hour, twenty minutes maximum.

'In any case,' she went on, 'Will said that this has nothing to do with Connell's murder and you're only linking the two because they happened around the same time and you haven't any other ideas. Didn't you, Will?'

Will looked embarrassed. 'I wouldn't have chosen to put it like that, but yes, I think you're barking up the wrong tree. It's much more likely that Mrs Margrave disturbed a burglar and it all went wrong. I was trained to look for a pattern in repeated crime and there's certainly none here.'

'And anyway, we're all each other's alibi,' Kendra said, 'especially me and Will.' She had given him a sidelong glance which, as Fleming said when they got back to the car afterwards, should have rung deafening alarm bells for her husband.

MacNee shook his head in disapproval. *'In temptation's path ye gang astray,'* he quoted portentously. 'What's that alibi worth?'

Fleming considered it. 'If one of them asked the other to lie I doubt if they'd get a refusal. On the other hand, it was risky – I can't see the husband being part of it and they both went into the kitchen occasionally.'

'Time unspecified,' MacNee pointed out. 'Still, Logie's alibi is solid. We can eliminate him, at least.'

'He wasn't really part of the Cyrenaics either – too busy working to be anything but a hanger-on.'

'What did you think to Will's claim that it was a burglar?'

'Well, he's wrong, of course – you don't invite a burglar in and start making them tea, but he

217

didn't know that and I suppose he may believe it. We certainly don't have the luxury of a neat pattern but I don't believe it's unrelated. Anyway, back to the station. I'll have to see the super and find something she can tell the press conference.'

'Several active lines of enquiry?'

'Several active lines of enquiry – absolutely. Someone should write a guide to standard phrases: Police Officers: For the Use of.'

'Numbered, so you could just tell the press "Number Twenty-Four and Number Thirty-Two" and you wouldn't have to say anything at all. Here, I like the idea. Might even write it myself.'

Louise Hepburn was washing her hair. If a girl was going to a party, even if not for the usual reasons, she had to look good and Louise's hair – the bane of her life – needed proper styling if she wasn't to look as if she'd been hauled through a hedge backwards and then had mussed it up a bit.

When the phone rang, she let it go to voicemail. Randall again, no doubt. He'd rung her four or five times before he gave up and left a message withdrawing his invitation. She'd been expecting that – he wasn't stupid and once he heard about Eleanor Margrave's murder he'd realise why she'd accepted – so she'd ignored that too.

The last message he'd left had been nastier. He'd said, coldly, calmly and unpleasantly, that he knew why she wanted to come and that he'd make it his business to see to it that she'd regret it if she did.

She would have preferred rage and expletives.

His tone made her uneasy; perhaps to go anyway was foolish, just asking for trouble. On the other hand, she wasn't going to let a little sod like Randall Lindsay tell her what she wasn't going to do. Maybe there were bouncers on the door to throw her out, but it wouldn't actually be a new experience. They were unlikely to be as rough as the ones in Glasgow had been after that particularly raucous night at uni.

She wasn't going to answer the phone and let him abuse her directly, though. She sprayed on half a ton of frizz-taming mousse and went on styling her hair.

But when she did pick up the phone and check it wasn't Randall, Andy Macdonald was asking her to call him back urgently. It must be business; she and Andy didn't have any social contact.

His first remark put her back right up. 'Oh, Louise, good! Look, you can't go to this party tonight.'

'I can't?' she said sweetly.

'We've just been interviewing Randall Lindsay. Has he spoken to you?'

'No.' That was true, sort of.

'He's making threats and he sounded as if he meant them. I would assess him as volatile – he's lost his job and he's not taking it well. It would simply be too risky to take him on.'

'Do you think so?'

'Oh, definitely. I'm not sure what you'd gain from it, anyway – at a party no one's going to go confessing to murder, are they?'

'Who knows? Anything could happen, if it's a good party.'

Andy's voice sharpened. 'Louise, you're not

219

taking this seriously, are you?'

'Thought you'd never notice. He's asked me and I've accepted. I'm going.'

'No, you're not. As your superior officer, I'm forbidding it.'

She had to take a deep breath and count to ten. 'It may come as a shock, Sergeant, but even if I'm only a humble constable your awesome power doesn't extend to my social life. Though of course, it's awfully sweet of you to be concerned.'

'Louise—'

'Of course, you can go and clype to Mummy. "Boss, Louise won't do what I tell her! It's not fair!" But she can't do anything if I don't answer the phone – and I won't. I'm switching it off right now. And don't come round – I'm not answering the door. Sorry – must dash. I'm just going to have a lovely relaxing bath before I get my slap on.'

Grinning, she could hear his bleating protests as she rang off. The smile only faded as she went through to the bathroom. Andy had sounded really concerned. Was she just letting her contrary nature override her common sense? She was, of course she was.

But she couldn't climb down now. And anyway, she'd known Randall since uni and at bottom he was just a pussycat. Wasn't he?

DC Lizzie Weston finished taking the statement from a householder whose garden ornaments had been stolen, assured him, untruthfully, that they would indeed be investigating the case and then before someone else could nobble her, slipped outside again.

It was a different person who took her call to the Kirkluce headquarters, but the message was exactly the same. She could talk to someone who would take it forward to DI Fleming if necessary.

That wasn't the point. Well, it was partly the point, of course: she had important information relating to a murder enquiry and it was her duty to pass it on to the appropriate authority.

But she wanted DI Fleming to know that it was her, Lizzie Weston, who'd taken the risk of incurring the vengeance of her inspector by doing her duty. She wanted to be able to ask her directly about a transfer and even if she hadn't quite decided how she'd do it, she wasn't going to give up yet.

Her husband was a farmer, wasn't he? Surely she could find out the name of the farm and get the phone number.

DI Fleming was in an irritable mood by the time Macdonald, Campbell and MacNee arrived in her office. DSI Rowley was on her back already, demanding miracles, and she'd been forced to endure a gleeful phone call from DI Taylor in Dumfries, washing his hands of the Connell Kane case so energetically that she could almost hear the water splashing.

To add to her annoyance, the SOCOs were dragging their feet. She'd hoped to find the papers that had been removed from Sea House on her desk by now, but they hadn't appeared.

'For the moment there's little to go on,' she told her team. 'No useful fingerprints or footprints and the fingertip search didn't produce anything either.'

She gave Macdonald and Campbell a brief report on the woman who had arrived on Eleanor Margrave's doorstep on the night of the storm and the outcome of the interviews with Skye Falconer, Jen Wilson and the Stewarts. Macdonald reported on Philippa and Randall Lindsay, including his threats.

Fleming listened, frowning. 'I don't like the sound of that. I'll tell Louise not to go.'

Macdonald looked uncomfortable. 'I tried that. She's made up her mind – said it's her social life, not official, and it's none of my business.'

She knew it was unfair to feel annoyed with Andy when he'd only done what any responsible sergeant would have, but with the situation he and Louise had set up between them, he should have been able to predict her reaction if he tried telling her what to do.

She sighed. 'Oh, for goodness' sake! I'd better have a word with her myself.'

Macdonald cleared his throat. 'Er ... she said she was going to be incommunicado.'

'Did she?' Fleming said grimly. 'Tam, what do you reckon?'

MacNee considered. 'It's not exactly the Glasgow East End on a Saturday night when Celtic's lost, is it? It's a nice wee village with party guests who aren't going to stand by and watch someone being duffed up. Anyway, what do you reckon to your chances of stopping her if she's got the bit between her teeth?'

'You've got a point there. Right – there's not a

lot more we can do tonight, then. I've got someone on to the Border Agency to find out when Skye Falconer came back from France, and it occurred to me that with Jen Wilson's car being parked outside the house, one of the neighbours might have noticed if it wasn't there, so the uniforms are asking about that. Anything else?'

'Lindsay,' Macdonald said. 'He admitted that he's lost his job, by the way, or "resigned" as he put it and I wondered about embezzlement – he's just the sort. He told us when he travelled back from France so we ought to check that too.'

'And when Will Stewart came in from Canada,' MacNee put in.

Fleming nodded. 'I'll put that in hand now. I'm going to take the briefing in half an hour but I don't see why you shouldn't knock off now. I'll want you in promptly in the morning.'

The atmosphere in Jen Wilson's house had felt strained since the police visit in the morning. They were both being too chatty in a forced sort of way, Jen thought, as if they were afraid of what might slip into any silence. They said things like, 'So lucky the weather's holding up for the party,' and 'How many people do you think they're expecting?'

She had taken most of the afternoon to do a much-needed tidy-up of her little courtyard garden and Skye had spent it baking, though to Jen's certain knowledge the tins were all full already.

The trouble about gardening, and baking too she suspected, though she'd never tried it herself, was that it left your mind free to wander and there were a lot of places that were mental mine-fields just at the moment.

What was happening wasn't her fault, Jen told herself. She hadn't been party to the worst of what had gone on; faced with competing impera-tives, she had done her best. It was beyond any control and she was frightened now, as well as being tortured by grief and regrets. It was as if a huge boulder was starting to roll down a hillside, and she couldn't do anything to stop it.

As she came in, grubby and tired, and went to run a bath, she thought longingly of just chang-ing into her pyjamas and snuggling down on the sofa to watch some mindless TV. There was no one to stop her doing just that.

She daren't, though. After what had happened, and given some of the people who would be gathering tonight, the party risked producing the effect of a lit match thrown into a tank of petrol. She might find herself caught up in the confla-gration but it would be worse not to know what was happening.

Cat Fleming and Nick Canton were sitting at the kitchen table still surrounded by the debris from tea – dirty mugs, a plate with three biscuits left on it and a fruit cake, diminished considerably from its original size – though it was almost six o'clock when Marjory Fleming came in.

She laughed and took the last flapjack. 'Gran's obviously been here. Lucky you, Nick – it would have been jammie dodgers from a packet if she hadn't refilled her famous tin and done a mercy run.' Despite her advanced age, Marjory's mother

Janet Laird still kept up the supply of home bakes for her daughter's deprived family.

'Oh yes,' Nick said smoothly. 'Cat said you were a hopeless cook.'

It was quite unreasonable that Marjory's hackles should rise. Her lack of culinary skills was a standing joke in the family, one she played up herself too. Coming from a stranger, it was different, though. The way he said it was plain rude and she found herself remembering wistfully Cammie's one-time girlfriend Zoë who had struggled so valiantly to find something good to say about Marjory's veggie lasagne.

'After that remark, I shall make a point of ruining your steak, Nick,' she said, trying not to sound as if she meant it. 'That's what we're having tonight and I'm on.'

Cat said sharply, 'I can do it. I thought you wouldn't be back till late anyway, Mum, with all the important stuff you have to do.' Clearly Marjory hadn't been forgiven for her sharp remark last night.

'It's the eye of the storm, really. There's not much we can do until evidence starts coming in and we have lines to follow.'

'Don't you have a "hunch"?' Nick said, doing quotes with his fingers. 'I thought detectives always had "hunches" that miraculously turned out to be right.'

'No, not actually. I'm afraid we have to be boring and work on the evidence.' For the sake of her relationship with her daughter, she mustn't lose her temper. 'Cat, perhaps you could clear the table, instead. You could put away the bakes

225

before I'm tempted to have another one. Where are Dad and Cammie?'

'Oh, up the hill,' Cat said. 'There's a sheep with the botts or rabies or something. Or maybe just a heavy cold.'

'Or hiccups,' Nick said. 'Your dad needs your brother along to say "Boo!"'

They both found that uproariously funny; Marjory smiled dutifully at the feeble joke. Perhaps she was losing her sense of humour.

'And you two townies didn't feel you needed some fresh air? Shame on you,' she said lightly. 'Got any plans for this evening?'

'We thought we'd go into Kirkluce and look for a pub,' Nick said. 'That's if we survive supper, of course.'

Oh, very funny. Marjory managed to join in the laughter. 'Just for you, I'll hold the arsenic,' she said, then seeing Cat's suspicious frown, went on hastily, 'There are a couple of nice pubs – I think the Black Bull has live music on a Saturday night.'

'Some of the old gang are around. I'm going to text round and see if we can get together. I want them to meet Nick.' Cat smiled up at him proudly.

Feeling guilty, Fleming made a mental 'must try harder' note. She went to fetch the steaks from the fridge. 'Want a beer while I'm here?' she said over her shoulder.

'Thanks,' Cat said. 'We'll take it through to the sitting room. Come on, Nick.' Just as she opened the door, she turned.

'Oh, I forgot. Someone phoned wanting to speak to you. A woman – she wouldn't leave a message.'

'Oh?' Marjory said, without much interest. 'A journalist, probably. No doubt she'll phone back. Say I'm still out if she does.'

'Well, ready to go?' Jen Wilson said as Skye Falconer came downstairs. Her friend really was looking very pretty tonight, with her hair loose and curling round her shoulders, tendrils framing her delicate features. Her sea-green eyes were sparkling and the patches of nervous colour on the cheekbones warmed her pale skin. As she reached the bottom step Jen could see that she was trembling a little.

She looked so fragile; despite her own concern, Jen reached out a hand to touch her arm comfortingly. 'It'll be all right,' she said.

Skye looked at her for a long moment. 'Do you think so?' she said, her voice flat, and she walked past Jen to the front door.

CHAPTER FOURTEEN

Timing was key to this whole thing. As she sat in her car, parked a little way along the lane that led to Ballinbreck House, Louise Hepburn looked at her watch for the tenth time. She didn't want to miss anything, but if she arrived too early Randall Lindsay would have no difficulty in spotting her and chucking her out.

The trouble was that she had no idea what their checking system would be. Informal, no doubt, but gatecrashers would obviously be a problem so the most likely thing was a list at the door with names ticked off against arrivals.

There had been only a trickle of guests coming along the road to start with but it was becoming a flood. In a few minutes Louise would have to make her move.

It was dusk now as she walked along the inside verge beside the other parked cars. Just ahead of her, she could see the entrance to the drive and yes, there was a table where a woman with a list was sitting, a couple of sturdy-looking men standing beside her. It was all very relaxed, though: if they were bouncers they were more interested in chatting to friends as they appeared than keeping an eagle eye on all comers.

Dare she risk Randall having forgotten to take her off the list? No, she decided, she couldn't. He had been too angry to forget to do that. Gatecrashing was the only possibility; she'd had quite a talent for it during a misspent youth and she considered tactics now.

Over the wall that bordered the rough ground beside the house? Awkward, when she didn't know what lay on the other side of it, and very conspicuous if there was no cover. Saying 'Press' and vaguely waving a card had worked in the past at small events – people were usually so ludicrously flattered to think they might be in the papers that they waved you through – but the consequences if she was caught doing that would probably include dismissal from the Force. Blagging was out.

Getting in with a noisy group that would confuse the checkers was the most promising, she thought, as a gang of young adults came along the road, laughing and pushing each other. They'd obviously got up to flying speed before the party and it was easy for Louise Hepburn to move out from behind the cars unnoticed and tag on the end.

It was getting dark now, anyway, and in the confusion of so many people arriving together there was no problem about ducking into the shrubbery by the gate. She worked her way along, looking for a quiet area before she emerged onto the lawn.

Light was pouring from every window in the house and huddles had gathered under the little gazebos and the outdoor heaters. An orderly queue had formed round the barbecues and the delicious smell of chargrilled meat filled the air.

Louise felt her stomach groan, but having been disinvited to the party she didn't really feel she could eat food she hadn't paid for. She was grateful, though, when a jovial man said, 'Hey! You haven't anything to drink – that won't do!' as she passed and pressed a bottle of lager into her hand. It made her less conspicuous.

The Homecoming party was warming up. It was going well: there were a lot of reunions under way with exclamations of surprise and hugs of greeting. Whatever anyone said about Philippa Lindsay, she'd made a lot of people happy tonight.

As Louise moved about in the gathering shadows, she had two objectives: one, to avoid being spotted by Randall and unceremoniously ejected; two, to get up close to the Lindsays and the Stewarts, the only Cyrenaics she knew by sight, who with any luck would attract the others to them at some stage.

Louise spotted Kendra immediately. She was standing on the gravel in the pool of light just in front of the sitting-room window, holding on to a man's arm and laughing up at him – Will Stewart, perhaps? He was certainly buff, with an attractively warm smile; Louise wouldn't have minded doing a bit of hanging on his arm herself. Logie was there too, talking to another couple but Louise could see his eyes flicking constantly to his wife. She made her way towards them, apparently casually.

And there was Randall, a cigarette in his mouth, coming out of the front door and heading straight towards them – and her. He was casting a swift look around the garden as he approached, eyes narrowed against the smoke – checking to see if she'd defied him and got past the gate, no doubt. Louise's heart skipped a beat and she melted quietly round the side of the house.

She could hear their greetings quite clearly – yes, the man was Will – and could hear, too, the couple who had been talking to Logie being hailed by another couple then excusing themselves and moving away, across her line of sight. She had found, she realised, an ideal position; there was a large bush just behind her where she could take refuge if anyone came too close.

Randall and the Stewarts were talking more quietly now. Straining her ears, she could hear comments about the police enquiries, but there was nothing, as far as she could tell, that was anything out of the ordinary in what they said.

Suddenly she heard Randall say, 'Well, well,

well! Look at this!'

Risking a peep round the corner, she could see him striding across the gravel towards two women. The taller one he ignored; he bent to embrace the smaller, slighter one, sweeping her right off her feet.

'Skye! I don't believe it! I didn't know you were back, sweetie. Why didn't you tell me?' He set her down and escorted her back to the Stewarts, his arm possessively round her waist. 'Look what I've found!'

'Hello, Randall. Nice to see you too.' That came from the taller woman, sounding acerbic as she followed them across the gravel.

Randall half-turned and said over his shoulder, 'Oh, sorry, Jen. Just so surprised to see Skye, you know.'

With every eye riveted on the new arrival, Louise was emboldened to work her way a little closer. Will was facing her way and she saw a quizzical look on his face. She could see, too, Skye's expression as she approached. Her eyes seemed luminous with some intense emotion – anxiety, fear, even. She stared at him as if he were the only person there.

At his side, Kendra visibly tightened her grip. Her voice was shrill as she said, 'I thought you'd abandoned us for good, Skye. What's brought you back?'

She got no answer; Skye didn't even turn her head.

'Darling, you haven't anything to drink.' Randall squeezed Skye closer to him, as if to break the spell. 'Red, white, beer?'

She ignored him, moving now towards Will. She held her arms up like a child and he shook Kendra off and went to meet Skye. As he embraced her she gave a little sob.

'Hey, hey!' Will laughed down at her, holding her to his side. 'What's all this? It's a party – no tears allowed! Randall, where's the wine you were talking about for the ladies?'

It broke the tension. Reluctantly, Louise moved back into the darkness, but not before she had seen the look of fury on Randall's face as he went to fetch the wine, the ugly pursing of Kendra's lips – and the small, satisfied smile Logie gave as he turned to talk to Jen.

'I've been watching you,' an unwelcome voice said in her ear as a hand touched her shoulder. 'You don't seem to know anyone. Are you shy?'

The man who spoke was middle-aged, kindly-looking. Taking her cue from him, Louise looked down modestly. 'I hate parties, really,' she murmured. 'I just thought there would be people I know, but–'

'Come on, love, there are now,' he said. 'I'm Mike. What's your name?'

'Samantha.' She heard herself say it with astonishment. Where had that come from?

'OK, Sam – come and meet the lads. Need another beer?' Helpless in the face of such relentless kindness, Louise gave in.

She hadn't expected it to be quite so hard to bear. There they all were, the Cyrenaics – with two missing. Julia – well, Julia had to some extent opened herself to destruction, but Connell, Connell! The thought of him stabbed her with a spasm of pain as if someone had turned a blade to deepen the wound in her heart.

Randall handed her a glass of wine without looking at her so that she had to make a grab at it and even so, slopped it on her shirt. He was making a fool of himself over Skye; she had eyes for no one except Will and they had drawn a little away from the others to have a quiet conversation, but Randall had butted in crudely, with the excuse of bringing her wine. He set down a bottle of red and a bottle of white at his feet so that there could be no excuse for sending him away again.

Mechanically making conversation with Logie, who was in a happy mood now Kendra had been frozen out and had come to join him, Jen saw Will give a little shrug as Randall monopolised the conversation, then hail someone across on the lawn and move off, with Skye's eyes following him.

Kendra gave a spiteful little titter. 'My goodness, I don't think I've ever seen anyone make such a dead set at a man! Will's obviously embarrassed.'

'Oh, Will's used to it,' Logie said jovially. 'Has to beat them off with a stick. Though I think myself he's got a bit of a soft spot for little Skye there. Wonder where she's been hiding all this time? Do you know, Jen?'

'She's staying with me at the moment, but she hasn't wanted to talk about it,' Jen said with perfect truth. 'Randall certainly has a soft spot for her too, doesn't he?'

'Such a little tramp!' Kendra oozed venom.

Logie laughed. 'Oh well, we were all pretty relaxed about it, back in the day. And look, here comes another of Will's conquests.'

Philippa Lindsay, trim in tight-fitting jeans and a fuchsia silk shirt, was standing on the front doorstep, her blonde hair gleaming under the overhead lamp. Her eyes raked the garden, then as she homed in on her prey she called 'Will! Will!' and hurried over to him.

Kendra turned to stare up at her husband. 'Philippa? But she was never one of the Cyrenaics!'

'Well,' Logie said, with what Jen thought was a smug smirk, 'not officially, maybe, but...' He shrugged.

His wife's eyes went to slits. 'You didn't, did you?'

He had drunk enough to be unwise. 'Oh, sauce for the goose, sweetie. Water under the bridge now.'

Giving him the sort of look that could strip paint, Kendra walked off. Would she, Jen wondered nervously, go over to Will and Philippa, talking earnestly together now, and cause a scene?

No, she wouldn't. She had gone to talk to an older couple, clients of the restaurant, perhaps. Logie looked after her, blinking.

'Shouldn't have said that, should I?' he said. 'I just get so sick of her going on, Will this, Will that. Sooner he goes back to Canada the better.'

'Mmm,' Jen agreed. 'Oh look, my glass is empty. I'm just going to get a refill.'

She moved off, then paused, looking round. Randall had Skye to himself, her back right against the wall of the house now; she was looking trapped, making restless, fluttering movements like a butterfly pinned alive to a board. Logie had bumbled off after Kendra, who ignored him as he joined in the conversation.

And Philippa and Will – Kendra might not have known what had gone on there, but Jen certainly had and she believed that the whole ghastly chain of events had been put in motion by Philippa's determination to entice Will back.

They were certainly engrossed in their conversation. Men weren't very good at disguising boredom, eyes always roving to find an excuse to move on, but Will's eyes were fixed on Philippa's face.

Did Charles Lindsay know about this? It was no wonder that he wasn't here. Lucky man, Jen thought bitterly. She'd give a lot not to be here herself.

No one, no one at all, had mentioned poor Eleanor Margrave, or Connell either. She could almost smell the sweet, sickly odour of death: the flowers of evil were blooming in this garden tonight.

And who, Jen wondered uneasily, was that woman she had noticed earlier taking a keen interest in their conversation when they were standing in front of the house, who was now positioned a little back from a knot of cheerful partygoers, obviously eavesdropping on what Philippa and Will were saying to each other?

Apart from the initial problem of having to invent Sam's CV on the spot in answer to friendly questioning, Louise felt she had landed on her feet. Mike and his pals, old school chums, were easy-going and chatty and with her declared shyness she was able to stand on the edge of the group nodding, laughing and not saying much.

In fact, it had been interesting to hear local opinion on the subject of Eleanor Margrave's murder. It had naturally caused a considerable sensation but the consensus was that she'd disturbed a burglar, up from the south likely and planning to do over the prosperous-looking houses round the edge of the bay.

'Just unlucky she disturbed him, if you ask me. And he's probably away back there by now,' Mike said comfortably.

'One of these unsolved crimes, likely,' another man said. 'The police nowadays are useless unless someone walks in and confesses.'

It was hard not to rise in her own defence, but Louise managed to nod wisely and sip at her lager. She had positioned herself so that she had a clear view towards the house and across the front garden, and though she couldn't hear anything that was being said she could observe the silent dramas: Will walking off; Randall downing glasses of wine much too quickly; Skye retreating from him until there was no space to retreat further; some sort of spat taking place between Logie and Kendra.

Then she heard someone calling, 'Will! Will!' A tall, blonde woman was coming out of the house, a woman who bore a strong resemblance to Randall Lindsay. Philippa, she guessed, and a moment later heard Will say her name as he came to meet her and kiss her on both cheeks. Then, with a stroke of luck, they stopped and stood together only a few feet away from Louise.

Her only problem was that Mike and his

friends were getting, if not drunk, certainly very cheerful indeed. Their voices were rising, their laughter was getting louder, and anyway the conversation Philippa and Will were having clearly wasn't intended for a wider audience.

There seemed to be a lot about places and times – trying to arrange some sort of meeting, Louise guessed. It seemed to her that Will was causing the difficulty – even stalling, she thought.

She missed the next bit as Mike asked her if she wanted another lager and when she said no, tried to persuade her until she agreed just to shut him up. When she was able to tune in again the conversation had moved on. She heard the word 'police' and risked taking a sideways step towards them.

'You know how they can...' Philippa was saying '...don't want...'

She had turned her head and Louise couldn't hear the rest. Then Will said, 'Yes, absolutely ... not at all ... leave it at that.'

'Of course ... mustn't let...'

The gaps were infuriating. Will was agreeing with whatever it was. 'No – absolutely right ... I can't have ... questions. I know ... that's important.'

Philippa had her hand on his arm. 'Definitely, Will. But Randall, you see ... again...'

Straining to hear, Louise took another step sideways in their direction. Wrongly: it had opened up a gap between her and the rest of Mike's group and suddenly Will and Philippa stopped talking and looked directly at her, a frown gathering between Philippa's brows.

Louise gave a feeble smile then stepped back to

237

Mike's side, joining in the conversation with an enthusiasm he clearly found surprising.

'There you are, you see, pet! All you needed was another drink to loosen your inhibitions. You'll be the life and soul of the party before you know it.'

Philippa and Will separated almost immediately after that. Jen, having got herself another glass of wine and spoken for a few minutes to the parents of a child in her class, saw that Will was going back to where Randall was still holding Skye prisoner.

With a surge of guilt, Jen made an excuse and followed him across. She should really have mounted a rescue mission herself but after the ruthless way Skye had forced her to lie to the police this morning she was much less inclined to be protective than once she would have been. This was going to be trouble, though; she'd seen Randall in a drunken temper before and chairs had got smashed that time.

Skye gave a little cry of, 'Will!' as he approached.

'Skye!' he said, gently mocking, then went to put a hand on Randall's arm. 'Not sure about your tactics, dude! Let the lady breathe, why don't you!'

Randall turned on him, his face suffused with rage. He picked up Will's arm between two fingers, held it out then dropped it, snarling, 'Keep your filthy hands off me, Stewart!'

Will stepped back. 'OK, OK, calm down. It's just that I don't think Skye was too happy with the situation.'

Jen had just reached them and Skye, seizing her opportunity, moved away from Randall. 'Hey,

Jen!' Her voice was shaking. 'Where have you been? Randall and I were just catching up...'

Neither of the men was paying any attention to her. Randall said, 'And you have a right to speak for her – how? You're nothing but a lousy, stinking bent copper, you bastard!' He launched into a stream of obscenities.

For a moment Will let him rave. Then he said, his voice dangerously quiet, 'Shut up. If you don't shut up of your own accord, I'll make you.'

'That's a joke!' Without warning, Randall took a swing at him.

Will dodged, but took a heavy blow on the shoulder. 'That's it!' he yelled. His punch caught Randall on the side of the face.

'Will!' Skye wailed. 'Randall – don't!'

They were wrestling now. The raised voices attracted attention; conversations died as people turned to stare. Kendra and Logie came hurrying over and then Philippa arrived, looking furious herself. 'Will you both stop that at once! Someone's going to call the police if this goes on.'

Neither man paid any attention. Randall was taller and heavier but Will was strong enough to push Randall off, letting him land a telling hit that split his lip.

'Logie – take Will,' Philippa said tersely, moving round behind her son to imprison his arms.

Randall struggled for a moment, but Will submitted readily enough as Philippa called briskly to the ring of onlookers that had collected, 'Right. Show's over. Sorry about that, folks.' She wagged her finger at the two men. 'And it's Diet Coke for you two for the rest of the evening.' She got her laugh and the little knot of people dispersed.

Randall took out a handkerchief to dab at his swelling lip and without another word swung round to stalk away, then stopped, his eyes widening.

She hadn't moved quickly enough. Louise had gone towards the fight in case she would have to blow her cover and break it up before real harm was done and his sudden pivot had taken her by surprise.

He had spotted her immediately. He crossed the garden towards her in three strides and there was no mistaking his threatening attitude.

'Get out of here!' he yelled. 'I warned you!'

As she shrank away from him, Mike moved in front of her. 'Now now, laddie,' he said. 'Calm down. There's been enough nonsense tonight. Maybe you should just go and sleep it off.'

Another three men moved forward, forming a barrier. Louise stepped behind them and Randall had no alternative but to stop.

Ignoring them, he called, 'You'll suffer for this! Dirty little spy!' But then he strode off back to the group and with distinct unease, Louise saw that they were all staring at her.

She said, 'Thank you,' a little shakily to Mike and his cohort, uncertain how they would react to what Randall had said.

But Mike was amused. 'Got another girlfriend then, has he, and didn't want you turning up? Oh dear, who would be young, eh? Never you mind, Sam, there's better fish in the sea than him.'

'Toffee-nosed git!' another man said, and there was more laughter. 'Have another drink, lassie.'

Louise said she was driving but allowed them to cheer her up. She didn't want to leave while Randall had his eye on her; she was afraid he might follow her out and, drunk and belligerent as he was, anything could happen.

Some of the guests were starting to drift away, though there were others who looked prepared to party till dawn. Her present friends seemed to be among them, unfortunately; it would have been reassuring to go out in their company but she was desperate now to get away.

At last she saw Randall go back into the house. She said goodbye as quickly as she could, given that she had seven men to kiss and in Mike's case give a grateful hug to as well, and went out into the darkness of the narrow lane.

Here, right on the edge of the village, there were no street lamps. It was a fine starlit night but she'd have welcomed a moon to light the uneven footing of the verge as she stumbled along, and headlight beams as the occasional car drove past were very welcome.

Louise didn't have the confidence to go down the road side of the cars that were still parked; she'd be too easily visible if Randall, bent on vengeance, had come back out of the house and noticed her leaving.

She would certainly be grateful to get back to the safety of her car. She had been forced to park some way from the gate and her progress along the verge was slow – and unpleasant, too. She swore as she stepped into a little ditch running across it that was full of water, then squelched on.

She would have plenty to think about on her

way home. The party had been a fascinating exposé of the relationships within the one-time Cyrenaics. A lot of the tension seemed centred on Will; he looked to be having some sort of relationship with Kendra and with Skye as well – a very intense one, at least on her part – though what sort of relationship he had with Philippa was less clear. She needed to get back and write down everything she could remember of their conversation while it was fresh in her memory. It would provide plenty of material for Big Marge's morning meeting.

And then there was Randall – she was inclined to discount him. He was plainly besotted with Skye and she, equally plainly, found him as unappealing as Louise did herself. He was just a pompous oaf and he was never going to have any romantic success until he stopped thinking of himself as God's gift. Though the insult he'd hurled at Will Stewart, 'bent copper', was interesting – what did that mean? Maybe it was just a random insult because he'd been sacked.

There was the car now, thank goodness. Home, and bed. Louise tried not to think about a nice, peaceful cigarette while she wrote up her notes; she was proud of herself for managing to get right through the evening without trying to bum one from one of the smokers. She'd decided, at last, to give it up – even if Andy Mac would crow – and she was doing it cold turkey. This would be a demonstration of her amazing willpower, not relying on chemical help, and so far she was doing pretty well.

Louise was definitely feeling smug, both

personally and professionally, as she went to get out her car keys. They'd slipped to the bottom of her bag; she bent over to rummage through it.

Was that a sound, from the rough ground at her back? She straightened up, alarmed, but couldn't pin down the direction. There were scrubby bushes and a little clump of low trees nearby; just an animal, she told herself, but she scrabbled for the key with renewed urgency.

She had no warning, no sense of anyone nearby. But as she found the key at last something came over her head and around her neck, pulling her backwards, then a gloved hand came across her nose and mouth with a strong, merciless grip, stifling her. She collapsed on to her knees, struggling helplessly, her hands scrabbling at her throat. Then the glove was removed from her face but the loop tightened and tightened so that though she screamed, all that emerged was a strangled groan. Then she had no more breath to scream, no more breath for anything except the urgency of getting air to her tortured lungs. And she was failing there too.

CHAPTER FIFTEEN

Dear God! He'd got it wrong! He'd been so anxious that Louise wouldn't see him doing his self-imposed surveillance that he'd let her get herself killed.

From the field gate near the entrance to Ballinbreck House where he'd parked – in his mother's little Honda, not his own recognisable car – Andy Macdonald had monitored her progress back to the car, sunk down in his seat.

There was no sign of Randall following her. When Louise was only a few steps away from her car he'd decided enough was enough: he'd spent a long, cold, miserable evening being tormented by the sounds of merriment and the barbecue fragrance on the air, all for nothing. She'd been right; he'd overreacted. Chippie on the way home, he decided.

He'd just started the car when a movement caught his eye. All he could make out was that there was a dark shadow behind Louise – a shadow that shouldn't be there.

He gunned the engine, put his hand on the horn and blasted the few yards down the road, leaping out without shutting the door almost before it had stopped. As he reached the car something moved rapidly away, an amorphous shape vanishing into the surrounding darkness.

Louise was there, lying on the verge: a limp, sprawled body. He dropped to his knees beside her, feeling desperately for a pulse. Then he heard the rasping sound of her straining breath.

'Oh, thank God for that! Louise–'

She was struggling to sit up, coughing painfully. He put his arm round her in support and she sagged against his shoulder.

'Did you see who it was?'

'No,' she croaked. 'Just – something here–'

Louise put a hand up to her throat. In the beam from his headlights he could see a deep-red pressure line but any ligature had gone. He scanned the rough ground over her shoulder but couldn't see anything. He didn't want to leave her like this but she said, 'I'm – I'm fine. Go on.'

Andy sprinted across the scrub, scanning the bushes, looking ahead and all round, but there was no telltale movement, no sign of any dark figure. The assailant seemed to have vanished into thin air – then he realised there was a track that ran at right angles to the lane and as he got nearer he could see that it led to a big double gate in the wall of the house. He could see the roof of a garage beyond.

While he had been so confidently watching the main gate, Randall Lindsay had been able to slip out at the side and attack Louise. He turned back; no point in going in there. He could put out an emergency call from his mobile in the car.

He had left it blocking the road, but it had been driven in to the side and Louise was getting out of it, looking shaky admittedly but waving an apology to the car that had been waiting to get past.

'For goodness' sake, sit down!' he exclaimed. 'You're not fit–'

'I'll recover.' Her voice was hoarse. 'I just want to get home.'

'I'll phone the guys to come and deal with this and we'll get you to hospital…'

She was shaking her head. 'Don't need hospital. It's just bruising. And if you bring in the mob it won't do any good. The ground's dry so there won't be footprints, I can't ID my attacker – couldn't see him, hear him, smell him even – and he wore gloves, so there won't be fingerprints or even DNA. With all the people in there you won't be able to pin down where anyone was for a given five minutes. And taking statements from everyone and checking them will tie up all the manpower we've got for a week.'

Andy stared at her. 'You're taking this remarkably calmly. We could pick up Randall, bring him in for questioning – he uttered threats about you–'

'Not convinced it's Randall. Lot of things happened. And I'm not calm, not inside, but I'm alive.' She paused. 'Thanks to you. Andy, what were you doing here, anyway?'

'Wasn't happy,' he said gruffly. 'I thought I'd just hang about and see you were all right.'

Louise was silent for a moment. Then she said, 'Not sure how you thank someone for saving your life. Isn't that meant to put you under an obligation to look after me from now on, or something?' She tried to laugh then began to cough, her face screwed up in pain. 'Thanks, anyway.'

'Aw, shucks! All part of the service. Look, you obviously feel strongly about this. Are you really saying – just let it go?'

Louise nodded. 'I'll report it, of course. But I know it's a dead end and it'll only be a distraction.'

'You're quite a woman,' he said. 'Insane, of course. Anyone else would be in a state of collapse and whimpering. Home, then?'

She smiled and nodded, but he realised she was sagging against her car and starting to shake. 'You may think you're all right,' he said, 'but you're going into shock. You're certainly not fit to drive. I'll take you home and we'll arrange to get your car back tomorrow.'

He was afraid she might argue, but she only said, 'Does it have a good heater? I'm awfully cold.'

'There's a rug. Smells a bit of my mum's dog, but it's warm.'

He tucked her into the passenger seat, then locked up her car before he drove off. He could hear her teeth chattering as he put the heater up to maximum.

After a moment or two, Louise said, 'That's better. Andy, it was fascinating–' She started to cough again, her eyes watering with the effort.

He was intrigued to know what she had to say but he said firmly, 'Save your voice. You'll hurt your throat. In the nicest possible way, shut up.'

A minute later, he saw that she had fallen into an exhausted sleep.

Bill was in the kitchen making a cup of tea when his wife came downstairs on Sunday morning, yawning. She had slept badly, her mind too full of problems that had scampered around her troubled dreams, turning back on themselves like rats in a maze.

'Didn't hear you getting up,' she said, taking the mug he was holding out to her.

'Wanted to have a look at the ewe I was worried about yesterday, but she's fine today. Just her little bit of fun.'

Marjory laughed. Farming wisdom always had it that sheep had one aim in life: to find a way of dying, preferably as expensively as possible. 'At least you didn't call the vet,' she said.

'Oh, that ewe's always a wee drama queen – goes into decline at the least thing. Worried well, the doctors call it when it's people.'

'I love it when you talk about their personalities. I can't tell one from another.'

Bill smiled. 'Professional skill. There's a couple I'd call the vet for right away if they were drooping.'

'Stoic sheep – I like the idea.' Marjory pulled the steeping porridge on to the hotplate and started stirring it. 'Bill, what do you think of Cat's Nick now?'

'Seems a nice lad,' Bill said happily. 'When you think what he might have been like! And he's having a good effect on Cat – she didn't jump down my throat once at supper last night. That's a record.'

'Mmm,' Marjory said. Farmers weren't famous for their modern and liberal views but Bill was normally kept in check by his wife as well as his daughter. With Nick's constant encouragement he had become expansive.

She had flinched at the sly, sidelong glances he directed at Cat, unnoticed by Bill. Even Cat, she thought, was uneasy about it. If she hadn't been, she'd have launched into a tirade when Bill said that if you were able-bodied you should have to choose between working and starving.

Nick had agreed. 'Absolutely.'

'How interesting,' Marjory said sweetly. 'And you go along with that, do you, Cat? Bit of a turnaround.'

Cat went pink, muttered something and changed the subject, but Marjory felt so uncomfortable, it was as if she'd had ants crawling across her skin all evening.

Her mother had been there too; she hadn't said much but then Janet Laird had always been quiet. It didn't mean she wasn't paying sharp attention to all that was going on, though, and she was a shrewd judge of character – perhaps as a result. Marjory decided she'd make time as soon as possible to pop in to see her and get her verdict.

Now she said, 'I'm not sure I'd take him at face value, Bill. I think he's a bit sleekit.'

'Sleekit?' Bill looked affronted. 'Having nice manners hardly makes him untrustworthy. I certainly appreciate it.'

'You don't think it's funny that a boyfriend of Cat's should have the sort of views that Cat absolutely despises? It wasn't like her to be so quiet.'

Giving him a sideways glance Marjory saw, from his faint flush, that she had sown a doubt in his mind. But he said stubbornly, 'Maybe he'll make her a bit more down to earth. And anyway, maybe he's just been brought up to believe it's polite to not disagree with his elders and betters.' He was looking thoughtful, though.

Satisfied with her groundwork, Marjory said, 'Could be,' as she put out the porridge. 'Bill, pass me up Meg's bowl for the scrapings.'

Hearing her name, the collie jumped up, circling her mistress hopefully.

'Not yet, Meggie, it's too hot. It'll hurt your nose. You'll just have to be patient.'

Her eyes on Marjory's face, the dog gave a heavy sigh and lay down again.

'Understands every word you say,' Bill said fondly.

'Of course she does. She's a highly intelligent animal,' Marjory agreed. She'd also noticed that Nick Carlton hadn't got the effusive greetings Meg normally gave visitors to the house.

Louise Hepburn awoke with an achingly dry throat and a stiff, bruised neck. She swallowed, wincing, as she opened her eyes. It took her a second to realise where she was, and when she did the pain of embarrassment gripped her too.

He'd taken her to his mum's last night, instead of delivering her home. She'd been livid with Andy but she hadn't been strong enough to argue last night and even if she had been, his mum was so nice and concerned it would have been downright rude. She was a retired nurse, apparently, and she checked Louise out and confirmed that no real harm had been done, then supplied a nightie and a toothbrush and tucked her up in bed with a couple of paracetamols, a soothing hot drink and a hot-water bottle.

Louise admitted to herself that it had been good to be cosseted, but after Andy had picked up his own car and gone back to his flat it had got a little alarming. May Macdonald had laughed as she said goodnight. 'I'm so glad to meet you, Louise. Andy's always been an awful boy for keeping his cards close to his chest. Sleep well, dear.'

Somehow she was going to have to make it plain that they only worked together and didn't really get on, even as colleagues.

What really got to her, though, was being under such an obligation to him. She'd insisted, quite

250

rudely, that she was able to look after herself and then had conclusively proved that she wasn't. If he hadn't been there – Louise shuddered.

When she thought about how close it had been, how she had felt as the band across her throat squeezed tighter and tighter, how easily this morning could have been a day she didn't see... She mustn't think, that was all.

She had to put it right out of her mind, concentrate on the information she'd collected last night and the leads it suggested. After all, she couldn't be sure that her attacker wouldn't strike again as long as he was still at large.

Andy had promised to come in to see how she was on his way to work and if he thought Louise was just going to accept meekly that she should stay at home and nurse her injuries, he had another think coming.

She moved very gingerly, though, as she got out of bed. Her throat, her neck, her back were all painful but at least not incapacitating. And the last thing she wanted was time to think about her injuries.

It was still early, but May Macdonald must have heard her moving and greeted her when she came downstairs with more paracetamol, the fluffiest scrambled eggs Louise had ever tasted and lots of anxious enquiries.

Louise assured her she'd managed to sleep, ate her eggs and tried, as subtly as she could, to disabuse May of the assumption she had obviously made. The trouble was she really didn't want to upset her; May was lovely and it was a treat, too, to be cosseted, as she hadn't been since her poor mother's mind had become clouded.

She was almost sorry when Andy appeared, still looking anxious and insisting that she took the day off.

'I'm absolutely fine,' she protested. 'It only lasted a few seconds, for heaven's sake.'

She was even more grateful to May when she told her son to stop fussing. 'Louise knows her own mind, Andy. She doesn't need bossing about – not out of office hours.' She gave Louise a mischievous look. 'Oh, he was always like that, you know, even as a wee boy. He–'

'Mum!' Andy said in exasperation. 'Oh, all right, Louise. If the two of you have ganged up I don't suppose there's anything I can do. If you want to go to your flat to change we'd better get a move on or we'll be late for the team meeting.'

As he left the kitchen, Louise made her thanks to May and was warmly embraced. 'It's been lovely to meet you – come back any time, dear,' she said. 'Someone with a bit of a spark is just what that boy's needing.'

Louise gulped. 'Er – yes. Thanks again,' and bolted for the car.

It was a shame, though, she thought as they drove away. She'd have loved to accept the invitation, if the bargain hadn't included Andy.

Horrified at what had happened, DI Fleming had been inclined to overrule her constable about not following it up. Hepburn, though, with her voice still rough and a scarf wrapped round her neck that didn't quite cover up the bruising, had pointed out that with nothing to go on it would make more sense to focus their efforts on the original cases.

In a sense she was right; it was a fairly safe assumption that the person who had strangled Eleanor Margrave had tried again. Something had spooked the killer; Hepburn must have gleaned some information so significant that she had to be silenced, even at the cost of focusing police attention on the suspects present. The challenge now was to recognise what that had been.

Hepburn was still in danger, though probably less so now she had got a chance to report in. She'd said that Randall didn't know her address, only her mobile number, and as she was insistent that the flat had an entryphone and she would be careful, Fleming allowed herself to be satisfied with that. The best protection they could give Hepburn was to get the perpetrator in a cell with the door locked.

The information Hepburn had obtained was impressive. She'd reported the general points and then gone off to cudgel her brains and record every possible scrap of overheard conversation as well as a statement about the attack.

The SOCOs had sent over all the papers found in Eleanor Margrave's house and Fleming had sent Macdonald and Campbell to do a quick check through them, though not before commending Macdonald on his initiative.

'I'm very grateful,' she finished, then smiled. 'I just hope Louise is.'

Macdonald grinned. 'Theoretically, absolutely,' he said.

When they had gone, Fleming turned to Mac-

Nee with a gesture of despair. 'Oh Tam, I feel awful. I should never have suggested it! I was concerned afterwards, as you know, but I didn't stop her. We might have been dealing with her death right now and I'd have been responsible.'

'Every time you send an officer out of that door it's the risk they're taking,' MacNee pointed out. 'You know that. It's the job. It happens.'

Fleming knew that, just as she was, he was remembering the officer who had been gunned down a few years back, saving Fleming's life.

After a moment he went on, 'Anyway, I'm not just sure how you thought you were going to stop her. She wasn't answering the door or the phone and I have my doubts that you could have justified forced entry. She's come out of it with some great stuff, anyway.'

'That's certainly true. So – where do we go from here?'

'We nail the bastard,' he said fiercely. 'And give me ten minutes with him round the back before we reach the security cameras.'

'Ten?' Fleming said, raising her eyebrows. 'Slowing up in your old age? Five would have been enough, once. Seriously, though – what did you see as most significant?'

MacNee thought about it. 'I'll tell you the obvious line – the "bent copper" remark. That's easy to check. There'd be gossip at the Kirkcudbright station at the time – Mike Wallace would know. I can get on to him.'

'Good idea. And his alibi – we both reckoned he and Kendra could have agreed it, if necessary. It did strike me that according to Louise she was

254

furious with him about Skye so it might be worth getting her on her own and finding out if she was sticking to her story. And I'd like to know where Philippa Lindsay fitted in to all that too.'

She got up. 'I've got to take the morning meeting first but we can get away after that.'

'You're on.' Then MacNee paused. 'What about Skye Falconer?'

'Certainly questions there we need to ask, but that can wait. We should get information back from the Border Agency quite soon.'

About half of Philippa Lindsay's task force had failed to appear this morning and she was in such a sour mood, the half that had were regretting it.

'We're not the ones she's needing to go on at,' one woman muttered to another as they collected up discarded beer bottles from round the garden. 'And you'll notice her own son's nowhere to be seen.'

'The drink he had on him last night, he'll not be much use to anyone for a good wee while yet.'

They both sniggered. Philippa, coming unexpectedly out of the house, heard them and flushed. Randall, though she had mercilessly hounded him out of bed, was indeed in no state to do anything much beyond groaning. She'd poured him a mug of coffee and told him where the Alka Seltzer was half an hour ago and she was hoping that when she went back he'd be capable of coherent speech.

There had been a lot she'd wanted to ask him the night before but by the time she got him on his own he was incoherent and weepy, oozing self-pity as he dabbed his injured lip. In disgust, she'd sent him up to bed.

She went over to have a word with the men who were taking away the barbecues.

'Great night last night,' one of them said cheerily, and Philippa tried not to make her agreement sound hollow. She'd no one to blame but herself; it had been all her own idea and now she had to live with the consequences.

The state her son was in was one of them. When she went back to the kitchen he was a pitiable sight: grey-faced, red-eyed and with a badly swollen lip. He was smoking, which she hated in the house, but he was at least on his feet, making himself breakfast.

Philippa looked contemptuously at the fried bread and frizzled eggs. 'It won't help, you know. But if you can keep it down, you're fit to talk to me. Tell me all about your little friend.'

She sat down at the table as her son, eyeing his plate a little uncertainly, stubbed out his cigarette and took his place opposite, saying 'Ow, ow, ow!' as he put the fork to his mouth.

His mother ignored him. 'She's a detective, is she?'

He nodded.

'And why was she there?'

'Good question,' he said bitterly. 'I met her in Paris ages ago – we were at the uni together. When I asked her if she'd like to come to the party I didn't know her little pals were going to start giving us the third degree and after that I left half a dozen messages telling her not to come if she knew what was good for her – took her name off the list. She must have sneaked in. We should make a complaint – get her suspended...'

Philippa considered that. 'No,' she said at last. 'She'd claim she didn't get the messages, and if they were at all threatening you'd probably find you were arrested instead. But it's upset everyone – being spied on like that. Kendra was throwing an absolute fit. Oh, you screwed up, as usual.'

She stood up, then without warning suddenly banged the table and yelled, 'Do you know how often I've had to say that, thanks to you? I'm sick of it – sick of you! Finish your breakfast and get out there to pick up some litter. It's all you're good for.'

For once, DS Macdonald didn't mind the pile of paper waiting on their attention, though it represented hours of work. He dumped half of it on the desk next to him for DC Campbell and settled down to it.

DC Hepburn was bashing away at a terminal in the other half of the room. As he looked across, she sat back rolling her head, as if her neck were hurting.

'All right?' he called across and she said, 'Yeah, fine,' and quickly went back to her task. He suspected that wasn't true – she was looking drained and pale – but there wasn't a lot he could do about it just at the moment.

'See this,' Campbell said, pointing to his screen.

Macdonald glanced at it sideways. It was a report just in that there was no record of Skye Falconer having crossed the Channel around the time she had indicated.

Macdonald raised his eyebrows. 'Interesting. Though to be fair, she was pretty vague about the times.'

Campbell scrolled on down. 'Nor any time in the last six months.'

'Really? So she's lying – wonder where she really was? Make a note of that – we'll have to pin her down.'

'Checked Randall Lindsay too. Came back last week.'

'Could have come over and gone back earlier some other way, I suppose,' Macdonald said, 'but at least it squares with what he said.'

He went back to sorting what was on his own desk. Most of it was the sort of stuff any house-holder would have: invoices, insurance policies, travel documents, even a copy of a brief will, leaving everything to a charity for rehabilitating addicts.

'Wasn't killed for an inheritance, anyway,' he commented to Campbell. 'Unless the charity's more than usually proactive.'

Campbell grunted, but it surprised a small laugh out of Hepburn. Gratified, Macdonald went on sifting through.

'Hey, look at this,' he said. 'She was a bit of an artist, seemingly.' He held up a watercolour, a sea-scape. 'That's the view from the house, I think.'

Hepburn looked across. 'It's quite good, isn't it?'

'Lots more like that.' Macdonald went through them, holding up the better ones. 'That's the lighthouse down at the Mull of Galloway – I recognise it. Wasn't like that when I went there, though – it was blowing a gale. Oh look, this one's a bit different. Rather sweet, really – it's a mermaid.'

Hepburn's ears pricked up. 'A mermaid?' She got up and came across to look over his shoulder.

It looked as if it might be an illustration from a children's book, a conventional mermaid with the statutory elegantly curving tail, long flowing hair and huge sea-green eyes.

Macdonald heard Hepburn's indrawn breath. 'Bridget James said Eleanor described the woman who came in from the storm as a mermaid. And I saw her last night. This is Skye Falconer.'

CHAPTER SIXTEEN

'Get her brought in for questioning,' DI Fleming said tersely. 'Right now. Ewan, make the arrangements – liaise with Inspector Wallace at Kirkcudbright. And I want fingerprints taken first thing – they've sent through prints from Eleanor Margrave's house and I want to check if we have a match before I speak to her.'

DC Campbell nodded and went out. The drawing of the mermaid was on Fleming's desk; Macdonald, Campbell and Hepburn had appeared with it, triumphant, and MacNee was on his way. Hepburn was still hollow-eyed but there was a flush of excitement in her cheeks and her eyes were bright.

'Tell me everything you observed about Skye,' Fleming said. 'Conversation, interaction – anything at all.'

Hepburn thought for a moment. 'The meeting with Will Stewart – she fixed him with these great, burning eyes and went towards him, as if she wasn't aware of anything else. Everyone was sort of struck dumb. Kendra looked ready to kill her. Will was just staring at her.'

'Was he surprised, pleased?' Fleming asked.

'Surprised – not sure. Pleased – yes, I'd say so. Kendra was holding his arm and he certainly pushed her aside quite roughly. He hugged Skye and they were talking away together until Randall cut in – and then of course Will got into the fist fight over her. We definitely need history on the relationship.'

'And to check out his alibi too. We thought at the time it was suspiciously pat.'

MacNee appeared, a little out of breath. His eye fell on the mermaid drawing. 'Well, well, well,' he said. 'Better than a photofit, eh?'

'And there's no record of her crossing the Channel,' Fleming told him. 'She may not even have left the country at all. Go on, Louise.'

'There's not much more to say. She got trapped by Randall and I didn't hear her say anything at all after that, except when he and Will squared up and she moved out of the way to talk to Jen Wilson.'

'Jen Wilson,' MacNee said. 'I'd like to know where she fits in – how much she knew about where her wee pal was for the last couple of years, that kind of thing. She's a bit of a dark horse, that one. I never like that.'

'Rock-solid alibi,' Macdonald said. 'You can't convince a class of children to say their teacher was there when she wasn't.'

'They don't know where she was in the middle of the night when her friend went to visit Eleanor Margrave,' MacNee argued. 'I think she might have a story to tell.'

'I think they all have a story to tell,' Fleming said darkly, 'and I don't think any of them have even begun to tell it.

'Andy, I want you and Ewan to get down there and talk to the Lindsays and the Stewarts, for a start. Turn up the heat on Kendra – if Louise is right that she was consumed with jealousy we may even find Will's alibi isn't quite so solid after all. Give her the charm, Andy – you've got form for softening up female witnesses.'

Macdonald grinned sheepishly as she went on, 'Then see what you can get out of Will.

'Louise, finish the reports and then I want you to go home. No–' as Hepburn started to protest, 'I'm not going to argue about it. You need some rest, whatever you think now. Andy will give you an update later on.'

Jen Wilson got up with a hangover that was only partly physical. She was suffering a sort of emotional nausea too after everything that had happened the night before, compounded by the dread of what might happen today. The boulder she'd imagined before was gathering pace now as it hurtled down the hill, and they were all trapped in its path.

There were games going on, games she knew nothing about, and that unsettled her too. The trouble last night hadn't been exactly Skye's fault;

she couldn't help it that Randall had always obsessed about her and you could hardly ask her to put up with him pawing her to keep the peace. But she'd got Kendra so jealous she could hardly contain herself; she and Logie were probably at each other's throats today and that needn't have happened if Skye hadn't been so dramatic about Will.

And what about Jen herself? Skye had dumped her in it, got her involved, when Jen had tried so hard to hold herself apart. Yes, Skye was actually poison.

She could hear her moving upstairs. It was going to be difficult to keep up the social front, given the resentment she was feeling this morning. Jen made herself a mug of coffee – she couldn't face breakfast – and went out into the little courtyard at the back.

It was another glorious morning, the sort of spell of weather you sometimes got in May, if you were lucky. There was blossom on the cherry tree in the next-door garden, the birds were singing their hearts out and there was a bullfinch on her bird table that didn't fly away even when she came out. The beauty of it all was like a benison, a respite from the ugliness of a threatening world.

Skye appeared in the kitchen and Jen gave an unenthusiastic wave, hoping she wouldn't come out to disturb her. Sooner or later there was going to have to be straight talking about the situation with Will, but it would be good to sit enjoying the tranquillity for just a little longer.

The doorbell rang. Once she'd have assumed it was a neighbour; now her heart gave a lurch. What now?

Skye went to answer it. Jen felt tempted to stay where she was but her peace was shattered already. She went through the kitchen to the hall.

The front door was open and there were two large policemen blocking the light. She heard one say, 'I am detaining you under Section 14 of the Criminal Procedure Scotland Act on suspicion of murder. You do not have to say anything...'

Skye turned a white, frightened face to Jen as the caution was recited to her. 'Jen, what am I going to do?'

Jen's heart hardened. 'You're going to go with them, Skye,' she said. 'I don't think you'll find you have any alternative.'

Then she turned and left her and went back to the garden.

The lawn in front of Ballinbreck House had suffered from the party last night, with trampled grass and holes where the garden tents and canopies had been put up, but apart from that the place was looking pretty good and there was no one to be seen.

'Someone must have gone round cracking the whip this morning,' DS Macdonald said to DC Campbell. 'They've done a good job clearing up.'

He went over and rang the doorbell. It was answered by a middle-aged man with a harassed expression.

'Yes?' he said shortly.

'DS Macdonald and DC Campbell.' They showed their warrant cards. 'We were wanting a word with Philippa or Randall Lindsay.'

A look of horror came over the man's face.

'Police? Oh my God, what happened last night?'

'Nothing to worry about,' Macdonald said soothingly. 'Are you Mr Lindsay?'

'Charles, yes. I don't know where Philippa is – she was here earlier doing the slave-driving bit but now she's disappeared. Randall said he was going to the pub.'

Macdonald was about to thank him and leave when Campbell unexpectedly said, 'Maybe you'll do.'

Macdonald gave him a quizzical glance even as he agreed. Campbell must have something in mind but as usual he would be relying on Macdonald's mind-reading skills to drive the interview.

Charles Lindsay was certainly cooperative, taking them through to the kitchen and pouring them coffee. While Macdonald was still trying to work out what he should be asking, he said awkwardly, 'Look, I don't know what all this is about but I've been uneasy ever since Philippa got this notion about a Homecoming party. After all that went on in the past, I thought it was crazy to stir it up again, and now look what's happened – that fellow Kane dead, Eleanor Margrave too – a lovely lady, Eleanor–' He gave a shudder. 'I'd like to think you could get to the bottom of this before some other horror happens and if there's anything I can tell you that will help I'm only too happy to do it.'

Macdonald found his line. 'Why did she want to do it, do you think?'

Charles hesitated, then said quietly, 'Oh, I think I know the answer – Will Stewart. She thought I didn't know but of course I did. It was all part of that sick little group Randall belonged to – dressing up sex and drugs as a philosophy of life. She wasn't one of them but she hovered on the fringes – envious, I think, and resented the fact that she was too old. Will got drugs for her–'

'Will did? Not Connell Kane?'

'No.' Charles gave a wry smile. 'She despised him – "a drug dealer and uncouth with it" was her description. Her little arrangement with Will was "just a bit of fun", she told me when I challenged her once. And of course that led on to the sex. Our marriage – well, it hasn't worked for years. The business is what binds us together, though the way things are at the moment I can't see it surviving and then our marriage won't either. There will be an up side to going bankrupt as well as a down side.'

Macdonald made a sympathetic murmur. The guy was doing his job for him; he deserved encouragement. 'But – why the Homecoming party?'

'Didn't I say? I worked it out – she just wanted to get Will back again. She didn't know where he was and she thought that the word would get to him if there was this party. I don't know – perhaps she was fooling herself into thinking that he would be looking for a signal from her to return. Or perhaps he was, and I'm fooling myself, though I think that's unlikely – I don't care either way. But that's what it was all about. Just because a middle-aged woman had a passion for an attractive younger man, two people have died.'

And nearly three, Macdonald thought. 'Were you here yourself last night, sir?' he asked hopefully. Charles would be a great witness.

'No. I cleared out the day before yesterday – only got back this morning. Couldn't take it. Did – did something happen?'

Remembering how nearly something had, Macdonald was thankful he could say no. 'We're just asking some routine questions. Did you know Skye Falconer?'

Charles's face softened. 'Little Skye? Oh yes, of course. I've known her since she was a child – a charmer even then. Poor Randall's always been smitten–' He stopped. 'Oh God, nothing's happened to her, has it?'

'No, no,' Macdonald said, adding silently, 'not yet.' 'Do you know if she knew Mrs Margrave?'

He thought for a moment. 'I shouldn't think so. Eleanor had lived here a long time but she hasn't been around much of late.'

'Right. Well, I think that's all–' He glanced at Campbell but he had got up without showing signs of wanting to ask anything more.

Back in the car, Macdonald said, 'As simple as that! It squares with what Louise said about their conversation – neither she nor Stewart would want the drug stuff coming out. And of course it would have been an excuse for her to meet him, which was the whole object of the exercise.

'That was an unexpected bonus – well done! I couldn't think to start with what you were wanting me to ask him. What made you think he'd have something useful to tell us?'

Campbell looked blank. 'I didn't.'

'What do you mean? You said maybe he'd do to talk to.'

'Hoped we'd get coffee. Not even a biscuit,

though.' Campbell's voice was bitter.

Macdonald opened his mouth to say something, then thought the better of it and shut it again.

Kendra Stewart was checking stock behind the bar of The Albatross. Her head was aching and her eyes were still stinging from the bitter tears she'd shed the night before, once Logie had passed out in the middle of the row they'd been having after the party last night.

He'd had the nerve to behave this morning as if nothing had happened but she'd frozen him out and he'd retreated to the kitchen. Will was no-where to be seen this morning – probably gone off with that little slut Skye.

Did their own very special relationship mean nothing to him? She'd cherished the thought of his devotion for two whole years, and when he told her that at last he was coming home she had really believed that he was returning for her. She loved the idea of Canada – somewhere different, excit-ing, not this stifling little place with a husband who made her want to scream with boredom.

And last night – she'd even seen Philippa Stew-art, with her hair bleached to cover up the grey and her scraggy old neck, coming on to Will, and he hadn't repulsed her.

So if Kendra wasn't The One, just – well, one of his women, what was she to do? What sort of future did she have with Logie who'd even been shagging Philippa too? And he'd said it in front of Jen – the humiliation was unbearable.

She sort of hated Will now – but only sort of. She knew that if he smiled into her eyes, told her that she'd got it all wrong, started making proper plans about taking her back to Canada, not finding excuses the way he had been, she'd forgive him. They'd all been drinking, after all.

The optic she was trying to fix to the new gin bottle was proving awkward and she was wrestling with it when there was a knock on the door of the pub. When she looked there were two men standing there; she'd never seen them before but she guessed at once they were police officers and went to open it with a bad grace.

'What do you want now?' she said.

The taller of the two went through the usual rigmarole then asked if they could 'have a word'. For a moment she was tempted to say, 'Yes of course. "Encyclopaedia" – will that do?' but it was never smart to be smart with the police.

'I suppose so, though I can't think what I could add to the statement I gave.' She stood aside to admit them but didn't ask them to sit down, standing near the entrance with her arms folded forbiddingly across her chest.

'We just wanted to ask you a little bit about last night,' the taller, dark one said. 'I gather things were – er, a bit difficult. Sorry to have to take you back to it but – well, it's the job, you know?' He smiled at her; he wasn't bad-looking, in fact, and he had a nice, sympathetic smile.

Kendra warmed to him. 'It was very upsetting,' she murmured, giving him a sideways glance from under her eyelashes.

'Poor you,' he said. 'I gather there was a fist fight – what was it all about?'

At the question, it all rushed back. 'Oh, it was

268

over that little tramp Skye Falconer. First she came on to Will and then she was all over Randall. It was bound to cause trouble.'

'And then Will waded in? Jealous, I suppose?'

She opened her mouth to deny it, then found she couldn't. She'd been trying to pretend that he might come back and beg her to run away with him, but she knew really that he wasn't going to. Her eyes welled with tears and she put up her hand to brush the tears away.

'I've ... I've been stupid,' she faltered. 'I thought he loved me, and all the time it was really Skye. I don't even know where he is this morning – he's just gone out without saying a word to me about last night. I'd have left Logie for him if he'd asked me–'

'Lucky he didn't, then,' the other policeman, the one with the red hair said.

She bridled at his brusqueness and the tall one said hastily, 'He's taken some care to deceive you, hasn't he? You must be finding this pretty hard.'

He was very understanding. Kendra gave a little sob and took out a tissue to blow her nose as he went on, 'Look, it's tricky asking you this, but – you gave a very full statement to my colleagues about what the three of you were doing on Friday afternoon. You said that though you and Will were in separate areas you could confirm that he was there all afternoon. On reflection, is it possible that he might have been away from the place for, say, half an hour, three-quarters of an hour?

'I tell you why – I'm just wondering if he might have popped out for a bit to see Skye? She was here at the time and if they were – you know, in a relationship...'

That hadn't occurred to her. Kendra stared at him, thinking furiously. They'd decided together to create a watertight alibi; it was Will who had said, 'I didn't kill Eleanor Margrave and I don't suppose either of you did. I know how the system works – it will save a lot of hassle if we don't leave any gaps,' and she and Logie had been happy to agree.

She owed Will precisely nothing. 'I suppose so,' she said slowly. 'He's probably gone to her this morning too – he certainly isn't here. Last Friday – well, I did spend quite a bit of time in the kitchen doing preparation for the Saturday night dining menu with Logie. I couldn't say definitely that Will didn't go out then.'

'Time?' the red-haired constable asked. He had started taking notes.

He was rude, that was his problem. Her voice was cold as she said, 'Oh, I couldn't be sure.'

'Do you think we can work it out together?' the taller one said. 'How long was it after lunch, say?'

'A little while. I was up with Will talking about the table settings in the restaurant first, then I was checking supplies in the bar. So I suppose it would have been after three when I went to the kitchen.'

'And you were there for – how long?'

She gave it some thought. 'I suppose – well, it could have been as much as an hour.'

The sergeant beamed at her. 'Thank you so much, Mrs Stewart. You've been incredibly helpful.'

They left quite abruptly after that, once they

had her assurance that she would sign an amended statement.

After they had gone Kendra felt a pang of guilt. It seemed so disloyal not to be on Will's side! But he'd betrayed her and she wasn't going to say she knew where he was all the time when actually she didn't.

It was only then that she wondered why the police should want to know if Will had gone off to see Skye that afternoon.

The fingerprint information came through only minutes after DI Fleming had been informed that Skye Falconer was at the charge bar going through the formalities.

'It's amazing, when you think how long it used to take to get confirmation like this,' she said to DS MacNee. 'How on earth did we ever get anyone back then?'

MacNee looked gloomy. 'Used to get folk coming in to tell us stuff. They don't now, unless they're paid for it. It's not all progress.'

'Tam, I'm not going to let you depress me. Look at this – she's got a lot of explaining to do.'

They both looked at the printout on her desk; the comparison between the two sets of prints was so clear that they didn't need the expert report below to tell them that they both belonged to Skye Falconer.

'Right,' Fleming said. 'Let's get down there and see what she has to say for herself.'

But when they reached the interview room, there was a hold-up. A constable was waiting to tell them that Skye had exercised her right to have a solicitor present while she was questioned. Worse, when Fleming asked who it was, the one she had chosen was one of the more able and aggressive practitioners.

'Damn!' Fleming said. 'I know he's there to defend his client but no one seems to have told him that making personal attacks isn't actually part of the job description.'

'Does it as a hobby,' MacNee said darkly.

Damien Thomson arrived quarter of an hour later. He took his time over talking to his client and when at last he expressed himself ready to allow her to be questioned, MacNee was frustrated enough to take exception to anything, even the tone in which he said good morning.

'Afternoon by now,' he said.

Thomson made a pantomime of looking at his watch. 'Goodness, Sergeant, you're absolutely right. How time flies when you're enjoying yourself.'

'Are you, Mr Thomson?' Fleming said coolly. 'How very strange.'

MacNee grinned as he performed the formalities for the video tape and saw the look of annoyance on Thomson's face. He never liked it when someone else did the sardonic bit.

Fleming began. 'Ms Falconer, you made a statement claiming that you had never met Eleanor Margrave. We now have fingerprint evidence that you were in her house. Perhaps you could explain to us how you can reconcile this?'

Sitting beside her solicitor, a tall, solid-looking young man, Skye looked smaller and frailer than

272

ever. She had deep shadows under her eyes and she shrank back into her seat at the direct question.

'No comment,' she muttered.

MacNee ground his teeth. 'Couldn't hear that properly. Could you speak up for the tape, please.'

Thomson stepped in. 'My client said, "No comment", and I shall resist any attempt to bully her.'

'*Bully* her?' MacNee gasped. Police brutality – that was to be his line, was it? He was about to defend himself when he encountered a steely look from his inspector and subsided.

'I'm sorry if you didn't understand, Mr Thomson,' Fleming said. 'It is a technical requirement that the answer to questions should be audible. I am going to put that question again, but before I do I would like to emphasise the seriousness of the charge on which you have been detained, Ms Falconer.

'It is the murder of an elderly lady – a frail elderly lady. She drew a picture of a mermaid that looks remarkably like you.' Fleming handed it across the table.

Thomson took it first, then pushed it contemptuously back. 'Is this what passes for evidence in Police Scotland? This is a fanciful drawing that looks nothing at all like my client and I fail to see what relevance it could have.'

But MacNee saw that Skye's eyes had widened in alarm and Fleming went on, 'She talked about you, you know, Skye. She described you arriving at her house, soaked to the skin that night.'

'What night is this?' Thomson said sharply, looking at Skye. 'I understood the time in question was last Friday afternoon.'

Fleming ignored him. 'Was that when the fingerprints got there? If it was, you know, that might help you as well as us. If you tell us now, perhaps we might be able to eliminate you from enquiries. I know you told us a lie, that you hadn't met her, but in the circumstances of someone just having been murdered, of course we understand that you might be frightened, might want to keep out of it, especially if you hadn't done anything wrong. You really would be wise to explain.'

MacNee glanced at his boss in admiration. She was leaning forward, her voice gentle, her eyes sympathetic. That was why she was so successful: folk got mesmerised.

Thomson turned to his client but before he could say anything, Skye spoke. She sat up very straight and said, loudly and clearly, 'No comment.'

And that was all she said for the whole of the rest of the interview. They couldn't charge her; they had placed her at the scene of the crime but there was no evidence to say when she had been there. She left with her smirking brief.

MacNee began a rant about the legislation that had robbed them of their precious six hours' questioning without a solicitor present. 'You'd have got it out of her if it hadn't been for him,' he finished.

Fleming shook her head. 'Oh no, Tam, I wouldn't. That was fascinating. She was tentative and scared over the question about Eleanor's murder, but when it got on to the night when Connell Kane was killed, something stiffened her

274

resolve. She didn't need her brief to tell her to say nothing, she said it immediately. So what do we make of that?'

'You tell me,' MacNee said blankly. '*I* don't know.'

DC Weston came off shift in Dumfries with her mind made up. Today she was going to go and squat outside the Kirkluce headquarters until someone agreed to take her in to see DI Fleming. If not, she'd wait until she saw her coming out to the car park and approach her directly, however long it took.

She had only been there for ten minutes when she saw a car slowing down to turn in, with two occupants who looked as if they might be detectives. She flagged them down and when they had confirmed that they were, said, 'Can you get me in to see DI Fleming? I've got important information to give her but no one will let me speak to her.'

The officer driving looked amused. 'If it's as important as all that and you tell me what it's about, I'll see if I can fix it.'

She shook her head vigorously. 'No. I need to speak to her.' She'd been fobbed off too many times already.

He glanced at the other detective, who shrugged. 'Oh, all right. Go round to reception and I'll see what I can do.'

Weston had only waited for ten minutes when he returned. 'Come on. She'll see you now.'

They introduced themselves as they went upstairs. On the top floor he opened an office door and ushered her in. 'DC Weston, ma'am.'

And here she was at last, Big Marge. She was looking at her coolly, and for a moment Weston felt overwhelmed at meeting her idol. But she knew that the evidence she had was gold dust and she felt quite confident as she told her all about the day she had found the car tracks leading down on to the Solway shore near to Ballinbreck. She'd had a long time to think about how to present her evidence and she delivered it clearly, without hesitation.

To start with, the result was all she could have hoped. Macdonald gaped and another detective, a short man in a black leather jacket, exclaimed, 'You wee dancer!'

Fleming, though she was obviously interested, said, 'I don't quite understand. Why didn't you report this to DI Harris at the time?'

'I did!' Weston cried. 'I told him and he said he'd checked it out and that it wasn't what I thought. But I don't believe he even went to look.'

She saw a glance pass between Fleming and MacNee, then Fleming said, 'I see. But I don't understand why this had to be reported directly to me.'

This was her big moment. She drew a deep breath. 'I really admire what you're doing here, ma'am. I don't rate DI Harris and I know he'll stand in the way of my promotion. I wanted to ask you direct to get me a transfer to Galloway division. I'd give anything to work on your team.'

DI Fleming didn't look gratified by her expression of admiration. She sounded quite cold as she said, 'As I understand it, you found this evidence, which I agree might be highly significant, on Friday morning. It is now Sunday afternoon. There are perfectly adequate procedures for dealing with the situation and even if you felt you wouldn't get a fair hearing, you could have explained what it was about to the first person you spoke to here and we wouldn't have lost two valuable days before following it up. I can only hope nothing has deteriorated meanwhile.

'There's nothing wrong with ambition, DC Weston, but I don't like prima donnas. You have a lot to learn about judgement and professionalism. Now, perhaps you could give DS Macdonald the details on your way out.'

Red-faced and utterly crushed, Weston muttered something and went to the door that Macdonald was holding open for her. Just as she reached it, Fleming said in a much kinder voice, 'I do admire your determination, though. If you take a lesson from this you could be a useful detective and I'd consider your request. Not just yet, though.'

A little comforted, Weston thanked her. She even heard, before the door shut, the short man saying exultantly, 'If that's right, I reckon we've got her!'

CHAPTER SEVENTEEN

'With all that, I forgot to ask you if you'd managed to speak to Mike Wallace,' Fleming said as she and MacNee set off once again on the road to Ballinbreck.

She had decided to go herself to check on DC Weston's evidence, though this was an indulgence when she had so much to do and Macdonald and Campbell were perfectly competent to check and report. But the Connell Kane case had been so much on her mind that she wanted to see her theory justified for herself – supposing DC Weston was right.

'He's a good lad, Mike,' MacNee said. 'Came up with the goods immediately. There was never evidence to pass up the line but there'd been rumours about Will Stewart not maybe being just what you'd call pernickety when it came to the rules about confiscated drugs.'

'Wouldn't be unique in that,' Fleming said dryly.

'Right enough. But there was a story too that he wasn't as keen as he might have been about following up where they came from either, so when him being a wee pal of Kane's came out and he resigned, no one was exactly begging him to stay.'

'Fits with what we know already.' Fleming said. 'He told us quite openly about turning a blind eye to Kane's activities. And he only flew in from Canada last Friday afternoon – Ewan checked that out. So really, it leaves us with Skye. And she's not about to give us any help.'

'Aye, you could say.'

'Macdonald will let us know about the finger-print evidence from the car once Len Harris deigns to respond. That would be the smoking gun.'

'He'll drag his feet.' MacNee was gloomy.

They drove on in silence. The rain had come on; the sky overhead was pewter-grey and Flem-ing switched the wipers to their fast setting. She wasn't happy, and not only about Skye's silence. This just wasn't fitting, somehow.

'I'll tell you what's bothering me,' she said at last.

MacNee interrupted. 'You needn't. It's bother-ing me too. Doesn't smell right.'

'Supposing Weston is right, we can place her near the scene of the crime at the time it was committed. We know she hasn't an alibi. To be honest, I'd be surprised if her fingerprints aren't in the car. But look at the size of her, Tam! She's tiny. Kane was, what – certainly above average height and quite solid with it, as I recall the report. Yet she comes out of a struggle with him all right, while he's dead?'

'She used a cosh,' MacNee pointed out. 'But what I'm asking myself is: who's more likely to have a cosh, someone who's in the drugs' under-world or a wee lassie like her?'

'Self-defence, you reckon? Then why not arrive on Eleanor Margrave's doorstep asking her to ring the police rather than pushing the car into the water to cover up the evidence? And she'd be able to move a car? I have my doubts.'

'Depend on the angle, I suppose. Downhill into the river, why not? Or she could rev up, get it going then bail out at the last minute.'

'But the other thing is Eleanor Margrave. Look, let's assume for a moment that she's got some obscure motive for killing her. But why would she choose to strangle someone when she had a cosh, especially being as slight as she is?'

'Right enough. And they said the body looked to have been half-dragged, half-carried – how could a wee smout like her carry the woman anyway?'

'And the attack on Louise too – she said she'd struggled but couldn't fight back. As you said, doesn't smell right. But if the car went in where Weston says it did, and her fingerprints are there, we'll have to charge her for Kane's murder at least, whatever misgivings we might have – you know that as well as I do. It's the fiscal's decision and he isn't going to listen to theoretical qualms.'

It was just before they arrived at the site that Macdonald's call came through on the speaker. He sounded jubilant.

'Prints match,' he said. 'Skye Falconer was in that car all right.'

Fleming should have been pleased. 'Good work,' she said, trying to make her voice enthusiastic. 'How did you get Harris to provide them so quickly?'

'Told him you knew about the report of the car tracks but you wouldn't be making an official complaint if we got this stuff quickly. Oh, and that if he victimised DC Weston you'd do it anyway.'

Fleming smiled. 'Taking my name in vain? OK,

thanks, Andy. We must be getting close to the site now.'

She was driving slowly, scanning the verge. And there it was: the broken branches, the double wheel track in the soft verge still clearly visible, just a little softened by rain, going down – yes, down, on to the muddy shore. On the night of the storm, that would have been a roaring tide.

She and MacNee got out to study it, then looked at each other, Fleming making a rueful face. 'They'll be able to match the tyre tracks, no problem. The report said there was a transverse cut on one of them – can't remember which...'

MacNee pointed. 'There.'

The small irregularity on the back left tyre was faint but definite. 'Oh,' Fleming said, her voice flat. 'That's it, then.'

She took out her mobile to call Inspector Wallace. 'Mike? We need someone along here ASAP, with scene-of-crime stuff. And I'll need a patrol car. If we can find her we're going to be arresting Skye Falconer.'

The early promise of the day hadn't been fulfilled and when the rain came on Jen Wilson had retreated inside. She lit the fire in the little sitting room and picked up a thriller, hoping that fictional suspense might blot out her thoughts of the real drama that kept crashing over her like waves in a stormy sea. It wasn't entirely successful; the room was cosy and she was tired after last night. Before long she drifted into a light doze.

She started awake at the sound of the front door opening, and then heard Skye's voice call-

281

ing, 'Jen? Are you there?'

She only realised just how unwelcome that was when she found she'd actually been *hoping* Skye was locked up – how shaming that she could think that about a friend! Trying to sound upbeat she called, 'In here.'

Skye was looking worse than ever, hollow-eyed and pale. But all she said was, 'I could murder a cup of tea. Want one?' She tried to smile.

Jen didn't. 'What happened, Skye?'

'Oh, they let me go. Can't think what that was all about.'

'Sit down.' Jen's voice was grim. As her friend complied, sinking into a chair as though she were afraid her legs wouldn't hold her up much longer, she went on, 'Don't lie to me, please. I need to know what's going on. You've involved me in it already, making me mislead the police.'

Skye's head had been bowed. Now she looked up. 'Jen, you were in it anyway.'

Jen's stomach lurched. 'I wasn't!' she protested. 'You can't say that! I have no idea what's been going on and being used makes me very angry. You have to be straight with me if you're to go on staying here, and if I'm not to tell the police next time they question me – and I've no doubt they will – that you came here long before you said you did.'

Skye began to cry quietly. 'You ... you don't understand–'

'I know I don't, Skye! That's what I've just said. You and Will strung me along before and I'm not prepared to put up with it any longer.'

'I'd tell you if I could, truly I would, but I can't.

Jen, you're my best friend. There's no one else.'

Still feeling bitter at the accusation of involvement, Jen said coldly, 'I may be your best friend. I don't really think you're mine any more. Anyway, what about Will? What's the position there?'

'I – I don't know...'

Jen got up. 'If that's the way you want it, fine. But I'm going to have to ask you to go. Apart from anything else, I'm a teacher. It won't do me any good to have everyone talking about me being linked to a murder.'

'Oh Jen!' She gave a wail of despair. '"What will the neighbours say?" Once you'd have laughed at the very idea of caring.'

'Oh yes, once.' Jen gave a mirthless smile. 'That was before Julia died and I thought Connell had killed himself. After that everything seemed very, very different to me and I think you might ask yourself why. I'll lend you money to get somewhere else to stay, if you need it.'

Skye dragged herself to her feet and trailed out of the room with one last, beseeching glance at her implacable friend.

Jen stood by the fireplace, her arms folded across in what was almost a hug, as if it might give her comfort. As she stared blankly out of the window her own eyes filled with tears, so that it took her a moment to register that a car had pulled up outside her house and DI Fleming and DS MacNee were getting out. Then she saw the police car pulling in behind them.

Fleming sensed that there was an atmosphere from the moment they stepped into the house. Jen

Wilson greeted their request to see Ms Falconer with nothing more than a nod, then opened the door on the left of the hall, gesturing them into a sitting room where a fire was burning, and called up the stairs, 'Skye! It's the police to speak to you.' She went through to the back of the house.

'Do I maybe jalouse they're not such great pals any more?' MacNee said.

'You certainly might guess it would put any friendship under a strain if the pal kept being arrested.' She heard slow footsteps coming downstairs and turned to face the door.

Skye came in with her head held high and Fleming could see that the muscles of her jaw were clenched. 'Yes? What now?'

More to please Tam who had a touching belief in her powers of persuasion than because she thought it would do any good, she said gently, 'Skye, you really need to talk to us.'

'I did. This morning. I said "No comment" and that's all I'm going to say now.'

'I'm sure that's what your lawyer would tell you to do, but even so I don't think it will be in your best interests. Let me explain. Why don't we sit down?'

Skye shrugged and sat on the sofa. Fleming took the chair nearest her and leant forward. 'You're in serious trouble, Skye. We've recorded your fingerprints in the car where Connell Kane's body was found.'

A quiver of shock went over Skye's face but she said nothing, and Fleming went on, 'And we can place you in Eleanor Margrave's house, just a short distance away from where the car went in to the water on the night we believe he died. It's enough for us to charge you with killing Connell Kane. I'm going to be open with you: I have doubts about your guilt. I haven't evidence to back them up, though, so I'm obliged to proceed on the evidence we do have.

'But I think there's a lot more to it than that. Talk to me, Skye. If you didn't kill Connell, tell me what happened. I believe in the principle that you're innocent till proved guilty. Oh, don't get me wrong – I can't give you any guarantees, but if you can give me something to back up the doubts I have already, I can promise that I'll do my best to make sure the truth comes out.'

She had made her voice as persuasive as she could but for all the reaction she got Skye's face could have been carved out of marble. 'Skye?' she prompted.

'No comment.'

MacNee gave an impatient, 'Tchah!' and looked meaningfully at Fleming. She sighed, and got up. 'I'm sorry about that. Very sorry.'

MacNee was already out of the door and beckoning to the officers in the car. Skye got up and walked after him, like a French aristocrat heading for the tumbrel.

Fleming stood warming her hands by the fire, her face sombre as she heard Skye being cautioned and charged, then went to find Jen Wilson. There would need to be an interview in depth later, but she couldn't afford the time now – there was too much to do back at the station, not least bringing the super and the procurator fiscal up to speed with developments.

She did, however, want to test Skye's claim that she had only arrived in Ballinbreck ten days before, and when she stepped into the hall Jen was standing at the open kitchen door watching Skye being taken away. Her eyes were narrowed and there was an expression of such venom on her face that Fleming was taken aback.

'Ms Wilson, could I have just a minute?' she said. 'Someone will be round later to take a further statement from you, but could I just briefly check – you confirmed yesterday that Ms Falconer had only been staying with you for about ten days. Is that right?'

'Oh no,' Jen said, her tone almost gleeful. 'I'm sorry I misled you last time but I was bounced into it. She lied about that, like she's lied about a lot of things. She came here the day after the one your officers asked me about – April 14th, wasn't it? And she had a bruise on her face that looked as if she might have been in a fight.'

'Where have you been?' Try as she might, Kendra Stewart couldn't stop herself from sounding accusatory.

Will, who had just come into their private sitting room, was looking tired and drained and he didn't take it well. 'Whoa, Kendra!' he said. 'That sounded almost like you thought you had a right to know. Back off!'

Kendra gave a little, false laugh. 'Oh, of course I didn't mean that, silly! It's just that the police were asking and I didn't know what to tell them.'

'The truth is usually safest.'

'Oh, I know. It's always so tiresome to have to

remember what you said if it wasn't true. But the trouble is – well, we didn't really exactly tell the truth last time, did we?'

'And what, *exactly,* do you mean by that?'

She didn't like the way he was looking at her. 'Well,' she said again, 'you know how we said we could all vouch for each other, all that afternoon when Eleanor Margrave died? But we couldn't, really, could we?'

Will went very still. 'What have you done?'

'Nothing!' she protested. 'Just ... when the police asked me if I could be absolutely sure that you hadn't popped out for a bit – to see your little friend Skye, maybe...' She invested the phrase with malevolence, glaring at him.

'Get on with it.'

She bridled. 'No need to be rude. You said yourself it was better to tell them the truth.'

'And?'

His eyes were glittering in a way that frightened her, but Logie was just through the wall and she would scream if he touched her. 'I didn't say you'd gone out or anything. I just said I was in the kitchen with Logie a lot of the time and I didn't know.'

'Oh God!' he said. 'You stupid, stupid little bitch! They arrested Skye this morning but of course they'd no evidence so they had to let her go. They're flailing, and you know what that means? They're going to cast around for someone else to arrest. We're all suspects and you don't seem to realise that if I don't have an alibi, then neither do you.'

'That's just silly,' she protested, though her

287

heart was beating faster. 'Anyway, you know I couldn't have gone out. A lot of the time I was with Logie.'

He smiled unpleasantly. 'A lot, perhaps. But there was quite a time when you weren't.'

'But I was in the bar all the time you were upstairs in the restaurant!'

'And I would know that – how?'

'Because – because if you came down and I wasn't here or in the kitchen you'd wonder where I was. And you didn't.'

'Didn't I? I did, actually, to collect some cutlery, and you weren't there.'

'I was, I was – or perhaps I was in the loo. It would only have been for a few minutes, that's all.'

'So you say. But if the police ask me, I'll have to say that I'm afraid I can't vouch for you either.'

She was shaking as he left the room, not only with anger. He couldn't do that, he couldn't! Her only satisfaction was that Skye was in big trouble, obviously, and it served her right.

Charles Lindsay had, as usual, retreated to his study, the only old-fashioned room in the house, with leather chairs and bookshelves its most striking features. When his wife came to find him, he looked up from the book he was reading.

'Did the police get hold of you? They came here looking for you and Randall.'

'Did they?' Philippa sounded weary. 'No, I've only just got back. Have you heard the news? They've arrested Skye Falconer.'

He looked up in genuine dismay. 'Oh no! They

288

did ask me about her but they didn't give me any idea that they were going to do that.'

'They were talking to you?'

Charles shifted in his seat. 'Just a short chat.'

'And what did you say, in this "short chat"?'

'Nothing much. Probably nothing they didn't know already.'

She sat down. 'Could you be a bit more specific?'

Irritated, he said, 'Since you ask, I told them it was a bloody silly idea of yours to have the party in the first place.'

'I daresay I might even agree with you about that. What else?'

He could tell her what he'd told them about her obsession with Will Stewart – well, he could if he wanted a full-scale row. 'Don't think there was much else, really. I couldn't tell them anything about last night, obviously.'

'Well, all I can tell them is that Randall and Will set about each other – Randall was totally out of his skull and I was afraid someone would call the police there and then. So humiliating!'

Charles hated being told about problems. 'Oh you know, young men,' he said vaguely. He hesitated before adding, with some reluctance, 'Is there anything else about last night that I absolutely need to know?'

'Just that it's over, thank God,' Philippa said. 'We need to have a talk about Randall, sometime, though.'

'Sometime,' Charles agreed. 'Where is he, anyway?'

'No idea. Drunk in a pub somewhere, I daresay. Seems to be all he's good for, these days.' She didn't seem to want to discuss it further.

'Where were you today, anyway?' he said idly.

'Oh, there were still a few people to see after last night. That's it pretty much wrapped up now.'

She was, he noticed, looking very tired and she'd been subdued in the morning too. He suspected that the rapturous reunion with Will Stewart that she'd spent so much time and energy in engineering hadn't quite worked out as she had hoped. He could almost bring himself to feel sorry for her – almost, but not quite.

Fleming had been foolish enough to mention some of her reservations about Skye Falconer's guilt to Detective Superintendent Christine Rowley and was subjected to a tirade.

Rowley's voice, shrill at the best of times, had gone up a couple of octaves when Fleming had talked about logistical problems.

'We've got this cleared up in nine days – less, in the case of Eleanor Margrave – when the Dumfries division has spent weeks going round in circles, and your clever idea is to drag your feet until some stupid little details have been ironed out! It's a triumph for me, for us, and I'm not going to let you spoil it. We have all the evidence we need–'

'Not in the Margrave case,' Fleming said unwisely. 'We haven't been able to charge her.'

'And whose fault is that? I'm expecting you to concentrate on nailing that one too, Marjory, instead of wasting time trying to undermine the solid case we do have.'

'There is the question of motivation–'

Rowley's eyes bulged with temper. 'Not our problem. Once the case preparation starts the procurator fiscal will be able to come up with something, I have no doubt.'

Gloomily, Fleming had to accept that she was right there. Sometimes she felt that like most lawyers the fiscal saw the process as something of a game with esoteric rules and winners and losers and he was always quite clear which he wanted to be.

She got out of Rowley's office as soon as she could. She went down to see how MacNee was getting on with Skye and her brief, but the situation was unchanged: she had said, 'No comment', and nothing else. After ten minutes she terminated the interview.

There wasn't much more that she could do tonight and she tied up a few loose ends, then headed home. It was just after six, too late to say goodbye to Cat and her guest, who had been planning to leave about four. She wasn't sorry to have an excuse for avoiding the warm farewells and pressing invitations to return that she might have been obliged to offer Nick.

Not having to rush back would give her time to pop in to see her mother too – always supposing she was in. She was certainly frailer than she had been but she still kept busy and drove her little car, with her doctor's blessing.

The front door wasn't locked, though, and there was a warm smell of baking when she opened it. Janet was taking a perfectly risen sponge out of the oven when Marjory went into the kitchen, calling, 'That smells wonderful!'

'Och, dearie, is that you?' Janet set the sponge down as her daughter bent to kiss her. 'You weren't needing to be coming to see me today. I've been hearing the news – you'll be run off your feet.'

'Difficult day,' Marjory said briefly. 'Anyway, I didn't think I had to. I wanted to. Something I needed to ask you.'

Janet's face brightened and Marjory felt a pang; her mother so loved to be needed – didn't everyone? And at her age, all too often you had to accept graciously that not only weren't you needed, you needed other people. Not easy.

'I'll just put the kettle on,' Janet said. 'I can't give you the sponge – it's for the Guild tomorrow night – but you'll find something if you look in the tins there.'

'Oh good. I missed lunch.' Janet tut-tutted as Marjory went scavenging. 'Mum, I wanted to ask you what you thought about Cat's Nick.'

Her mother didn't say anything for a moment, swilling water round the teapot to warm it and emptying it into the sink. When she turned round her gentle face was uncharacteristically stern but she was, as always, reluctant to say a bad word about anyone.

'I'm sure he's a very clever young man.'

Marjory was unburdened by such scruples. 'Oh yes, clever and arrogant and nasty. He spends his time making a fool of Bill and Bill just doesn't see it.'

Janet sighed. 'Bill wouldn't, bless him. He's too decent a man to understand that sort of thing.'

Marjory was well aware that her mother

believed her son-in-law to be little less than a saint, not least because of what he had to put up with from her only daughter. 'But that's what's so irritating,' she cried. 'Maybe if he made it clear to Cat that he didn't like Nick, she'd realise what he is.'

Her mother didn't say anything, just put down a mug of tea in front of her with a pitying smile.

'Oh, I know! We should have called her Mary – Cat's the most contrary person I've ever met. And before you say that you should have called me Mary too, I just want to say that I know how difficult I was. I struck it lucky with Bill but it could all have gone horribly wrong. I don't want that to happen to Cat.'

'We all want to protect our bairns – it's human nature. When I see you looking worn out and worried, I wish I could still just kiss it better and give you a sweetie like I used to. I can't, though, and you can't for Cat either.'

Marjory's eyes prickled. 'I know.'

'Of course you do. But our Cat's not daft. I've no doubt that like her mother she'll put a few through her hands before she finds the right one.'

She directed a meaningful look at her daughter and Marjory felt a positively teenage blush rise to her cheeks as Janet went on, 'And do you not think she was smart enough to notice what the lad was doing? I'll be quite surprised if we see him again.'

Marjory stared at her. 'Do you think so?'

'You wait and see. And if I were you, I'd not say a word against him.'

'You're right, of course.' Marjory took out her

mobile. 'I tell you what – I'll just send her a text saying I was sorry not to see them to say goodbye and I'll be looking forward to seeing Nick again. I won't add, "and maybe next time you'll realise what an unpleasant little creep he is."'

Smiling, her mother shook her head at her as Marjory texted. 'I seem to have a gey manipulative daughter.'

'And I can't think who I took it from,' Marjory said dryly.

CHAPTER EIGHTEEN

Louise Hepburn woke feeling confused, uncertain for a moment where she was, even. When she got back to her flat she had made herself some coffee and sat down on the sofa to drink it; it was there now on the coffee table, stone cold, and she straightened up painfully, rubbing at the crick in her neck.

She looked at her watch: nearly six o'clock. She must have crashed out for almost five hours, for heaven's sake, but it hadn't refreshed her; in fact, she felt worse than she had in the morning and her throat was dry and aching.

Andy's mum had popped a packet of paracetamol into her bag and she rooted for it now and went into the kitchen for water. She really, really wished that she hadn't thrown away the last of her Gitanes – but it wouldn't have done her throat any good, anyway. More coffee? Somehow she didn't want that either.

She ran a bath instead. Her back muscles felt stiff and strained and she tipped in a handful of Radox. She submerged, then lay back with her head on the bath pillow. It would be a good place to sort out the ideas that were buzzing in her head.

She was trying not to stress about her personal safety. The attack on her had been an attempt to stop her reporting something she had learnt – she only wished she knew what the 'something' had been – and now she had done that the threat would be removed. The only other worry was that her assailant might be afraid that she could make an identification – but then again, she told herself, when there was no immediate police investigation whoever did it would realise that she hadn't. At least, she hoped so.

It was intensely frustrating that she didn't know what had been going on at headquarters today. Probably Skye Falconer was under arrest for Eleanor Margrave's murder, but that wasn't really what that Louise had most on her mind. She didn't believe that it was Skye who'd tried to strangle her last night; the way she had resisted, she'd have had someone as slight as that off their feet.

So if not her, who? The why could come later, but she was highly trained in observation – surely she must have noticed something that would give her a clue.

Perhaps that was the trouble. She'd noticed so much that she couldn't separate the wheat from the chaff – the report she'd written this morning ran to several pages. So, ignore the detail. What, in terms of gut reaction, had seemed most significant?

There was no doubt about that. The fist fight had been a bit of drama but it was the meeting between Skye and Will Stewart that sprang immediately to mind. Why should it have seemed so important?

This was a reunion. There were always swirling undercurrents when the past intruded on the present and she'd watched all the Cyrenaics picking up their friendships again, with different emotions. Randall had seemed both excited and surprised to see Skye after such a long time, Kendra had been jealous, Jen had been annoyed at being ignored, Logie had been – well, indifferent.

Will had been – the word 'guarded' came into her head. He was throttling back his instinctive reaction. And what had that been? Skye's reaction – Louise closed her eyes, trying to picture it again – looked almost like relief. She had gone to him as if she were coming home.

Had he, like Randall, been surprised when she appeared? She didn't really know – and why would it matter that a police officer had seen their meeting? Given what had emerged at Julia Margrave's inquest, it was hardly a secret that they'd had an intimate relationship. Perhaps she was placing too much emphasis on Skye's intensity – it might be that she was just by nature a drama queen.

She sighed and ran in a little more hot water. The fight, then – what about that?

Straightforward enough – Randall was a prat, behaving prattishly. He obviously really fancied

296

Skye and refused to accept that she just wasn't into him. It was impossible to take Randall seriously.

That left the conversation between Will and Philippa Randall, before Louise's cover had been blown. She went through it all in her mind but she couldn't–

The entryphone buzzed. Swearing, Louise got out of the bath and pulled on her heavy bathrobe, remembering that Fleming had said Andy Macdonald would bring her up to speed with events.

'Louise?' his voice said. 'Is it all right to come up?'

She could hardly turn him away. 'Sure,' she said, and buzzed the latch release.

When he saw her, he looked embarrassed. 'Sorry – have I dragged you out of your bath?'

Putting her hand self-consciously to her hair, which was standing out like a bush round her head, she said, 'Oh, it's all right. Thanks for coming. I've been dying to know what's going on.'

'Oh, big stuff,' he said, following her in. 'How are you feeling, though?'

'Fine. Look, there are beers in the fridge – help yourself. Just let me get dressed.'

She fled to her bedroom to throw on jeans and a sweater, then went to the mirror with her hairbrush. After a couple of attempts she decided it was a lost cause, slapped on some lippy and went back. Something major had obviously happened and she couldn't wait to hear what it was, though she felt a jealous twinge that she hadn't been in on the action.

Andy, ensconced in the little sitting room, brought her up to date. 'But she's saying nothing this time either,' he finished. 'So that's where we are – looks as if we've got our man, or woman, rather.

'If she hasn't said anything by tomorrow morning, the boss will apply for an extension to hold her into Tuesday before she has to charge her. Maybe by the time Skye's been questioned half a dozen times she'll think of something to say apart from "no comment".'

Louise frowned. 'Do they really think that she did all that by herself? I just can't buy her attacking me – I'd have had her off her feet, no bother.'

'Yeah, I take the point. Don't think Big Marge is very happy with it either. But she was in the car with Connell Kane so...' He shrugged.

'Will has to have been in this with her.' Louise was very definite.

'He wasn't even in Britain at that time. Ewan checked. I reckon someone was, though – Randall?'

'Can't see it.'

'Who else, then?'

'I keep wondering what Will and Philippa Stewart were discussing–'

'Ah, I can help you there. I read through your transcript, and it all fits with what her husband told us this morning. She was crazy about him, apparently – set up this whole party thing to try to lure him back. They talked about the police investigation – well, I guess everyone was doing that on Saturday night – and it sounds as if she was trying to make an assignation and he was a bit reluctant.'

Louise gaped at him. 'You mean all this – two murders – was because a middle-aged woman was lovelorn? You're kidding.'

'Scouts' honour. That's life, isn't it – unintended consequences.'

'Certainly explains most of what comes our way.' Suddenly she gave an enormous yawn. 'Sorry – can't think why I did that. I slept all afternoon.'

Andy got up. 'Time I was off, anyway. Are you fit for tomorrow?'

She was surprised. 'Oh, are we still on to go to Edinburgh? Is there not backup we should be doing here?'

'The other lads and the uniforms are on to that. Big Marge still wants to see what we can dig up about the whole banking background.'

Louise wrinkled her nose. 'Waste of time. I'd far rather be here, where it's all happening. Randall's just a klutz – and why would he want to kill either Eleanor Margrave or Connell Kane?'

'Don't know why Skye Falconer would either,' Andy pointed out.

'I know, but...' Louise was slipping into contrary mode but she checked herself; how could she have a barney with him when he'd saved her life yesterday? It was going to cramp her style something rotten, she reflected as she showed him out.

The mood in the morning meeting had been buoyant and while DI Fleming didn't want to dampen their enthusiasm, she warned them not to think the job was done.

'I'm not optimistic that we'll get anything out of Skye Falconer but we have an extension and we'll be arranging sessions during the day when we can establish whether there's any point in my questioning her again, but anyway I'll be planning to charge her tomorrow.

'We're still at the stage where the defence can drive a coach and horses through our case, though. We've no chance of charging her with Mrs Margrave's murder unless we can place her in the area at the relevant time, so I want the neighbours near Sea House questioned and near Jen Wilson's cottage too – did they see her around, did they see the car going out? You know the sort of thing.

'I want all the main people in the frame interviewed again. Neighbours near them too – did they see them coming and going, was there anything they noticed. Try to pick up any rumours – you'll get help there from the Kirkcudbright lads. Right – any questions?'

A young DC asked, 'Do we think someone else was involved? I saw her yesterday and she looked kind of wee to go around murdering folk.'

It got a laugh and Fleming smiled. 'Open mind, I think. Anything else?'

There were one or two minor queries but they were easily dealt with and she was finished by half past eight.

MacNee was waiting for her as she went out and she jerked her head. 'Come on. I'm ducking out before the super calls me in to discuss the media coverage. Her picture was on the front page of the *Herald.*'

He fell into step beside her. 'You won't get me stopping you. Where are we going?'

'I want to see how the search is progressing at Jen Wilson's. It's kind of a delicate one, that, and I need to make sure they're making a distinction between what's Skye's stuff and what's Jen's or we'll be landed with a complaint – the sheriff was very particular about that when the warrant was sworn out.

'And I really want to see the woman herself. She may have gone to the school but if she has they'll have to do without her for a bit. I want an in-depth conversation with that young woman. I have a feeling that she could be key to the whole thing. She's hard to read, with that quiet manner.'

'Never trust those ones – *"grave, tideless-blooded, calm and cool"*,' MacNee said. 'And school-teachers – I've never been overfond of them either, except my old English teacher – I'd never have heard of Rabbie Burns if it wasn't for him.'

'I wondered whose fault it was,' Fleming said as they left the building and walked to her car. 'That's good – I was afraid I might get stopped on the way out. Now, we've got time to plan what we need to ask her. She and Skye are obviously good mates – or at least were. From the way she was speaking yesterday she's gone off her a bit.'

'You would, wouldn't you? If one of my pals was arrested for murder it would make me just a wee bit cagey, to say the least.'

'The priority for me is how much she knew about Skye in the last two years – where she was, who she was in contact with – not her father, certainly.'

301

'The party,' MacNee said. 'I want her to talk us through that, see how it squares with Louise's report. Here – I wonder how the pair of them are getting on? Squabbling all the way to Edinburgh?'

Fleming grinned. 'Could be. On the other hand, maybe Louise will be inhibited by gratitude.'

MacNee snorted. 'Won't last long, if she is. She's given up smoking so she'll be tetchy anyway. Want to have a sweepstake? Twenty miles, that's my bet.'

'Mmm. A bit more than that, I reckon. But we're not likely to find out.'

Presented with the search warrant, Jen Wilson felt sick. The calm, polite officers were behaving as if this was merest routine, which it presumably was for them, but to her it felt an intolerable intrusion, a sort of rape of her privacy.

'But I haven't anything to do with this,' she protested.

'Of course not, miss,' one said reassuringly. 'If you can identify your computer, your phone and your personal papers we can mark them to make sure no one accesses them.'

'But what about my bedroom? Skye was never in there – her things are all in the spare room.'

'I'm afraid you don't know that, miss.' He was very firm. 'She could have been anywhere while you were out. We have instructions to be very respectful of your property, though.'

'So I should hope,' she snarled, rudely. It wasn't his fault, but she just felt so helpless, so angry about the unfairness of it all. And she knew whose fault it really was.

She was due at school. They assured her that she wasn't needed at the cottage and she went, but not directly to her classroom. Wisdom dictated that she should tell the head teacher what was happening rather than leaving her to get an even more lurid version on the grapevine that was probably spreading its tendrils even now.

Mrs Pearson was horrified. 'I'm aghast!' she said. 'You teach small children – how could you get mixed up in something like this?'

'I'm not. One of my friends is, somehow, but it's absolutely nothing to do with me. I don't know anything about it.'

Mrs Pearson gave her a sharp look. 'The woman who has been arrested – was she one of the group we all heard about two years ago?'

Jen could feel her cheeks turning red. 'Yes.'

'I see.' Mrs Pearson fiddled with a pen on her desk. 'I shall have to take advice about this, Jen. On the face of it, I don't think it constitutes gross misconduct but for the moment, at least, it wouldn't be acceptable to have you in the class-room – we will have to arrange for a supply teacher. I shall, of course, keep you fully informed of whatever discussions I have.'

Her cheeks still flaming, Jen walked back home. Her anger against Skye was building; she owed her nothing, nothing. She wasn't going to cover for her any longer.

But as she got near to it she saw a car pull in and DI Fleming and DS MacNee get out and go into the house. She stopped.

Yes, she was angry with Skye, but she would need to keep her wits about her; she mustn't get drawn into this any deeper. The police could turn anything to suit their theories.

Jen took a deep breath, then walked on to face her inquisitors.

There was a scarf round DC Hepburn's neck but as she got into the car it slipped. The line of bruising had deepened to livid blacks and purples and DS Macdonald, reminded of what she had been through, decided he must tiptoe round any subject that seemed likely to be provocative. She didn't look strong enough for the usual no-holds-barred approach.

It certainly helped that she wasn't stinking of smoke. 'Have you given up, then?' he said and saw Hepburn give him a sharp look.

'Yes,' she said. 'You–'

She stopped, but from the look on her face he could complete the sentence 'want to make something of it?'

She was clearly tiptoeing too. It felt unnatural but perhaps it was better for them to be biting off their words rather than each other's heads.

To move away from the subject he said, 'What do we need to find out about Randall? It's probably too much to hope for that there would be someone that knew something about the drugs business, but that's obviously where the whole thing started.'

'I expect it is. But a) I don't think a bank employee is going to admit to knowing anything about it, even if they do, and b) I don't think that's got anything to do with it except tangentially. I can't imagine Randall going round with a cosh in his pocket. Where would he get it from? Wander into a low life pub in Glasgow and say, "Any of you dudes got a cosh you could flog me?"'

Why did she always have to be so bloody aggressive? 'I'm not suggesting that. I just think it won't do any harm to try to learn a bit more about him, that's all. After all, you were attacked and he was the one making threats before you went.'

Hepburn snorted. *'Post hoc ergo propter hoc.'*

He knew what that meant now – she'd used it before – but he hated it when she flaunted her superior education. 'Why can't you just say that I'm making an assumption that because something happened after something else, it happened because of it?' he said, then could have kicked himself because he'd left himself open to her riposte.

'Not really snappy, though, is it? Why shouldn't I use a nice neat phrase just because it's in Latin? You have some sort of problem with that?'

Macdonald gritted his teeth. 'Say whatever you like. Anyway, whether you want to be here or not we have a job to do. What do we need to ask?'

'The sort of smoothie they'll send along to talk to us will be programmed not to tell us anything anyway.'

He'd had enough. 'Fine. No point in talking about it, then.'

With Ewan as his partner, he was used to silence in the car, but sometimes he'd thought lively conversation would pass the time a bit more quickly. 'Come back, Ewan, all is forgiven,' he thought. And they were barely twenty miles into their journey.

What struck Fleming most about Jen Wilson, now she was studying her, was that she was very controlled. Probably you had to be when you spent your life dealing with young children; the level of patience teachers had to show day in day out would have driven her screaming up the wall.

She must have been both irritated and upset about her home being searched, but despite the noise of heavy footsteps on the stairs and people calling to each other, she showed no sign of that, sitting waiting for their questions with her hands folded in her lap.

They'd decide MacNee should start off, leaving Fleming to observe. The answers were coming readily enough: Jen had checked the date she'd been hesitant about yesterday – April 15th – and described clearly Skye Falconer's arrival on her doorstep.

'She was looking terrible. She had a great bruise on one side of her face, a bit grazed–'

'Like someone had punched her, maybe?' MacNee offered.

She considered that. 'It could be, I suppose, or she might have fallen – she wouldn't tell me. She'd been crying a lot; her eyes were all red and sore and she went on crying for days afterwards. She got better at controlling it, but she didn't stop. I'd hear her in her room at night. But then something happened – I don't know what it was, but she began to cheer up. She'd been refusing even to set foot outside but then suddenly she decided she wanted to go to the party – she wouldn't even consider it before that.'

'And you've no idea why?' MacNee probed, but Jen only shook her head. She confirmed her previous statements when he checked, then he looked towards Fleming.

'Thanks, that's all very helpful,' she said. 'But now I'd just like to take it all back a little further. Were you very surprised when Skye turned up on your doorstep? She'd been missing for a couple of years – you must have been happy to see her.'

Jen was visibly taken aback. 'Well...' she floundered.

Fleming didn't fill the silence. She watched Jen's eyes, flickering up and down as she calculated her response.

'Not really, to be honest. I knew Skye was all right. We were old friends – we kept in touch by email – oh, in a very casual sort of way. Like at Christmas, maybe. Nothing more. We weren't, like, confidantes or anything.'

Why, Fleming wondered, was she so keen to emphasise that? 'But you must have known her parents were worried about her? You didn't tell them?'

'Oh, I know I should have. But when I went round there they were so nasty I decided just to leave them to stew. And I never thought of telling the police – I'm sorry. I expect that was wasting police time. I hope I'm not in trouble.'

She looked at Fleming with a placatory smile.

Fleming ignored it. 'And where was she?'

Jen opened her eyes very wide. '*I* don't know. She never said.'

And that, Fleming thought, was a big, black, thumping lie. She raised her eyebrows. 'Really? And you didn't ask?'

'Oh, I did, once or twice. But she obviously didn't want to tell me, so...' She shrugged.

Trying again to underline how little she knew? She'd got her defence in place now, though, and there was little point in challenging her; shifting the ground might be more useful.

'I want to take you further back now,' Fleming said. 'In fact, right back to the night Julia Margrave died.'

That shocked Jen out of her composure. 'Oh no, please!' she wailed. 'It was such an awful, awful time.'

'Yes it was. Tell me about it.'

Jen drew a deep, shuddering breath. 'We were in the wood, looking at the stars—'

'No, before that. Talk me through, from the start of the evening.'

'We met in The Albatross, as usual – just the pub, not the room upstairs: that was only if we were having, well, a special evening.' She hesitated, but when Fleming didn't press her on that she went on. 'We were all there. Julia and Randall and Connell had come down from Edinburgh and Will from Kirkcudbright, and of course Kendra and Logie were there – Logie was working. And Randall's mother was having a drink at the bar and of course she pounced on Will.'

Jen smiled. 'It was a bit of a joke, you know. She obviously fancied him and kept trying to gatecrash the group – we all used to snigger about it, and Randall would go mental. We were talking about going out to see the stars and she was hinting about going along too until Randall turned on her. I think they'd been rowing earlier and he was in a bad mood. I really thought he was going to hit her – he'd drunk quite a lot already. So then she flounced out in a huff and we all left for the forest. And then ... that was it, really. Julia was–' Jen choked. 'Sorry, sorry.'

'Take your time.'

'Yes.' She licked dry lips. 'She was ... beyond anything. Crazy. Skye was too, well away.'

Her voice had hardened when she said her name.

'And you?'

'I was... Well, I'm not going to try to pretend I didn't join in – you wouldn't believe me if I did. I was coming down off a high and suddenly it all seemed a bit silly. I wanted to go home, and Randall had been banging on about leaving too, so we went together.'

'And was he high too?'

'No. Just drunk. Randall was more that way inclined. Then ... we heard the scream–' She stopped, again visibly distressed.

Fleming was unmoved. 'We know about the rest. Tell me about the relationships.'

'Relationships? Huh! We didn't exactly have *relationships*, except of what you might call a very fluid sort. I reckon Will had a bit of a fling with Philippa, even though he didn't admit to it. Connell was the only one who didn't – it was Julia or no one.' Suddenly she began to cry, bowed over, her hands up to her face.

Ignoring her distress, Fleming persisted. 'And yet it was the drugs he gave her that killed her.'

Jen's head came up sharply and just for a moment Fleming thought she had her breakthrough, but then all she said was, 'I suppose so,' her voice flat.

Time to shift the ground again. 'You said you believed Connell Kane had killed himself, is that right?'

'Yes, oh yes!'

Fleming had no doubt that she was a very calculating woman, but she hadn't worked out that this immediate, convincing response would highlight the more equivocal nature of others she had made.

'At least we got a truthful response to that, Ms Wilson.'

'I don't know what you mean,' Jen protested, but her face turned a dull red.

'So you must have been very surprised when you heard what had happened to him?'

'I was, yes. I was so "surprised" I fainted.' Her tone was hostile.

'Do you have any idea why he should have come back to the area? In the light of what happened to him afterwards it wasn't a very wise decision.'

'No, it wasn't. Perhaps you should be asking Skye about it.' She was on her guard now. 'I understood she was the person being charged with his murder, not me, though it hasn't really felt like that this morning. I've been suspended from school too, just for associating with her. I can promise you that I'll do anything I can to see that she pays for what she's done.'

Again Fleming saw the venomous look on her face and drew her own conclusions. As she and MacNee went back to the car, she said, 'Can we assume that Connell's faithfulness to Julia was a sore point?'

'Oh aye,' MacNee said. 'So if she wouldn't have killed him and she wants him to have justice, why is she lying about not knowing where her one-time pal spent her gap years?'

CHAPTER NINETEEN

Mrs Jennifer Brunton, Head of Human Resources at Rutherford's, wasn't at all what DC Hepburn had expected. In her mind, anyone working in a merchant bank would be slim, sleek and sophisticated, but none of these words applied to Mrs Brunton, who was middle-aged, small and plump with curly grey hair, and her business suit though good quality – Jaeger, probably – wasn't what anyone would describe as a fashion statement.

Her cosy appearance, Hepburn suspected, masked a tough character, though. She was certainly very direct.

'I have two obligations to consider,' she explained. 'One is my duty to see to it that Rutherford's isn't brought into any sort of disrepute. The other is my duty as a citizen to help the police. I'm hoping that you don't plan to put me in a position where the two would conflict. But you look like nice young people – can I hope you're discreet as well?' There was a smile lurking as she looked from one to the other.

Hepburn warmed to her. 'If it's the press you're worried about, we won't be telling them,' she assured her.

Macdonald frowned her down. 'If there is evidence that relates to our enquiry, we couldn't suppress it, but since what we're talking about is very general background I can't see that it would be an issue.'

Hepburn subsided into her chair. Of course, he was quite right. She'd done it again, just what Fleming had warned her against – acted on an emotional response. She bit her lip miserably; things hadn't gone well today. She'd started by planning to change the relationship she had with Andy, but somehow it just hadn't worked.

Brunton looked from one to the other with obvious amusement, but said only, 'I'll help as much as I can. What do you need to know?'

Macdonald said, 'As we explained, we're concerned with Julia Margrave and Randall Lindsay. What can you tell us about them?'

'Oh dear me – Julia!' Brunton shook her head. 'So desperately, desperately sad. She was such a talented young woman, so pretty and charming – and able too, very able. But our young staff work hard and play hard, and with the sort of money we pay them – well, you know the sort of thing that can happen.'

'Indeed.' Macdonald moved on to ask about the drug scene.

Waste of time, Hepburn thought sulkily. What would a nice middle-aged, middle-class lady know about that?

Jennifer Brunton surprised her. She knew a great deal about it, and had Hepburn wanted to go out and score she now knew which two pubs, within a few hundred yards of this West End bank, to go to. Respect!

'Were Julia and Randall in the drug scene to-gether?' Macdonald asked.

Brunton hesitated. 'She was, primarily. I'd been worried about her for some time, though she wasn't falling down on the job or anything. But when you've been in the personnel business as long as I have you get to recognise the signs – too many "colds" in the winter and "hay fever" in the summer.

'Randall, I suspect, just went along with her. She was his mentor, you see – got him the job, basically. I think they were friends at home.'

'I believe he's out of a job now,' Macdonald said. 'Resigned, allegedly.'

'Really? I hadn't heard, but of course I don't have anything to do with staff at the Paris branch. You don't surprise me.'

'Because…?'

'There were question marks over the quality of his work. Julia was his line manager and there were a couple of occasions I'm quite sure she covered up for him. But then she came to me and said there were questions he needed to answer.'

'What sort of questions?'

For the first time, she went vague on them. 'Oh, just general – lateness, carelessness, that sort of thing. In a way, I suppose the whole dreadful business did him a favour.'

'Yes?'

'I need to watch my words here.' Brunton stopped and looked from one to the other, assessing them. Then she said, 'Can this be off the record? I should flatly deny it if you quoted me.'

'Unless you're planning to tell us you've been breaking the law, I think we can agree to that,' Macdonald said, smiling.

She looked shocked. 'Oh, dear me no, Sergeant. If I'd committed a crime I would *never* be stupid enough to confess. This is merely an indiscretion.

'The bank was very unhappy about the publicity when Julia died. They decided that the best thing to do with Randall Lindsay was to shunt him off to Paris rather than having a review of his performance first. If it had come out badly and they'd had to sack him, the press would have been on to it. That's it, really. I think I've told you all I know.'

Hepburn cleared her throat. 'Just one thing. You talked about Randall Lindsay's carelessness. Did that by any chance extend to carelessness about assigning funds to the appropriate accounts?'

Jennifer Brunton gave her a long look. Then she said, 'You might very well think so. I couldn't possibly comment.'

'Heading back now, are we?' MacNee said provocatively as they drove away. 'You said you just wanted to check on operations at the house and speak to Jen Wilson.'

'I know I did. But–' Then she caught sight of MacNee's expression and laughed. 'Yeah, OK, I know I told the lads to follow up on the Cyrenaics but when I'm here anyway...'

MacNee settled back contentedly into his seat. 'Fine. Just watch when you take their nice juicy bone away from them that you don't lose half your fingers.'

314

'I don't suppose they'll be pleased. I'd have been looking forward to getting right in on the action too, when I was a DC. But I don't care – I'm just going to pull rank. Anyway, if there's anything to dig out, we're more likely to get to it than they are.

'I've got my eye on Will Stewart first. I may get a call that I can't ignore from headquarters at any time, so let's go straight to that.'

There was a familiar car in the car park and when they went in they found that two of the DCs were there before them. Fortunately they had started by interviewing Kendra Stewart, and Fleming, drawing them aside, offered them a sop in the form of going on to interview her husband as well.

MacNee saw the disappointment on their faces when she said, 'I'll speak to Will Stewart myself,' but they knew better than to say anything other than, 'Yes, boss.' He'd like to be a fly on the wall when they were back in the car afterwards, though.

They hadn't got anything more out of Kendra, they reported. MacNee glanced at her: she was sitting at the other end of the bar now, *nursing her wrath to keep it warm*,' like Tam o' Shanter's wife. You wouldn't want to be that one's husband: the poor man must be pecked half to death, from the looks of her. He recognised the type – all smiles till something didn't suit her.

When he went across to speak to her she gave him the sort of look that could curdle milk.

'Could we maybe see Mr Will Stewart upstairs in the restaurant if he's in?' he said and she shrugged her shoulders.

'If you like.'

'Could you tell him, maybe?'

Kendra gave a put-upon sigh and got up as MacNee went back to Fleming.

'I was just wanting you to see this,' he said, leading the way upstairs. 'Tells you all you need to know about that lot.'

He enjoyed the expression of amazement on Fleming's face as she took in the velvet drapes, the glittering mirrors and the prints of insectivorous plants on the purple-black walls.

'I don't think my mother would like me being in a place like this,' she said primly, making MacNee laugh. 'You get hardened to all kinds of depravity in our line of work but – I don't know, there just seems to be something particularly sick about this.'

'It stinks,' MacNee said bluntly. 'All the fancy stuff is to show it's a joke for them, all clever and sophisticated, not like it is for the pathetic losers out there in the gutter. Joke was on them in the end, though.'

'They're not the first people to discover that the hard way.'

They heard footsteps on the stairs and Will Stewart appeared. The man who had been so easy, so relaxed and friendly, had changed markedly; his body language as he came in, shoulders braced and chin stuck out, was hostile.

'Do we really have to go all through this over again? It's verging on harassment – my sister-in-law is getting quite upset by it.'

Fleming brushed his objection aside. 'I hardly need to explain to you the demands of a murder investigation. I want to you to focus on relationships this time.'

She got him on the raw. *'Relationships?* What relationships?'

'Oh, yours, Will. They seem to have been – how can I put this? Complex.'

She was, MacNee noticed with interest, going straight for the jugular. She only did that when she reckoned someone was seriously rattled already. He hadn't picked up on that himself – he'd have served up a few easy balls first – but her antennae were better than his and studying the man now he could see that he looked strained and tired.

'Oh, for God's sake!' There were ornate chairs, purple velvet with gold frames, placed round the tables and he flung himself into one; it rocked under the impact. 'Let's just get this over with, if prurience floats your boat. What do you want to know?'

Fleming pulled out another chair to sit next him and moved it rather too close; MacNee did the same on the other side, so that Stewart couldn't put distance between them.

'I'd much rather not go into the sordid details,' she said, 'but you've made that inevitable. Start with your sister-in-law – a bit incestuous, wouldn't you say?'

Stewart choked. 'I do not have an inappropriate relationship with Kendra.'

'Really?' Fleming's raised eyebrows conveyed flat disbelief. 'I have reason to believe that's untrue.'

Stewart had begun shifting in his seat. 'I don't see how you can have,' he said weakly.

317

'Oh I do, believe me. She was possessive at first, then jealous as a cat on Saturday night, I was told.'

Throwing in Hepburn's observations at the party so early in the interview was unexpected and MacNee looked at her sharply, then at Will. It took him a moment to register the hand grenade rolling towards his feet.

'How did you–' he began, then it hit him. 'Oh, your rotten little spy. Of course.'

Fleming raised her brows. 'I'm surprised you would describe an undercover officer as that, but yes. We've had a rigorous debriefing since the party.'

Top marks for that, MacNee thought; Louise will be safer if it gets about that she doesn't have any information she hasn't shared.

Will's eyes narrowed. 'I didn't say that Kendra wasn't jealous. That's her problem. It's not mine.'

'It suggests you may have given her cause.'

He opened his mouth to speak but Fleming didn't give him the chance to argue. 'Let's move on to Skye Falconer.'

MacNee saw Stewart's hands, resting on the arms of the chair, tighten their grip. 'I had a relationship with her, yes. As far as I know there's no law against sex between consenting adults even if it's with someone who's been fitted up for a murder rap.'

'Are you accusing us of corruption now?' Fleming's voice was icy cold.

He put his hands to his head. 'No, no, of course not. But you can't think she could have done that! Look at her, for God's sake – it's bloody well obvious! She's a gentle creature – wouldn't hurt a fly, let alone a man like Connell – and no doubt you're planning to add in Eleanor Margrave. You'll never make it stick. It's – it's crazy!'

'So how do you suggest her fingerprints got into Connell Kane's car?'

He sprang up and walked away from them, obviously unaware that the mirrors gave them a clear view of his face, twisted into a mask of agony. After a moment he turned, the expression gone.

'I can only think she had one of the "relationships" with him that you're so keen on.'

'And with you as well?'

Relentless, she was, MacNee thought admiringly. Stewart was starting to sweat.

'Yes. Like I said, we're casual that way.'

'Her greeting of you was far from casual, I understand.'

Stewart gave a short laugh. 'Skye – well, she likes a bit of theatre. Doesn't mean much.'

'Let's move on to Philippa Lindsay, then, shall we?'

He didn't say anything but his Adam's apple bobbed up and down nervously.

'What were you two talking about?'

'Oh – just chat, you know.'

'What does "chat" mean?'

'If you want me to spell it out, it means that she fancies me and I don't fancy her. Mostly I was trying to brush her off without being rude.'

That squared pretty much with what Hepburn had said. Fleming left it at that and moved on.

'Randall Lindsay – did Skye have one of her "relationships" with him too? Where did he fit into all this?'

Stewart stared at her, then turned his head away. The silence this time went on for an uncomfortable length of time; he was still standing and in the mirror they could both see that something had struck him forcibly. When he turned back to face them, it was to change tack.

'Look, let's put this on a better footing. I was one of you lot and of course I know what you're doing – you're trying to confuse me, break me down for some sort of confession.

'You can weave all sorts of fancy theories around a crime. And yes, I have a problem with women. I'm not by nature faithful but Kendra and Philippa both feel they've got "rights". I don't suppose I'm blameless. But when it comes right down to it, you'd have to prove that I had opportunity and I didn't. I arrived from Canada after Connell died – I can show you the ticket stub, if you haven't checked already–'

'Oh, we checked,' Fleming said.

'Good. That's clear, then. And I was here at The Albatross all the afternoon when Eleanor Margrave died. Oh, I know,' as MacNee opened his mouth to speak, 'Kendra was playing games with the alibi. Yes, there were long spells when we didn't see each other, and she's jealous, like you said, and feeling spiteful, but I was here all right. That's it. OK?'

'Not quite. Where was Skye during the two years when she was away?'

Stewart had been standing, his hands spread wide in an open gesture, urging his case. Now he sagged like a puppet whose strings had been cut,

320

his shoulders slumping. 'I don't know. But I can tell you you've got the wrong person.'

Fleming got up. 'I'm tired of this. I don't believe you don't know. I am inviting you to attend at the Kirkluce headquarters at four o'clock this afternoon for formal questioning. I would stress that this is an invitation you would be very wise to accept.'

She walked off downstairs. MacNee who, unusually, had not spoken once in the whole interview, said, 'Not smart, laddie,' with a certain amount of sympathy as he left.

Back in the car, he said, 'Phew! You gave him laldy! What were you trying to do?'

She looked at him with a quizzical smile. 'Trying to save Skye Falconer – what do you think?'

Will sat down after they had gone, his head in his hands, his mind spinning. He'd hoped there was an easy way out but that last, unpleasant quarter of an hour had shown him that it was firmly closed. It had also started him wondering, joining up loose threads. He knew what he had to do, but it was going to be rough.

The sun was shining when Hepburn and Macdonald came out of the bank and the Georgian elegance of Charlotte Square was showing to its best advantage, but she wasn't really in a mood to appreciate it. As the interview with Mrs Brunton went on, she had felt more and more embarrassed about the way she had rubbished Macdonald's ideas about Randall Lindsay.

Just because the man was a buffoon, it didn't

mean that he wasn't capable of murderous violence. He was certainly strong enough to overpower Connell Kane, to transport Eleanor Margrave to the shore, to pull the noose tight about her own neck from behind. She gulped, and her hand went unconsciously to touch her throat.

He'd even given notice of his intentions but she hadn't believed him, and hadn't believed Andy when he'd warned her. She'd brushed any suspicion about Randall patronisingly aside; she could hear her own voice saying mockingly, 'Any of you dudes got a cosh you could flog me?'

As they walked back to the car, Macdonald said, 'Nice lady.'

'Mmm.'

'Food for thought.'

'Mmm.'

He glanced down at her, eyebrows raised; she knew such reticence was unlike her but she couldn't begin an apology out here in the street. They had found a parking place just across the square, and walked there in silence.

As Macdonald manoeuvred the car out, Hepburn said in a small voice, 'Sorry.'

Macdonald frowned, then his face cleared. 'Ah,' he said. 'I thought for a minute we were going to drive back in silence – though I should be used to it, with Ewan.'

'You were right about Randall. I've been an idiot. It's all there, isn't it, and we're looking at another murder too – the reason behind it all. Julia was going to shop him for theft and he had to stop her.'

'Nothing easier than to murder a drug addict

322

by engineering an overdose, certainly,' Macdonald said grimly.

'And if Connell Kane somehow got suspicious, Randall would have to do away with him as well. But Eleanor Margrave – how did she come into it? And Skye's fingerprints were in Kane's car–' Hepburn stopped.

Macdonald turned his head to look at her. 'Yes?'

'Hang on, let me think about this.' She could sense his impatience as she sat, her brows furrowed in concentration, but he didn't speak.

At last she said, 'I was just running through Randall's interaction with Skye at the party. The way I read it was that he was besotted with her, trapping her in a corner so that she couldn't get away while he was chatting her up. But what if it was all about this – that he was threatening her, perhaps, warning her not to say anything to anyone? It would explain why she was so thankful to escape when Will came back to rescue her, and why Randall was angry enough to provoke a fight.'

Macdonald was impressed. 'And maybe it explains Eleanor Margrave too, if something Skye said that night when she came in from the rain was going to make Eleanor realise that her daughter had been murdered. He left it a long time, though. Why?'

'He didn't know immediately.' Hepburn was getting excited. 'She was lying low at Jen Wilson's – he probably didn't even know she was there, then when he found out he acted immediately.'

They looked at each other. 'We could have this whole thing worked out, right there,' Macdonald said. 'We're a good team, you know that? I can't wait to get back and tell the boss.' He accelerated as he reached the Edinburgh bypass.

'Watch out – you're over the speed limit,' Hepburn pointed out. 'It would take the gilt off the gingerbread if the Lothian lads booked you. Hyacinth would go spare and Big Marge would have your guts for garters.'

Macdonald laughed. They drove on more sedately, and in perfect harmony.

'Ewan!' DI Fleming exclaimed, spotting DC Campbell working at a computer as she and MacNee walked past the CID room. 'I thought you were off today.'

'Was. I'm back now.'

'Are you – are you all right, son?' MacNee asked. 'Don't want to probe, but–' He stopped in confusion. 'I mean...'

'I'm fine.' He pointed to the screen. 'Got something to show you, boss.'

Fleming and MacNee came to look over his shoulder. He pointed to what seemed to be an airline's passenger manifest, detailing a flight from Toronto to London on April 10th.

'Wondered if we were looking in the right place.' Fleming looked where he was pointing and there was Will Stewart's name.

'And this.' He flipped to another screen; the manifest this time was for a flight from Edinburgh to Toronto on April 15th. He pointed.

'Flew back, after Kane's murder, then flew over again,' Fleming said slowly. 'Well, well.'

'There's more.' Campbell went back to the first

screen. 'She's here too.'

MacNee let out a low whistle of amazement. 'She was in Toronto after all – left with Will when he did, can we suppose? Lying bastard – said he didn't know where she was.'

'We can't assume anything now, can we?' Fleming said. 'This turns the whole thing upside down.'

'But she's not going to open up now,' MacNee said. 'Will Stewart, though–'

Fleming had picked up her phone. 'I'm calling Mike Wallace. I want Stewart picked up immediately.'

Macdonald and Hepburn were cock-a-hoop when they came into the CID room. They too were surprised to find Campbell there but their solicitude produced the same laconic response as the senior officers' had.

'Where's Big Marge?' Hepburn asked. 'We think we've pretty much cracked it.'

'So does she,' Campbell said. 'Arresting Will Stewart.'

Macdonald and Hepburn exchanged blank looks. 'Why?' she said.

Campbell demonstrated his discoveries once more.

'What do we make of that?' Macdonald said. 'Are they all in this together, or something?'

'One more thing,' Campbell said. 'I'd an idea, after the boss left.'

He opened another file. 'See this?'

'The exclusivity list!' Macdonald exclaimed. 'Of course, our fingerprints are all on file, for elimination. And they didn't wipe Stewart's when he left. So – don't tell me…?'

'Ucha.' Campbell demonstrated, then opened up a new window on the other half of the screen, clicked a couple of times and there, among the fingerprints taken from Connell Kane's car, was a set that looked to the untrained eye remarkably like Will Stewart's.

Linda Morrison was in a bad mood before she even got back into the car. Martin had said he'd only be a minute fetching it but she'd spent fully ten waiting on the appointed corner of the High Street in Dalbeattie.

'What took you all that time?' she demanded as she got in. 'We were only parked at the far end.'

'You could have walked there, then,' Martin said disagreeably, as he set out on the back road home.

'I would've, only I just wanted to pop into that shop for a wee minute and you were being so ill-natured I thought I'd get on better with you out the way. What was keeping you, anyway?'

'Met Rab Johnston – couldn't just walk past him, could I?'

'You could have said your wife was waiting, couldn't you?'

'How was I to know you were waiting? When you go in a shop you could be half an hour.'

'Not in that shop – there wasn't a thing I wanted to look at.'

'And I was supposed to know that – how? Anyway, why is it all right for you to keep me waiting, but I've to jump to it the minute you crook your pinkie finger?' Martin's face was dark with temper.

'Now you're just being nasty for the sake of it. And you're driving too fast.'

'While I'm behind the wheel of this car, I'll do the driving. You're–'

'Martin!' she screamed. 'Stop!'

They had just rounded a corner and there right in front of them was a man lying in the road. Martin swore, slamming on the brakes and swerving violently. Linda screamed again but there was nothing anyone could do. The car hit the man hard and ran over the body with a couple of sickening bumps before it juddered to a standstill, stewed across the road.

In the terrible silence that followed, the Morrisons sat transfixed. Then Martin said hoarsely, 'Stay where you are,' and got out, his legs shaking so that he could hardly stand.

He bent over the mangled body then turned away and was violently sick.

CHAPTER TWENTY

'So you see,' DS Macdonald said, 'I think we need to consider that Julia Margrave's death could well have been murder, rather than an accidental overdose. Nothing easier than to spike a drink – if she was high anyway she certainly wouldn't notice.'

DI Fleming listened with some fascination as he and Hepburn tumbled over each other in their anxiety to tell her their theory; first one, then the other, but in perfect agreement. At last they were performing as a team, playing to their strengths as she had always wanted them to do: Hepburn sparking off the ideas and Macdonald tidying up the details. It was probably too much to hope that it would last, but it was good while it did.

'But what about our pal Will Stewart now Ewan's got him placed in the car?' MacNee said. 'That was good work, lad.'

Campbell only grunted, but he looked pleased.

There was silence for a moment, then Hepburn said, 'Murder on the Orient Express? They're all in it together?'

'Car would be a bit crowded, would it not?' Macdonald spoke dismissively and Fleming braced herself for an explosion.

But Hepburn said only, 'Take your point.'

'The problem is,' Fleming said, 'that we've got almost too much evidence.'

MacNee nodded. 'Aye, and it's pointing in different directions. So where do we go from here?'

Fleming thought for a moment. 'Stewart's being picked up. We need to get hold of Randall too. Louise, can you liaise with the lads who were doing interviews in Ballinbreck and find out if they've talked to him today? Andy and Ewan, check out any reports that have come in – there should be stuff from the door-to-doors by now and the technical stuff will be trickling in before long. Skye's still steadfastly refusing to talk but I'm going to see that she's brought along and asked at intervals until the extension runs out.' She gave an evil grin. 'Apart from anything else it will annoy the hell out of Damien Thomson if he keeps being dragged in.

'OK, that's it. It's been an interesting day and I daresay it's not over yet.'

When they had gone, she turned to MacNee. 'What's your take on this? I feel I'm going round in circles.'

MacNee shrugged. 'It's a fine wee theory Andy and Louise have come up with – and they're agreeing for once. Wonders will never cease.'

'It's almost too neat, though. We don't know that Julia was murdered–'

'Don't know she wasn't, either.'

'Fair enough. Certainly Randall Lindsay's possible motive for disposing of her is clear enough and if we accept Louise's idea about Skye letting something slip to Eleanor Margrave, and him not finding that out until later, it's a motive for that one too. But Connell Kane, two years after all this happened? That's my sticking point. It's just starting to seem too elaborate. And after all these years with Donald Bailey as super, going on at me about Ockham's Razor–'

'Remind me.'

'Oh, this guy Ockham just said that the simple explanation is likely to be the right one.'

MacNee snorted. 'Let me know when you find it, all right? Here – it's past my lunchtime. Are you coming down to the canteen?'

'Not just now. I went off to Ballinbreck when I should have been working through this stuff and I'll have to pay for my pleasures now.'

She picked up the pile of papers on her desk and put them firmly in front of her, picking up a pen. But her mind kept drifting off.

Randall's guilt was a pretty theory, with everything to recommend it to the procurator fiscal: means, motive and opportunity all neatly parcelled up. Just no actual evidence.

And according to Louise, Skye had shown signs of distaste in her dealings with Randall at the party. Why would she allow herself to be charged with murder without using his guilt to prove she had been an innocent bystander – if innocent she was? The more that emerged, the stronger Fleming's instinctive feeling grew, reinforced by what Will Stewart had said – they had the wrong person.

But why would Randall have decided to murder Connell *two years* after it had all happened? Water under the bridge, you would have thought. Except somehow it wasn't.

Which brought her right back to the root of the problem: why had Connell decided on resurrection, only to meet with death? He must have had a reason.

Blackmail? He bleeds Randall for years, Randall can't pay any more because he's lost his job and murder is the obvious way out? Bank account details would show that, but they'd need a lot more evidence to get an access warrant – and it still didn't explain why Kane would obligingly turn up to put his head on the block.

And if she didn't process the paper on her desk right now the whole investigation would grind to a standstill. She returned to it with grim determination.

DC Hepburn said, 'Thanks, anyway,' and switched off the phone. 'They haven't managed to raise Randall Lindsay yet,' she said.

'Not at home?' Macdonald looked up from sifting through a pile of reports; Campbell at another desk was working at a computer terminal.

'There was no one at the house and when they went to the warehouse where the Lindsays have their business, his father said he hadn't seen him at all today. He can't have bolted, can he?' Hepburn said. 'That would be equivalent to an admission of guilt.'

'More likely keeping out the way,' Campbell said.

Macdonald ignored that. 'We haven't seen him since the night of the party. He could be scared that you've worked out about him and Skye – he'd know that would bust the whole thing wide open.'

'He has to be worried too about what she might say. She could have decided to tell us all about it to save herself – he doesn't know that she hasn't. He could be – I don't know, on his way to France, or Spain, even. Villains do that. So what do we do now?'

'Better tell the boss,' Macdonald said, getting up.

Campbell looked at them both with exasperation. 'Better look around for him first. Ask his mum.'

Hepburn stared at him. 'Why his mum?'

Macdonald, more skilled at reading Campbell's gnomic comments, said, 'I see what you mean. It was uncanny – my mum always knew where I'd be if she wanted to find me. I'll try phoning the business and asking to speak to her. Number?'

After a couple of clicks, Campbell read it out to

him. He was put through promptly and Macdonald identified himself, explaining that they wanted to speak to her son. 'Do you have any idea where he's likely to be?'

Philippa Lindsay, it appeared, was not a mother of Mrs Macdonald's stamp. She hadn't seen him today, she had no idea where he was and no suggestions to make. When Macdonald asked whether it was possible he had left Ballinbreck House she was sceptical– 'Why would he? It's free board and lodging,' – but on being pressed agreed that it was theoretically possible.

'When was the last time you saw him?' Macdonald asked.

It had been yesterday, the morning after the party, she said, then, in mocking tones asked if they thought he had done a runner, adding that he was dumb enough to think it was a good idea.

Macdonald said stiffly, 'Not at present, no. But if you hear from him would you please tell him to contact us as a matter of urgency.'

He disconnected, then said, 'Wow! I'm glad she's not my mum. No wonder Randall's such a tosser.'

'I'll give the boss a buzz,' Hepburn said.

Fleming asked her a few brief questions. 'She's not getting excited about it,' Hepburn reported, 'but she's going to get the uniforms to look for him. So now we just have to wait and see. I hate that.'

Macdonald bundled together a pile of papers. 'You work through those. It'll take your mind off it.'

It was more than an hour since Martin and Linda Morrison had arrived at the police station in Kirkcudbright, but Linda was still on the verge of hysteria. She had been given hot sweet tea, though she looked at it askance.

'Brandy's what I need, not tea, after all I've been through,' she said, but even mentioning what had happened had been enough to set her off again.

The traffic officer was having to extract the necessary information. 'And you said he was just lying in the road?' she said patiently. 'Was he lying on his back or his front?'

'Oh, I can still see his face!' Linda wailed. 'Just lying there, his eyes open–'

'On his back, then? Stretched out, not huddled up or anything?'

'Just ... just lying there.' Linda grabbed another handful of tissues from the box at her side.

'And he couldn't have been – well, sort of at the side of the road?'

Linda's tears dried instantly. She sat up straight and glared at her questioner. 'If you're trying to pin it on Martin, trying to say it was him knocked the man down – well, you're a liar, that's all. Oh, I know what they say about the police, just wanting a conviction, no matter who it is! I didn't believe it before, but I do now.'

'No, no, Mrs Morrison, really we don't,' the policewoman said hurriedly. 'We're just trying to establish if perhaps the man had been taken ill, fallen into the road – a heart attack, or something...'

Only slightly mollified, Linda sniffed. 'If he had a heart attack, it was before we came round the corner. That's all I can tell you.'

Martin Morrison was more controlled, but even more anxious. 'I can see you've only got my word for it, and Linda's, that he was lying in the road when we arrived. But I can assure you that he was, flat on his back, not moving.'

'Yes sir,' the traffic sergeant said. 'We've got all that written down. The post-mortem will no doubt be able to tell us exactly what happened.'

At the mention of the words 'post-mortem' Martin flinched, but then it seemed to trigger a memory. 'Is it right what they say in *CSI* – that you don't bleed after you're dead? Well, there wasn't much blood, even after both wheels going over him.' He gulped. 'I felt it happening, you know. Twice.'

Inspector Mike Wallace looked up as one of his sergeants came in carrying a plastic folder.

'Ah, good,' he said. 'Is that the man's ID? Messy business, I gather.'

'Certainly was. One of our new lads was in the car that went out to it – doesn't want his lunch.' He took a wallet out of the folder and laid it on the desk. 'This is all they found on the body – back pocket of his jeans. Getting them out wasn't a nice job either.'

Wallace grimaced, picked up the wallet, took out a credit card and read the name. 'Oh,' he said flatly.

'Know him, boss?'

'You do too. It's Will Stewart.'

'I hadn't really planned to drive this road again today,' Fleming said as she and MacNee headed down to Kirkcudbright. 'Maybe I should just take a room down there.' She was feeling faintly sick, with a headache forming a tight band round her head.

'We didn't see it coming,' MacNee said.

'Should have, according to the super. She's taken all the credit for Skye Falconer's arrest and now she's afraid it's starting to fall apart. She can hardly claim the girl did this, after all.'

'Maybe it was an accident,' MacNee said hopefully. 'Maybe he just took a heart attack, with us asking questions.'

'I scared him to death, you mean?' She gave a bitter laugh. 'Oh, great! Thanks, Tam. But I don't believe it, any more than you do.'

'What are we going to do there, anyway?'

'See Mike Wallace to get full details, then find Randall Lindsay and force the truth out of him. Or if we can't find him, see whether the Macdonald–Hepburn sensationalist version is right and he's taken his passport and bolted. Can you imagine what the press would make of that?'

'No bother. They'd say–'

'Don't tell me,' she snarled. 'I can work it out myself.' Then she sighed. 'Sorry, Tam. I didn't mean to snap at you.'

'Didn't get your lunch, did you? Here...'He rooted in his pocket and took out two Penguin biscuits. 'Picked them up from the canteen for our tea. You can have them both, if you like.'

'Greater love – you're a good man. One'll do, though. And I'm sorry to be in such a mood, but

I'm worried sick. If Randall's realised he's in the frame and is just lashing out frantically...'

'What was Stewart going to do, if someone hadn't killed him?'

'Talk to us. That's the obvious thing. But who would have known that was going to happen?' Then she stopped. 'Ah.'

'Yes?'

'Logie and Kendra, that's who. And if you remember what he said, Kendra doesn't have an alibi for Eleanor Margrave's murder any more than he did. She was certainly here at the time Kane was killed–'

'And that alibi was kinda vague, too. And perhaps it wasn't that he was going to disclose something, perhaps she was afraid he'd blow her alibi and point us in her direction. But why would she want to kill Eleanor Margrave?'

'Why would anyone? Oh God, Tam, we need more than this. I know I was complaining we had too much evidence, but in some ways we haven't enough.'

'Don't know where we're going to get it from, though. Skye's not telling.'

'The minute he hears about this her brief's going to ask for her release on an undertaking to appear, and I can't see how we could oppose. Hyacinth will go spare.'

MacNee grinned. 'My, you are in a bad mood!'

Fleming looked rueful. 'Oh, I do try not to use the nickname but sometimes it just slips out when she's being more than usually shrill and demanding.

'But could Kendra have had a reason to kill

Julia? Jealousy again, I suppose, but that's flimsy.'

'The whole Julia theory's flimsy, if you ask me,' MacNee said. 'Macdonald and Hepburn were egging each other on to work something up. Nothing in the autopsy report suggested murder.'

Fleming rubbed tiredly at the frown line between her eyebrows. 'No, of course it didn't. We could be back to square one.

'There's just one thing that keeps nagging at me, Tam. No, two things. First, why did Connell Kane come back? And why do I keep thinking that Jen Wilson is more involved in this than she'd like us to think?'

'Hit on the back of the head with a stone, or something like that, according to the doc,' Inspector Mike Wallace said. 'Quite large, with rugged edges. Muddy, too.'

'Killed on the spot?' Fleming asked.

Wallace shook his head. 'The pathologist said there's blood spatter on the clothes but there's none in the surrounding area and no pool of blood beside the body. There's no lividity evidence to show it was moved, but that takes time to get established – if the body was moved almost immediately there wouldn't be any sign. There's no disturbance on the road edges where it was found and given it was a quiet road his suggestion is that the man was killed elsewhere and then dumped from a car.'

'So we're looking for a large stone with traces of blood and tissue, somewhere in the Galloway countryside?' Fleming said hollowly. Today was getting worse and worse, and it wasn't just because the sugar rush from the chocolate biscuit was wearing off.

Wallace was tactfully silent. MacNee, with an anxious glance at his boss, said, 'Have the lads turned up Randall Lindsay yet? We're hoping for a wee word with him.'

But they hadn't. Fleming pulled a face. 'We'll go and call again at the house. It's almost seven o'clock – he could just have been out for the day.'

When they reached Ballinbreck House, though, there was no one in. 'Maybe they've all done a runner together,' MacNee suggested facetiously, but Fleming wasn't in the mood for jokes.

'Could be working late at the office,' she said. 'Find out where it is and we'll go there now.'

The warehouse was in a road parallel to the main street, near the centre of the village and the board outside read 'Etcetera – Interior Design by Philippa Lindsay' and though the main building had no windows, one small window on an upper level at the side had a light burning.

The outer door of the warehouse was open, too, and when they pressed the bell beside it, there was a pause, then round the edges of the inner door light showed in the main part of the building and it was opened cautiously by Philippa herself. She began, 'Sorry – we're closed,' then recognised them. 'Oh, I see. What is it this time?'

'We were just wanting a word with your son,' Fleming said. 'Is he here?'

'Here?' Philippa gave a bitter laugh. 'You'd think, if you had a son who was a banker that he'd be able to take over at least some of the business side, but not a chance. I sell all day and then work on the books at night.'

The woman seemed weary and distinctly fed up with her son, Fleming thought. Through the open door she could see into the warehouse and it was impressive: fabrics beautifully displayed, room settings laid out to highlight elegant lamps and vases made of heavy glass or Chinese blue-and-white ceramic, and sculptures in alabaster and black polished stone on dark-wood coffee tables. Philippa certainly had good taste.

'He's probably at the house,' she went on. 'And I don't suppose he's making supper either.'

'No one there,' MacNee said.

'Oh?' she didn't seem very interested. 'Of course, Charles was golfing this afternoon – he's probably eating at the club. And I've no idea about Randall – haven't seen him since yesterday morning.'

The two officers exchanged glances. 'I wonder,' Fleming said, 'if it would be possible for us to have a look in his bedroom? We haven't applied for a search warrant as yet but we are very eager to speak to him and if he's gone off somewhere it would be helpful to know if his bags are missing.'

Philippa frowned. 'What's this about?' she asked, her voice sharp. Fleming told her smoothly that it was just routine enquiries, and after giving her a long, cool look Philippa shrugged.

'I was more or less finished here anyway and if it's just looking I don't have any objection. If you wait a minute for me to lock up, I'll walk along and let you in.'

As they waited in the car, MacNee said, 'Know something? Never took to her before but I feel quite sorry for her today with those two freeloaders round her neck.'

'She obviously works hard. And I think she's ready to give up on Randall. I wonder if there's something she knows that we don't.'

Philippa went ahead of them into the house. The sun was still shining outside but the hall was gloomy and she went to switch on a huge, deep-blue glass lamp with a white linen shade that stood on a heavily carved chest at the foot of the staircase.

'Up there,' she pointed. 'Second door on the left – help yourself. His car isn't here so I don't suppose he is. I'm going to get a drink. You'll find me in the drawing room, through there.'

'One of our more trusting clients,' Fleming said as they climbed the stairs. 'How does she know we're not going to take his room apart?'

'Doesn't care,' MacNee said.

Philippa's clever hand was evident here too. With its French-Grey walls and white bedlinen, the room would have looked like a picture from an interiors magazine if it hadn't been for the fact that the bed wasn't made, cushions were thrown carelessly about the floor and there were dirty footprints on the silver-grey carpet and dirty smears on the white duvet cover. It stank of cigarette smoke; there was an ashtray full of stubs on the bedside table. There was a well-worn sweater, along with a pair of mud-stained jeans slung over the back of a neat little grey velour tub chair.

'Slob,' Fleming said crisply. 'Poor woman.'

They looked around. 'Can't see any bags,' MacNee said, 'but maybe he's put everything neatly away in the drawers.'

With a sinking heart, Fleming acknowledged that this was possible, though definitely unlikely. When they opened the doors of the carved armoire, which had shelves beside the hanging space, there was nothing there apart from a couple of folded blankets, a thin dressing gown and a hairdryer, clearly put there for guests.

'Taken off,' MacNee said.

'Yes. So – put out all the usual alerts, I suppose.' She had been almost expecting it, but it still managed to be a shock.

They went back downstairs and Fleming stuck her head round the door of the drawing room, tranquil and pleasing with its turquoise silk curtains and cream sofas. 'Thank you very much, Mrs Lindsay. That's all.'

Philippa, lounging on a turquoise linen upholstered chair with a large glass of white wine in her hand, said, 'I suppose I should ask you what you found.'

'I didn't see any bags, so I think your son may be away somewhere. Would you have any idea where?'

'Sorry, no.'

'Perhaps you could let us know if you hear from him, or if he returns?'

'Certainly.'

Fleming turned to go, then paused. 'Just for the record, Mrs Lindsay, would you be willing to tell us what you were doing today, say from ten o'clock to about two?'

'It's not difficult. I drove to Kirkcudbright to the antiques centre, did a couple of things there,

341

then visited two art galleries. I had a sandwich with the owner at one of them, then came home.'

Then she sat up straight. 'Hang on – routine? Why did you want to know? Has something happened? Randall?'

'No, no, Mrs Lindsay, as far as we know Randall is perfectly all right. Just routine, as I said. Thank you again.'

They left before she could ask anything more.

Back in the car, Fleming said, 'I just want to go along to The Albatross before we set off back. I'd like to see how Kendra's taking all this.'

When they reached the darkened pub, though, a police liaison officer told them that she had taken the news badly and was now in sedated sleep. 'Mr Stewart's through the back, if you want me to fetch him.'

'It'll wait,' Fleming said. There was probably little useful that he could tell them and it was time she went back to face all the explanations and arrangements she would have to make.

It was late and Marjory Fleming was very tired when she got back to Mains of Craigie. Bill was on his way to bed, but came back downstairs when he heard her arrive.

'Bad day?' he said sympathetically as he saw her white face.

'Grim,' she said, patting the collie, who had pranced across to greet her. 'Yes, Meggie, I see you.'

'Dram?' Bill offered but she shook her head.

'Just something to eat and a mug of tea.'

As she made a cheese sandwich she told him

briefly what had happened: that one of the suspects had been killed and another had disappeared, that there was an alert out to have him picked up.

'Want to talk about it?'

Marjory shook her head. 'It's all too muddled and I'm too tired. You go on up – I won't be long. How was your day?'

'Just the usual. Cammie's gone to some do or other in Glasgow. Oh, and Cat's Nick phoned to thank us for the weekend. Very nice manners, I thought.'

'Oh.'

Bill frowned. 'You don't think so?'

She was too tired to be diplomatic. 'I think he's a smarmy little creep and I think he's making fun of you behind your back.'

Her husband's face darkened. Famed for his even temper, Bill had been more irritable since his illness and he was annoyed now.

'And I'm just too stupid to notice – is that what you think?'

'No, of course I don't think you're stupid!' Marjory cried. 'I think you're too nice, that's the problem.'

'Better than being too nasty. You've got to the point where you're suspicious of everyone. Perhaps it's the job, but you're going to wreck your relationship with your daughter completely if you go on like this. She's not stupid either, you know. She's a grown woman and if she thinks this young man is right for her I'm happy to accept her judgement. If you're wise you will as well, but I'm not sure you are.'

'Bill–'

He shook his head. 'No. I don't think there's any point in discussing it – you have your view and I have mine. I think I'll just go on up to bed. Goodnight – I shut up the hens.'

Marjory looked after him miserably as he went out. The cheese sandwich seemed supremely unappealing but she forced herself to eat it; if she hadn't been so tired and hungry none of this would have happened.

She and Bill rowed so seldom that when they did it really hurt. And they'd always agreed that they shouldn't go to bed on a quarrel but he seemed to have forgotten that tonight. She could go up now and say sorry, but it would be meaningless unless she was planning to change her mind about Nick Carlton, and she couldn't do that.

And she was so tired! She really didn't need this, to add to all she was coping with at the moment. Her eyes prickling, she put her head in her hands and groaned, then felt a nudge on her knee from Meg's nose.

She laughed, then sniffed, looking down into the dog's anxious eyes and stroking her head. 'I'm all right, Meg, really,' she said as she bent down to have her cheek licked. 'Look, what about a bit of cheese sandwich?'

Meg, reassured, accepted it gratefully and went back to her bed by the Aga. Marjory refilled her mug and her mind slid away from her domestic problems, back to the professional ones.

She knew she wasn't thinking straight. There was something blocking her, something stopping her seeing the way ahead. She needed to think this through, here in the quiet house where the only sound was Meg starting to snore gently.

There was a pile of accumulated bumf on the kitchen dresser and she sorted through it until she found a circular with a side left blank, then tried two or three dried-out ballpoints standing in a mug beside the phone until she found one that still worked and went back to the table.

Mind maps had always been Marjory's way of clearing her brain and she drew one now: the victims, the suspects, the links between them. And as she stared at it, the picture began to clear before her eyes. She drew two separate circles and then drew a sharp, decisive line.

That would do. She had a new direction to go in tomorrow.

Marjory got up, put her mind map into her bag then her mug and plate into the dishwasher and switched it on. As she turned off the light she decided that if Bill was still awake, she'd say sorry anyway and hope he wouldn't ask her to be too specific about what she was apologising for.

He was sound asleep, though, of course. She gave a little sigh then dropped a gentle kiss on the top of his head before she got into bed.

CHAPTER TWENTY-ONE

Louise Hepburn, a glass of white wine in front of her, watched as Ewan Campbell set about a pie and chips.

'I don't know how you're not obese,' she said, torn between admiration and revulsion. 'You had a bridie for lunch – if I ate like that I'd be the size of a house.'

Ewan, thin and wiry still, if starting to show a paunch ignored her but Andy Macdonald, eating crisps along with his pint, grinned. 'And he'll be away off home to his tea in a minute.'

Ewan paused long enough to say, with some bitterness, 'Aye, but what'll it be? *Salad!*'Then he turned his attention back to his plate.

Louise and Andy both laughed. It gave her a warm feeling; it was the first time she'd ever been asked to join them for a drink after work. She'd made a virtue out of her independence, prided herself on her mates being outside the Force, but it was undeniably good to be part of the gang.

'So – what's Big Marge going to do now?' Andy said. 'She was a bit antsy at the briefing. Unless they pick up Randall tonight there's going to be a big media stushie tomorrow.'

'No wonder. A serial murderer on the loose is enough to get any sub with a headline to write to start drooling,' Louise said. 'And no one seems to have seen him for a couple of days – could be anywhere by now.'

'If he's taken his car abroad it'll be on a ferry list,' Andy pointed out. 'And my guess is he wouldn't go without it.'

'You'd feel sort of vulnerable, escaping on foot,' Louise agreed. 'It's not logical – you're actually more anonymous on public transport. But I can understand it.'

Ewan cleared his plate, set down his knife and fork and said, 'Why's he gone?'

The others stared at him. 'Because he knows we're on to him,' Andy said patiently.

'How?' Ewan said. Then he got up. 'Better get home.' He walked out.

Louise looked at Andy. 'Is he always like that?'

'Yup. Always.'

'I don't feel I know him at all, really. I've never been partnered with him and he says so little in meetings that the only impression I have of him is from isolated remarks like that.'

'Not sure I know him either. We go around the place in silence, mostly, or with me doing a sort of stream-of-consciousness monologue in the hope he'll come out with one of his remarks to shed a new light. If he actually says something it's always worth hearing, I can tell you that.'

'So what do we make of that last remark?'

They were both silent for a minute, then Andy said, 'He's got a point, you know. How would Randall know we were out to get him? He'd be far smarter to carry on as normal.' He drained his pint then said, 'Fancy the other half? My shout.'

'Thanks,' Louise said. 'You get them in and I'll think about that.'

When Andy came back, she had developed a theory. 'Randall hasn't actually been around since just after the party, has he? He could think we'd be on to him after his attack on me – I could have realised, you could have seen him. He'd issued threats.'

'But he must have been in touch with Will Stewart or he couldn't have killed him. And we know Will and Skye were both in the car with Connell Kane – are we assuming that Randall was there too?'

'We won't know till we get a search warrant and can find his prints to check against the records from the car. But if Kane's murder was some sort of follow-up from Julia's – and I can't imagine there's not a connection – Randall only had to know that Will had been summoned to the station yesterday afternoon to need to get rid of him.

'And it wasn't premeditated.' Louise was warming to her theory. 'He met him to check that he'd keep schtum, then found out he wasn't planning to – wasn't prepared to leave Skye to carry the can, say – and he picked up a handy stone.'

'That works for me. It looks like a panicky impulse – and once he realised what he'd done, that Skye couldn't be blamed this time, he took off. We're a good team – you know that?' Andy held his glass across to clink with hers. 'Cheers!'

'Will you tell the boss tomorrow, or will I?'

'You can,' Andy said graciously. 'Provided, of course, that you give full acknowledgement to the brilliance of my input.'

'Naturally. And Ewan's, of course. Wonder how he's enjoying his salad?'

There was something very comforting about hens, Marjory Fleming thought, as she watched her little flock mill around her, waiting for her to fill the feeding trough, shoving and jostling. Cherie the alpha hen was there in the forefront, having trampled right over Sam Cam, a new arrival who was hanging back with what Marjory would like to think was well-bred politeness but was presumably terror.

It gave you a sense of perspective: whatever un-pleasantness lay ahead of her in the world outside today, tomorrow the chookies would still be here, scratching and pecking and squabbling and mak-ing that soothing crooning sound when they were happy.

Marjory allowed herself just a few moments to watch them as she ate a slice of toast, then with some reluctance went back to the house. She hadn't time to check for eggs today; she'd have to leave a note for Bill. Unfortunately she'd over-slept and he'd gone up the hill before she woke.

The drive into Kirkluce gave her time to collect her thoughts for the morning briefing. She wasn't quite ready yet to share generally what she'd been considering last night, not before she'd had a chance to kick the idea around with her team. It felt right, but there were still too many pieces that didn't fit into the jigsaw.

So today she would make time for review and meticulous examination of the evidence they had. Not exciting, but this was the stuff real police work was made of. So unless some other disaster happened – she winced at the thought – she would just have to resign herself to a very dull day ahead.

'The informal report we have, that Will Stewart was killed with a blow from a large stone, suggests that this wasn't premeditated,' Fleming told the morning briefing. 'There was mud in the wound so it was probably snatched up from the ground at the time – the result of an argument, perhaps, or even because the killer discovered that Stewart was to attend here for questioning yesterday afternoon and there was something incriminating that he could tell us.

'Two obvious questions: what might he have been going to say, and who was he going to say it about? So far we don't have the answer to either of these so keep them in mind as you go about your interviews today.

'His hire car isn't at The Albatross and the number's been circulated locally but we haven't found it yet. Randall Lindsay's car licence number has been circulated too and Border Force has been alerted, though there's a danger he may have left the country already. We want to know of any sightings of him since Sunday morning and there's a dedicated phone number being broadcast for information from the public. It's possible – just! – that there may be gold in the avalanche of dross.'

That got a polite ripple of amusement. She went on, 'So it's pretty much routine legwork today. Don't despise it – that's where the dramatic breakthroughs come from.

'Right. Questions?'

A hand was raised. 'Is Skye Falconer still our prime suspect for Connell Kane's murder?'

It was an entirely legitimate, not to say obvious, question, but it was one Fleming had hoped wouldn't be asked directly. 'For the moment, yes,' she said. 'Anyone else?'

The rest only needed routine responses and she gave them with brusque efficiency, then went up to her room to wait for her team to join her.

DC Hepburn was first and when DS Macdonald appeared he took the chair next to her, to Fleming's quiet amusement. Could peace really have been declared at last?

MacNee came next, leaving Campbell to pull forward one of the chairs by the table and Hepburn moved hers to widen the circle. A nice, cooperative grouping, Fleming thought with satisfaction.

She launched straight in. 'I want to look at connections. Four acts of violence: Kane's murder; Eleanor Margrave's murder; the attack on Louise after the party; Will Stewart's murder yesterday.

'Weapons: a cosh, almost certainly; a ligature twice; a random rock, probably, though we're waiting for further tests. Comments?'

There was a brief silence, then Hepburn said, 'The attack on me had to be unpremeditated, at least to the extent that no one knew until quite late in the evening that I was there. It would be easy enough to find something and head out after me, like a belt or a scarf, say, or even a thin rope – there were lots of tents and things in the garden.'

'And even if you'd gone to Sea House with the intention of killing Eleanor Margrave, you could easily conceal any of these,' Macdonald offered.

'The cosh,' Campbell said. 'Odd one out.'

Fleming nodded. 'Precisely. There is no innocent reason for acquiring a cosh. You might, I suppose, carry it for protection but that too sheds a light on your activities. The fingerprints of Kane, Stewart and Falconer were all in the car. It's possible there may have been someone else – Randall, say – but the unidentified fingerprints there are could be perfectly innocent, relating to a previous owner, say. So that's the assembled cast.'

Hepburn was thoughtful. 'You wouldn't be likely to have a cosh, would you, unless you were a professional, so to speak.'

'Or a cop,' Campbell said.

'I hadn't thought of that,' Fleming admitted, 'but it's true, of course. Will Stewart could easily have had access to confiscated weapons.'

'But if he had it,' Hepburn argued, 'why wouldn't he use it on Eleanor Margrave? I think it's far more likely it belonged to Kane.'

Macdonald was the only one who hadn't spoken. 'I agree with Louise. Stewart was unlikely still to have had it to hand, after two years.'

This came under the heading of 'remarks least likely for Andy Macdonald to make' and Fleming sensed, rather than saw, MacNee's quiet smile. However, she said only, 'So – are we talking self-defence? For some reason, Kane goes for Stewart and Skye gets caught up in it somehow?'

Hepburn went on, 'And then either she or Stewart or possibly even Randall throws the cosh away, into the Solway probably, to get rid of the evidence. They don't know they're going to need to kill Eleanor Margrave, so–'

'Or they didn't do it.' That was Campbell.

Fleming pounced on the remark. 'That's what I was mulling over last night. There are two very different MOs. The blow to Kane's head worked, so why change to strangulation?'

'Circumstances.' MacNee was unconvinced. 'Stewart's murder – blow to the head too, but unplanned. The murderer just lost it for some reason and grabbed what came to hand. But like Andy said, if you'd a surprise attack in mind you could easy hide a ligature.

'Say Randall goes out from the party to nobble Louise here, if he was carrying a hammer or something he could be noticed and he couldn't rely on finding a handy stone. Scarf in his pocket and then – aargh!' His hand went to his throat in a pantomime of strangulation.

Fleming saw Hepburn go pale and Macdonald protested, 'For goodness' sake, Tam!'

'Oh, sorry, sorry, lass.' MacNee was immediately penitent. 'Got a wee bit carried away there. But I still don't think we need to complicate things. Find Randall and squeeze him till the pips squeak.'

Fleming glanced at the clock. 'This has been useful, and it's opened up the discussion but that's about as far as we can go for the moment.

'There's going to be a lot of stuff coming in today and I'm going to be stuck at the desk. Tam, I want you and Louise to interview Jen Wilson again. Try to get the truth this time – I have a gut feeling that there's something there that we need to know.

'Andy, could you and Ewan go to The Albatross and lean on the Stewarts again? I reckon Logie's alibi is solid for Eleanor Margrave's murder but it might be as well to check up on what he was doing yesterday. He can't have felt a lot of brotherly love towards Will if he was carrying on with Kendra. I wouldn't put money on him but the MO's different this time so we have to take that into account.

'I'm more interested in Kendra. Her alibi is shaky for that afternoon and she would know that Will was coming in to talk to us.'

'And the way she was looking yesterday, she'd be ready to take a knife to anyone who happened to be passing,' MacNee said. 'You might need body armour.'

'Anyway, that's it,' Fleming said, 'except that you could touch base with the uniforms – they should be all over the place like a rash. And be sure you're up to date with the reports of all the interviews before you go. Tam, you filed the Will Stewart one, didn't you?'

MacNee nodded, and she finished, 'And spare a thought for me stuck here all day, ploughing through paper.'

'I felt as if I were going round in a tumble dryer in that meeting,' Hepburn grumbled as she drove with Tam down the now overfamiliar road to Ballinbreck. 'Whenever I thought I had something straight in my mind and was following a line, something else came up to confuse me all over again.'

'Aye, it's kind of a mess, this one,' MacNee agreed. 'But I think the boss is getting there. She's a lot more upbeat this morning than she was last night.'

'I wish I was. If Randall really has managed to vanish, it could be tied up for weeks. Months, even.'

'Oh, we'll get him. It's what we're best at, picking people up, unless they've got professional help to cover their tracks. He's an amateur.'

'Why's the boss so set on Jen Wilson, anyway? She's got thirty kids as an alibi for the Margrave murder.'

MacNee thought for a moment. 'Has she, though? She told us she was in school but we didn't check. Teachers have free periods, don't they – pop out for a bit of shopping, maybe. And she was definitely in the area on the night Kane was killed.

'I tell you something else – she was ducking and diving when we questioned her, and hell-bent on dumping her pal Skye right in it. But she still wasn't prepared to give us the full story.'

'Mmm.'

Hepburn fell silent and after a moment Mac-Nee glanced at her. 'You're doing that thinking thing again. Want to share it?'

'It was just what the boss said about MO. Suppose there are two people involved, Killer A who bashed Connell Kane and Will Stewart over the head, and Killer B who strangled Eleanor Margrave and tried to strangle me?'

MacNee nodded. 'I think the boss is playing with that idea. But I'm not just sure you'd say using a stone was the same as using a cosh – you couldn't carry a bloody great boulder in your hip pocket ready for use.'

'You might be more inclined to think that way

355

if you'd done it before, though,' Hepburn argued. 'We know Skye didn't kill Will Stewart and if we find who has a solid alibi for yesterday afternoon, we could at least establish they weren't Killer A and concentrate on finding Killer B.'

'It'd be fine and handy, right enough. But you've been in the job long enough to know by now that unless someone's locked up or standing in full view of an audience of independent witnesses, preferably including a couple of justices and a minister from the Free Kirk, there's no such thing as a solid alibi.'

Deflated, Hepburn sank down in her seat and looked at her watch impatiently. 'You know something – you can get really sick of driving down this road. Are we nearly there yet?'

Kendra Stewart came into the bar where DS Macdonald and DC Campbell were waiting, wearing a pair of dark glasses. Her face was pale, though that could just be because she'd left off her make-up, Macdonald thought cynically.

She sat down on the banquette at one of the tables and waved them to the seats opposite. Her voice, when she spoke after receiving their formal condolences, was soft and shaky.

'It's hard for me to even think about this, let alone talk about it, but to bring Will's – killer,' she faltered on the word, 'to justice, I'll do anything – anything!'

Repressing the urge to say, 'Just tell the truth and ditch the histrionics,' Macdonald said gravely, 'I appreciate that. It must be very hard for you.'

'It is, it is!' She took out a tissue and dabbed at

the corner of her eyes under the glasses. 'He was
– well, he was my brother, quite simply.'

Which raised all sorts of interesting questions
about incest and if she went on like this sooner or
later Campbell was going to pose them. Macdonald hurried on, 'I don't want to make this any
more difficult than it is already, so if I can just ask
you a few routine questions first. Where were you
yesterday afternoon?'

Kendra bridled. 'I don't believe this!' she said,
her voice suddenly much stronger. 'You can't
possibly think that I – *I* would have– Oh, it's too
ridiculous.'

'No, no,' Macdonald said soothingly. 'This is
purely a matter of routine. You and your husband
were probably the last people to see your brother-
in-law alive so we have to ask these questions.'

'Where were you?' Campbell said.

Kendra shifted in her seat. 'When do you mean?
It's difficult to tell you just like that – I don't wear
a watch. Though I probably would have if I'd
known there was going to be this sort of fuss.'

'So you weren't here, then?' Macdonald asked.

'I'm not tied to the place, you know – my
husband does let me out sometimes.' Kendra was
visibly recovering her energy, with bitterness
replacing the hushed tones of grief. 'Occasionally
I'm even allowed to spend money, you know.'

'Shopping spree, was it?' Campbell said.

She took exception to that. 'If you call buying
one dress that I need for professional reasons a
shopping spree, you and my husband would get
on just fine.'

'Mrs Stewart, it would be helpful if could just

tell us straightforwardly where you were and what you did yesterday afternoon.' Macdonald decided there was no further need for tact.

'I was trying to. I left here just after lunch and drove to Kirkcudbright. There is a little boutique there run by a friend who knows my taste and I found a dress–'

'Time?' Macdonald said.

'*I* don't know. I told you I don't wear a watch. If you know how long it takes to drive from here to Kirkcudbright and then back, after about half an hour in the shop, that's how long it took.'

Campbell, who had been taking notes, scribbled something while Macdonald went on, 'And when did you last see your brother-in-law?'

It had been just before lunch, she said, 'And I never said goodbye!' That produced another bout of eye-dabbing.

'And did he tell you that he was going to be formally questioned in Kirkluce yesterday afternoon?'

Kendra hesitated. It wasn't a difficult question; was she, Macdonald wondered, weighing up whether she could lie about it?

'Yes,' she said at last. 'He told us both that there was some sort of witch-hunt going on. Since you've arrested Skye Falconer, I shouldn't have thought there was any need to persecute the rest of us.'

Campbell looked up from his scribbling. 'Didn't kill Stewart, did she? And that's an hour and ten.'

'What is?' Kendra said blankly.

Macdonald interpreted. 'The time it would take to get to and from Kirkcudbright, with half an hour in the shop. So when did you get back here?'

'I don't know!' she said wildly. 'And I probably spent a bit of time shopping – food and stuff, you know? Oh, and I had a cup of tea somewhere, probably.'

'Probably?' Macdonald raised his eyebrows. 'This was only yesterday, Mrs Stewart.'

'I came home to hear my brother-in-law had been killed. I'm still confused. Yes, yes I did. And,' she said triumphantly, 'and I waved to a friend of mine who was passing. I can give you her name–'

'We'll send someone to take a formal statement,' Macdonald said. 'Perhaps before that you could jot down a timetable of your movements, along with any confirmation you can think of, while it's still fresh in your memory.'

He was braced for an outburst, but it didn't come. For the first time, she seemed to be taking this seriously.

'What was your relationship with Julia Margrave?' he asked.

'*Julia?*' She looked shocked. 'Why are you asking about her? It was two years ago – it was an accident.'

'Just tying up loose ends. Did you get on with her?'

'Absolutely. She was a close friend.'

'Did she have a relationship with Will?'

Colour flooded Kendra's pale cheeks. 'I don't know. It was none of my business.'

'You weren't jealous of her?'

'Jealous? Me?' She gave a high-pitched laugh.

'Why should I be?'

'But you were jealous of Skye, I understand.'

'Oh, I suppose your snooper told you that. She doesn't seem to have been much of a detective – Will said she'd trotted back to you with all sorts of poisonous suggestions that weren't even remotely true. That was certainly one of them.'

'You see, Mrs Stewart, in an interview yesterday morning Mr Stewart admitted that you were jealous. And we have to ask ourselves whether the jealousy you showed at the party might have spilt over into the anger of a woman who has been dumped?'

'That's – that's preposterous!' she spluttered. 'I would never have hurt Will! You can see how I've been ripped apart by his death!' She began to cry.

Because you have taken great care to demonstrate it, Macdonald thought. 'And you see, when you told me that you couldn't absolutely swear to it that he was here all the afternoon when Mrs Margrave was killed, you destroyed your own alibi as well.'

Kendra recoiled as if he had slapped her. Then she got up. 'When you said you wanted my help, I hadn't realised that you were intending to accuse me of murder.'

'We haven't,' Campbell said, but Kendra paid no attention.

'I'm not going to say another word without a lawyer to protect me. And I shall advise my husband to do the same.'

She went out through the door to the back of the pub, slamming it behind her. Macdonald looked at Campbell.

'Interesting! Has that worried her, or is she just the huffy type?'

'Could be both,' Campbell said, as the door opened again and Logie Stewart appeared. If he didn't look completely broken by grief, he did look grey and weary and, at the moment, anxious.

He was wringing his hands as he said, 'I'm sorry about my wife. She doesn't mean anything, you know – just tends to fire up, and she's very upset about Will. I told her she's being stupid but that didn't go down well either.'

He slumped down on the bench. 'What is it you wanted to ask me?'

'Where were you yesterday afternoon, Mr Stewart?'

'Where I always am.' He sounded very weary. 'Preparing for the evening's service, with Maggie. She'll confirm that.'

'Thank you, Mr Stewart. And are you able to give us any idea of your wife's movements – what time she left here, when she came back?'

'Oh – left after lunch, came back before tea. That's all I can tell you, really. But there's no way Kendra would have hurt Will. If I'm to be honest, it worried me that she was a little too fond of him. Nothing serious, of course,' he gave a nervous laugh, 'but just – you know, he's younger, smarter, slimmer – but it would never have come to anything. Will would have discouraged her.'

'Wouldn't like that, would she?' Campbell said.

Logie went quiet. 'Maybe not. But I can tell you it's preposterous to suppose she would have killed him. You don't seriously think that, do you?'

'We're following several active lines of enquiry,' Macdonald said. 'Thank you for your cooperation, sir.'

As they went back to the car he said to Campbell, 'Should I have left them guessing? I can't quite see her wielding a boulder, can you?'

Campbell, in his usual provoking way, shrugged and said nothing.

When the phone rang in DI Fleming's office and she was told that Damien Thomson, Skye Falconer's solicitor, was at the other end of the line, her heart plummeted, even though she had been expecting it. Time had almost run out; he had every right to demand they charge her or release her and it was a hard call.

'Mr Thomson,' she said stiffly.

He sounded irritated. 'I want to make it clear to you from the start that I have most strongly advised my client against the course of action she is proposing to take.'

Fleming's heart lifted just a fraction. 'Yes?'

'She says that she wants to talk to you. As far as I can make out, what she is going to say amounts to a defence of incrimination, though she has been less than specific to me. I shall, of course, attend the interview so I need to know when this will be.'

'I'll arrange for it immediately,' she said, then paused. 'Can I just ask, has she been told that Will Stewart is dead?'

'Yes,' he said stiffly. 'But I wouldn't wish you to draw any adverse inference from this.'

'Of course not,' Fleming said.

As she rang off, a little bubble of excitement was building inside her. Was she, at last, going to get the information she needed?

CHAPTER TWENTY-TWO

'We'd better have a word with the heidie at the school first,' DS MacNee said to DC Hepburn. 'Supposing Miss's alibi doesn't look as watertight as we'd thought, we could use that to twist her arm.'

Their reception, when they were shown into the head teacher's office, was less than cordial. The secretary looked alarmed as they identified themselves and when they were shown in, Mrs Pearson's manner was distinctly frosty.

She looked quite a cuddly figure, wearing the kind of clothes MacNee's own Bunty might put on if she were having coffee out with her pals, but the eyes had a gimlet glare that reminded him of Miss McGregor, one of his own primary school teachers – and he could almost feel now the sting of the leather tawse, wielded with enthusiasm across the palm of his hand.

'Is this something further to do with Miss Wilson?' she demanded. 'You know that she is not teaching here at the moment?'

'Yes, we know that,' MacNee said. 'We were just wanting to check with you – does your staff have free periods in the course of the teaching day?'

She looked affronted at the term. 'Non-pupil-contact modules, yes. Not everyone realises that modern educational standards demand a great deal more planning and preparation than was once necessary, so of course time has to be allocated to that.'

MacNee felt a temptation to ask how come half of them couldn't read and write properly, then, but remembering Miss McGregor he didn't yield to it. Instead, he said, 'There's a particular day we're interested in – last Friday. Would Miss Wilson have had a – thingamabob that afternoon?'

'I would have to check. Friday, – oh, that wasn't the day that poor woman was killed, was it?' She looked shocked. 'Oh, please don't tell me that Miss Wilson is a suspect! Of course, I wasn't happy about keeping her on after that sordid business two years ago – we did worry about her influence on the children, but employment law makes everything very difficult these days. I never imagined this, though–'

'No, no,' MacNee said hastily. 'There's no implication that she was involved. It is purely routine to check on alibis. We just need to know that she would have been in school that afternoon.'

A little mollified, Mrs Pearson said, 'Of course she would, on any weekday.' She got up and went to consult a noticeboard on one wall. 'Here we are,' she said. 'Friday ... oh Miss Wilson's class has PE, last lesson.' There was a little silence.

'Right,' MacNee said, and Hepburn asked, 'What time does the PE class start?'

'Two-thirty, finishing at three-twenty. Of course staff are not permitted to leave the premises until the end of the school day,' she said, but without much conviction.

They repeated their assurances that it was purely routine, but they left her looking shaken.

'Oh yeah, like no member of staff who had a free last thing on Friday would dream of skipping out and starting the weekend early,' Hepburn said acidly.

'Or bunking off to rub out an inconvenient old body. Time we went and turned the heat up.'

But they were just getting into the car when MacNee's mobile rang and Fleming's voice said, 'Tam? Get back here right now. Skye wants to talk.'

'Let's go in to Ballinbreck House and see whether anyone's heard from Randall,' Macdonald said. 'Wouldn't trust our Philippa to bother to lift the phone if he turned up.'

Campbell nodded though without much enthusiasm, remembering presumably the defects of the hospitality on the last occasion.

The village as they passed through it was busy, with a little knot of people standing outside the general store, and several squad cars whose lucky occupants would be off knocking on doors. Seeing a sergeant he recognised, Macdonald pulled over and opened his window.

'Any luck, Donnie?'

The sergeant pulled a face. 'A couple of people claim to have seen Randall Lindsay on Sunday afternoon but nothing since. No joy on tracing Will Stewart's movements – the car hasn't turned up yet and no sightings yesterday.'

'Thanks. We'll be here for another half hour or

so – keep in touch.'

There were no cars parked outside Ballinbreck House when they reached it and there was no answer when they rang the doorbell.

'At the business, maybe,' Macdonald said. 'Unless they've all done a runner. Directions?'

As they drove along the main street a standing board, grey with fancy white lettering, was standing on the pavement with an arrow directing them down the side street.

'Looks like it's open, anyway,' Macdonald said, and when he turned in there were five cars in the car park at the front already, including two 4x4s and a BMW. The outer door to the warehouse was fixed back; they opened the inner door and went into the shop. It was windowless but brilliantly lit, with spotlights and lamps everywhere.

'Posh,' Campbell said, and indeed the clientele, as well as the woman who was showing a fabric book to one particularly yummy mummy, suggested that his diagnosis was spot on. There was no sign of Philippa Lindsay.

Conversation died as they appeared and after an uncertain glance at her client the assistant came over. Macdonald could feel the eyes of the other customers suddenly bore in on them.

'Can I help you?' the assistant said.

'Wanting a word with Mrs Lindsay,' Macdonald said. 'Is she here?'

'Er ... yes, well, she's upstairs in her office. She did say she wasn't to be disturbed, but I suppose...'

'Yes.'

The firm response sent her scurrying to an

intercom, and they heard Philippa's sigh before she said, 'Send them up, then.'

It was, Macdonald thought, a remarkably stylish outfit. There were even mock rooms laid out, sitting rooms and bedrooms to show off different colour schemes. He hadn't much of an eye himself but even he could see that having a room that looked like one of these would be more restful than the shabby shambles that passed for decor in his own flat.

As they reached the top of the stairs to a sort of mezzanine that ran along one side of the building, Philippa opened the door of a small office. 'Thanks, Suzanne,' she said to their escort. 'And if you could possibly damp down the gossip when you go back? I'm not about to be arrested yet – at least, as far as I know.'

As Suzanne nodded and hurried back to her customer, she added wryly, 'Unless, of course, you know different? You'd better come in, I suppose, and shut the door. I should think there will be someone wanting to "browse" up here any moment now.'

'Just a few questions,' Macdonald said stolidly.

The office was very small but immaculately tidy. Apart from the contents of two trays, one on either side of the desk, there was no paper visible; she had been working on a laptop which she closed down as she took her seat.

When they had interviewed her previously, Macdonald had been struck by her confident, almost aggressive attitude. She had been, he had thought unkindly, reasonably well preserved. Today she looked years older and quite vulnerable, with dark shadows under heavy eyes.

'We just wondered if you had any news of your son,' Macdonald said, and saw a spark of her former aggression appear.

'I told your inspector that if I heard from him I would let you know immediately. Do you think I'm concealing him somewhere?'

'Has been known,' Campbell said.

'It would show a level of stupidity I don't possess. What good would it do? I suppose he could hide but he'd have to come out eventually. You seem to have made sure that he can't go anywhere without being spotted. Are you planning to arrest him?'

'We're anxious for his help with our enquiries.'

'If that's all, you could have done it without making a circus out of it. I've had to switch off my phone and poor Suzanne's even had to rebuff some oik from one of the newspapers who turned up here. If it gets any worse I'll have to close for the day and drive yet another nail into the coffin.'

'Business difficult?' Macdonald asked.

She gave a snort of bitter laughter. 'Do you lavish money on decor when there's a downturn? But presumably you didn't come here to talk about my turnover. What do you want?'

'You know that Will Stewart was killed yesterday?'

Philippa compressed her lips and Macdonald saw a look of pain on her face. She didn't look at him as she said, 'Yes.'

The time to put the boot in was when someone was down. 'Your husband said you had an affair with him.'

She gave a gasp of outrage. 'How dare he!' she said, then, defiantly, 'And if I did? So?'

'And at the party you were trying to arrange a meeting with him because you fancied him.'

'I suppose this was from your undercover chum. Or "spy", as normal people would call it. Slimy little bitch! Don't you ever feel dirty, just being part of the job you do?' The aggression was back, all right; she was coldly furious.

'No,' Campbell said flatly, while Macdonald ignored it.

'But Will himself told my inspector that he was trying to brush you off without being rude, which backs up our officer's report.'

He saw that one go home. Philippa curled forward, her arms across her chest, and tears sprang to her eyes. 'I don't believe you,' she said.

Oh yes, she did. 'When was the last time you saw him, Mrs Stewart?'

Her head bowed, she didn't speak for a moment. When she looked up her eyes were hard again.

'At the party. I never saw him again. We were hoping to meet but–' she bit her lip, 'for one reason and another it didn't work out.'

Macdonald nodded. 'You told my colleague yesterday that you'd been in Kirkcudbright?'

'Yes, Sergeant, I was. And I gather, from the phone calls I had this morning from a couple of friends that your efficient colleagues have checked it out already. Look, I've been generous with my time. Is there anything else, or can I get back to my work?'

'Just one more thing. What was your son's

relationship with Julia Margrave?'

Philippa hadn't expected that and it threw her. 'J-Julia?' she said, then stopped, as if she were considering it. 'I don't know – he doesn't confide in me. He certainly owed her a lot, getting him the job in the bank and so on, but...' She paused again, then gave a tight-lipped smile. 'But, as I know all too well, he isn't the grateful type. Why do you want to know?'

'Routine,' Macdonald said. 'But if you do hear from Randall it would be very much in his interests to persuade him to contact us immediately.'

She wasn't a stupid woman and he could see that she was making connections but she said nothing more than, 'I see,' and then, 'Goodbye,' as they left.

There was, Macdonald thought, real anger there, but by the end of the interview she had looked very weary, defeated almost. Given her problems – her business, her lover, her son – it wasn't surprising.

Skye Falconer looked as if the puff of air from the door closing as Fleming and MacNee entered the interview room might blow her off her seat. She was thinner than ever; her eyes were swollen and her cheeks hollow and raw from the salt of tears.

As Fleming sat down and MacNee performed the formalities for the tape, including repeating that the interview was taking place under caution, her brief jutted his chin aggressively.

'As I told you on the phone, my client is ignoring my advice in deciding to talk to you. In her best interests, I will be repeating that recommendation. I beg you to listen to me, Skye!'

Damien Thomson turned to try to catch her eye, but Skye gave no sign of having heard him. He sat back, throwing his hands up in a gesture of despair.

Fleming could understand his protective instincts. In the face of this small, broken creature, who could help it? From the look on MacNee's face, she could tell that the words, 'Poor wee soul!' were forming in his mind.

She had to harden her heart, though, and remember that this was a suspect who had at the very least been present at one of the murders and had a strong connection with a second. She could go easy to start with, anyway. But just as she opened her mouth to ask the first question, Skye began.

'I want to tell you it all. I don't care what happens to me. Will's dead – nothing matters any more.' Tears started as she said the words but, uncannily, she didn't sob; she didn't seem to notice she was crying though the tears must have stung her sore cheeks as they spilt over.

'We kept in touch with Connell, a bit, after he did his disappearing act and I persuaded Will to take me with him to Canada. Will had helped him to do it, you see – there was – it would have been...'

She hesitated. Fleming said gently, 'He couldn't afford an investigation that would have implicated him too?'

'Yes, well, I suppose so. But Will didn't deal in drugs, really – he just, well, had them, sometimes. Not much.'

'Where was Connell, during the time he was

away?' Fleming asked.

'Living in a flat in Birmingham. We never e-mailed or phoned, just in case it got tracked, but we had his address if we needed to get in touch. Actually, we never used it. We weren't really friends. I was always kind of scared of him, to be honest. Don't know what he was doing – he didn't tell us.'

No prizes for guessing, Fleming thought, with a significant glance at MacNee.

'Then we got this letter,' Skye went on. 'It was back in March. Just – out of the blue. A letter ... and it said–'

Without warning, she broke down, uttering great wrenching cries, hunching over as if in terrible pain.

'That's enough.' Thomson stood up. 'I insist that we terminate the interview here. My client isn't fit–'

'I have to! You can't stop me.' Shuddering, Skye sat up, struggling for control. 'I need to get it over with, to explain.

'Oh God, the letter! If it hadn't been for that, and carelessness – it was my fault, my fault, of course it was, but it didn't deserve punishment like this for me or for–' She choked.

Thomson, who had sat down again, was starting to look almost as distressed as his client. 'This is intolerable–'

'Do you wish to terminate the interview, Skye?' Fleming said.

Skye shook her head vehemently. 'No, no! It'll be worse if I put it off.'

MacNee poured her a glass of water from a

carafe on a side table, and drinking it seemed to calm her.

'What did the letter say?' Fleming was anxious to divert her from the tidal wave of guilt that had clearly overpowered her.

Skye took a deep breath. 'It said, "What I gave to Julia wasn't fatal. I didn't kill her. I want to know who did."'

It was all Fleming could do not to gasp. It was MacNee who said, 'Did you know?'

'No, of course not! It was rubbish. She wasn't *killed*, she'd just taken too much stuff–'

'Did Will believe it?' Fleming cut in.

'No.' Then she paused. 'I don't think so. He said he didn't, but with what happened...' Her voice tailed away.

'So, you arranged to meet Connell?'

'Yes. There was the Homecoming Party, you see. Kendra sent Will the invitation and he'd been thinking maybe of trying to get a job back here. So we could do that and see Connell at the same time, sort out what he was talking about, get the others to talk to him too, if need be. He was always besotted about Julia and we needed to reassure him – no one would hurt her, she was a lovely girl.

'We came over a bit beforehand. Will had a couple of people in Glasgow he was going to talk to about a job. Then Connell wanted us to meet him down here. We ... we didn't know why at the time, why not Glasgow? But he'd been planning it all along. We just didn't realise–'

She broke off to bite at her thumbnail, tearing a sliver of skin away until it bled. The other nails, too, were ragged and bitten down to the quick.

The tension in the room was palpable. MacNee was leaning forward as if that would let him catch her words more quickly, Thomson was rigid in his chair and Fleming felt her own pulse quicken.

Thomson spoke first. 'Stop! Don't say anything else until I've talked to you, Skye.'

She dismissed him with a gesture, like someone swatting away an irritating fly.

'We met in a pub in Castle Douglas – nine o'clock. Not very convenient – we'd have a long drive back to Glasgow – but it was an edgy situation, you know?

'We didn't like to argue. Connell was always...' She paused. 'It's hard to explain, sort of dangerous. I think that's why Julia liked him, the excitement of it, the buzz, but I don't think any of the rest of us did – oh, except Jen. I think she seriously fancied him, but with Connell it was always Julia.

'He was looking really haggard, and his eyes – he'd these very dark eyes and now they looked...' she considered the next word, 'haunted – haunted by Julia's memory, I suppose.

'He got in the drinks and then he started talking about the Cyrenaics, asking about what the others were doing. It felt uncomfortable, like he was making small talk to put off discussing it, but he was watching us all the time. It was giving me the creeps. At last Will asked him what he'd meant about Julia's death? Connell stared right at him. He looked – oh, I don't know, sort of lit up from inside with anger or something. He started talking about Ecstasy in Julia's system that night.

'Well, everyone knew he didn't deal in E – too unpredictable, he always said. You'd have to be crazy to give it to Julia on top of what she was taking already – but quite honestly, that wouldn't have stopped Julia taking it herself. She was – well, just away, really.

'He said he'd only just discovered that the inquest had found it was the combination that killed her, and then he accused Will of giving it to her.'

'Had he?' Fleming asked, her voice as gentle as she could make it.

'No,' Skye said, then hesitated. 'Well, he said he hadn't but – Will wasn't always – straight-forward.' Her mouth twisted in pain, at some memory, perhaps. But she went on, 'I could see he was sweating, wiping his forehead and his mouth. I didn't think anything of it, just that he was under a lot of pressure, that he was upset.

'Oh, maybe he had done it – he did have drugs, sometimes. And Julia was always – sort of *hungry*, if you know what I mean.'

Fleming nodded. 'Go on.'

'Then Connell just said flatly, "You're lying." He wanted us all to go to The Albatross so he could talk to Logie and Kendra, see what they'd say when he challenged Will. "They were there – they'll know what you did." He kept saying that whenever we tried to say it wouldn't help.

'Will and I looked at each other. I was really uncomfortable, I didn't want to go – I was scared of Connell, really, but Will just said we should go with him, that they might know where she really

375

got it from. He was looking a bit strange but I just thought it was because Connell was getting to him.

'So we went out to his car – he insisted that we could talk on the way and he'd bring us back. I got in the front beside Connell, Will was in the back.

'It was a terrible night – rain, wind, storm. We drove down through Dalbeattie, then on to the road towards Ballinbreck. There was lightning and the river was running high – I could hear it even above the engine of the car.

'Connell had said we were going to talk but then he didn't say anything and Will didn't either. I didn't think anything about that – we hadn't got anywhere arguing with him before.

'We were a few miles from Ballinbreck when suddenly Connell stopped. He leant across me and opened the door and told me to get out. I thought he'd gone mad.

'I said, "What do you mean, Connell? It's pouring with rain, we're in the middle of nowhere." He said he meant that I should get out of the car – he started pushing me. I screamed, "Will!" but he didn't answer and Connell just laughed.

'I was desperate, clinging on to the door, but when I looked round I could see Will was fast asleep. I kept screaming and screaming but he didn't react and then I saw that Connell had something in his hand, a sort of stick thing with a knob at the end–'

'A cosh?' MacNee suggested.

Skye shrugged. 'Probably. He threatened to hit me with it and then he gave me such a hard push that I fell out – landed on the side of my face against a stone. He chucked my bag out after me and then he slammed the door and drove on.

'I was distraught. He must have spiked Will's drink and I could see what he was going to do but I was helpless. I didn't even have my mobile – it was back in the car at the pub.

'I walked and walked, for hours, it felt like, hoping for a house or a car I could flag down – though what could they do, anyway? But it was such a terrible night – only two cars passed and I don't think they even noticed me.

'Then I saw the tracks. There were broken branches and tyre marks, and I just knew – Connell had driven it into the water. He really had committed suicide this time and taken Will with him. I peered through the hedge but there was no sign of the car, just black water, running fast and high.

'I think I went into shock. I just walked on, and then I saw the lights of a house and – well, the rest you know.'

Skye slumped and her solicitor, who was looking shocked himself, stepped in. 'Miss Falconer has been cooperative beyond your wildest dreams, Inspector. I think she's had enough – more than enough.'

Fleming ignored him. 'Tell me about Mrs Margrave, Skye.'

'Oh, she was a lovely lady – so kind. I couldn't tell her, I couldn't thank her, even. I just – just couldn't speak. I felt like I was paralysed. Shock, I suppose. I stayed the night and then left in the morning.'

'But you didn't contact us, once you'd recovered?'

'What would be the point? He was dead and I didn't care about anything else, just wanted to cower away like a sick animal – and Jen was a true friend...' She gave a sad little smile. 'Not sure she is now, though.'

'When did you realise that Will wasn't dead after all?'

'Oh, I'll never forget it – that moment! Jen just came in and mentioned she'd seen Will and it was – I don't know, like the sun had come out or a brass band had started playing. I hadn't told her what had happened and she'd been good about not quizzing me, so I just acted casual. I don't know what she thought. I just felt dazed. The drug must have been wearing off, I suppose, and my screaming woke him – and it was Connell went into the river, not Will. I was so happy.

'But then I wondered – why hadn't he been looking for me? He hadn't asked Jen about me and he knew she'd be more likely to know than anyone else.

'You see–' Skye faltered, and tears gathered in her eyes again. 'I was never sure of him. Perhaps he was tired of me, glad of the excuse to get rid of me. I had to work so hard, so hard to keep him. And I'm not sure I did, really.

'There was the party – I thought I'd go looking my best and surprise him. Then–' Her hands went up to cover her face.

After a moment Fleming said softly, 'Then...?'

Skye gave a great sigh. 'Connell's letter,' she said. 'I'd had the letter in my bag. I'd forgotten all about it until I was looking for a top to wear to the party and I suddenly realised it wasn't there. It wasn't anywhere in the room, either.

'I realised I must have dropped it when I took my stuff out of my bag at Mrs Musgrave's house to let it dry by the heater. Julia's mother was going to find a letter that said someone had killed Julia.'

Thomson looked aghast. 'Skye, stop there,' he said, though without much conviction.

Fleming said quickly, 'So what did you do?'

'I had to phone Will. He was stunned to hear my voice, said he'd thought Connell had killed me earlier. And then I had to tell him what had happened with the letter.'

'How did he react?' Fleming asked.

'Shocked, I think. Then he just said there was nothing we could do.'

'That was all?'

'Yes. That's all I know.' Skye sagged in her chair as if she no longer had the strength to sit upright.

Even so, Fleming went on, 'And do you think Will might have killed her even so, wanted to stop someone investigating Julia's death?'

She gave a little sob. 'Oh please, no! Surely he couldn't... She was such a kind lady. I could have died of cold – and I didn't even thank her. What she thought–' She was starting to slur her words from sheer exhaustion.

You could only feel pity. Fleming said gently, 'I think she was very sorry for you. She called you her little mermaid.'

Skye's eyes, too big for her pinched face, filled again. 'The little mermaid! Oh God, yes. Every

379

day with Will, it was as if I were walking on knives too, just like she was with her prince, afraid he would leave me. And now he's gone!'

As she broke down completely, Fleming got up. 'I will put in hand Miss Falconer's release on bail and I'll make an immediate report to the fiscal. Interview terminated, 15.25 p.m.'

CHAPTER TWENTY-THREE

'I'm still feeling dazed, to be honest,' DI Fleming said, when she had briefed her team on Skye Falconer's confession.

'The best bit was her brief's face,' MacNee said. 'Thought he was going to have a coronary a couple of times.'

'So are we accepting this – that Will Stewart killed Kane in self-defence?' Macdonald asked.

'Having killed Julia, maybe even accidentally, then went on to strangle her mother to stop questions being asked?' Hepburn was enthusiastic. 'That would all fit.'

'Didn't kill himself, though,' Campbell pointed out.

'Exactly,' Fleming said. 'I don't buy it, Louise. Apart from anything else, Stewart's not a stupid man and he was a copper – he knew perfectly well about standards of proof. A letter like that from a convicted drug dealer isn't evidence. He'd have to have been mad to take the risk of committing murder instead of simply stating that Kane was

380

delusional. No, I'm afraid nothing's that simple. OK, we know now why Kane came back but we're no nearer to understanding why he only recently found out about the inquest verdict. Did someone contact him? And if so, why.'

'And why now?' said Campbell.

'That's a bit weird,' MacNee agreed. 'Suddenly someone just takes a wee notion to stir up trouble? Nothing on the telly and they got bored?'

'I could understand that, with all this referendum stuff,' Hepburn said with feeling. 'But there must have been a trigger, surely.'

'The Homecoming party?' Macdonald suggested. 'Whoever wrote it knew that the Cyrenaics would be coming back together again.'

'Philippa Lindsay would definitely know,' Hepburn said. 'And Randall, possibly. And of course Kendra and Logie would hear from Will that he was coming. Jen Wilson – maybe, maybe not. But why would you want to cause trouble just because they were going to be together again?'

'There's folks just like trouble,' MacNee said darkly.

'Hey, wait a minute!' Hepburn was off again. 'Will was killed in the end, right? Maybe someone planned to kill him all along – like Philippa, say, being mad jealous because he'd gone off with someone else, or Kendra, even – and one of them wrote the letter hoping that if Connell thought Will had killed Julia that he'd do it for them?'

Macdonald was impressed. 'And then, I suppose, things just went wrong and the rest could have followed from that. So we need to ask who might want Stewart dead, and why?'

Fleming had listened, saying nothing. Now she said, 'I think starting another hare running about motivation is counterproductive. Let's focus on what we can establish from Skye's evidence. We know that Stewart helped Kane to disappear. We know that he had Kane's address. Who else had it? Who knew where he was and knew he wasn't dead?'

'Not Jen Wilson, anyway,' Macdonald said confidently. 'She passed out with shock when we told her.'

'Didn't,' Campbell said.

Macdonald bristled. 'What do you mean? I only just caught her before she hit the floor.'

'Passed out when you told her he was dead. Again.'

'Oh.' Macdonald thought about it. 'I suppose that's right.'

Fleming said sharply, 'Suggesting she'd thought he was alive? If you believed someone was dead anyway, I can't see that being told he'd been alive before but was dead now would make you faint. That's quite significant.

'Tam, did–' She broke off as the phone on her desk rang and she took the call, scribbling down a note as she listened, finishing, 'Thanks, Mike.' She put it down.

'They've found Will Stewart's hired car. It's in the Balcary Bay car park – good spot for starting a walk along the Solway coastline, but of course it's still quiet at this time of year. Pure luck they found it, Mike says – a sharp-eyed constable on his day off. He's arranging a fingertip search so we may have some joy with forensics at last.'

There were murmurs of satisfaction and Mac-Nee said, 'So – what now?'

Fleming thought for a moment. 'Mike's calling in the SOCOs so for the moment there's nothing we could do at the site except get in the way. Tam, I was going to ask you how you and Louise got on with Jen Wilson?'

MacNee smote his head. 'I meant to tell you – with all this it slipped my mind. I'd a brainwave about teachers' free periods – only they've got some fancy name for them nowadays. When we checked at the school the heidie told us she's got one last thing on a Friday, so maybe her alibi's not just so great after all. But we never got to speak to her before you phoned.'

Fleming raised her eyebrows. 'Didn't mention that to anyone, did she?'

Macdonald and Campbell shook their heads.

'Right. I'll get down there, then – Tam, I'll need you. Bring a tape recorder. The rest of you – just clock off. Tomorrow may be a busy day if we get reports on Stewart's car.'

She sensed a certain reluctance as they got to their feet and shuffled out. Hepburn hung back.

'Randall,' she said. 'There isn't any news of him, is there?'

'Not that's reached me.'

'What do we think about him now, with all that Skye said? He certainly had a motive to kill Julia but Will clearly didn't think he had, so why would Randall want to kill him? And how would he know that Mrs Margrave had found the letter?'

'I take your point. The letter certainly seems to have been the triggering incident and it's hard to see how he would have been involved in that. The most damning thing was him suddenly disappearing – if he would just make contact and answer a few questions, my guess is that we could rule him out.'

Hepburn nodded. 'Right. Never seemed the type to me, to be honest. Thanks, boss.'

DC Campbell clocked off with the others but then went back to the CID room via the canteen to collect a couple of KitKats. He was in no hurry to get home: his mother-in-law was coming the next day and his wife had been bellyaching on about the lawn needing mowing.

The room was quiet and he settled down at a terminal in perfect contentment. He was at his happiest just ferreting through files, trying to spot what others might have missed, and Eleanor Margrave's murder had produced extensive reports, offering hours of pleasurable trawling ahead.

It was six o'clock when, going through the records, he suddenly stopped. He checked what it said, frowning, and then recollected an interview they'd done. He accessed it and read it, nodding with satisfaction.

That could be worth following up. He flagged it up so the boss would see it in the morning, then with some reluctance logged out and went home to face the domestic storm.

For once, Fleming chucked the keys to MacNee when they reached the car park. Knowing her dislike of being driven, he looked surprised.

'I just want to think really hard about this next

interview,' she said. 'I've got a feeling it's crucial and I don't want to be distracted while I work out the line I want to take.'

'Good,' MacNee said. 'Maybe that'll stop you giving a running commentary on when I should change gear.'

She pulled a face at him and settled back in her seat.

She ought to be feeling elated that they had the evidence now to close the Connell Kane enquiry but she hadn't time for that. Yes, it was satisfying, but it shed very little light on what had happened afterwards – and she hated being in the dark.

Once the news of Skye's release got out, someone would be afraid, scrabbling for safety in the shadows like some frightened animal; she could almost sense the small panicky movements, the shifting patterns.

Frightened creatures were dangerous. It scared her when she saw no obvious way forward – with reason, since there were previous cases where she had failed to prevent a tragedy. She needed to think clearly, and she needed to think fast.

She'd had a feeling all along that Jen Wilson wasn't the bystander she appeared to be, and now she hadn't that solid alibi for Eleanor Margrave's murder it was getting stronger.

This was all about connections – who knew what, and when? The letter, as quoted by Skye, indicated that Kane had only recently found out that there had been Ecstasy as well as cocaine in Julia's system. That had been published in the report from the inquest two years ago but Kane would have been 'dead' before that; perhaps he hadn't known then about the report. Skye and Will Stewart self-evidently hadn't told him.

Jen Wilson could have known Kane was alive despite her claims that she hadn't – and even known where he was. But then, why wait until now to tell him that the drugs he'd given her weren't what killed Julia? And what was the point? Why would she have wanted to rake it all up again?

Fleming thought back to their earlier interview with her. She had checked back on it before she left and once more was struck forcibly by how defensive she had been, how determined to distance herself from it all. Some of her answers just hadn't been credible; indeed there had been only one that had shone out as truth – that she had, at least at one stage, believed Kane was dead.

Suppose she'd discovered he was alive, what had she thought the result of contacting him would be? What would it achieve?

'Tam,' she said, so suddenly that he jumped, 'if you got, say, a letter, telling you that the woman you loved had died because someone gave her a large dose of E on top of the stuff she was taking, what would you do?'

MacNee's reply was prompt. 'Same as he did. Come back to kill the bastard. Mind you, it's kind of hard to imagine Bunty OD'ing on cocaine and Ecstasy. Cupcakes, now...'

Fleming smiled. 'Her and the rest of the Women's Guild. Anyway, I agree – that's what the sender would guess Kane would be likely to do. And say you were Jen Wilson, why would you want that?'

'If she'd some kind of grudge against Will

Stewart, maybe? If they all knew Kane didn't deal in E, if he was the obvious source...?'

'Mmm. Not convinced. Too many "ifs" there.' Fleming was frowning. 'Tam, she passed out when she was told Kane really was dead – and after Skye had been arrested for his murder, she was venomous about her, remember. She cared a lot.'

'So she's daft about him, jealous of Julia – answer, get rid of the competition. Fair enough – but she's hardly going to draw a wee map with arrows on for him saying look what happened, is she?'

Fleming said suddenly, 'Did you read that report of the interview the lads did with Charles Lindsay? He said that Philippa had set up the whole Homecoming thing because she was in love with Will Stewart and it was the way she hoped to get him back. Could that apply to Jen as well, do you reckon?'

'So she uses it to lure him home, then the whole thing kicks off and Kane's dead for real? All her fault?'

'She's been insisting all along that it's nothing to do with her. Maybe she even needs to believe that. And the more I think about it the more I like it. Skye knew Kane's address; what would be more likely than that she'd tell her best friend after all the fuss had died down?

'The connections are falling into place. She's right in there, Tam.' Somehow, she'd known that all along; now she needed to play her hunch. Fleming could feel the excitement building.

As she let herself into her flat, Louise Hepburn

was feeling bored and restless, at a loose end. This was always a danger point: the desire for a cigarette kicked in and there was a newsagent's two minutes away – but having come so far that really would be a crass thing to do.

Instead, she went to scrabble in the kitchen drawer where she kept the nicotine patches and slapped one on to blunt the craving, while she made a cup of coffee and went through to her little sitting room to drink it. The ghost of past cigarettes still hung on the air, which didn't help.

It had been such an interesting day with the new developments in the case and she'd been hoping they'd all go off together and discuss it, but Ewan had gone back to the CID room and Andy had seemed pleased to get away early and driven off. Probably had a date, or something.

Louise didn't. The nice guy she'd gone out with a couple of times hadn't been in touch since she'd had to cancel their cinema plan to go to the Homecoming party. He'd probably found someone else to take who didn't have a ridiculously demanding job.

She was definitely feeling flat. Apart from anything else she'd been looking forward to interviewing Jen Wilson and now Fleming was going to do it herself.

The idea about Will Stewart having killed Julia – she knew she'd only been flying a kite and Ewan and Big Marge between them had sent it fluttering down in flames. And when you really thought about it, Jen hadn't been properly scrutinised, lurking there on the fringes with her perfect alibi.

She thought back to the night of the party. Jen

had been on the fringes then too, she realised, watching but uninvolved. Had she always been like that, the one nobody noticed? If she cared enough about Connell to faint when told he was dead, she'd have been bitterly jealous of his adored Julia. There was nothing simpler than to give a druggie an overdose – and, it suddenly struck her, if PC Will was a bit free with drugs, it would be simple enough to get a tab or two of E from him and reckon that no one would ever know Julia hadn't taken it herself.

No one except Will. They'd been at a loss to understand why he should have been killed, but you could have the answer right there.

What Louise needed now was a Gitane to help her think it through. In desperation, she found some nicotine chewing gum and didn't sit down again, pacing restlessly to and fro as she masticated it. The taste really was pretty revolting.

She knew there were still gaping holes in her theory and she wished she had Andy here to bounce it off; joining the gaps was his speciality. She wasn't going to phone him, though. She could just imagine him rolling his eyes at his date and saying, 'This stupid woman from work,' after he'd brushed her off.

No, it would have to wait till the morning. There was nothing else she could do except see if for once there was something on the box that wasn't either football or politicians slagging each other off.

Or maybe there was. Fleming had said that if they could just get Randall Lindsay to come forward and explain, they might be able to score him off the list. She hadn't wiped her messages and if she checked back, she should find the ones he had sent.

Louise picked up her bag and rummaged for her phone. She scrolled through, found the message and pressed the call-back number.

There was, predictably, no response. When it went to voicemail she said carefully, 'Randall, it's Louise. Please listen to me. I want to help you. I guess you'll have been scared because we've been hunting for you but there have been new developments that could let you off the hook, if you would just explain why you haven't come forward. You'd be doing yourself a favour. And I promise if you talk to me I won't bring out the handcuffs.'

He didn't pick up and he didn't ring back immediately. But perhaps, once he'd thought about it, he might. Always supposing he was as innocent as she believed him to be.

There was a wildlife programme on BBC4. It told Louise more than she wanted to know about invertebrates, but at least it would pass the time.

Jen Wilson was looking sullen. When she opened the door she stood in front of it, blocking the way in.

'Yes? What do you want now?'

'If we could have a word,' Fleming said.

'Go on.'

'Inside, if you don't mind.'

Jen sighed elaborately. 'If you must, you must, I suppose. But I can't think what more you imagine I could tell you.'

'Oh, this and that,' Fleming said silkily, walking

into the sitting room and sitting down uninvited. MacNee followed her example and Jen, after standing for a minute with her arms folded, sat down herself with a bad grace.

'You won't mind if we record this? Saves DS MacNee having to decipher his own handwriting.'

Jen eyed the small machine he set down on the coffee table between them as someone might eye a poisonous spider, but she didn't object.

Fleming took a deep breath. 'Jen, tell us why you contacted Connell Kane to tell him it was Ecstasy that caused Julia Margrave's death.' She knew it was a high risk strategy. The calm, controlled Miss Wilson had only to keep her cool and deny it and there would be nowhere to go.

She didn't. Jen's face flared red and she stammered, 'I-I– How could I? I thought he was dead.'

'Oh, at first. When did you discover that he wasn't?'

'I-I didn't–'

'Of course you did. Skye told you. Quite recently.' Fleming was careful not to say that Skye had told them, but Jen would assume that she had. She was biting her lip now.

'You're a bad liar, Jen,' Fleming said conversationally. 'A good liar doesn't show relief when they're asked a question they can answer truthfully and you did that last time. You told quite needless lies to try to distance yourself from everything that happened, didn't you? And I wonder whether that was as much for your benefit as ours – you were in love with Connell and you can't bear to think that you caused his death.'

Would it work? There was a silence while Jen stared at her. Then she burst into tears and covered her face with her hands.

'I didn't, I didn't,' she sobbed. 'Yes, I sent him a letter. Dear God, I wish I hadn't now. But what happened wasn't anything to do with me. You can't make me feel guilty about it, you can't! It wasn't me that killed him – it was Skye.'

Fleming was pitiless. 'No, we don't believe it was. It seems that Connell tried to kill Will, Jen, and it was Will who killed him in self-defence.'

'No, no!' There was anguish in Jen's voice. 'He wouldn't, he wouldn't...' But it was clear she didn't believe what she was saying.

Fleming had her admission about the letter. Her gut feeling had been to focus on Jen and she'd been right. Now it was getting stronger; she felt a sudden surge of adrenalin.

'You were in love with Connell.' It was a flat statement, not a question and Jen didn't deny it. She bowed her head, wiping her eyes and her nose with the back of her hand.

'Did you send him the letter just so that he would come back to you?'

She looked up and her face told the truth, but she denied it. 'No, no. It was just – Skye didn't tell me until recently, just casually, in an email, as if it didn't matter. It was so cruel of her, so cruel, when she knew I'd thought he was dead.' She choked up again.

'And then you sent the letter. So what happened – did he reply?'

Jen said nothing, only shook her head.

'So there wasn't much point in it, then?'

There was still no response but Fleming waited, like a cat watching a mouse hole, until Jen went on haltingly. 'It just seemed so wrong he should be haunted by guilt when–' She stopped.

'When it was someone else? Who, Jen?' Fleming held her breath. She was getting close to it now.

'I ... I don't know. How would I?'

'Because you did it yourself? And it was worth taking the risk of telling him what had happened for the sake of seeing him again, perhaps making him look at you when he wasn't dazzled by Julia any more?'

Jen was staring at her as if transfixed. Fleming sensed MacNee moving uneasily beside her but she ignored him.

'But then Skye arrived. You knew it had all gone wrong, you heard that she had dropped the letter at Eleanor Margrave's house and knew that she would report it, you knew that Will had given you the Ecstasy and that now, with Skye being charged with murder, he was going to tell us, so he had to die too.'

Fleming believed it as she said it. She was totally unprepared for Jen's response.

She was patently amazed. 'Me – do all that? You must be barking.'

The praying mantis was holding a transparent grub between its front legs, nibbling at it delicately as the victim squirmed and writhed. Revolted, Louise Hepburn switched channels to what looked like a reality show of some kind unless, of course, there was a directive about lookism that meant that the new TV stars had to be obese, ugly people, then switched back, hoping the mantis had finished its meal. It hadn't. She switched off.

She couldn't sit here all evening just trying not to yield to the temptation to go out and buy a pack of cigarettes. Surely one of her girlfriends would be up for an evening in the pub! She got up to fetch her phone, which gave a 'ping' just as she reached it.

A text message – probably one of her friends with a similar idea, she told herself, but her hands were shaking a little as she opened it.

'Why would I trust you? R,' was all it said.

Yes! Louise punched the air. She thought for a moment. Text back? But she'd rather talk to him and he was probably holding his phone right now. She dialled his number.

At least he picked up, but there was only silence at the other end. 'Randall,' she said, 'listen to me. You can't spend your life in hiding. Move, and you'll be picked up – we're good at that. And my boss actually said that it was disappearing that made you a prime suspect. Talk to me, and we can get it all cleared up. Where are you?'

There was another long silence but she waited it out. At last he said, 'You'll send someone to arrest me. Why should I believe you? You spied on me.'

'Yes, I went to the party after you said you didn't want me there, but I didn't lie to you, Randall, and I'm not lying now. Tell me where you are.'

Again, there was the pause. 'You'll come yourself?'

So he was still in the area! Excitement bubbled through her. 'I promise.'

'If you send in the mob, I'll just vanish again, believe me. I've got my escape worked out.'

He paused, and Louise held her breath.

'All right,' he said at last. 'I'll trust you. Come to my mother's business – just off the main street in Ballinbreck. Wait till it's dark – and park round the back.'

Louise agreed and rang off. She looked impatiently at her watch, then at the sky outside that was still provokingly bright. It would be ages yet.

Cigarette, cigarette, cigarette! The word was beating a sort of tattoo in her brain. With a groan she broke out another stick of chewing gum and gloomily switched the TV back on.

It was showing the most enormous spider this time, trussing up its prey, in such vivid close-up that she sat mesmerised, almost able to feel the sticky strands tightening around her too, until with a shudder she killed the programme.

CHAPTER TWENTY-FOUR

Fleming and MacNee didn't speak as they went back to the car. Fleming held out her hand for the keys and MacNee handed them over.

She couldn't remember the last time she had felt so humiliated. She'd let herself get carried away by her pride in being instinctively right about Jen Wilson's crucial role. She'd gone on what men unkindly called 'female intuition' instead of hard evidence, and she'd got what she deserved.

There was no doubt that Jen was innocent. Her comment, after her initial reaction – 'Ask Skye! She'll tell you that's total rubbish' – had left Fleming deflated and struggling to preserve some sort of dignity, with Jen sitting in self-righteous silence as she terminated the interview.

MacNee was tactfully saying nothing. At last she said, 'Made a right fool of myself there. Rookie mistake. Sorry, Sarge.'

MacNee laughed. Back in the day, he'd been her sergeant when she arrived in the CID. 'Maybe I should have pulled rank and stopped you, lass,' he said. 'That wasn't like you.'

'It just suddenly seemed to be falling into place. The admission about the letter, the gap in her alibi for the time of Eleanor Margrave's death – I suppose I had a rush of blood to the head.'

'Happens to us all. I remember there was the once when I even did it myself – ooh, twenty years ago – or was it twenty-five?'

She smiled weakly. 'I wouldn't feel quite so bad if I hadn't been hard on Louise for being impulsive. But Tam, the situation hasn't changed. You know what I'm going to say – it's highly likely that whoever killed Will and Eleanor – and possibly even Julia as well – knows now that Skye's out on a reduced charge. The super drafted a statement so it would be on the evening news.'

'There's someone who'll have been spooked by that. What's likely to happen, if we seem to be closing in?'

MacNee gave her a cynical look. 'Chance would be a fine thing.'

Fleming winced. 'Back to square one, I suppose.'

'Och, come on, lass!' His tone was bracing. 'We've come a long way. We know who killed Connell Kane and we know it was the letter Jen Wilson sent that started it all and that likely Eleanor Margrave was killed because she saw it. And I'll tell you the other thing we know.'

Fleming looked at him hopefully.

'Folk don't stop being jealous just because they talk about "free love". Free? It's had a pretty fancy price tag for them.'

Fleming's face was sober. 'What they used to call the wages of sin, I suppose.' Then she smiled. 'In spite of all your friend Rabbie Burns had to say in favour of it.'

'Aye, well, that never did him any good neither.'

After they had gone, Jen Wilson was seized by a shaking fit. She collapsed into a chair as her knees failed her and her teeth began to chatter as if she was cold.

Shock, she told herself. There was some cheap brandy she'd bought in a duty-free; she found it and poured out half a tumbler then sat down at the kitchen table.

She could have been in prison tonight. For a moment she'd thought she was going to be, when she'd done nothing. Nothing!

'Apart from bringing the man you loved back to his death and causing an old lady, who'd suffered more than enough already, to be killed,' murmured a small, ugly voice in her head. 'It wasn't about justice for Julia either – you just thought she'd persuaded Will to give her the extra stuff, and you hated her anyway. You were perfectly happy to cause mayhem if it gave you a chance to see him again – and you despised Philippa Lindsay for doing just that to get Will. He died too, remember? If it hadn't been for you, he'd still be alive and so would Connell. And if you'd told the police the truth at the start–'

Jen swallowed half the brandy in one go. She choked and her eyes watered at the rough spirit, but she could feel its warmth spreading through her.

She *wasn't* a bad person. She'd done what was right, told Connell a truth he had every right to know. What other people did then was their own affair; she wasn't responsible. It was their fault, not hers.

She took a more cautious sip of her brandy. Yes, she was blameless. She had nothing to reproach herself with. Nothing at all.

But even so, Connell was still dead and she couldn't even dream of the day when her steadfast love might miraculously be rewarded. She put her head down on the kitchen table and wept.

The evening service at The Albatross was in full swing. Logie Stewart was putting a basket of battered fish into the fryer when Kendra burst into the kitchen. Her face was flushed and she was in a state of agitation.

'Logie, I need to speak to you right now.'

'But–' he protested.

'Right now.'

She turned and walked through the door that led to their private flat. With a shrug, Logie summoned his sous chef to take over and followed her out. She had been very fragile since Will's death; he hadn't even been sure that she'd be up to running front of house tonight.

'I can only take a minute, Kendra,' he warned her. 'We're busy–'

She didn't let him finish his sentence. 'You know what they've done? They've let Skye out and even dropped the murder charge. There was someone who heard it on the news.' She was very agitated, rubbing her hands together restlessly.

'Well, she didn't kill Will, did she?' Logie pointed out. 'Seems reasonable enough.'

'But she was involved, of course she was! I don't know, perhaps she got someone to do it for her. What happens now?'

'I expect the police just carry on with the enquiry, like they're doing now.'

'It was so horrible, the questioning.' She was beginning to cry. 'And I know they didn't believe my alibi. I can't bear it if they start again. You know the reputation the police have for stitching up innocent people, just to improve their clean-up record!'

Controlling his impatience, Logie said, 'No one thinks for a moment that you would kill anyone, let alone Will who you were so fond of. It's routine, that's all. Now make yourself a cup of tea, or something, while you calm down. I've got to get back.'

He could feel her glaring at him as he returned thankfully to the familiar frenzy of the evening service.

She had dropped MacNee off at home despite

his protests.

'Leave it for tonight,' Fleming had said. 'Get in promptly in the morning, though. We'll have at least some of the evidence from Stewart's car to follow up by then.'

'Right enough – maybe fingerprints and DNA that tells us everything we need to know, with a name and address attached. And Santa'll likely be dropping by with the presents later. But get back home yourself. Give my best to the *hardy son of rustic toil.*'

It was his favourite epithet for Bill and Fleming had nodded and waved as she drove off, though she had no intention of doing as she was told.

There were fences that needed mending where Bill was concerned and she didn't feel strong enough for that, just at the moment. It was rarely that Bill took up a stand but when he did he dug in his toes like one of his own stirks refusing to get into a trailer. She knew from experience that putting things right would mean a concession from her and her pride had suffered enough today already.

She drove back to the headquarters, parked her car and switched off the engine, but she didn't get out. Did she really want to spend another half hour, beating her brains out at her desk?

No, she didn't. She needed a shot in the arm, something to give more focus to the investigation. At least she could set aside the Connell Kane case, at any rate until the procurator fiscal started demanding the file.

So take it a step at a time. Concentrate on Eleanor Margrave next; look at the small particulars of the case instead of trying to figure out the larger picture. Perhaps it was her obsession with connections that had led her so badly astray with Jen Wilson.

She could go down and take another look round Sea House, just to concentrate her mind. If she phoned ahead, Mike Wallace could arrange to have it opened up for her.

And by the time she got back, surely she'd feel ready to go home and say whatever it took to get back on good terms with Bill.

There was a uniformed constable waiting at the gate of Sea House when Fleming arrived. He didn't look thrilled with his assignment; he looked cold and bored but dutifully logged her visit and brightened visibly when she told him he could wait in the car and that she would only be taking a quick look round.

It didn't take long for a house to take on the smell of abandonment – fusty, unaired and hushed so that Fleming almost felt she could hear the dust falling and settling. There were signs of intrusive police activity everywhere, an assault on its former order and elegance – drawers and cupboard doors standing open, greasy smears on the furniture, a small table upended having been checked for prints, a chair knocked over and left. Automatically Fleming set it back on its feet as she walked through to the hall to the drawing room.

She could hear the sound of the Solway now, murmuring gently tonight, and she went over to the big window to look out. It was bathed in the soft golden summer light that the Scots call the gloaming, after the sun has set and before the light has gone, beautiful and peaceful – and how strange to think that Eleanor and Connell Kane, who for all their differences had been united in love for Julia, were united again after death in the waters of the firth. She turned back to look at the room.

Eleanor's 'shrine' to her daughter's memory, which she had looked at before with deep pity, had been dismantled and the photographs of Julia were now piled randomly on a sofa, the snapshot of the toddler on top. Poor, poor woman, she thought, her life so marred by tragedy. It would be good to think that she had managed to take some comfort from the beauty that lay about her.

She had created beauty in the house too. Fleming's eyes lingered with pleasure on the furnishings, the pictures, the ornaments Eleanor had chosen to harmonise with the elegance of the house itself. They would all be dispersed now, sent to a saleroom where they would fetch little: a couple of hundred pounds, perhaps, for the watercolours which would be nothing special out of their setting.

She sighed and turned to go, taking one last look before she went through to the kitchen where Eleanor had been struck down.

Then she stopped, her eyes narrowing and her pulse quickening. It was a little thing, a nothing, perhaps. But – connections, connections. Just maybe she hadn't been wrong to let that shape her thinking after all.

This time, though, she wasn't going to jump to any conclusions. She was going to go back and ferret through everything she could find on the files about Eleanor Margrave.

She signalled to the constable that she was finished, jumped into her car and set off back up the road to Kirkluce.

The sky was still provokingly bright. At this time of year it would be eleven o'clock before it was properly dark and Louise Hepburn had never known an evening pass so slowly.

She had been staring at the TV without really seeing it, checking her watch every ten minutes, her mind whizzing. At half past nine she could bear it no longer; it would take a good while to get down to Ballinbreck and she could always hang around there if she arrived too early. Anything would be better than sitting here trying not to think how much she wanted a smoke.

She got up, switched off the set and got ready to go. She was just taking her car keys out of her handbag when the reality hit her.

She knew Randall was harmless – of course he was. She could handle herself and the man was just a joke, always had been, with his silly pretensions and his attempts to look cool – but on the other hand, the dumb heroine walking in blind innocence into the dark house where the villain is waiting for her was a standard trope. Suddenly the memory of the ligature around her neck, tightening and tightening, and of her own helplessness and terror struck her, so forcibly that she put her hands up to her neck as if to loosen the circle of fading bruises that still marked it.

Perhaps she was being dumb. She certainly

403

couldn't rely on Andy happening to turn up just in time to rescue her. She needn't go. She could just tip off the lads in Kirkcudbright to go round and bring Randall in – but he'd said he'd an escape plan ready to put into action in case she had shopped him. Then she wouldn't get the kudos for finding him after the police force up and down the country had failed – and after all, the boss had pretty much dismissed him as a suspect.

Even so, she hesitated. She wasn't a coward, but... Slowly, she reached for her phone.

May Macdonald's birthday party was in full swing now. The cake had been cut some time ago but it was still mild enough for everyone to be lingering on around the barbecue and with seventies hits blaring out from a speaker by the French doors a singalong had developed.

'The neighbours'll be complaining,' Andy warned his mother. 'I'll be dead embarrassed if the lads appear to tell you to turn it down.'

'They won't,' May said airily. 'The neighbours are all here.' She flung herself into 'Y.M.C.A.', making up with enthusiasm for what she might lack in grace.

Andy groaned and went to find another beer. When his phone rang, he was positively hoping he was being called back on duty – though they'd need to come and fetch him. He certainly wasn't about to drive anywhere.

Louise Hepburn sounded stiff. 'Oh – sorry to have disturbed you. You're obviously having a good time – it doesn't matter.'

'No, no!' Andy said hastily before she could

ring off. 'It's my mum's birthday party and it's getting more excruciating by the minute. Please tell me they need me down the station.'

'Well, not exactly. The thing is–'

'Hang on. I'll just try to find somewhere quieter – though it probably means walking half a mile to get out of earshot. They're worse than teenagers.'

He went inside and shut every door he could find then went upstairs to a bedroom at the front. 'I can more or less hear you now,' he said.

As he listened his first thought was, thank God she called me; his second, she's crazy!

'Look, Louise, it's quite straightforward. Get him picked up and then Big Marge can grill him in the morning. Where is he?'

'I'm not telling you.'

'Oh, for God's sake, stop mucking about. This is a safety issue. Do I need to remind you what happened last time?'

'No, of course you don't. I put it on record that I was very thankful you saved my life – still am. Permanent debt of gratitude. OK? Now could we take it as read?'

She always had the power to get under his skin. 'I never wanted thanks,' he said coldly.

'Sorry, sorry,' she said. 'I know you didn't. I didn't mean it to come out like that. It's only that I'm so keen to take this opportunity because he could just disappear again. And this time I promise you that I'm not going to be caught off my guard – as I've told you before, he's a pussycat. Talks a good line but I've known him since he was eighteen and that's all it is – a good line.

'He's not really even a suspect. It's just it would

be nice to get him ruled out, and anyway, I wouldn't be going on my own. If you come with me you can guard my back.'

'Why not wait till tomorrow and clear it with the boss? Much more sensible.'

'Because he'll be gone by then. I told you.' He could hear the exasperation in Louise's elaborately patient voice, as if she was having to explain to a dim-witted six-year-old. 'He's agreed to talk to me tonight and if you won't come with me I'll go myself. I promise you I'll be fine – just don't tip off the uniforms to intercept me or I'll never speak to you again.'

She really was the most infuriating woman! But the horror of seeing her collapsing, fighting for breath, was still vividly in his mind and there was no doubt she meant what she said about going on her own. He wouldn't be able to live with himself if anything happened to her.

Andy groaned. 'Oh, all right then. You'll have to pick me up and I warn you I'll be reeking of beer.'

'That's all right. I'm much more tolerant than some people are about others' personal habits,' she said sweetly. 'I'll be there in five minutes.'

Andy went back to the party to make his excuses to his mother, pleading tiredness. She trilled, 'No stamina, you young folk,' and went back to her dancing. They were on to 'Hi Ho, Silver Lining'.

He went outside to wait. It was typical Louise, coming up with something like this, but when he considered it calmly he didn't think it was actually dangerous – certainly not with the two of them to conduct what would be just a standard interview.

And she was right – the latest developments had all but cleared Randall and scoring him off the list would save hassle in the long run. He was just an irritating nuisance. Anyway, Andy had to confess to some mild curiosity about what sort of story he would come up with to explain why he'd been hiding when the whole of the Force was after him – and where.

When Fleming reached her desk there was a note waiting for her. The SOCOs at Balcary Bay had found a stone that was showing traces of blood and tissue. With its rough surface they had as yet failed to find fingerprints but they were hopeful that more detailed forensic investigation might produce evidence from it later.

The hire car had a superfluity of prints, but the victim's were on the steering wheel and the handle of the car door, so the perpetrator might not even have been in it. They were taking tyre moulds from a muddy puddle in one area of the car park but there was, of course, nothing to indicate that this had any relevance.

Fleming sighed. Not much to go on there, and even forensic magic would struggle to lift finger-prints from a rough surface like stone; DNA was more likely, but getting it would take days if not weeks.

She wasn't ready to consider that case anyway. Her mind was busy with her new idea, making – yes – connections. She'd learnt her lesson, though; an idea wasn't enough to go on.

She switched on her computer eagerly and scrolled through to find the labelled files she wanted. There was a huge number of them – probably more than she could even skim through now, unless she planned to spend the night at her desk. Her spirits sank. Tomorrow she could set everyone on to it, but she'd been so impatient to get some results tonight.

But when she opened the first one, a message came up. It was from DC Campbell, who must have gone back to his desk after she'd dismissed them earlier, and it said, with his usual laconic style, 'Tagged a couple of things. Worth checking out.'

She clicked on them, and there, before her eyes, was exactly the kind of evidence she had been hoping to find. Trust Ewan – always one step ahead.

There were gaps that needed to be filled in but as her mind raced she could see how it might fit together. Mentally reviewing the evidence they already had, piece after piece slotted into place. It was a whole new angle for the investigation, following a line they'd dismissed before.

Then, with a sudden chill her own words came back to her. That conversation with Louise after the last briefing: she'd answered her question carelessly, with her mind not fully engaged – too busy with her obsession about Jen.

She'd agreed with Louise's assessment that Randall was out of the frame, even said that if he gave a satisfactory account of himself they'd be able to rule him out of their enquiries. And now she thought about it, there had been something odd about the response she'd got.

Louise, who had form for impulsively taking

matters into her own hands, had said – what was it? Never believed it was him, something like that. Could she have taken their conversation as giving tacit permission to try to contact him herself? Now she thought about it, Louise certainly had his phone number and though official attempts had been made – and ignored – he might answer if it was her.

She could be putting herself in deadly danger. She had to be warned off immediately. But when Fleming phoned it rang briefly then went to voicemail.

She tried to tell herself that it was of no significance, that there were lots of reasons why Louise might have her phone switched off, that she was only being neurotic, but that was one more reason for setting off for Ballinbreck immediately. She stood up and scrolled down to Mac-Nee's number as she went to the door.

'Tam? I'm coming to pick you up. I think we're on to something.'

CHAPTER TWENTY-FIVE

'So it's Ballinbreck?' DS Andy Macdonald turned to look at DC Louise Hepburn as she drove out of Kirkcudbright and took the A711. 'Hiding in plain view, is he? I think you could afford to tell me exactly where we're going.'

She had told him what little she knew, except that last detail. Now she grinned. 'I think it's safe

409

enough now. I didn't trust you not to tip off the uniforms. And I switched off my phone so if you had grassed to Big Marge she couldn't order me to stop.'

'Oh, I know better than that,' he said wryly. 'So...?'

'The decor shop – you know, where their business is. Just off the High Street, he said.'

'I've been there. Very posh – room settings all laid out, everything costing a week's wages. So are we to think now his mother was shielding him, after all? She sounded as if she didn't like him much.'

'I never got the impression they were close, certainly. He may just have thought it was a discreet place for us to meet – out of the way, and he'd have the keys I suppose.'

'I certainly can't see where he could have been hidden while we were there, and I think the uniforms checked it out at the time too. It's just a big warehouse with an office up a stair – and he wasn't hiding under the desk while we interviewed her. If she really was protecting him, I have to say her attitude of indifference fooled me.'

'I don't think it's going to matter anyway. Big Marge clearly reckons Jen Wilson's going to give her the answers and for all we know it may be done and dusted by now. How much do you bet she's been arrested for murder?'

Speculating on the outcome kept them talking until they reached Ballinbreck and Macdonald was able to direct Hepburn to the warehouse. The car park at the front was empty when she turned in, but Lindsay, she said, had told her to go round the back. There was only a narrow, weed-grown path along the farther side of the building but it was wide enough, just, to allow a car to pass through to a sort of paved yard. There was another car there: Lindsay's car, with the number plate they had all been told to look out for.

Macdonald gave a low whistle. 'Been here all the time, do you reckon? Hoping to bunk up till we'd all forgotten about it?'

'Not very smart, if so.' Hepburn parked the car and got out. 'Look, let me go to the door to talk to him first. I don't want him to think we're just going to burst in and arrest him.'

That seemed fair enough. He walked with her to the end of the building and then hung back.

It was very dark now. The street lamps from the High Street were a glow in the sky but there was no moon and in the pale starlight the scrubby bushes round the edge of the car park waved in the night breeze, casting shifting shadows. As he watched Hepburn cross confidently to the door, Macdonald moved from foot to foot. He was feeling edgy – just the atmosphere, he told himself, since there was nothing to worry about. He wasn't going to let Hepburn go into the place alone.

He could see the door opening now, but no light spilt out. She had stepped forward so that she was blocked from his view and he didn't hesitate. She could have been pulled in, attacked – he was across the car park in a few strides.

She turned her head to scowl at him. He didn't see Lindsay just at first, standing in the darkness of the warehouse, but as he reached Hepburn's side the man stepped forward.

Macdonald would hardly have recognised him. When last he'd spoken to him he'd been arrogant, sneering. This man was unshaven and dishevelled; he looked desperate and, with the sixth sense for trouble that police officers develop, Macdonald stiffened. He didn't like it; a cornered rat has nothing to lose.

'So – you lied to me,' Lindsay snarled at Hepburn. 'You said you weren't going to turn me in.'

Really! Hepburn thought, with extreme exasperation, why couldn't Andy have waited long enough to give her time to explain before he appeared? To protect her, presumably, and that was frankly patronising. She gave him a dirty look.

'Randall, let me explain,' she said. 'I haven't lied to you – this isn't a raiding party. We just want to interview you and two officers is standard procedure. All we want is for you to explain why you went into hiding and then we can probably sort things out. All right?'

She was crossing her fingers. They could, of course, go down the arrest route but that would mean lawyers and all sorts of complications.

Lindsay looked from one to the other. After a long pause, he said, 'Do I have an alternative? Oh, you'd better come in, I suppose.'

Hepburn followed him as he picked his way across the pitch-dark showroom. She could just make out the white-painted railings of a staircase as Lindsay started up it and behind her she heard Macdonald swear as he bumped into something.

Lindsay opened a door at the top and went forward to switch on a table light on a desk; this must be his mother's office. There was some dark fabric draped across the window to conceal the light and the air was heavy with the stale smell of cigarettes. Hepburn tried not to think about that, even when Lindsay reached in a packet that lay on the desk and lit one. His hands, she noticed, were trembling.

'Have you been here all the time, Randall?' She tried to make it sound as casual as a social enquiry as she sat down on a neat little sofa and Macdonald took a chair.

Lindsay didn't sit. He was pacing to and fro taking nervous drags at his cigarette as if he couldn't keep still.

'No, no,' he said. 'I only came late last night.'

'Where were you before?' Hepburn asked. 'Why did you take off after the party?'

He turned on her. 'Because I was sodding-well fed up, that's why! My mother was treating me like a slave and when I was absolutely wrecked the morning after the party she told me to go out there and clear up litter as if I were a binman. I wasn't going to put up with it. All right?'

'It hadn't anything to do with trying to strangle Louise the night before, by any chance?' Macdonald's tone was coldly cynical.

Again, Hepburn glared at him. She wanted Lindsay chatty, not defensive. Now all he said, with a touch of his old loftiness, was, 'I'm afraid I haven't the faintest clue what you're talking about,' and she had no idea whether he was telling the truth or not.

'So – where did you go, then?' she said.

'Went to stay with a mate in Glasgow, that's all. For obvious reasons I didn't tell my mother where I was going and it wasn't until I was driving back here yesterday that I heard on the radio that everyone was looking for me.

'You don't know what it's like, do you, being hunted – when I hadn't done anything! So I just parked up out of the way, lay low till it was dark. I didn't know what it was all about, didn't know what to do. Then last night I phoned my mother and she said I was in trouble – you were looking for me, that my room had just been searched, that they were asking questions about Julia–'

'Oh yes, Julia,' Macdonald said. 'Why don't you tell us what happened with Julia?'

'Andy!' Hepburn muttered in a furious undertone. 'Let me take this–'

'Julia? Nothing happened with Julia. We worked together, that's all.'

And now she was sure he was lying. She felt a cold chill; perhaps this hadn't been such a straightforward, ticking-the-boxes exercise as she had thought. At least she had been wise enough not to come alone.

'She can't have been your favourite person though, could she? She was going to get you sacked for dishonesty. Prosecuted, probably.' Macdonald was determined to needle him.

She'd never have asked him along if she'd known he was going to take over like this. Before Lindsay could reply, Hepburn cut in, 'What happened after you contacted your mother?'

'She said if I managed to get here without being picked up she'd let me stay, just for a bit, to decide the best thing to do. So I drove here then hid the car round the back and slept on one of the showroom beds. Then I was stuck hiding in the office all today, just wondering what would happen next.

'I told her you'd contacted me and she said talking to you would be a good idea, to tell you to come here so I could explain and we could get everything straightened out.'

There was something about the way he said that – almost as if it had been memorised – that made the hairs stand up on the back of Hepburn's neck. Perhaps, after all, this wasn't the smartest idea she'd had all year.

Macdonald had noticed it too. She saw him sit up straight, quietly moving nearer the edge of his seat. Unobtrusively, she uncrossed her own legs so that her feet were flat on the floor in case sudden action was needed.

Lindsay was sounding more confident now. 'You see, this is all a wild goose chase. I've had nothing to do with this, start to finish. I know I was a fool not to contact you immediately, but–'

Macdonald was on his feet. 'What was that?' he said sharply.

Hepburn had heard nothing. As she started to get up Macdonald said, 'Back in a minute,' and went out of the door.

Philippa Lindsay let herself out of the back door of Ballinbreck House, shutting it quietly behind her even though Charles, in his study upstairs with the TV on, wouldn't have heard her if she'd slammed it.

She was wearing dark trousers and a black jacket and she walked across the lawn, a shadow herself in the shadow cast by the trees, towards

415

the door by the garage that opened on to the scrubland on the other side of the high wall. There was a rough path through fields and a copse behind the houses on the street that would take her directly to the warehouse; she enjoyed the walk there on sunny mornings.

Tonight, though, it was dark and the path was rutted and muddy but it wasn't overlooked and she couldn't risk the quicker route along the main street; even in quiet Ballinbreck at this time of night there were people moving about and if she was seen it would be the end of everything.

Philippa ought to have been feeling nervous but she wasn't. She felt totally cold and calm, perhaps because she hadn't allowed herself to feel anything since Will had had to die. It shouldn't have happened, she should never have been in this position. God knew she'd begged and begged him to leave it alone... But he wouldn't, and she knew who to blame – that silly little bitch Skye. And the police spy too, with the threats she posed. She'd got Will spooked and now–

She daren't let herself think about it, let the waves of grief and bitterness pour over her. Philippa had a job to do – a simple enough job, in all conscience, and provided she kept calm, did it quickly and neatly, and her idiot son played his part, it would work perfectly. She smiled grimly.

She allowed herself one neurosis – patting her pocket to check that what she needed was there, even though she knew it was.

There was the warehouse now, its bulk dark against the night sky. She could see light seeping from round the square of her office window and frowned. She'd impressed on Randall that the place needed to be absolutely dark and he couldn't even do that – typical! Probably it wouldn't matter.

At the gate she stopped by the board that stood there. 'Etcetera: Interior Design by Philippa Lindsay', it read. She had taken so much trouble over choosing the colour of the paint, the style of the lettering. She had really loved her business.

Philippa gave a deep sigh, then keeping in the shadows she walked the length of the building and looked round the corner. There were two cars there, Randall's and another she didn't recognise.

With a nod of satisfaction she walked back and opened the door. She winced as it gave a little creak, but it didn't matter. There was no way back now.

'You'll tell me if I'm getting carried away by my theory this time, won't you, Tam?' Fleming said. 'I don't want to go making a fool of myself again.'

'I wonder you have to ask me,' MacNee said dryly. 'When have I ever been backward in coming forward?'

'Ah, but I know how it goes against your shy and bashful nature. Anyway, this is what I've turned up.

'I went back to Sea House, just to get myself grounded again after the Jen Wilson fiasco. I was looking round the sitting room and I suddenly noticed an ornament she had – a lovely thing, a sculpture of a seal in polished stone. I'd seen these in Philippa Lindsay's shop so that had to be a connection – worth following up, at least.

'I went back to the station to go through the notes and found that Ewan was ahead of me. He'd flagged up two things for me to look at: the interview he and Andy had done with Philippa where she'd said Eleanor was "an acquaintance" – natural enough, why not?

'But then he'd spotted that the day she was killed Eleanor had made a phone call to Philippa. Eleanor didn't make many phone calls – just hair-dresser, doctor, routine things. She didn't seem to have many friends, apart from Bridget James.'

'Aye, Mrs James thought she didn't have any locally. Was Philippa the only one, maybe?'

'She certainly didn't say that in the interview – stressed it was only a very casual acquaintance-ship – and this was the only call listed to her number. So what I want to know is what Eleanor talked to her about in that call.'

'Hmm. I can tell you what she'll say, if you ask her.' MacNee was sceptical.

'Oh, I know – that Eleanor wanted to know if there was a new shipment of sculptures or some such thing. But they knew each other, and the timing of the call could be significant.

'These are the only two pointers we've got and you don't need to tell me they're flimsy. But I have a scenario I want to run past you. Shoot it down in flames if you want.

'We know Skye dropped the letter when she was staying at Sea House back in April. Now, if Eleanor had found it then, why didn't she men-tion it to her friend Biddy in one of their many phone calls?

'Supposing she didn't find it immediately. Sup-

418

pose she finds it later – on the morning she died, say. She reads it, she's shocked, of course. And suppose she decides to phone Philippa to ask her if she knew anything about this? She knew her slightly and she'd certainly have known about the connection with the Cyrenaics from the inquest.'

MacNee grunted. 'Reaching a bit, there.'

'I know. But listen, Tam. Jen Wilson told us Randall was in a bad mood the night Julia died. He probably knew she was probably going to get him sacked. And he and his mother had been having a row – had he confessed to her, and she had been furious with him?

'Now don't tell me there isn't much love lost between them because I agree with you. But I'll tell you what Philippa does love – she loves her lifestyle, being lady of the manor, and I don't think she could keep that going on. Since the recession hit the business was struggling. Randall was earning a fat-cat salary; she'd be reckoning that he'd keep the business afloat, if not for love then for the sake of inheriting a going concern.'

MacNee, whose attitude had definitely been sceptical, was starting to look interested.

'OK, I'll go along with that so far. And...?'

'She sees her chance when she's having drinks with the Cyrenaics before they went out to the forest – Jen told us that. She's a hanger-on, wants to be down with the kids because of Will. We know she got stuff from him from time to time – and she spotted her chance when Julia was obviously well away already.'

'Slipped it in her drink, do you mean?'

Fleming nodded. 'Or maybe even just offered it

to her. From what I can make out the woman was at the stage when she'd take anything. Kane was probably keeping her as short as he could for her own safety.

'And then everything's fine until Eleanor Margrave phones. Suddenly, it's all falling apart. An enquiry is the last thing Philippa can afford. So...?'

'She'd an alibi, though, didn't she?'

'I checked that this evening. It's porous, hard to pin down for times. Same with the one for Stewart's murder.'

'She kills Stewart too? When she's so daft about him that she stirs everything up again, arranges the whole Homecoming stuff to get him back, according to the husband?' MacNee was frankly incredulous.

'She thought she was safe by then. But when all this happened, Stewart started putting two and two together – he wasn't a stupid man. Kane has accused him of giving E to Julia. He knows he didn't, but–'

'He knows who he did give it to?' Suddenly MacNee was with her. 'He asks her about it at the party – the conversation Louise couldn't quite hear. But maybe he thought she had, and that we were going to throw the book at him– Here! You could be on to something there, you know that?'

'Tam, it's all speculative, like I said. But it works, and it gives her the commonest motive of all. Money. If I'm right about this, when it comes right down to it love means nothing by comparison. She's totally ruthless.

'And I tell you what's worrying me – Louise.'

420

She told him about the conversation she'd had with her about Randall. 'And I couldn't get hold of her tonight, Tam – her mobile's switched off.'

He shook his head. 'Naw! How's she going to find him anyway, when Britain's finest have failed? And even supposing she did, it's his mother that's the problem, not him.'

'Oh, you're probably right. And if we bring Philippa in for questioning it would solve the problem anyway.'

'Just ignore it,' Randall Lindsay called. 'The building creaks all the time!'

But his face was pale and sweaty, Hepburn saw, as she sprang to the door after her sergeant.

Below, the warehouse was a pit of darkness beyond the pool of light coming from the open door behind her. She saw Macdonald standing at the foot of the staircase, facing towards the warehouse door. She saw, in the darkness, a dark shape moving silently towards him, a shape holding something above its head, something it brought down on his head. He crumpled, falling to the floor with a groan.

The shadow's arm was raised again. 'Police – freeze!' Hepburn screamed at the top of her voice, launching herself down the stairs, throwing herself at the weapon and deflecting the blow with her shoulder.

She didn't even notice the pain. The force of her attack had knocked his assailant over and Hepburn threw herself on top. Scrabbling for purchase, she found hair under her hand and she grabbed it, pulling with all her might.

There was a scream, high-pitched – a woman's scream. Hepburn levered herself up, trying to smash the other's head down against the concrete floor, but the woman was tall and strong, fighting back. And now in the dim light she could make out her face – Philippa Lindsay. Who else?

'Andy!' Hepburn yelled, but there was only a sickening silence in response. She was still winning the struggle, but only just.

Lindsay had come down the stairs and was standing watching. He wasn't leaping to her aid, was he?

She tried, though. 'Randall, help me! I'll speak for you–'

A flailing arm caught her painfully on the face and a sharp, commanding voice said, 'Randall, get on with it! She's hurting me.'

And she could hear the smirk in Lindsay's voice as he said, 'Doubt if you'll be in a position to say very much, in my favour or otherwise,' and pulled Hepburn roughly off his mother up on to her feet, twisting her arms cruelly up behind her back.

Philippa stood up, dusting herself down and patting her hair back into place in a pantomime of calm, though Hepburn could see her shaking.

'Thank you, *sweetie!*' Her voice was icily sarcastic. 'You took your time about it.'

Hepburn, her own voice unsteady, said, 'Philippa Lindsay, Randall Lindsay, you are both under arrest. Release me immediately.' She felt stupid even as she said it.

'Oooh, I'm scared,' Lindsay sneered.

'Well, it's a pretty thought,' Philippa said. 'Pretty, but pointless.'

Stepping round Macdonald, she walked across to the wall by the door, a wall hung with sample curtains, and stopped about halfway along, stooping to check something on the floor.

Hepburn couldn't see what it was. A sense of unreality had come over her; she was fighting against Lindsay – kicking, trying to lean far enough forward to bite, but he was six inches taller and far stronger. He only jerked her arms up more painfully and held her off, laughing. No matter what she did, she couldn't break his grip.

And there was Macdonald, still not moving. She couldn't see whether he was breathing or not. He could be dead, and desolation engulfed her.

Philippa had moved now to the curtain nearest the door. She took a cigarette lighter out of her pocket and lit the edge. It flared immediately.

Some sort of accelerant, Hepburn thought numbly. *She's soaked them in it, planned to set the place on fire and burn us to death. And I've brought Andy into this.*

Philippa had opened the door, stepping quickly outside. Lindsay hurled Hepburn to the floor and, leaving her struggling to her feet, ran to the door after his mother.

It slammed in his face and Hepburn heard the click of a key turning. A second curtain was blazing now.

'Mother!' Randall screamed. 'Let me out! Mum! Mum!'

CHAPTER TWENTY-SIX

There were two cars parked outside Ballinbreck House and there were lights on, but it took three rings on the doorbell before Charles Lindsay appeared, apologetic.

'I'm so sorry, I was upstairs in my study with the TV on. I thought my wife would go – it's always more likely to be for her than it is for me. What can I do for you?'

'It is your wife we wanted, in fact,' Fleming said. 'Could we have a word with her?'

He didn't ask why. He gave them a level look then said only, 'She's upstairs. I'll go and dig her out. Just go and sit down.'

He waved them into the sitting room and disappeared upstairs, calling, 'Philippa! Philippa! That's the police, wanting to speak to you.'

MacNee looked doubtfully at the cream and turquoise linen chairs they had been invited to sit on. 'Places like this always make me feel I'm wearing my old tacketty boots,' he complained. 'You couldn't just relax in your socks with a beer in here, could you?'

'It's not meant for that. This is where you take people to impress them – or to sit admiring your own exquisite taste with a glass of chilled Pinot Grigio. But where is she?'

They could still hear Charles going round the house, calling her name. After a few minutes he reappeared, looking puzzled. 'I can't find her. She told me specifically that she was going to have a bath and an early night, but she seems to have gone out.'

'Her car's there,' Fleming said. 'Where would she have gone without it?'

'If there was a meeting or something in the village or she was going to see a neighbour, she'd probably walk, but she didn't mention that to me. She's probably at the shop – she seems to spend most of her time there these days. Not that it's doing any good. It's going to go under and she might as well face up to it.'

'You're not sounding much bothered, Mr Lindsay,' MacNee said.

Charles shrugged. 'Swings and roundabouts,' he said. 'It'll be the end of more than the business.'

He didn't expand on that. He bade them a polite good evening and went back, no doubt to his study and his TV programme.

'If he'd had a basin handy, you'd have seen him washing his hands. Nothing to do with him, whatever she's done, eh?' MacNee said.

'A seriously dysfunctional family. I suppose we try the warehouse. She's maybe preparing the books for the receiver.'

Randall was shaking the inner door, screaming obscenities. 'You can't do this! Come back!' The outer door shutting with a bang was the only response.

The fire was running right up the curtains, burning with a dense, choking smoke.

'Shut up!' Hepburn yelled at him. 'Fire exit?'

'Isn't one. What are we going to do? She wants to burn me alive – her own son!'

And two other people. Hepburn had her mobile out, ready to dial emergency but there was no signal inside the metal shell of the building. And by the time someone noticed and called the fire brigade they might be dead anyway from smoke inhalation. If they were lucky.

'Extinguishers?' There had to be, surely.

He looked around helplessly. She couldn't see any either; Philippa had thought of that, probably.

Terror was stopping her thinking straight. She needed to get a grip. 'Find something to batter down the door,' she screamed at him. 'Take this!'

She bent to pick up the weapon Philippa had used on Andy: a two-foot polished stone sculpture – an otter on its hind legs, she registered automatically. Randall snatched it from her and went to the door. The smoke was thicker there: he began to cough as he swung it at the lock.

Hepburn looked wildly about her. One of the curtains fell and a rug on the floor began to smoulder – smoulder, not burn. There were any number of rugs around the place, flameproof, even, perhaps.

She seized one, ran to the farther edge of the fire, pulled down the drapes nearest it to create a firebreak, then used the rug to beat at the licking flames.

'It's no use! She's shut the outer door!' Randall was panicking now.

'Leave it,' she ordered. 'Get a rug! Beat them down.'

But some flimsy drapes had caught now and in the draught from the spreading flames scraps were floating, alight like Chinese lanterns, across the room. The cover on one of the beds flared up as one landed and the ring of fire grew faster and faster about them. A floating rag fell on her arm and she brushed it off, barely registering the pain.

It was getting hotter now. Sweat pouring down her face, Hepburn raced round, swatting frantically at each new outburst, trying to keep ahead of the blaze as Randall stood uselessly by, paralysed by his terror.

She was losing the battle. The acrid smoke was getting thicker and Hepburn began to cough, tears pouring from her smarting eyes. She could feel her lips cracking, her skin drying out. It was so hot, so hot! There were burns on her hands now too and the pain was excruciating.

The floor – she remembered from her training; the air would be clearer nearer the floor. But you couldn't go on fighting if you lay down. She wasn't going to give up, not until she had to. She redoubled her efforts, snatching up another rug as the one she had been using began to smoulder, but with the pain, the lack of oxygen and the terrible heat her breathing was laboured and she was losing strength.

'You might – you might as well face it.' Lindsay was crouching halfway up the staircase, huddled now, crying hysterically, his arms wrapped round himself. 'We're finished. Damn her to hell! We're going to die!'

She ignored him. Coughing, retching, her

throat raw as if it was bleeding, she struggled on.

Then, from the floor she heard Macdonald's voice. 'Louise...?'

He sounded groggy but he was alive and for a fraction of a second her heart lifted. Then it hit her. He had come round, only to face the horror of choking to death or burning alive in the inferno of smoke and flame that surrounded them.

She went over to crouch down beside Macdonald, taking his hand. Randall was right. There was nothing more she could do.

'No one here,' MacNee said as Fleming drove into the car park of Etcetera. 'The outer door's shut.'

'Damn,' Fleming said. 'I was sure this was where she was going to be. So, what now? Do we go back to the house and wait until she comes home?'

'Do you think it's worth it?' It was all very well to indulge the boss in her fancy theories but MacNee was beginning to think longingly of his bed. 'Nothing's going to happen if we wait till the morning.'

Fleming sighed. 'You're probably right. OK.' She swung the car round to drive back out, then stopped. 'Look, Tam – there's a light up there.'

High on the side of the building, a small square window was outlined by light spilling round the edges of a curtain.

'That's her office,' Fleming said. 'She's here after all. Let's go and knock on the door.'

She parked the car. As they got out, they smelt smoke. Looking closer, they could see it seeping through the gaps around the door.

MacNee had his phone out of his pocket, dialling emergency and speaking urgently as they both sprinted across.

Fleming tugged at the door. 'It's locked. She must be inside. We need to break this down.'

'Ram it,' MacNee said, and she nodded, running back to start the car.

He stood waiting, poised for action. He was worried; there could be a fireball ready to explode and his first priority would be to rescue Marjory – Philippa Lindsay could take her chances.

It was only the slightest of sounds – the faint rustle of leaves underfoot, a tiny twig snapping. He spun round. A dark figure emerged from the shadows under the trees, moving fast and low across the car park.

At the same moment, Fleming's car hit the warehouse door. There was no fireball; the door, though it splintered, still held. Fleming reversed, ready to try again.

MacNee took off. As the figure ahead of him sped across the side road, he saw in the light from the lamps in the main street that it was unmistakably Philippa Lindsay.

There was no need to go in hot pursuit. He knew where to find her.

This was the oldest trick in the book – setting your failing business on fire so that you could claim the insurance money. He'd better stop the boss from dashing in to rescue someone who wasn't there and endangering her own life in the process.

The sound of the impact of Fleming's car on the door galvanised Hepburn. Screaming, 'Help!

Help!' at the top of her voice, she rushed to it, pulling her jacket across her face to give some sort of protection.

There were no drapes to the right of the door, and the curtains where the blaze had been started had burnt out so the smoke was, at least for the moment, thinner here, though behind her the ring of flame was growing faster and faster, right along the back wall now, engulfing sofas and chairs, beds and tables in its rage.

Whatever that noise had been, the inner door was still solidly in place; Hepburn had no idea what was happening. The flames were roaring like a stormy sea – would anyone hear her screams?

Behind her, Macdonald had staggered to the door beside her. Flat on the floor, he'd suffered less from smoke but he looked groggy; in the livid light of the flames she could see a great gash on his temple and he still didn't look as if he was focusing. But when she tried to pick up the sculpture again she hadn't the strength to lift it and he took it from her to swing it at the door.

A panel splintered. Now they could see that someone had battered the outer door – battered it, but not broken it down.

'Go on, go on!' she urged.

As air came in through the opening they gasped in its freshness greedily. If Macdonald took out another panel, if the door was hit again...

But the fire had been refreshed by the air too. It was raging even more fiercely now; the centre of the building was a sea of flame and only the farther wall by the staircase, where there were no drapes, had not yet caught.

Macdonald, too, was losing strength now. They were both coughing their lungs out.

Hepburn glanced over her shoulder. Randall had passed out and was lying on the floor a few feet away, overcome.

And in another moment, Hepburn realised bleakly, they would be too.

Running back to the car park, MacNee saw that Fleming had backed the car into position for a second attempt at the door. Waving his arms, he signalled to her to stop, came across and opened the car door.

'That was Philippa, running away. It's just good, old-fashioned arson,' he said. 'We might as well wait for the fire brigade.'

The second impact hadn't come. Even with their faces pressed to the gap in the inner door, breathing was getting more difficult and the heat was all but unbearable. Hepburn could smell her hair singeing

'One ... last ... try,' Macdonald wheezed. He took her hand and squeezed it. 'Scream – now!'

'Fine,' Fleming said. 'Wonder how long they'll be?'

When she switched off the engine, the noise of the raging flames filled the silence. MacNee, by the open car door, stood listening to it.

'Amazing, the racket it makes,' he said. 'I can feel the heat from here.'

'We'd better get out of the way, anyway – clear the space for the experts. Hop in, Tam.'

He hesitated. 'Hang on,' he said, taking a couple of paces nearer the building. He turned, his eyes wide in shock. 'There's someone in there! Hit it again!'

He leapt back from the car as Fleming slammed it into gear and accelerated. Someone in there – if they were close by, the falling door might kill them anyway. But anything was better than burning alive.

This time, they heard it coming. They were able to dodge to the left where the fire had already done its worst, and the inner door came in with the outer, crashing harmlessly to the floor.

Tongues of flame surged forward. The car backed up, out of reach, and Macdonald and Hepburn stumbled through the opening, out into the blessed fresh air.

CHAPTER TWENTY-SEVEN

Ballinbreck House was in darkness when Fleming and MacNee arrived, shaken, tired, and very, very angry at two in the morning.

The fire engines and ambulance had arrived with impressive speed and Andy Macdonald and Louise Hepburn were in hospital suffering from smoke inhalation, with concussion in Macdonald's case and burns in Hepburn's, but the outlook was good. Randall Lindsay, on the other hand, was fighting for his life.

'It's going to be hard keeping calm, dealing with this one,' MacNee said. 'I just want to get her by the throat. The woman's a monster.'

Fleming agreed. 'Nothing mattered more than her selfish interests – even her own son.'

'And a couple of random police officers, but I can see they wouldn't count,' MacNee said with considered irony. 'What's she going to say now?'

'She'll deny everything. Have we got uniforms around the house, though, just in case she makes a run for it?'

MacNee nodded. 'I did that whenever the lads arrived at the warehouse – though I was only assuming she would go straight home. I don't think she knew I saw her.'

'Well, we're going to find out now,' Fleming said grimly. She rang the bell, keeping it pressed even after a light came on in an upstairs room, watching other lights appear until the door opened and Philippa Lindsay stood there.

She was wearing a green silk dressing gown, cinched so tightly round her waist that it looked as if she was girded for battle. Her face was flushed.

'What is the meaning of this?' she demanded.

MacNee pushed past her into the house. 'In there,' he said, pushing her roughly towards the sitting room.

'How dare you!' she shouted. 'Take your hands off me, you disgusting little man!'

Fleming spoke from behind him. 'Philippa Lindsay, I am arresting you on suspicion of attempted murder. You are not obliged to say anything but anything you do say will be noted down and may be used in evidence. Do you understand?'

Shock showed in her face. 'I-I don't know what you mean.'

MacNee had his notebook out. Provocatively, he repeated, 'I – don't – know – what – you – mean,' as he wrote it down.

'Do you understand?' Fleming said again.

Philippa stood very still. When she spoke, her tone was different. 'Yes, of course I understand. I'm sorry for my reaction – it's just that it's really such a ridiculous accusation I couldn't believe it.

'Look, let's sit down, talk this through. There must be some silly misunderstanding.' She gave an unsteady laugh as she went to sit down, waving her hand for the officers to do the same.

They didn't move. 'Do you wish to make a statement?' Fleming said. 'You are entitled to representation from a solicitor before you do.'

'I don't want this to become official when I can probably give you a simple explanation.' Her face, flushed before, had become deathly pale. 'What can I tell you, to show you that you've got this all wrong?'

'For a start, you can tell us where you were tonight,' Fleming said.

'Here,' Philippa said confidently. 'I went up to have a bath and get an early night. My husband can bear me out.'

'He can't, you know.' Charles Lindsay had come quietly into the room. 'You didn't.'

She turned her head and gave him a look of purest rage. 'Of course I did, don't be stupid!'

'I'd be rather stupid to back up your story, since these officers came round to speak to you while you were out, doing whatever it is you've done

434

this time.'

He seemed, Fleming thought, to be taking a quiet satisfaction in saying it, and then in watching his wife crumple. She bent forward, putting her hands over her face as if overcome, but when she looked up again there were no signs of tears or despair.

'Oh God, it's about the warehouse, isn't it? I knew I'd be the first suspect, I knew it was wrong. But it was the only way I could rescue anything from the wreck of the business. I'm hardly the first to do that – to take on the robber barons who have us over a barrel for insurance and make their profits out of our losses.'

She was wringing her hands quite artistically and anguished guilt was beautifully depicted. 'Is that a confession?' Fleming said as MacNee scribbled earnestly.

'Oh, I'll put my hand up to that, Inspector – but the rest – I can't think what you're talking about.' Her hands fluttered helplessly but her eyes were pebble-hard.

'And I suppose you didn't know that your son and two police officers were in there at the time?'

Philippa's hand went to her throat this time. 'Oh – oh no!' she cried. 'You mean – you mean there was someone – someone inside? Not – not Randall! My boy – he'd have had the keys, he should have told me if he was hiding there!'

She collapsed into her chair and there were sobbing noises, but Fleming was ready to bet that her eyes were dry. She turned, a little anxiously, to look at Charles; this was a brutal way to break the news about his son.

435

Charles seemed oddly unmoved. 'Dead?' he asked her.

'In hospital. Critical.'

Philippa's head came up. She was dry-eyed and when she said, 'Critical?' Fleming had little doubt that this was unwelcome news.

'You haven't asked about the police officers,' she said. She was going to enjoy this next bit. 'Fortunately, they are in slightly better shape than your son and were able to give us perfectly coherent statements detailing your part in tonight's events. We have another eyewitness in the form of my sergeant here to your presence at the crime scene.'

MacNee gave Philippa a little mocking bow as Fleming went on, 'We will also be questioning you about the murders of Eleanor Margrave and William Stewart. At the police station, where we are taking you now.'

She could see the shock hitting her but when Philippa stood up her posture was rigid and her face a mask of contempt. 'I have nothing to say to you. I want a lawyer now. I assume I can change my clothes?'

Fleming gave MacNee a nod and he went out, returning with a policewoman ready to escort her upstairs.

Charles Lindsay stood silently aside in the doorway. His wife passed him without a word or even a glance.

MacNee put away his notebook, then burst out, 'Are you not wanting to go to your son? He's in a bad way.'

Charles raised his eyebrows. 'My son? Well, he may be or he may not. I've never really cared to find out. But she's been unfaithful to me from the start. Good business head, though.'

He walked out, leaving Fleming and MacNee staring after him.

It seemed a very long drive back to Kirkluce. Fleming and MacNee were both yawning.

'Talk to me, Tam,' she said. 'If you don't get a reply, I've fallen asleep.'

'At least we don't need to interview her tonight. If she'd been prepared to talk it would have had to be sensational to keep me awake.'

'If she'd told the truth, it would have been. But she'll be set to deny everything now.'

'You didn't mention Julia or the attack on Louise. Deliberate?'

'Don't think we've a chance of fingering her for Louise – not a scrap of evidence, though Philippa may have been worried that she'd remember something. Julia...' She shrugged. 'Now she's got rid of Will Stewart, there's no one to say she was in possession of Ecstasy that night, let alone that Julia didn't take it herself when it was offered.'

'Unless Randall knows different.'

'If he makes it.' Fleming sighed. 'And even so he's not likely to tell us – he'll be in the dock too, on Louise's evidence about him restraining her while Philippa lit the fire.'

'So we're pinning our hopes on forensics for the other two?'

'I suppose so. They're looking for traces of DNA from Eleanor's body and I suppose there may even be fingerprints we can identify once they take Philippa's. But she'll fight every step of

437

the way, that's for sure.'

It was half past three when Marjory Fleming crept into bed, moving gingerly so as not to disturb her sleeping husband.

But a voice spoke. 'And what time do you call this to be coming home, young lady?'

She laughed and snuggled into his arms. 'The only assignation I had was with a woman. Unless you count Tam MacNee.'

'I've always worried about his charismatic charm,' Bill muttered sleepily, kissed her and turned over.

A moment later she heard him snoring gently and smiled. Sometimes the best way to make up a row was just to say nothing and forget about it, she thought as she fell into exhausted sleep herself.

Everything hurt. Her face hurt, her shoulder hurt, her hands hurt, her chest hurt when she breathed and the nauseating smell of singed hair was all about her. She felt disgusting with the layers of greasy gunk they had put all over her face and across her split lips; it tasted disgusting too.

Louise Hepburn was trying to be grateful that she was still alive to experience all this pain and discomfort but it was easier to acknowledge that in theory than it was in practice.

Almost worse was the sense of guilt. With her arrogant contempt for Randall Lindsay she'd not only walked into deadly danger herself, she'd dragged Andy in as well. It was only luck that had saved his life.

She heard someone come into the room – a

nurse to carry out the exquisitely painful process of changing the dressings, probably. She opened her eyes reluctantly.

Instead, it was Andy's mother, May, who was looking down at her.

'I didn't mean to wake you,' she said. 'Oh, you poor wee soul!'

A huge wave of guilt swept over Louise. 'I'm sorry, I'm so sorry!' she cried.

May sat down on the chair beside the bed, looking puzzled. 'What for, dear?'

'If it wasn't for me, Andy wouldn't have gone there. I nearly got him killed.'

'Well, that's not what he said. He said you saved his life. After that woman hit him, he saw her all ready to hit him again, and you taking the blow to stop her, before he lost consciousness.'

'He wouldn't have been there at all if it wasn't for me,' Louise muttered.

'I don't know about that. He's a big lad now, you know, and he makes his own decisions. All Andy said was that it's just the job – don't know why you want to do it, myself.' May shook her head. 'But if you hadn't been there the other poor laddie whose own mother was going to kill him would just have been burnt to death.'

'Is there any word of how he is this morning?'

'Andy didn't know. But he's going to be fine, anyway, and he sent me along to tell you he's got to wait to see the doctor but that whenever they discharge him he'll be round to see you at once.'

Louise's hand went up to shield her face. 'Oh no!' she said.

May laughed. 'From the way he was speaking

about you, I doubt if you need to worry what you're looking like.' She got up.

'You need your rest. I'm not going to stay any longer. I just wanted to say that when they let you out you're coming home to me. You'll be needing a wee bit extra TLC and I'll just love having a daughter to spoil – you've no idea what it's like living in a household of menfolk.'

She winked and departed.

Louise settled back against her pillows, trying to blink away the tears – it was too painful to cry. She should really have corrected May when she said 'daughter' – but remembering how she had felt when she'd thought Andy was dead, she wasn't absolutely sure that one day it mightn't be right.

When Fleming and MacNee were at last admitted on Friday after a very long, tense wait there was oxygen by Randall Lindsay's bedside but he was not only able to talk, but keen. He had waved aside his solicitor's advice to say nothing.

'I want her locked up for the rest of her life,' was the first thing he said, and he was in a good position to make sure she would be. While flatly denying all knowledge of the murders of Eleanor Margrave and Will Stewart, he was able to quote his mother on Julia Margrave when she learnt that Randall's job was on the line: '"She's a druggie anyway – she's doomed, and if she's going to die it might as well be sooner as later."' He insisted he hadn't thought she really meant anything by it, at the time, though now, of course...

And it had been entirely Philippa's idea to

bring Louise to the warehouse – he had, of course, no idea she planned to set it on fire, obviously, and as for his restraining Louise – well, she was attacking his mother and he didn't know what had got into her. He hadn't seen anything happening to the other policeman – just thought he'd fallen or something.

It was difficult not to go in hard and challenge every lying word, but this wasn't the time or place. Fleming had to let it ride; no doubt there would be horse-trading over evidence provided and charges laid between his brief and the procurator fiscal but that wasn't her business.

'He's a thoroughly disgusting creature,' Fleming said as she and MacNee drove away from the hospital. 'But what can you expect if you have the sort of mother who'd be happy to burn you alive if it suited her business interests?'

'Right enough. And a father who couldn't be bothered to find out whether you were his son or not.'

'I still doubt if we can make the charge of murdering Julia stick, but his cooperation is a definite bonus. There's probably more circumstantial stuff we can get from him too, once he's fit for formal questioning.'

And there was better to come. The SOCOs had spent the day before taking apart Philippa Lindsay's car and there were bloodstains on the back seat that they could prove were from Will Stewart's body. The forensic team working on Eleanor Margrave had managed to lift a DNA contact from her skin, and though it would take some time to analyse it, there was reason to hope that the link with Philippa would be firmly established too.

Detective Superintendent Christine Rowley was ecstatic. 'You know, even *the chief constable* has sent a message congratulating me.' She named him in the tones a religious person might adopt to name the deity. 'He's *very* pleased with me.'

'That's good,' Fleming said hollowly, but she did say to MacNee afterwards that at least it might take Hyacinth a step nearer promotion, away from Galloway.

'Don't know if that's a good thing,' he pointed out. 'We were happy enough to see Donald Bailey retire as super and look what we got instead.'

Fleming groaned. 'Always the cock-eyed optimist. Thanks a lot.'

'Never mind. You weren't daft enough to expect a pat on the back, were you? And we've got Philippa bang to rights, anyway,' MacNee consoled her.

'She's a thoroughly evil woman. And she thought she would get away with it, you know. Did you see the fire chief's report? There was an ashtray full of stubs close to where she started the fire – presumably we were meant to conclude that Randall had been careless with a cigarette and it was all an accident.'

MacNee was impressed. 'Here, she wasn't daft, was she? If he got burnt to death it would be kinna hard for the insurers to claim it was just a scam.'

'And his evidence linking her to Julia's murder, and any threat Louise might present, would die with them. The best of all possible worlds, in her twisted universe.' Fleming sighed. 'I do wonder what made Philippa such a warped person.'

MacNee snorted. 'Easy! Money, money, money, if you ask me – if it hadn't been for that, there'd be three people still alive – four if you count Julia, though she'd probably have killed herself, given time.'

'It wasn't only down to her, Tam,' Fleming said slowly. 'It was Jen Wilson's obsession about Connell Kane that set the whole thing in motion.'

'Won't admit it, though, that one. Smug as you like.'

'No,' Fleming agreed. 'I think she's been able to convince herself that the sort of person she is would never cause anything like that, so she didn't. That's all.

'Now it's only the paperwork, really. You'd better let me get on with it.'

It had been a successful operation but as always at the ending of a case, Marjory Fleming was in sombre mood as she drove home, feeling low and depressed. So much damage, so much grief, so much pain.

But as she turned in at the track to Mains of Craigie, up to the farmhouse that she always thought looked like a child's drawing – a window on either side of the front door, three windows above – her mood lifted. Cat was coming home tonight, Cat by herself. She'd phoned Marjory the day before to tell her and when her mother had asked, sounding as upbeat as possible, 'And is Nick coming?' there had been an awkward pause.

At last, 'No, he isn't,' Cat had said. Then, in a sudden rush, she'd gone on, 'Actually, Mum, I dumped him after last weekend. He spent the whole time needling you and taking the piss out of Dad and what really finished it was that Dad didn't even realise and Nick thought it was funny. Don't tell Dad, though, will you?'

'Of course not,' Marjory had assured her. And as she parked the car she promised herself that even if Bill said what a shame it was they'd split up, she wouldn't so much as exchange glances with Cat. She'd just agree and smile.

Bill was coming across the yard, Meg at his heels. When they saw her Meg rushed over, barking joyfully and Bill followed her, beaming. He was always happy at the end of a case; increasingly, he hated watching her worry her way through all the problems, short of sleep and stressed.

'Good to see you! I thought you might have been a lot later, with all that. How did it go?'

'All right, I suppose – if you can say that. It's been – nasty.'

He eyed her narrowly. 'You're looking terrible.'

'Gee, thanks,' she said. 'Considering the lack of sleep, I'm looking pretty good, I think.'

Cat and Cammie were sitting at the kitchen table. Cat got up to kiss her, then gave her a hard look. 'God, you look awful!'

'I'm feeling worse by the minute, thank you,' Marjory said. 'Anything you'd like to add, Cammie?'

Cammie grinned. 'You look like a woman who needs a dram,' he said.

She smiled on him fondly. 'You get more and more like your dear father every day. Someone can bring it to me – I'm going to sit down.'

With Meg trotting importantly ahead, she went

through to the sitting room to sit down in the shabby armchair that they'd never got around to replacing. The dog threw herself down on the hearthrug then sat up again to look in disappointment at the unlit fire, then at her mistress.

'You don't need a fire, Meggie. It's a lovely warm evening,' Marjory told her firmly.

After a grey day, the sun had broken through, pale and tentative to be sure, but it was flooding the room with soft evening light. She leant back in the chair and shut her eyes, hearing the sounds of chat and laughter coming from the kitchen.

They had worked it out in the end. Everyone, from the chief constable down, was pleased with her. But she was always aware of her shortcomings: if she'd been quicker, cleverer, maybe... It was a punishing job, and the scars it left grew deeper, more painful, as time went on. If she allowed herself to think like that too much she'd be tempted to chuck the whole thing.

The sound of clinking glasses and cheerful voices was coming nearer and she opened her eyes and sat up, scolding herself. She was a lucky woman, beloved and cherished. Whatever happened outside, she had Bill and the children and this place, always the still centre of her troubled world.

There was a solid measure in the crystal glass Bill held out to her. 'I made it a double,' he said. 'And Cat's bringing the crisps.'

'Sour cream and chive?' Marjory asked. 'Then what more could any woman want?'

The publishers hope that this book has given you enjoyable reading. Large Print Books are especially designed to be as easy to see and hold as possible. If you wish a complete list of our books please ask at your local library or write directly to:

Magna Large Print Books
Magna House, Long Preston,
Skipton, North Yorkshire.
BD23 4ND

This Large Print Book for the partially sighted, who cannot read normal print, is published under the auspices of

THE ULVERSCROFT FOUNDATION